Collins

REVISED EDITION

COMPUTER WORLD 7

MOHINI ARORA

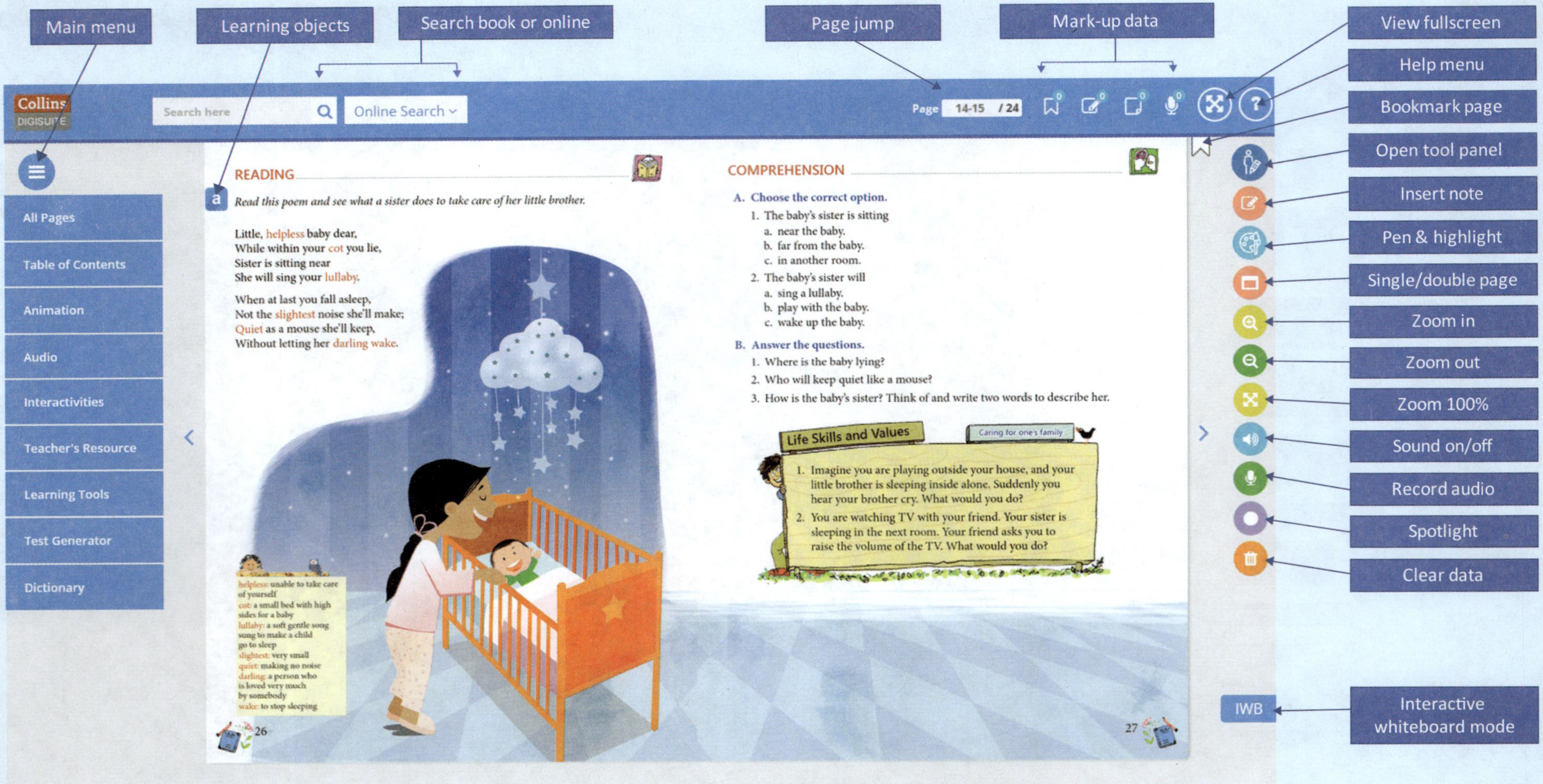

Student + Teacher			Teacher-only	
a animations	**ia** activities	**g** games	**lp** lesson plans	**tn** teacher's notes
ilt instructor-led tutorials	**w** worksheets	**v** videos	**w** worksheets	**ak** answer keys
	audio			

Preface

Computer World (Revised Edition), a series of eight books for Classes 1 to 8, familiarizes students with the latest trends in computer technology. This is a well- graded course that conforms to the latest syllabus requirements of various boards.

This revised edition builds on the strengths of the course while ensuring that the subject is updated to meet curriculum requirements. The end-of-chapter exercises have been expanded to support revision of the chapters. As with the previous edition, **Worksheets and Projects** have been interspersed within chapters for reinforcement of the concepts learnt.

Although the series continues to be based on Windows 2007 and MS Office 2010, a few changes have been introduced based on feedback from teachers and students across the country who have used this course. Popular features such as **Assessments**, **posters** and **National Cyber Olympiad** papers have been retained.

New to this Edition

1. Tux Paint and Tux Typing have been introduced from Class 1 onwards.
2. MSW Logo has been replaced with KTurtle, proprietary software such as Adobe Photoshop and Windows Movie Maker has been replaced with GIMP and OpenShot Video Editor, respectively.
3. Scratch and Python have been added to the series in keeping with the new curriculum requirements.
4. Labelled and numbered screenshots have been added to make it easier for students to navigate through the text.
5. Screenshots from LibreOffice have been included at the relevant places to ensure that students are able to use open-source software comfortably.
6. Pedagogical elements such as chapter-opening, warm-up exercises and concept-check questions within the chapter have been included.
7. Windows 10/Microsoft Office 2013 updates have been included from class 3 onwards.
8. Model test papers have been appended to the book to help students prepare for examinations.

The Teaching and Learning Package

Computer World (Revised Edition) comes bundled with teacher's manuals and Collins Digisuite. *Collins DigiSuite* is an interactive digital solution containing animations, test generator, and a host of other features designed to support teachers both within and outside the classroom.

Key Features

Learning Objectives

By the end of this chapter, you will be able to:

- identify and use the different keys on a keyboard.
- identify the different parts of a mouse and their functions.
- hold and use a mouse correctly.

Well-defined **Learning Objectives** make the teaching and learning process easier.

Warm Up

Join the dots from 1 to 30 and name the parts of the computer that you see.

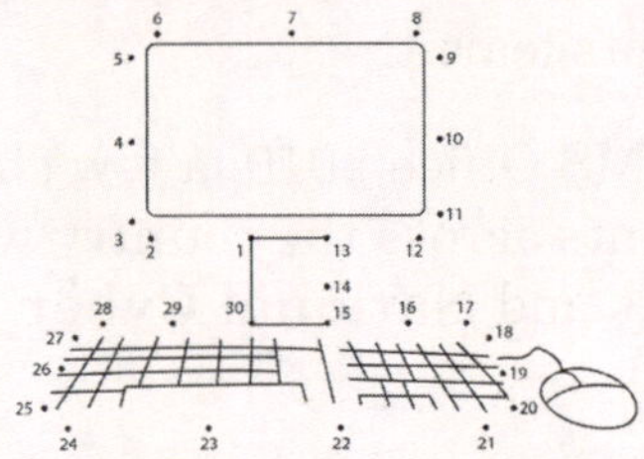

Age-appropriate **Warm-up** activities in a variety of formats for higher engagement.

Quick Way gives the keyboard shortcuts for commands.

To open a saved document, follow these steps (Fig. 7.10):

1. Click on the **File** tab. The Backstage view appears.
2. Click on the **Open** option. The **Open** dialog box appears.
3. Choose the file and folder you want to open.
4. Click on **Open**.

Quick Way

You can also press **Ctrl + O** on the keyboard to open an existing document.

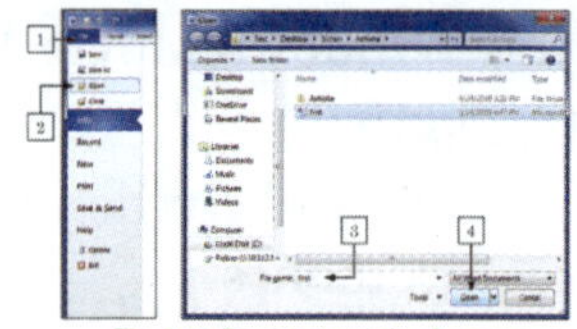

Fig. 7.10: Opening an existing document

LibreOffice Writer

Unlike MS Word, the LibreOffice Writer does not have tabs, groups or Ribbon. LibreOffice Writer contains a Menu bar, a Standard toolbar and a Formatting toolbar to work on the files. Here are the steps to create, save, open, close and print a document in LibreOffice Writer:

- Create a new document: Click on **File ▶ New ▶ Text Document**
- Save a document: Click on **File ▶ Save**
- Print a new document: Click on **File ▶ Print**
- Close a document: Click on **File ▶ Close**
- Exit a document: Click on **File ▶ Exit LibreOffice**
- Open an existing document: Click on **File ▶ Open**

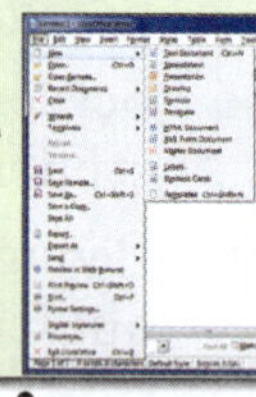

Open-source software included in the series.

Computer Etiquettes

Press the keys gently. Never bang or press the keys harshly.

Computer Etiquettes explains the etiquettes to be followed while using computers for classes 1 and 2.

PRACTICE TIME

In the image of the computer given below, identify two input devices and three output devices.

Practice Time includes hands-on tasks for revision.

You should know!

Data can be of four basic types:

- Text: words, numbers, sentences and paragraphs
- Graphics: images or pictures, like drawings, charts and photographs
- Audio: music, speech or any other sound
- Video: images that appear to be moving

You Should Know gives additional information about the topic.

Check your understanding!

Identify and label the following as Input, Processing or Output.

1. Making juice

2. Making lemonade

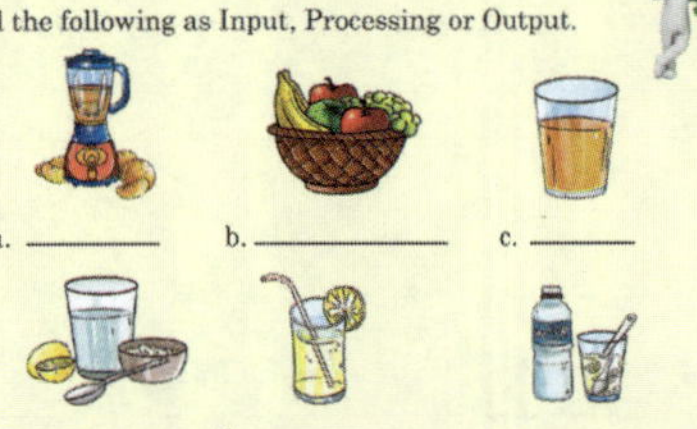

Check Your Understanding comprises short questions to revise the concept learnt

Web browser

A special application (or software) is required to view web pages or access information on the internet. This application is called a **web browser**. It allows us to browse the pages on the web.

Word Web
browsing: to move from one web page to another to search for specific information.

Computers running MS Windows come with a default web browser called the **Internet Explorer (IE)**. This is the default Microsoft web browser.

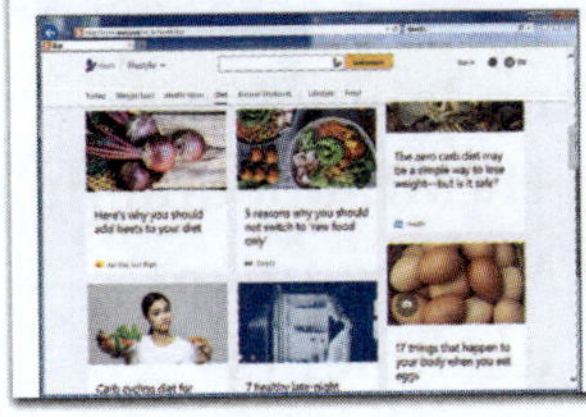

Cool Tip
The most recent version of Internet Explorer (IE) is Internet Explorer 11.

Word Web gives the contextual meaning of difficult words.

Cool Tip presents relevant tips.

Examples of **visual walkthroughs** using numbered steps with matching corresponding screenshots.

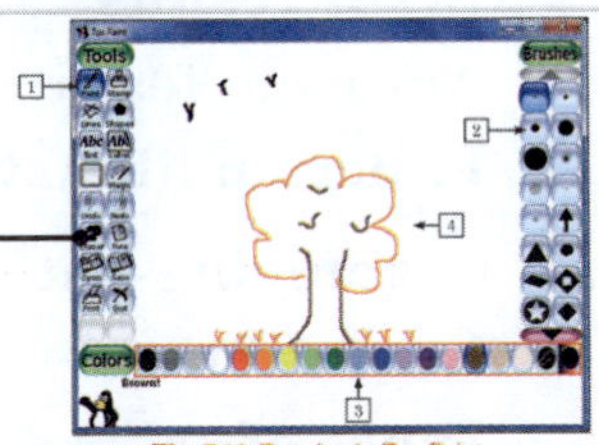

Fig. 7.13: Drawing in Tux Paint

Exhaustive revision **Exercises** comprising a blend of both fact-check and concept-check questions.

Exercises

A. Fill in the blanks using the words given below.

tr	File	fw	Canvas	console

1. We use the ________ command to turn the turtle towards its right.
2. ________ is the area where the drawing is created.
3. We use the ________ command to move the turtle forward.
4. The output of the command typed in the ________ is seen on the canvas.
5. The Save As option is present in ________ menu.

B. State whether the following statements are true (T) or false (F).

Quick Recap recapitulates all the important points covered in the chapter.

Quick Recap

1. MS Paint is used to draw and colour pictures on a computer.
2. To start Paint, click on Start ▸ All Programs ▸ Accessories ▸ Paint.
3. The important parts of the Paint window are the Title Bar, Drawing Area, Paint Button and Ribbon.
4. The Pencil or Brushes tools are used to draw lines.
5. The Paint button contains various options to open, save and close files.
6. Tux Paint is also a drawing program.
7. The main components of Tux Paint window are Toolbar, Drawing Canvas, Selector Toolbar, Colors Palette and Help Area.

Fun Time

1. Label the different components of a MS Word window.

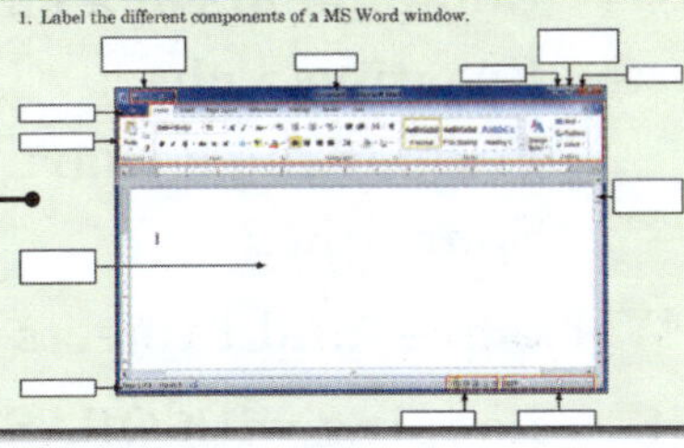

Fun Time facilitates recapitulation of key concepts/terms from the chapter in a simple, interesting manner.

Lab Activity

1. Draw a rectangle of width 60 steps and length 120 steps.
2. Complete the following programs by writing the missing commands.

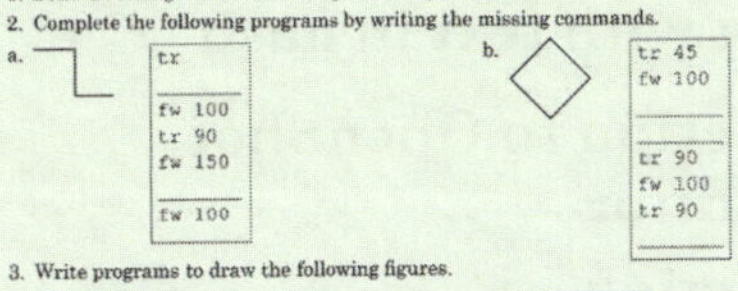

3. Write programs to draw the following figures.

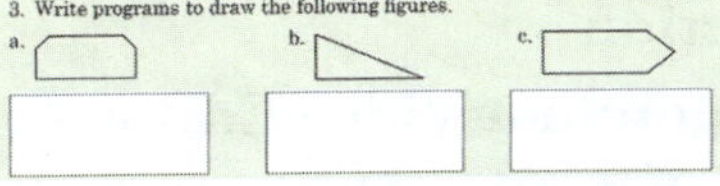

Lab Activity comprises hands-on tasks for students to practice.

Research Project requires students to go beyond the chapters and gather more information, solve a problem, etc.

Teacher's Notes include suggestions for teachers on tackling concepts from the chapter.

Online Link gives links to relevant additional material on the topic for students.

Research Project

1. Create a program to draw the letter 'T'. Execute it by selecting various options from the Run menu—Fast, Slow, Slower, Slowest and Step-by-step.
2. Which option do you find the most interesting and why? Discuss with your friends.

Teacher's Notes

1. The teacher should explain the importance of giving correct instructions in the correct sequence.
2. The concept of angles and degrees should be explained to the students before teaching turnright (tr) and turnleft (tl) commands.
3. The teacher should explain the steps to register with rollapp to run the KTurtle application online as KTurtle is not supported by Windows operating system.

Online Link

Go to https://www.rollapp.com/ to register yourself to run KTurtle online.

Contents

1 Formulas and Functions in MS Excel 2010

Learning Objectives

By the end of this chapter, you will be able to:

- understand cell and range references.
- use formulas—text and numeric.
- understand some error results.
- describe the AutoSum feature.
- use functions from Function Library.

Warm Up

Choose the correct option.

1. Which of the following is NOT present in the Delete dialog box of MS Excel?
   a. Shift cells left b. Entire row
   c. Shift cells up d. Shift cells bottom
2. Which of the following orientation options are available in MS Excel?
   a. Rotate Text Left b. Rotate Text Up
   c. Rotate Text Right d. Rotate Text Bottom
3. Which is the shortcut key for the partial modification of text in cells?
   a. F2 b. F3
   c. F4 d. F5
4. Which of the following features helps to fit long text into a cell?
   a. Live Preview b. Wrap Text
   c. Merge and Centre d. Both b. and c.
5. On which tab are all the formatting commands available?
   a. Home b. Insert
   c. Page Layout d. Formula

Introduction

You have already learnt to use formulas and their applications in mathematics. In this chapter you will learn how you can use formulas in Excel 2010 to perform various calculations.

A formula is a particular method which, when used, results in a new value from an existing range of values. A formula in MS Excel always starts with an 'equal to' sign (=) followed by one or more of the following constituents:

- Cell addresses or range references—A4, B9:B20, C:F
- Constant values—numeric (423, 90.9) and text ('Good and Bad')
- Mathematical operators—+, –, *, %, /, etc.
- Brackets—( )
- Functions—Sum, Average, Min, Max, Count, etc.

Cell and Range References

The data to be used within a formula may be placed in a single cell or a range of cells in an Excel worksheet. The values in these cell references or range of cell references are used in the formulas for computation of the result. Giving cell ranges in a formula saves a lot of time as there is no need to write individual references for each cell. Here are examples of cell addresses and range references:

- The cell in column D and row 6 — D6
- The range of cells in column F and rows 7 through 17 — F7:F17
- The range of cells in row 8 and columns A through F — A8:F8
- All cells in row 8 — 8:8
- All cells in columns A through D — A:D

You should know!

MS Excel 2010 has 1048576 rows and 16384 columns.

Using Formulas

A formula may be a simple formula containing just one operator or a compound formula with multiple operators. To enter a formula for a specified set of values, type the equal to (=) sign in the formula bar followed by the formula. Then press the **Enter** key or the click the ✔ button. For example, to calculate the sum of numbers in the cells A1, A2, A3, A4 and A5, follow these steps:

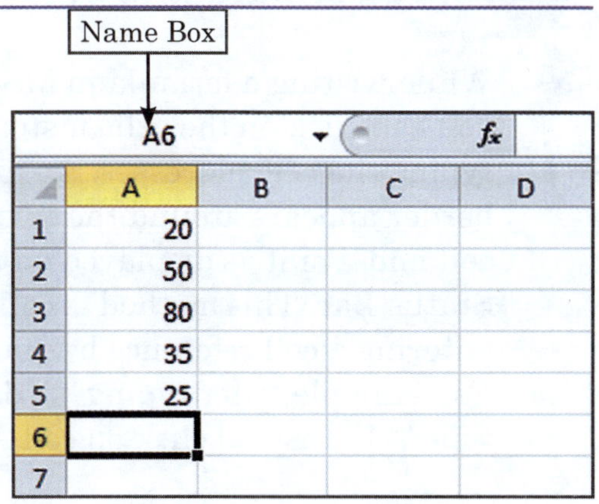

Fig. 1.1: Cell selection

1. Click the cell in which you want the sum to be displayed, say **A6**. You will see **A6** in the **Name Box** (Fig. 1.1).
2. Type the formula beginning with an equal to (=) sign. As you type the formula in the cell, it also appears in the **Formula Bar** simultaneously. You will notice that the colour of the cell name in the formula and the border colour of the corresponding cell is the same (Fig. 1.2).

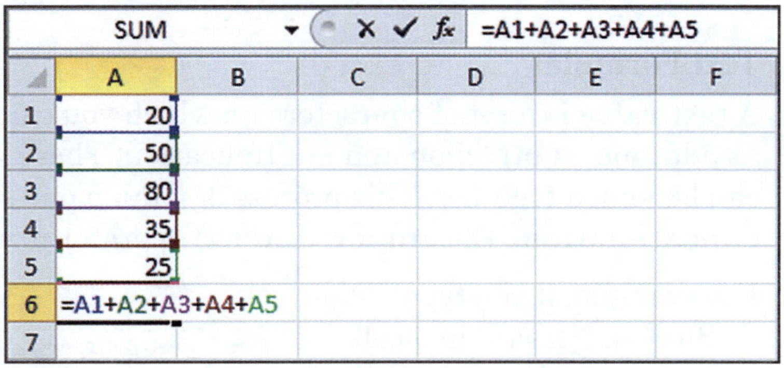

Fig. 1.2: Enter the formula

3. Click the ✔ or press the **Enter** key. The result will be displayed in the cell A6 (Fig. 1.3).

Once a formula is applied, Excel allows the results to be auto-edited. As you change the data in the cells containing input values, the result automatically changes in the cell where formula was entered.

In the example given, if you change any of the values of cells A1:A5, then the result in the cell A6 changes automatically.

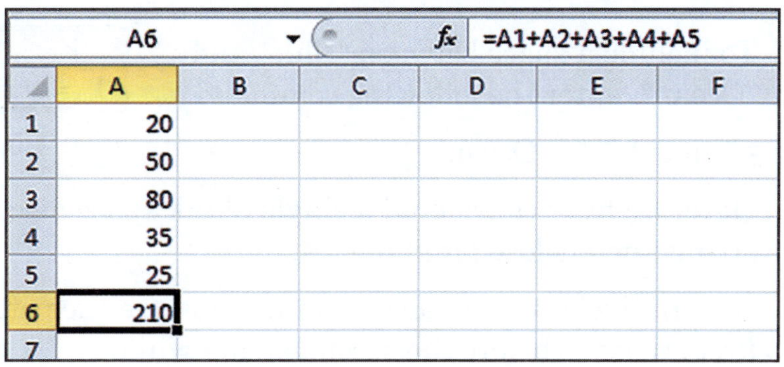

Fig. 1.3: Result

You should know!

Formulas in MS Excel are not case-sensitive. So, A1+A2 is same as a1+a2.

You should know!

While writing a formula in MS Excel, you can click on the cells instead of typing the cell addresses. An animated border appears around the selected cell and 'Point' is displayed on the Status Bar. This method is called entering a cell reference by pointing. For example, after typing '=', do not type 'A1'. Instead click on cell A1.

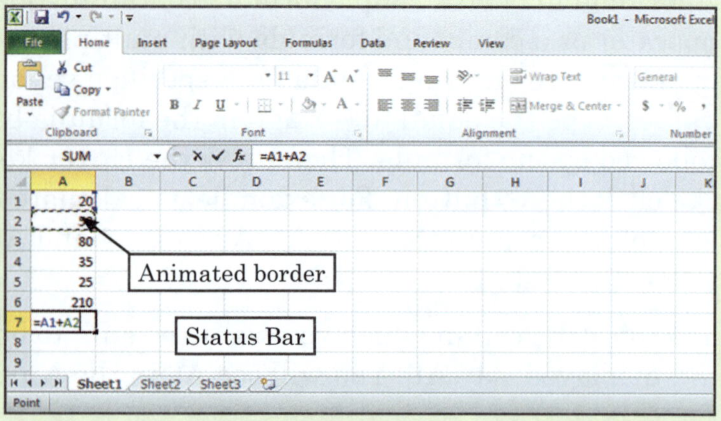

Text Formulas

A text value is a set of characters on which you cannot perform arithmetic operations such as addition, subtraction and multiplication. These values are also called **strings** and they can be joined together. This process of joining one string with another is called **concatenation**. The **ampersand** (&) operator is used to concatenate two strings.

For example, if you type = "Blue" & "Ocean" in a cell and press the **Enter** key, you get BlueOcean.

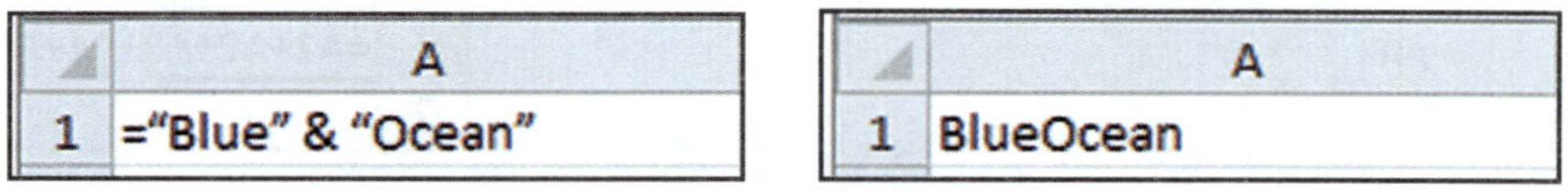

Fig. 1.4: String concatenation without space

To include a space between "Blue" and "Ocean", enter the following command:

="Blue"&" "&"Ocean"

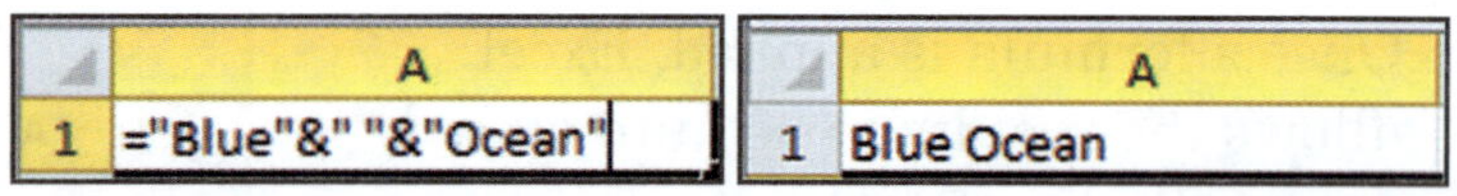

Fig. 1.5: String concatenation with a single space

Here, we have considered a single blank space also as a string and enclosed it in quotes.

Alternatively, we can also include a space either after the first string or before the second string while concatenating.

For example, both ="Blue "&"Ocean" and ="Blue"&" Ocean" will result in Blue Ocean.

You should know!

String values are always entered in double quotes.

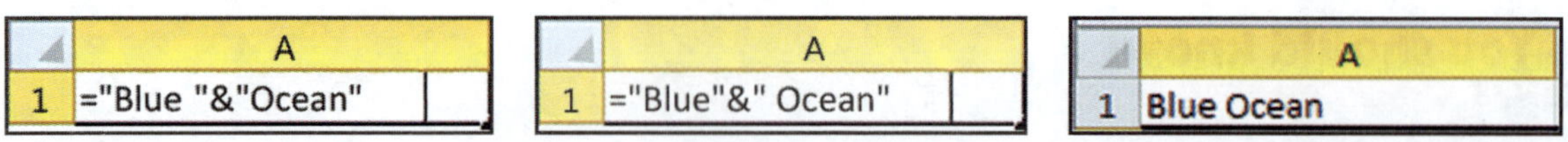

Fig. 1.6: Alternate method of adding a single space in string concatenation

You can also use cell references while concatenating strings.

Consider the example in which the score of the players and the time for which they played (in minutes) is stored. To use the text formula with cell references, follow the below steps given after creating the table containing name, score and minutes played:

1. Click the cell in which you want to display the result, say A10.
2. Type the text formula (Fig. 1.7):

   = A4&" scored "&B4&" runs "&" in "&C4 &" minutes."

   The spaces succeed and precede each word in the quotation marks except at the end of the last word, which uses a full stop.
3. Click ✔ or press the **Enter** key to view the result as shown in Fig. 1.8.

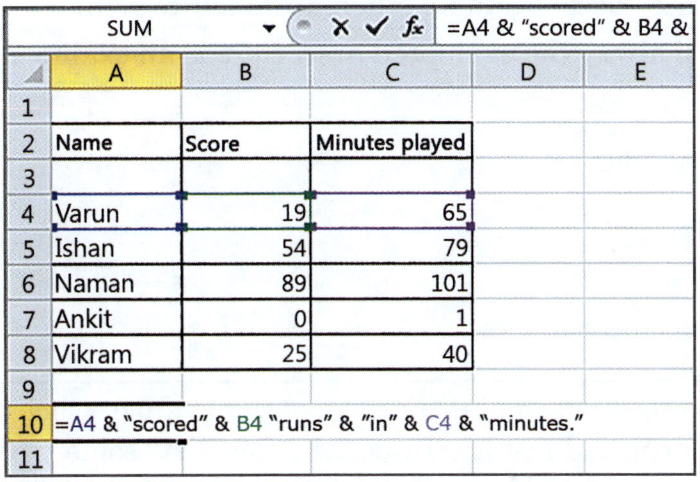

Fig. 1.7: Creating a text formula

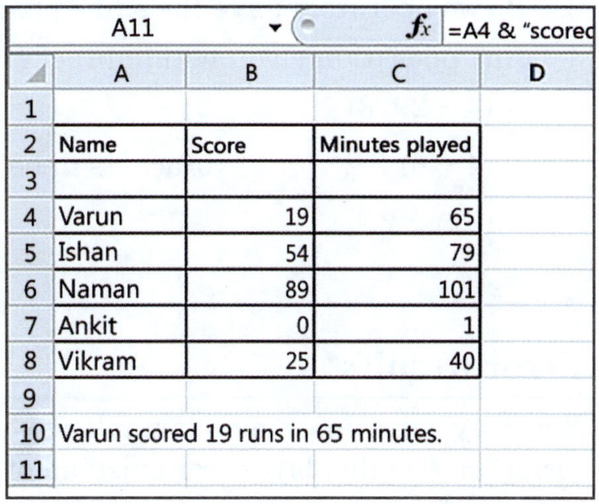

Fig. 1.8: Result of a text formula

Mathematical Operators Used in Numeric Formulas

Various mathematical operators can be used in Excel while creating and using formulas. Table 1.1 gives the list of arithmetic operators.

Table 1.1: Arithmetic operators in MS Excel

Operator	Operation	Example	Result
^	Exponent	2^5	32
*	Multiplication	2*5	10
/	Division	10/5	2
+	Addition	2+5	7
–	Subtraction	10–2	8

While creating numeric formulas, keep the following points in mind:

1. Evaluation is always carried out from left to right.
2. While evaluation, if multiple operators are present in a single formula, the operator with the higher order of precedence will be evaluated first. The order of precedence of

arithmetic operators is exponent (^), division (/) and multiplication, followed by addition (+) and subtraction (–).

Consider the expression: 2*5 + 3^2

It has three operators: *, + and ^. According to precedence rules, ^ will be evaluated first (as it has the highest precedence), then * and then +. So, the order of evaluation will be:

=2 * 5 + 3 ^ 2

2 * 5 + 9

10 + 9

19

3. If two operators have the same precedence, Excel evaluates them from left to right.
4. Any operation given within brackets will always be evaluated first. Here is an example:

   = (4 – 2 * 3) ^ 2

   = (4 – 6) ^ 2 (brackets to be evaluated first)

   = (–2) ^ 2

   = 4

Error Results

You may sometimes make mistakes while entering formulas. Excel does not evaluate such formulas and displays errors instead of the expected results. Table 1.2 below lists some common formula errors in Excel along with their possible reasons.

Table 1.2: Common formula errors in MS Excel

Error	Reason
#DIV/0!	Division by zero (An invalid operation)
#N/A	Data not available
#VALUE!	Formula contains invalid data

Cool Tip

Press **F2** to enter or modify a formula in a cell.

You should know!

If you see two or more '#' symbols in a cell, it means the column is not wide enough to display the resultant number. This is not considered a formula error. In this case, increase the width of the column so that the complete number is displayed.

Autosum Feature

The AutoSum feature is one of the most commonly used features of MS Excel. It automatically adds the numbers in the selected range of cells. Other than addition, the AutoSum feature can also be used to find the average, maximum value, minimum value, etc. for the selected range of cells. You can find the AutoSum button in the **Editing** group of buttons on the **Home** tab. It is also present in the **Function Library** group of buttons on the **Formulas** tab.

Household Expenditure						
Name	**Grocery**	**Electricity Bill**	**LPG**	**Vegetables & Fruits**	**Misc**	**Total**
Shiwali	3000	6000	2000	2000	4000	
Teena	2500	4500	1500	1800	3500	
Bhawna	4000	2900	1600	2300	4200	
Krishna	2700	5000	2500	2500	3800	

Fig. 1.9: List of expenses

To use the AutoSum feature, consider the following example containing the list of expenses of four homemakers (Fig. 1.9).

1. Select cell G5 and click **AutoSum** (not the arrow) in the **Editing** group of buttons on the **Home** tab. You will see a formula with the **Sum** function along with a cell range. An animated border surrounds the range of cells in the formula (B5:F5). A tool tip showing the syntax of the formula also appears under the active cell.

Household Expenditure						
Name	**Grocery**	**Electricity Bill**	**LPG**	**Vegetables & Fruits**	**Misc**	**Total**
Shiwali	3000	6000	2000	2000	4000	=SUM(B5:F5)
Teena	2500	4500	1500	1800	3500	SUM(number1, [number2], ...)
Bhawna	4000	2900	1600	2300	4200	
Krishna	2700	5000	2500	2500	3800	

Fig. 1.10: Creating the formula using AutoSum

2. Press the **Enter** key or click **AutoSum** button again to view the result (Fig. 1.11).

Household Expenditure						
Name	**Grocery**	**Electricity Bill**	**LPG**	**Vegetables & Fruits**	**Misc**	**Total**
Shiwali	3000	6000	2000	2000	4000	17000
Teena	2500	4500	1500	1800	3500	
Bhawna	4000	2900	1600	2300	4200	
Krishna	2700	5000	2500	2500	3800	

Fig. 1.11: Result of AutoSum

3. To further fill the range of cells G6:G8, you can use the **AutoFill** feature of MS Excel. Select cell G5. Drag the fill handle (the small black square at the lower right corner) to cell G8. While dragging, the fill handle changes to a small black cross as shown in Fig. 1.12.

Household Expenditure						
Name	**Grocery**	**Electricity Bill**	**LPG**	**Vegetables & Fruits**	**Misc**	**Total**
Shiwali	3000	6000	2000	2000	4000	17000
Teena	2500	4500	1500	1800	3500	13800
Bhawna	4000	2900	1600	2300	4200	15000
Krishna	2700	5000	2500	2500	3800	16500

Fig. 1.12: Copying the formula

4. Release the left mouse button. You will see that the AutoSum formula is copied to all the cells in the range.

Functions in Excel 2010

Functions are predefined formulas in MS Excel. Various functions are provided by MS Excel to perform various mathematical operations. One such function is Sum() that adds the numbers in a given range of cells.

Quick Way

The shortcut key for AutoSum is **Alt+ =**. This shortcut key can only be used for adding adjacent cells.

You have performed the addition operation in the previous section using AutoSum feature. The Sum function is inserted automatically on clicking the AutoSum button.

Other functions provided by Excel 2010 are available in the options of the AutoSum feature. For using them, click on the arrow to the right of the **AutoSum** button.

The following AutoSum options are displayed (Fig. 1.13):

a. **Sum**: Calculates the sum. (You have used this option by clicking directly on AutoSum). This is the default option of AutoSum feature.

b. **Average**: Calculates the average of the values in the selected range of cells.

c. **Count Numbers**: Counts the number of cells containing some values.

d. **Max**: Displays the highest value from the given range of cells.

e. **Min**: Displays the lowest value from the given range of cells.

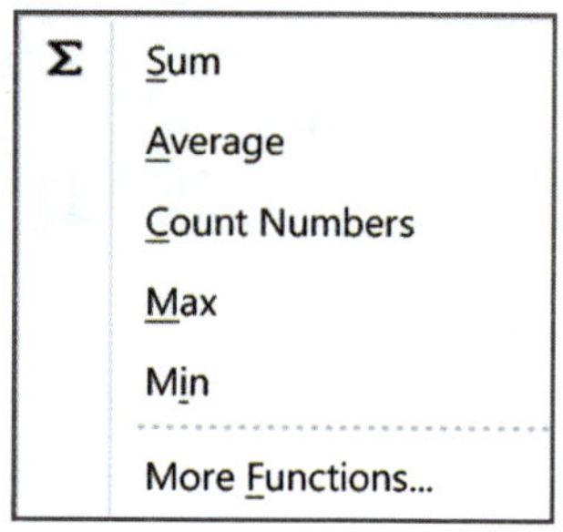

Fig. 1.13: AutoSum options

Consider an example to use the various options of the **AutoSum** button. Figure 1.14 shows an Excel sheet containing the details of household expenses. Follow these steps to find the average expenditure of each category:

1. In the Excel sheet of Household Expenditure, write *Average Expenditure* in cell A10, *Maximum Expenditure* in cell A12 and *Minimum Expenditure* in cell A13 (Fig. 1.14).

	A	B	C	D	E	F	G
1							
2	Household Expenditure						
3–4	Name	Grocery	Electricity Bill	LPG	Vegetables & Fruits	Misc	Total
5	Shiwali	3000	6000	2000	2000	4000	17000
6	Teena	2500	4500	1500	1800	3500	13800
7	Bhawna	4000	2900	1600	2300	4200	15000
8	Krishna	2700	5000	2500	2500	3800	16500
9							
10	Average Expenditure						
11							
12	Maximum Expenditure						
13	Minimum Expenditure						

Fig. 1.14: Data entry in Excel

2. Select cell B10. Click the arrow to the right of **AutoSum** button (Fig. 1.15). Select the **Average** option. The average function is inserted automatically.

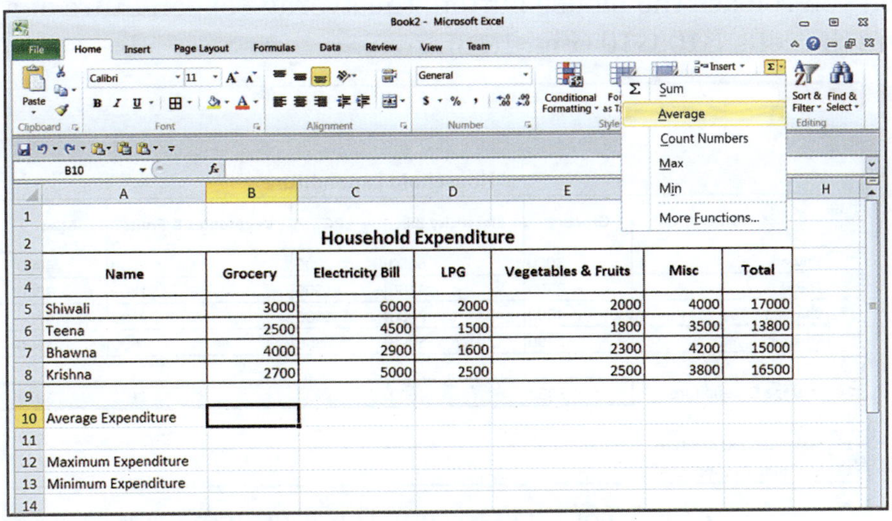

Fig. 1.15: Cell selection

3. The range in the formula is B5:B8. This range of cells will also have an animated border around it as shown in Fig. 1.16.

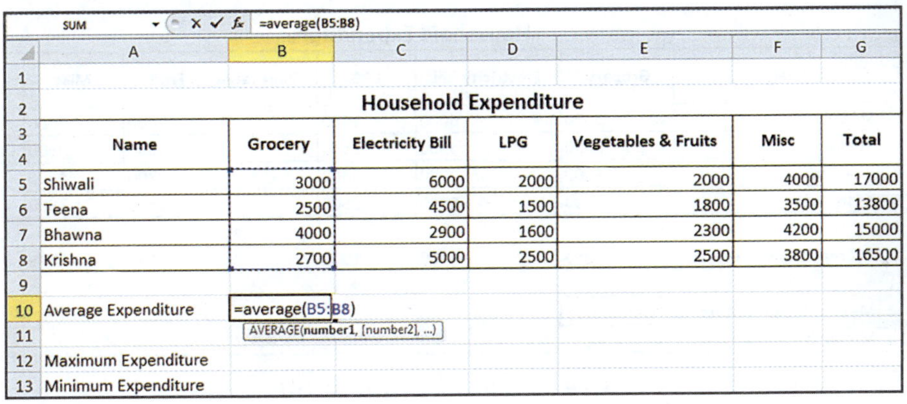

Fig. 1.16: Average formula

4. Press **Enter** to view the average grocery expenditure (Fig. 1.17).

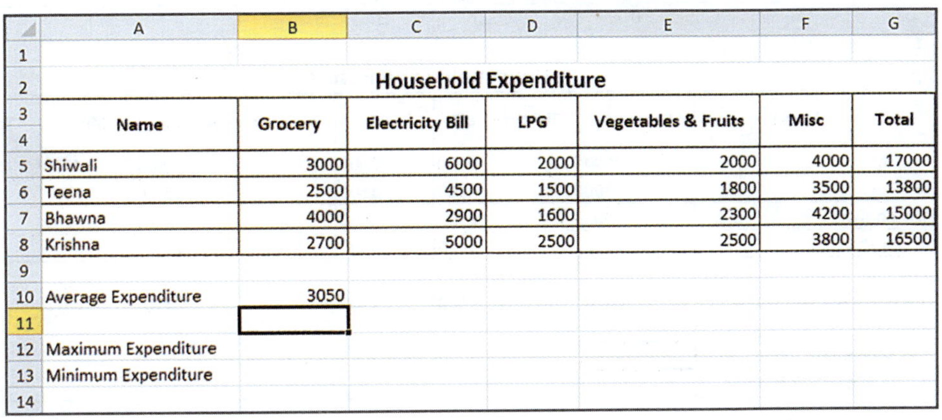

Fig. 1.17: Result of the Average formula

5. To find the average expenditure of other expense heads, use the AutoFill feature of MS Excel. Keeping the left mouse button pressed, drag the fill handle to cell G10 (Fig. 1.18). When you release the mouse button, the average expenditure of all the heads is displayed in the cells B10:G10 (Fig. 1.18).

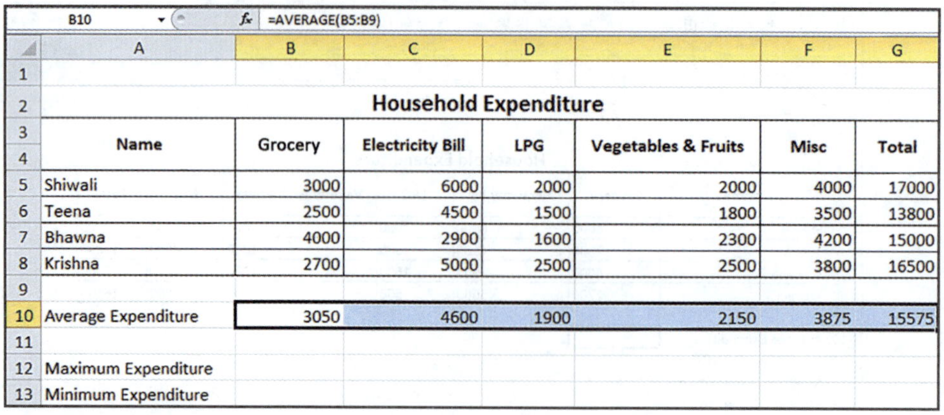

B10 | fx =AVERAGE(B5:B9)

	A	B	C	D	E	F	G
1							
2	Household Expenditure						
3–4	Name	Grocery	Electricity Bill	LPG	Vegetables & Fruits	Misc	Total
5	Shiwali	3000	6000	2000	2000	4000	17000
6	Teena	2500	4500	1500	1800	3500	13800
7	Bhawna	4000	2900	1600	2300	4200	15000
8	Krishna	2700	5000	2500	2500	3800	16500
9							
10	Average Expenditure	3050	4600	1900	2150	3875	15575
11							
12	Maximum Expenditure						
13	Minimum Expenditure						

Fig. 1.18: Drag to copy the Average formula

6. To find the maximum expenditure incurred under each head, select the **Max** option from the **AutoSum** drop-down menu (Fig. 1.19).

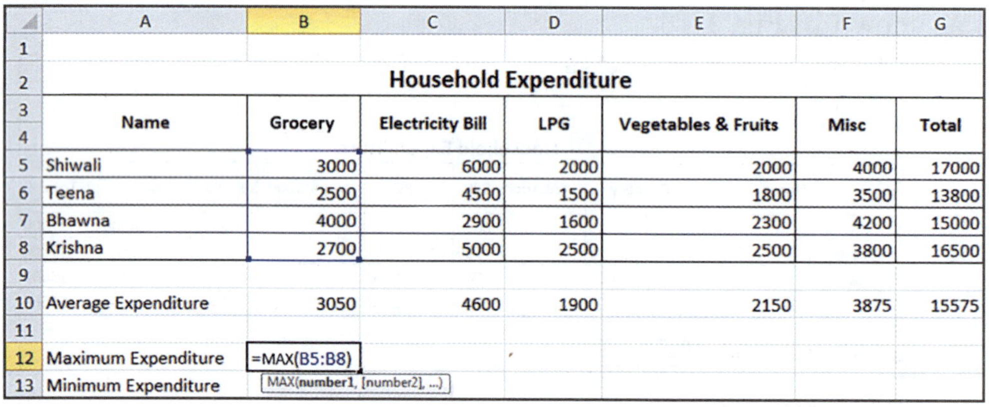

	A	B	C	D	E	F	G
1							
2	Household Expenditure						
3–4	Name	Grocery	Electricity Bill	LPG	Vegetables & Fruits	Misc	Total
5	Shiwali	3000	6000	2000	2000	4000	17000
6	Teena	2500	4500	1500	1800	3500	13800
7	Bhawna	4000	2900	1600	2300	4200	15000
8	Krishna	2700	5000	2500	2500	3800	16500
9							
10	Average Expenditure	3050	4600	1900	2150	3875	15575
11							
12	Maximum Expenditure	=MAX(B5:B8)					
13	Minimum Expenditure	MAX(number1, [number2], ...)					

Fig. 1.19: Max formula

7. Fill the correct range (B5:B8) and press **Enter** to view the result (Fig. 1.20).

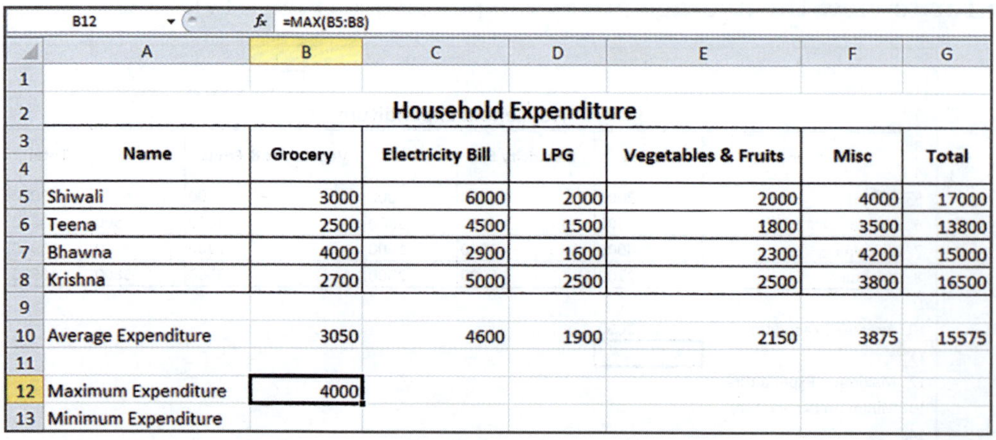

B12 | fx =MAX(B5:B8)

	A	B	C	D	E	F	G
1							
2	Household Expenditure						
3–4	Name	Grocery	Electricity Bill	LPG	Vegetables & Fruits	Misc	Total
5	Shiwali	3000	6000	2000	2000	4000	17000
6	Teena	2500	4500	1500	1800	3500	13800
7	Bhawna	4000	2900	1600	2300	4200	15000
8	Krishna	2700	5000	2500	2500	3800	16500
9							
10	Average Expenditure	3050	4600	1900	2150	3875	15575
11							
12	Maximum Expenditure	4000					
13	Minimum Expenditure						

Fig. 1.20: Result of the Max formula

8. Click and drag the fill handle to view the maximum expenditure under each head (Fig. 1.21).

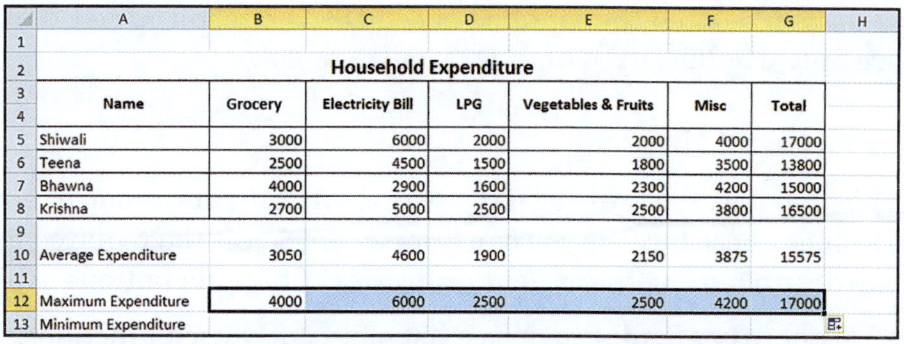

Household Expenditure

Name	Grocery	Electricity Bill	LPG	Vegetables & Fruits	Misc	Total
Shiwali	3000	6000	2000	2000	4000	17000
Teena	2500	4500	1500	1800	3500	13800
Bhawna	4000	2900	1600	2300	4200	15000
Krishna	2700	5000	2500	2500	3800	16500
Average Expenditure	3050	4600	1900	2150	3875	15575
Maximum Expenditure	4000	6000	2500	2500	4200	17000
Minimum Expenditure						

Fig. 1.21: Drag to copy the Max formula

9. Similarly, you can find out the minimum expenditure under each head by choosing the **Min** option from the **AutoSum** menu (Fig. 1.22).

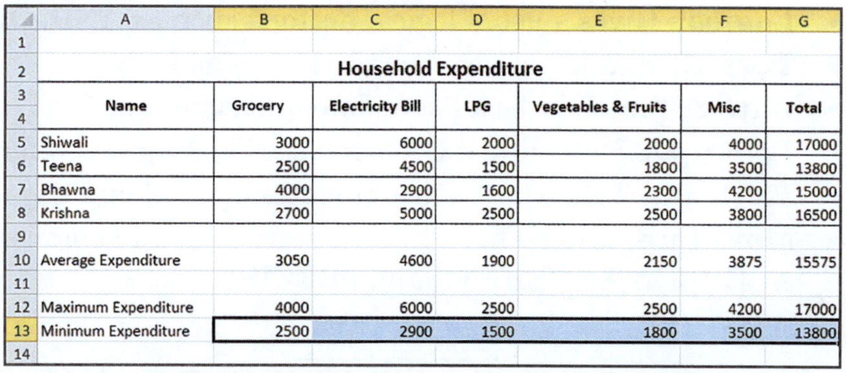

Household Expenditure

Name	Grocery	Electricity Bill	LPG	Vegetables & Fruits	Misc	Total
Shiwali	3000	6000	2000	2000	4000	17000
Teena	2500	4500	1500	1800	3500	13800
Bhawna	4000	2900	1600	2300	4200	15000
Krishna	2700	5000	2500	2500	3800	16500
Average Expenditure	3050	4600	1900	2150	3875	15575
Maximum Expenditure	4000	6000	2500	2500	4200	17000
Minimum Expenditure	2500	2900	1500	1800	3500	13800

Fig. 1.22: Result of the Min formula

10. The **Count Numbers** option in the AutoSum menu counts the number of numeric values in the range. To understand this, delete the contents of cell D6 under the LPG expenditure head. Now, select cell B16 and select **Count Numbers** from the **AutoSum** menu (Fig. 1.23).

11. Type the correct range (B5:B8) and press the **Enter** key. You will see the result as 4.

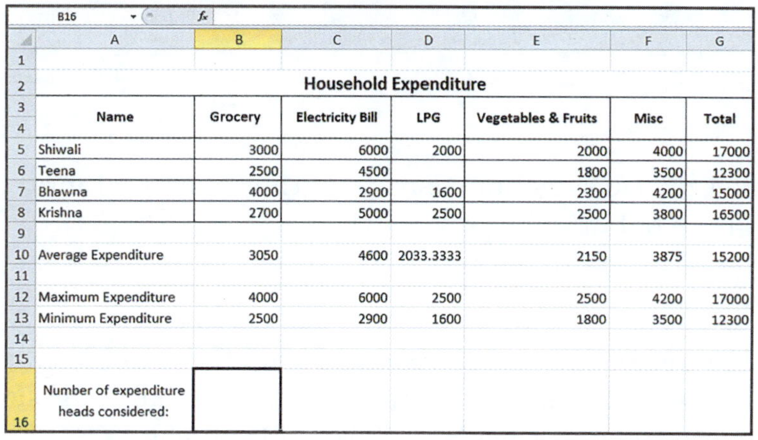

B16

Household Expenditure

Name	Grocery	Electricity Bill	LPG	Vegetables & Fruits	Misc	Total
Shiwali	3000	6000	2000	2000	4000	17000
Teena	2500	4500		1800	3500	12300
Bhawna	4000	2900	1600	2300	4200	15000
Krishna	2700	5000	2500	2500	3800	16500
Average Expenditure	3050	4600	2033.3333	2150	3875	15200
Maximum Expenditure	4000	6000	2500	2500	4200	17000
Minimum Expenditure	2500	2900	1600	1800	3500	12300
Number of expenditure heads considered:						

Fig. 1.23: Count Numbers from the AutoSum menu

12. Click and drag the fill handle to display the count of each expense head (Fig. 1.24).

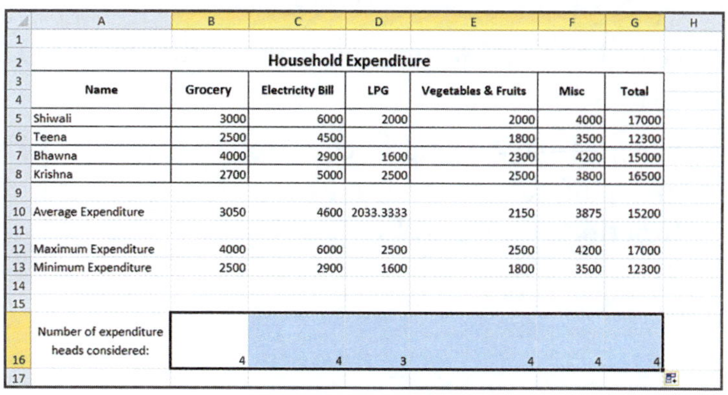

Household Expenditure

Name	Grocery	Electricity Bill	LPG	Vegetables & Fruits	Misc	Total
Shiwali	3000	6000	2000	2000	4000	17000
Teena	2500	4500		1800	3500	12300
Bhawna	4000	2900	1600	2300	4200	15000
Krishna	2700	5000	2500	2500	3800	16500
Average Expenditure	3050	4600	2033.3333	2150	3875	15200
Maximum Expenditure	4000	6000	2500	2500	4200	17000
Minimum Expenditure	2500	2900	1600	1800	3500	12300
Number of expenditure heads considered:	4	4	3	4	4	4

Fig. 1.24: Result of Count Numbers from the AutoSum menu

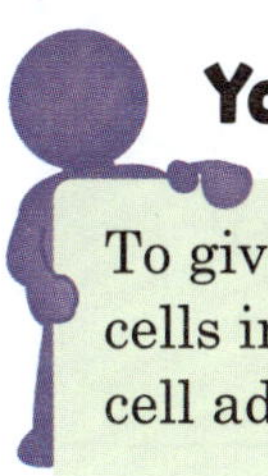

You should know!

To give a range of non-adjacent cells in a formula, separate each cell address by a **comma (,)**:

=AVERAGE(A1, C5, D3, E2)

Since you deleted the contents of cell D6, the result in cell D16 will be 3 because now there are only 3 values in column D from D5 to D8.

Function Library

The functions are present in the **Function Library** group of buttons on the **Formula** tab. Through these buttons you can browse and select the required formulas. Other than the **AutoSum** button, the various categories of formula buttons available are as follows (Fig. 1.25):

- **Recently Used**: Provides a list of recently used functions.
- **Financial**: Provides a list of financial functions to choose from such as INT.
- **Logical**: Gives a list of logical buttons such as AND, OR, NOT, etc.
- **Text**: Gives a list of text functions such as LEN.
- **Date & Time**: Gives a list of date and time functions.
- **Lookup & Reference**: Gives a list of look up and reference functions.
- **Math and Trig**: Gives a list of mathematical and trigonometric functions.
- **More Functions**: Gives a list of statistical and engineering functions such as AGGREGATE, CEILING and PRECISE.

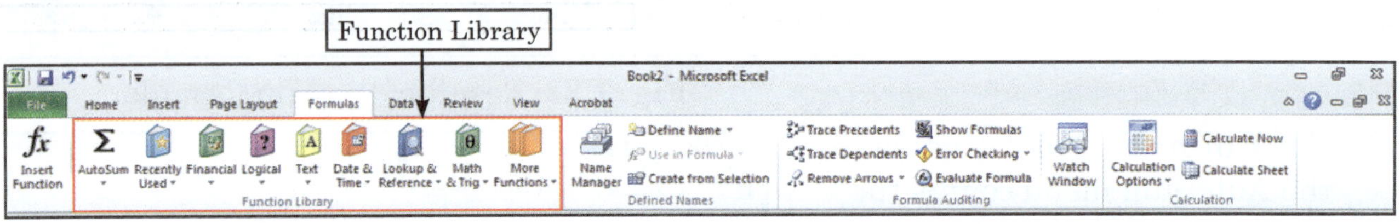

Fig. 1.25: Formulas tab

Let us use some functions from the Function Library group of buttons.

LCM

You must have calculated the Least Common Multiple (LCM) of two or more integers in mathematics. Follow these steps to calculate LCM in MS Excel:

1. Type the numbers in cells B1:B4.
2. Select the cell where you want to display the LCM, say B6.
3. Click **Math & Trig** button from **Function Library** group of buttons on the **Formulas** tab. A list of functions appears (Fig. 1.26).

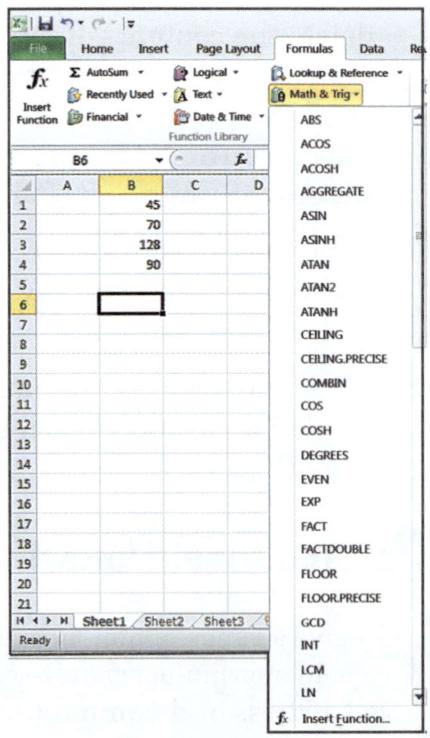

Fig. 1.26: Math & Trig drop-down list

4. Select LCM option from the drop-down list. The **Function Arguments** dialog box appears (Fig. 1.27).
5. Type the cell numbers B1, B2, B3 and B4 in the Number1, Number2, Number3 and Number4 text boxes respectively. The value in each cell is displayed on the right side of the text boxes itself.
6. Click **OK**. The result is displayed in the cell B6 on the spreadsheet (Fig. 1.28).

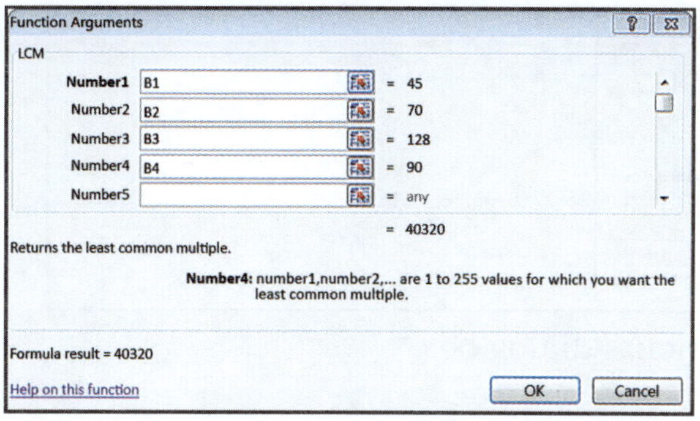

Fig. 1.27: Function Arguments dialog box

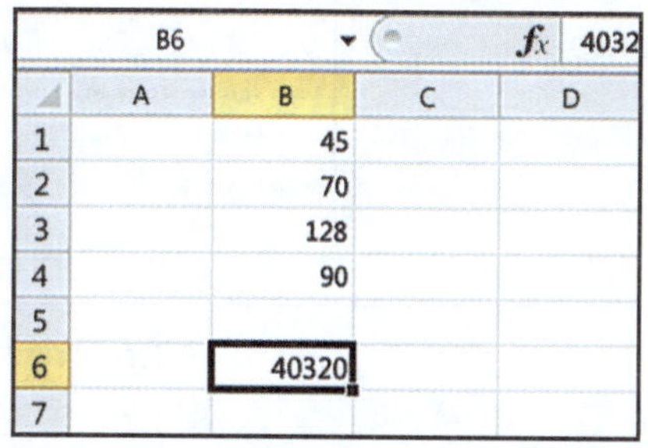

Fig. 1.28: LCM of the range of numbers

LEN

LEN is a text function which displays the number of characters in a cell. The steps are as follows:

1. Type the characters, say "This is my book." in cell A3. Increase the column width of column A to accommodate the entire text.
2. Click the cell where you want to display the string length, say B3 (Fig. 1.29). Click **Text** button in the **Function Library** group of buttons (Fig. 1.30).

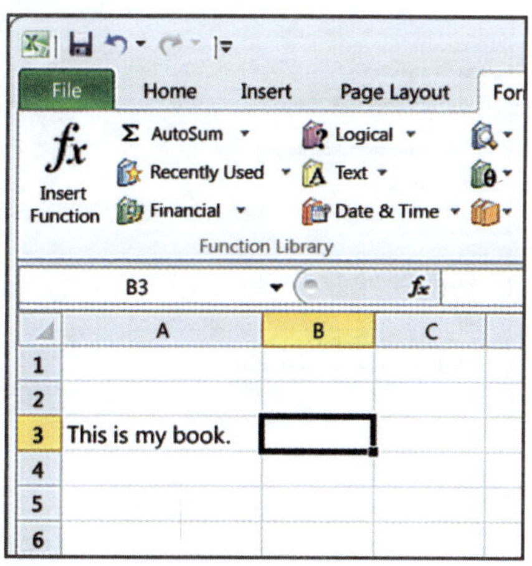

Fig. 1.29: Cell selection for result display

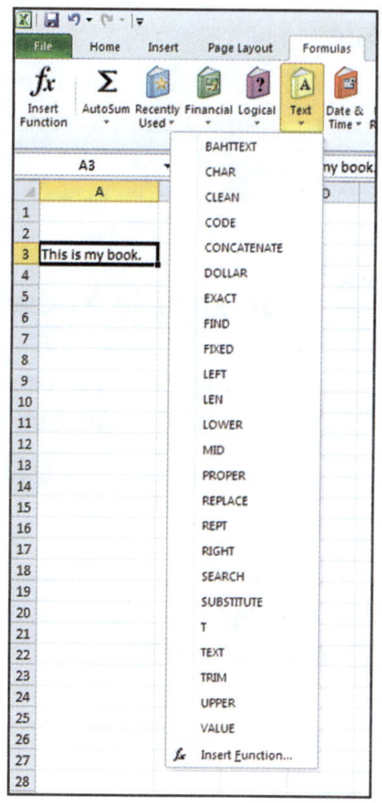

Fig. 1.30: Text drop-down list

3. Select the **LEN** option from the drop-down list. In the **Function Arguments** dialog box, type A3 (Fig. 1.31). You will see the result in the dialog box.

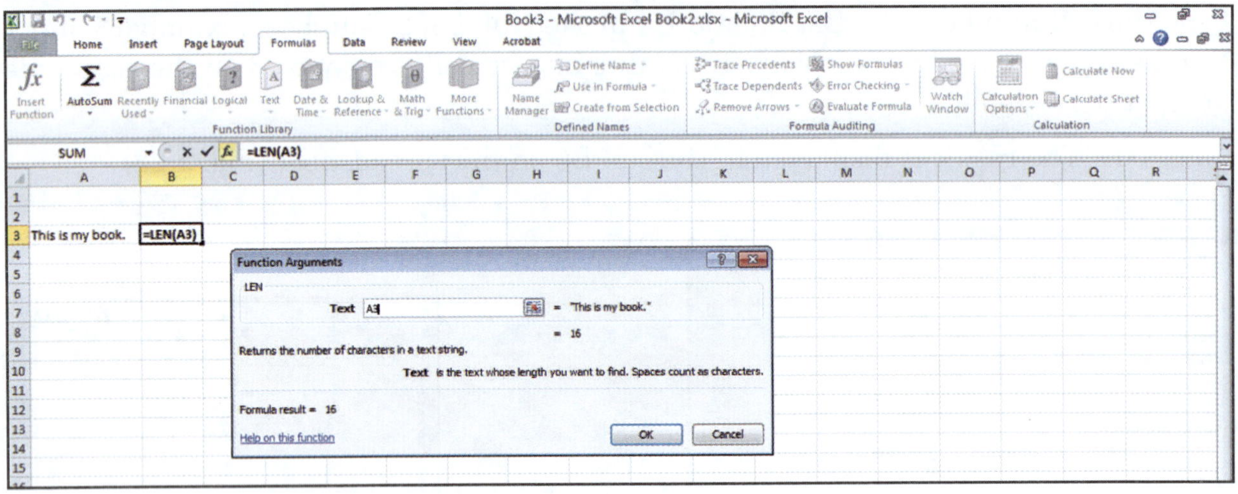

Fig. 1.31: Function Arguments dialog box

4. Click **OK**. The result is displayed in the cell B3 and the formula in the formula bar (Fig. 1.32).

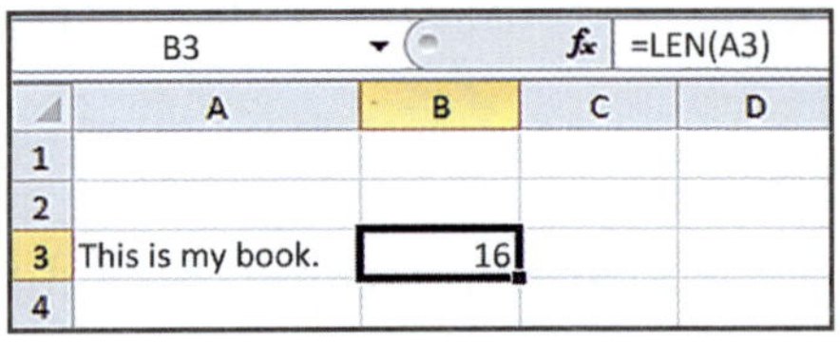

Fig. 1.32: Result of LEN function

Today

This is a **Date & Time** function that displays the current date. Click the cell where you want to display the current system date. From the **Date & Time** drop-down list, select **TODAY**.

You should know!

On the extreme left of the **Formulas tab** is the **Insert Function** button.

You can edit or choose any function in the **Insert Function** dialog box.

Through this dialog box, you can search for a particular function by giving a brief description of what you want to do.

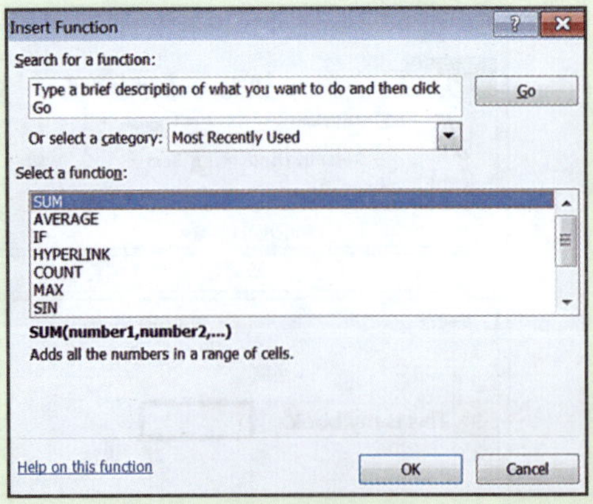

The **Function Arguments** dialog box is displayed (Fig. 1.33). Click **OK** and the current system date will be displayed in the active cell.

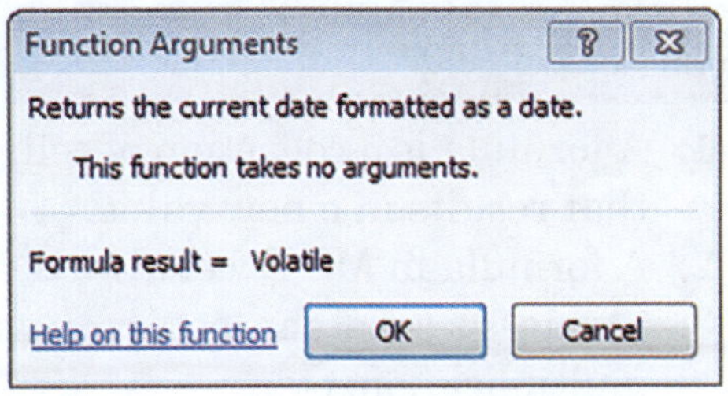

Fig. 1.33: Function Arguments dialog box

PRACTICE TIME

The computer teacher has asked you to create a worksheet containing a list of teachers and their number of periods per week. Find out the average teaching periods and the maximum and minimum number of periods.

SOLUTION

1. Type the data as shown in the worksheet.
2. Select cell E13. Click the arrow next to **AutoSum**.
3. From the drop-down menu, select **Average**.
4. The formula appears in the active cell. Check that the range in the formula is E5:E10. Press the **Enter** key. The average periods allocation appears in the active cell.

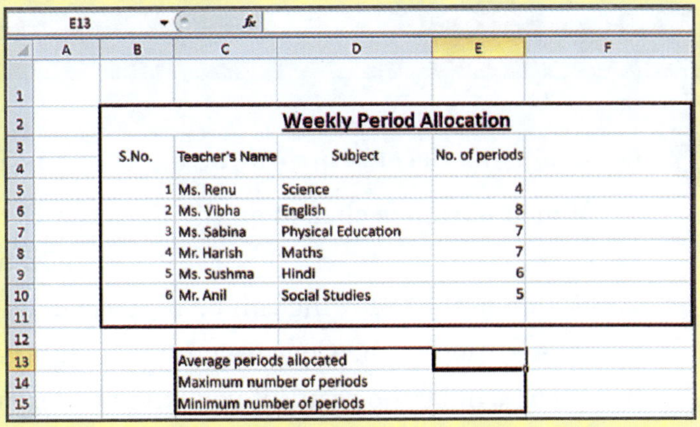

S.No.	Teacher's Name	Subject	No. of periods
1	Ms. Renu	Science	4
2	Ms. Vibha	English	8
3	Ms. Sabina	Physical Education	7
4	Mr. Harish	Maths	7
5	Ms. Sushma	Hindi	6
6	Mr. Anil	Social Studies	5

Average periods allocated	
Maximum number of periods	
Minimum number of periods	

5. Select cell E14. Click the arrow next to **AutoSum** button and choose **Max** from the drop-down menu.
6. The formula appears in the active cell. Click cell E5. Drag the fill handle till E10. The range in the formula changes to E5:E10. Press the **Enter** key. The maximum number of periods appears in E14.
7. Select cell E15. Click the arrow next to **AutoSum** button and choose **Min** from the drop-down menu.
8. The formula appears in the active cell. Click cell E5. Drag the fill handle till E10. The range in the formula changes to E5:E10. Press the **Enter** key. The minimum number of periods appears in E15.

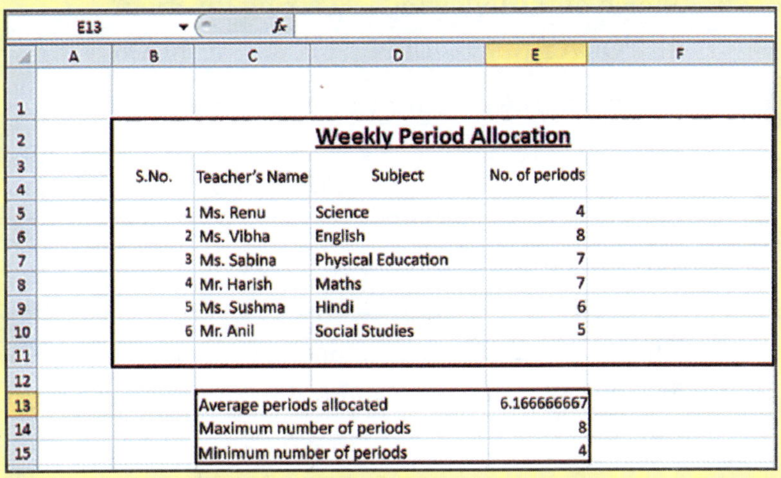

S.No.	Teacher's Name	Subject	No. of periods
1	Ms. Renu	Science	4
2	Ms. Vibha	English	8
3	Ms. Sabina	Physical Education	7
4	Mr. Harish	Maths	7
5	Ms. Sushma	Hindi	6
6	Mr. Anil	Social Studies	5

Average periods allocated	6.166666667
Maximum number of periods	8
Minimum number of periods	4

Quick Recap

1. A formula is a collection of cell references, constant values, operators and functions in a cell that results in a new value.
2. A formula in MS Excel always starts with an equal to (=) sign.
3. String is a set of characters on which you cannot do arithmetic operations such as subtraction, multiplication, etc.
4. Joining of strings is called concatenation. In Excel, the '&' operator is used to concatenate strings.
5. The AutoSum feature adds the numbers in the selected range of cells.
6. The options provided by the AutoSum drop-down menu are Sum, Average, Count Numbers, Max, Min and More Functions.
7. Functions are predefined formulas to perform certain operations.
8. Functions are present in the Function Library group of buttons on the Formula tab.

Exercises

A Choose the correct option for each of the following.

1. Which button is clicked on the Formula Bar to see the result of a formula?
   a. ✓ b. H c. Both a. and b. d. Neither a. nor b.
2. Which of the following can be performed on a string?
   a. Addition b. Concatenation c. Subtraction d. Division
3. What will be the result if you enter ="Best"&"Friend"?
   a. Best Friend b. BESTFRIEND
   c. BestFriend d. Bestfriend
4. Which of the following is not an option in the AutoSum drop-down menu?
   a. Sum b. Count c. Average d. Max
5. Which of the following is a string function?
   a. TODAY b. LEN c. MAX d. LCM

B Fill in the blanks using the words given below.

=	Functions	Enter	&	Home

1. A formula in MS Excel starts with the ____________ sign.
2. Press the ____________ key to view the result of the formula in the active cell.
3. The ____________ operator is used to join two strings.
4. The AutoSum button is found in the Editing group of buttons on the ____________ tab.
5. ____________ are predefined formulas in MS Excel.

C **State whether the following statements are true (T) or false (F).**

1. The data to be used within a formula should always be placed in a single cell. ☐
2. Providing cell ranges in the formula saves a lot of time. ☐
3. A formula can contain just one operator. ☐
4. You cannot join multiple strings. ☐
5. The evaluation of a formula is always from left to right. ☐

D **Answer the following questions.**

1. How can you enter formulas in MS Excel? Explain with an example.
2. 'Excel gives an advantage of auto editing the result.' Explain.
3. Define a string.
4. What will you infer if you see a couple of '#' in a cell?
5. Explain the AutoSum feature of MS Excel.

Lab Activity

1. Nikhil's father is the president of Vidya Housing Society. He has to make a list of flat owners who have paid maintenance charges of the society.

	A	B	C	D
1				
2		**Vidya Housing Society**		
3				
4–5		**Flat No.**	**Owner**	**Maintenance Charges**
6		1	Mr. Manish	20000
7		2	Mr. Karan	Not Paid
8		3	Ms. Mallika	22000
9		4	Ms. Kiran	10000
10		5	Ms. Bharti	13000
11		6	Mr. Deepak	Not Paid
12				
13				
14		No. of flat owners who have paid		
15		Total Collection		
16				

Research Project

Try to understand the use of the various statistical and engineering functions available under the More Functions category in the Function Library of MS Excel 2010.
[***Hint:*** *Select More Functions from the AutoSum group and search for specific categories of functions to use.*]

Teacher's Notes

1. Discuss the benefits of using formulas and functions.
2. Demonstrate with examples how formula errors can be rectified.

LibreOffice Calc

Cell and Range References

The procedure of **Cell and Range References** in LibreOffice Calc is the same as that in MS Excel 2010.

Using Formulas

The procedure of **Using Formulas** in LibreOffice Calc is the same as that in MS Excel 2010.

Text Formulas

The procedure of using **Text formulas** in LibreOffice Calc is the same as that in MS Excel 2010.

Mathematical Operators Used in Numeric Formulas

The procedure of using **Mathematical Operators Used in Numeric Formulas** in LibreOffice Calc is the same as that in MS Excel 2010.

Error Results

The **Error Results** produced in LibreOffice Calc is the same as that in MS Excel 2010.

AutoSum Feature

To use the AutoSum feature in LibreOffice Calc, follow these steps:

1. Select the cell or range of cells.
2. Press the **Sum** Σ from the **Formula bar**.

Functions in LibreOffice Calc

To use the functions in LibreOffice Calc, follow these steps:

1. Select the cell or range of cells.
2. Click on the **Function Wizard** command from the **Formula bar**. The **Function Wizard** dialog box appears.
3. Click on **Functions** tab and type the function name in the **Search** box. The search result appears under **Function** section.
4. Choose the required function and click on the **Next** button.
5. Type the new range in **Number 1** text box (as shown).
6. Click on **OK**.

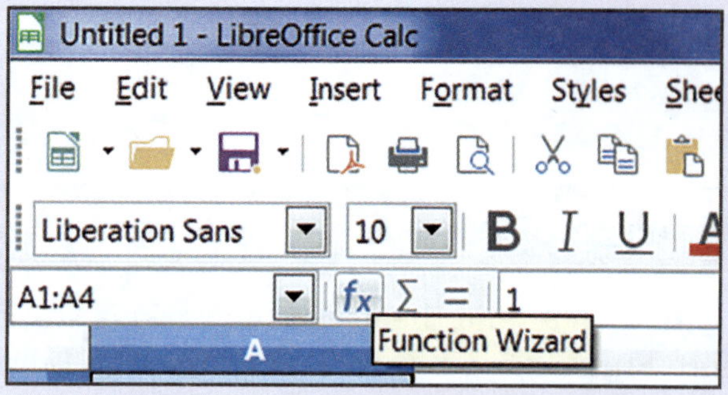

Alternatively, you can also use the **Functions** option from the **Sidebar** to use the functions.

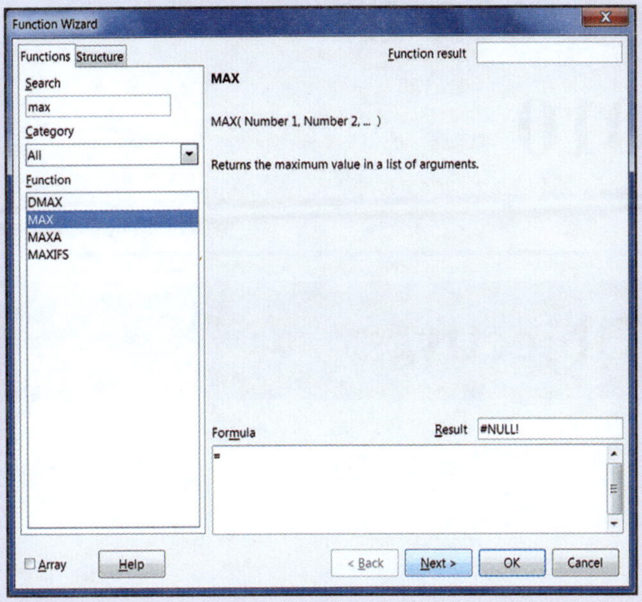
Function Wizard
Functions
Structure
Function result
Search
max
Category
All
Function
DMAX
MAX
MAXA
MAXIFS
MAX
MAX(Number 1, Number 2, ...)
Returns the maximum value in a list of arguments.
Formula
Result
#NULL!
=
Array
Help
< Back
Next >
OK
Cancel

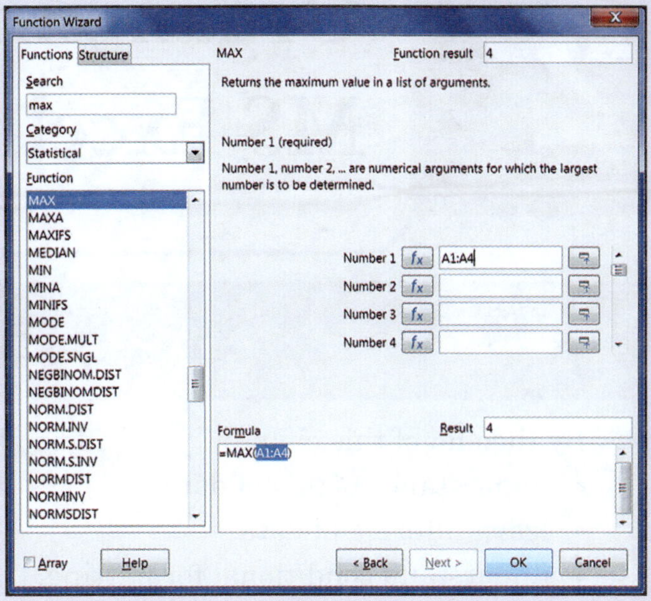
Function Wizard
Functions
Structure
MAX
Function result
4
Search
max
Category
Statistical
Function
MAX
MAXA
MAXIFS
MEDIAN
MIN
MINA
MINIFS
MODE
MODE.MULT
MODE.SNGL
NEGBINOM.DIST
NEGBINOMDIST
NORM.DIST
NORM.INV
NORM.S.DIST
NORM.S.INV
NORMDIST
NORMINV
NORMSDIST
Returns the maximum value in a list of arguments.
Number 1 (required)
Number 1, number 2, ... are numerical arguments for which the largest number is to be determined.
Number 1
A1:A4
Number 2
Number 3
Number 4
Formula
Result
4
=MAX(A1:A4)
Array
Help
< Back
Next >
OK
Cancel

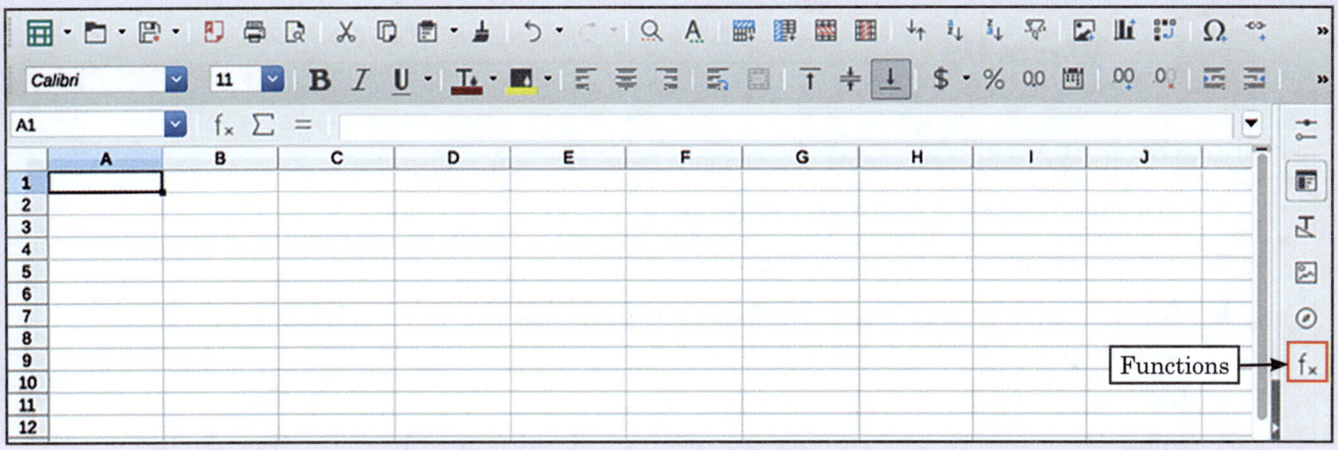
Calibri
11
A1
Functions

2 Organizing Data in MS Excel 2010

Learning Objectives

By the end of this chapter, you will be able to:

- understand sorting of data.
- learn filtering of data.
- understand conditional formatting.

Warm Up

Fill in the blanks.

1. All formulas in Excel begin with an ____________ sign.
2. Formulas cannot be applied to ________________.
3. The __________ group of buttons on the Formula Tab contain the various categories of formula buttons.
4. AND, OR, NOT, etc. are examples of _________________ functions.
5. The ______________ feature automatically adds numbers in the selected range of cells.

Introduction

Data looks presentable when it is organized in a particular order. The process of arranging data in a particular order is called **sorting**. Data in MS Excel can be sorted in ascending or descending order.

MS Excel also gives users the option of viewing selective data. This feature is called **filtering of data**.

Both sorting and filtering of data help in organizing it. Another way of making data more useful is by formatting, which helps to draw the attention of users. **Formatting** is the process of making changes in a worksheet in order to enhance its appearance or lay focus on specific data in the worksheet. In this chapter, you will learn **conditional formatting** where cells are formatted according to some specific conditions.

Types of Cell Referencing

The address of a cell used in calculating formulas is called a **cell reference**. A formula can be copied from one part of the worksheet to another. It may even be copied from one worksheet to another. Based on how a cell reference in the formula is copied and used, there are three types of cell referencing techniques—relative, absolute and mixed.

Relative Referencing

This type of referencing is based on the relative position of the cell in which the formula is being written, with respect to the cell address appearing in the formula. When the formula is moved or copied to other cells, the reference automatically changes according to the relative position. For example in Fig. 2.1, the formula in the cell F6 is (=E6/50*100). If the formula is copied for the cells F7 to F17, the relative referencing would change the formula accordingly and replace the row 6 of Column E in the formula with corresponding row values of the column E. So the formula in cell F7 will be = F6 / 50 * 100.

	A	B	C	D	E	F
1						
2			Class VII - Result			
3						
4			Maximum Marks :		50	
5		S. No	Name	Class	Marks	Percentage
6		8	Anirudh	VII C	49	=E6/50*100
7		3	Astha	VII A	48	
8		12	Dhruv	VII D	45.5	
9		6	Chandni	VII B	43.5	
10		5	Jia	VII B	42	
11		9	Tejasvi	VII C	42	
12		10	Soumya	VII D	42	
13		11	Allen	VII D	41	
14		4	Tanvi	VII B	39.5	
15		2	Aarav	VII A	36	
16		1	Pooja	VII A	35	
17		7	Supriya	VII C	30	

Fig. 2.1: Relative Referencing

Absolute Referencing

This type of referencing is used when we do not want to change the address of the cell while copying the formula to another cell. To implement absolute referencing, make absolute reference of a formula, that is, add a dollar sign **($)** before the column and the row number. For example in Fig. 2.2, $E$4 can be used instead of the number 50 for calculating

You should know!

To refer to a cell in another worksheet, use the sheet number followed by an exclamation mark (!) and then the cell address. For example, if you want to refer to cell A1 in Sheet 2, the cell reference will be Sheet2!A1 or Sheet2!$A$1.

percentage in Column F. When a formula containing absolute reference of a cell is copied, the address of this cell will not change anywhere.

Mixed Referencing

This type of cell referencing is the combination of absolute and relative referencing. While implementing mixed referencing, either the row or the column of the cell reference being used in the formula is fixed. Cell references such as $A5 or A$5 are examples of mixed referencing.

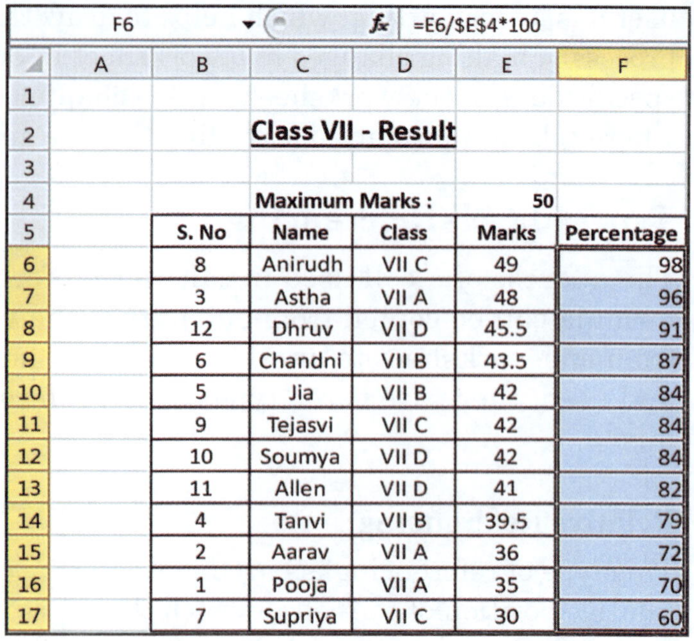

F6 =E6/$E$4*100

	A	B	C	D	E	F
1						
2			Class VII - Result			
3						
4			Maximum Marks :		50	
5		S. No	Name	Class	Marks	Percentage
6		8	Anirudh	VII C	49	98
7		3	Astha	VII A	48	96
8		12	Dhruv	VII D	45.5	91
9		6	Chandni	VII B	43.5	87
10		5	Jia	VII B	42	84
11		9	Tejasvi	VII C	42	84
12		10	Soumya	VII D	42	84
13		11	Allen	VII D	41	82
14		4	Tanvi	VII B	39.5	79
15		2	Aarav	VII A	36	72
16		1	Pooja	VII A	35	70
17		7	Supriya	VII C	30	60

Fig. 2.2: Absolute referencing

Sorting Data

Sorting of data is done to arrange data in ascending or descending order. The data in the cells being sorted may be numeric or textual or both. There are three buttons to sort data in the **Sort & Filter** group of buttons on the **Data** tab:

a. **Sort** : This displays a **Sort dialog box** to sort data based on various criteria at one go.

b. **Sort Smallest to Largest** : Sorts the data in ascending order.

c. **Sort Largest to Smallest** : Sorts the data in descending order.

Sorting can be done in any way—single-column sorting and multiple-column sorting.

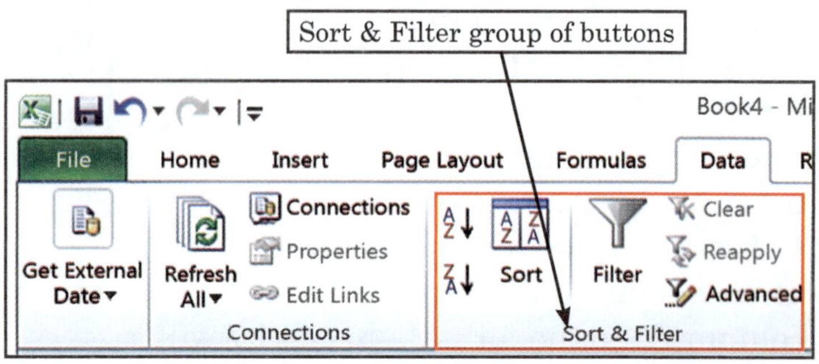

Fig. 2.3: Sort & Filter group of buttons

Single-column Sorting

In this type of sorting, data is sorted according to the values in one column only. Consider the table shown in Fig. 2.4. It contains the average temperature and the average rainfall of India in each month. In this example, we will be sorting the data in ascending order of temperature. To do so, follow these steps:

1. Select the cell in the column according to which you want to sort the data. Since data is to be sorted according to average temperature, so select any cell in column C, say C7.

2. Click **Select Smallest to Largest** button to sort data in ascending order of temperature. You will see that the entire data is arranged according to the data values in a single column (C) containing average temperature.

	A	B	C	D
1				
2		Average Temperature and Rainfall In India		
3				
4		Month	Average Temperature (°F)	Average Rainfall (in mm)
5				
6		January	65	0.7
7		February	68.4	0.8
8		March	75.1	1.1
9		April	81.3	2.1
10		May	84.7	3.9
11		June	83.8	9.8
12		July	80.9	13.9
13		August	80.1	11.5
14		September	79.7	7.8
15		October	77.2	4.1
16		November	71.3	2
17		December	66.2	1

Fig. 2.4: Unsorted data

	A	B	C	D
1				
2		Average Temperature and Rainfall In India		
3				
4		Month	Average Temperature (°F)	Average Rainfall (in mm)
5				
6		January	65	0.7
7		December	66.2	1
8		February	68.4	0.8
9		November	71.3	2
10		March	75.1	1.1
11		October	77.2	4.1
12		September	79.7	7.8
13		August	80.1	11.5
14		July	80.9	13.9
15		April	81.3	2.1
16		June	83.8	9.8
17		May	84.7	3.9

Fig. 2.5: Data sorted in ascending order of temperature

Multiple-column Sorting

In this type of sorting technique, data is sorted according to values in multiple columns. For example, in Fig. 2.6, the data has to be sorted in ascending order of month and in descending order of average temperature.

To understand the concept of multiple-column sorting, first add two rows in the table containing data for any two months, say August and November.

D17 fx 2.1

	A	B	C	D
1				
2		Average Temperature and Rainfall In India		
3				
4		Month	Average Temperature (°F)	Average Rainfall (in mm)
5				
6		January	65	0.7
7		February	68.4	0.8
8		March	75.1	1.1
9		April	81.3	2.1
10		May	84.7	3.9
11		June	83.8	9.8
12		July	80.9	13.9
13		August	82.3	12.6
14		August	80.1	11.5
15		September	79.7	7.8
16		October	77.2	4.1
17		November	69.4	2.1
18		November	71.3	2
19		December	66.2	1

Fig. 2.6: Unsorted data

Follow these steps to sort data according to values in multiple columns:

1. Select the range of cells that need to be sorted. Alternatively, users can also select any cell in the range. For example, select B4:D19.
2. Click the **Sort** button in the **Sort & Filter** group of buttons on the **Data** tab. The **Sort** dialog box appears (Fig. 2.7).
3. On the top right corner of the dialog box there is an option—**My data has headers**. This option should be checked if the selected range consists of column headings in the top row of the selected

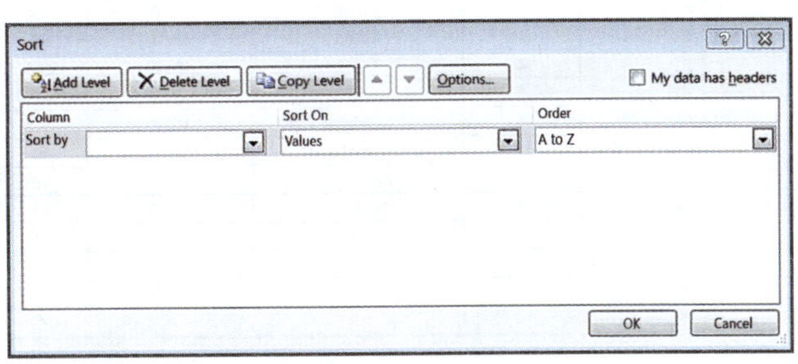

Fig. 2.7: Sort dialog box

range. Since the selected range consists of column headings, so check the option (Fig. 2.8).

4. Under the **Column** section, there is the **Sort by** list box. Choose the column to be used to sort the data. You will have all the column headings in the list box to choose from. Select Month from the available list of options.

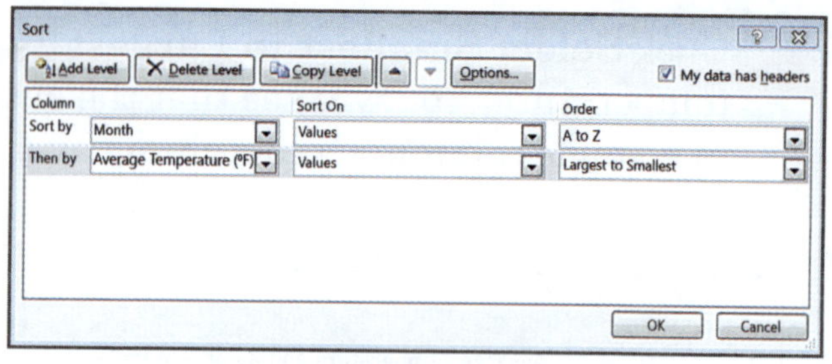

Fig. 2.8: Adding another column in Sort dialog box

5. Under **Order**, A to Z is already selected. To sort in descending order, then choose Z to A.
6. Click **Add Level** button on the top left corner of the dialog box. A new row appears as shown in Fig. 2.8. Select Average Temperature for **Then by** list box in **Column** section. Under **Order**, select **Largest to Smallest**.
7. Click **OK**. The data is arranged in ascending order of month (alphabetically) and in descending order of average temperature as shown in Fig. 2.9.

B6 — April

Average Temperature and Rainfall In India

Month	Average Temperature (°F)	Average Rainfall (in mm)
April	81.3	2.1
August	82.3	12.6
August	80.1	11.5
December	66.2	1
February	68.4	0.8
January	65	0.7
July	80.9	13.9
June	83.8	9.8
March	75.1	1.1

Fig. 2.9: Sorted data

PRACTICE TIME

For an interclass competition, Geetika's teacher wants the list of participants to be arranged in order of their score, so that the prize winners can be identified easily. The teacher has asked Geetika to complete the task using MS Excel. Help Geetika complete the task.

SOLUTION

1. Enter the data in an Excel worksheet.
2. Select a cell in column E.
3. Click ZA↓ in the **Sort & Filter** group under the **Data** tab. The data will be sorted in descending order.

Interclass Declamation Competition

S. No.	Name	Class	Score
1	Pooja	VII A	35
2	Aarav	VII A	36
3	Astha	VII A	48
4	Tanvi	VII B	39.5
5	Jia	VII B	42
6	Chandni	VII B	43.5
7	Supriya	VII C	30
8	Anirudh	VII C	49
9	Tejasvi	VII C	42
10	Soumya	VII D	42
11	Allen	VII D	41
12	Dhruv	VII D	45.5

Original data

Interclass Declamation Competition

S. No.	Name	Class	Score	
8	Anirudh	VII C	49	FIRST
3	Astha	VII A	48	SECOND
12	Dhruv	VII D	45.5	THIRD
6	Chandni	VII B	43.5	
5	Jia	VII B	42	
9	Tejasvi	VII C	42	
10	Soumya	VII D	42	
11	Allen	VII D	41	
4	Tanvi	VII B	39.5	
2	Aarav	VII A	36	
1	Pooja	VII A	36	
7	Supriya	VII C	30	

Sorted data

Filtering Data

The Filter feature of MS Excel selectively blocks or hides data. Only that part of data which meets the specified criteria for a column is displayed. This feature helps to retrieve and work with selected subsets of data as the unwanted data is temporarily hidden from the view. Users can edit, analyse, format and even print the filtered data. Filtering does not rearrange data as is done while sorting. The filtering of data can be done on the basis of any or both of the following:

a. Data values in cells, for example, cells with values greater than 50 to be filtered
b. Different cell formats, for example, red-coloured cells to be filtered

In the **Sort & Filter** group of buttons, **AutoFilter**, **Advanced Filter** and **Custom Filtering** are the three commands (Fig. 2.10) available to filter data ranges. In the former, a simple criteria is given for filtering while in the latter case, a more complex criteria is given for filtering.

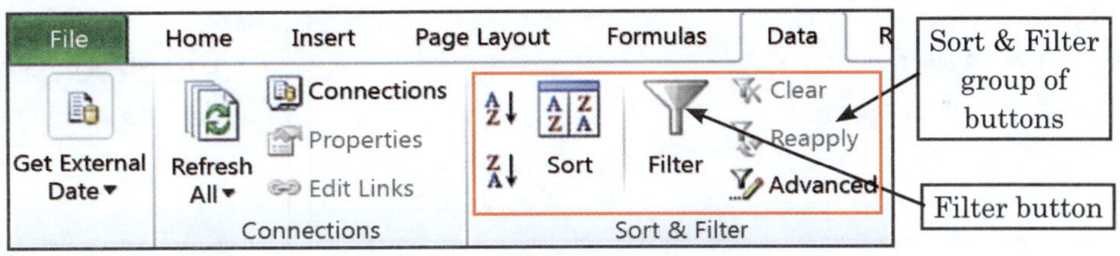

Fig. 2.10: Filter commands in Sort & Filter group of buttons

AutoFilter Command

The AutoFilter command is used to filter a column or row to view the data that meets a specific criteria. To use the AutoFilter command, follow these steps:

H9

	A	B	C	D	E	F
1						
2						
3	Roll No	Name	FA1	FA2	SA1	SA2
4	2	Abhishek	20	22	46	58
5	5	Ritu	19	24	60	59
6	7	Ankit	13	15	30	40
7	10	Vaishvanee	23	24	59	58
8	8	Subhash	20	20	51	53
9	14	Anuj	9	6	19	17

Fig. 2.11: Unfiltered data

1. Create a table (as shown in Fig. 2.11) containing marks of students in FA1, FA2, SA1 and SA2.

2. Select any cell in the range A3:F9, say C5 (Fig. 2.12).

3. Under the **Data** tab, click the **Filter** button in the **Sort & Filter** group of buttons. Small arrows are seen next to each column heading with the filter icon. This indicates that the filtering has been turned on. Once filtering is turned on, click the arrow in the column header to choose the filter for the column, say SA2. A drop-down menu is displayed (Fig. 2.13).

C5 | f_x 19

	A	B	C	D	E	F
4	2	Abhishek	20	22	46	58
5	5	Ritu	19	24	60	59
6	7	Ankit	13	15	30	40
7	10	Vaishvanee	23	24	59	58
8	8	Subhash	20	20	51	53
9	14	Anuj	9	6	19	17

Fig. 2.12: Selecting a cell to apply filter criteria

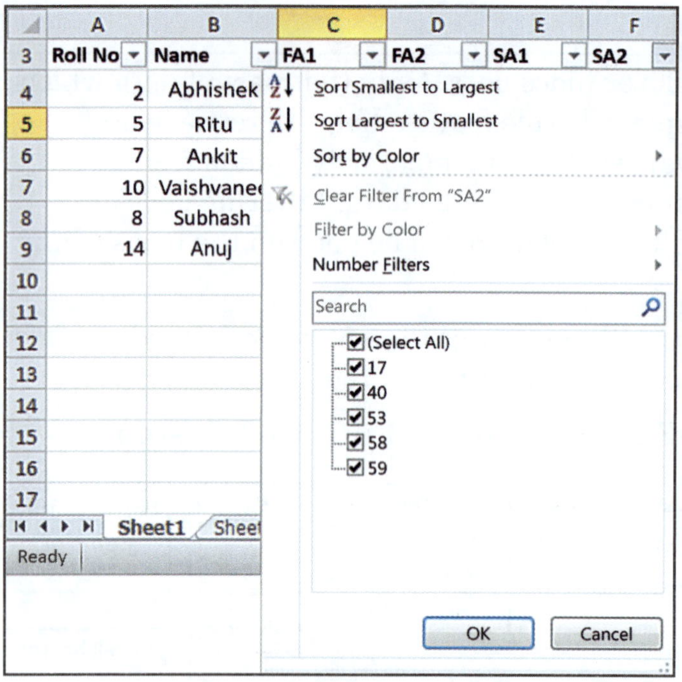

Fig. 2.13: Filter drop-down menu

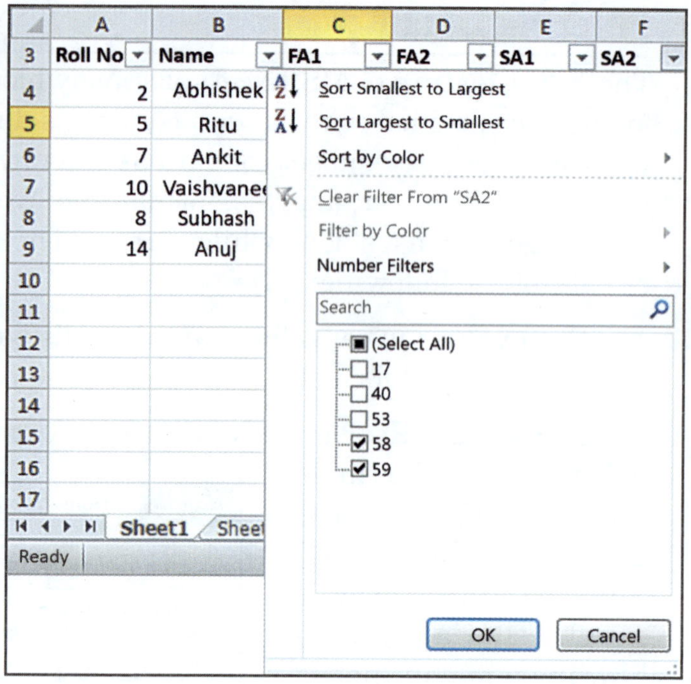

Fig. 2.14: Deselect Select All

4. You will see that **Select All** option is checked. Deselect **Select All** and select 58 and 59 from the drop-down menu to retain only the numbers which are more than 55 (Fig. 2.14). You can even type the value in the **Search pane** given in the drop-down menu.

5. Click **OK**. The rows with more than 55 marks in SA2 will be filtered from the original table and displayed (Fig. 2.15).

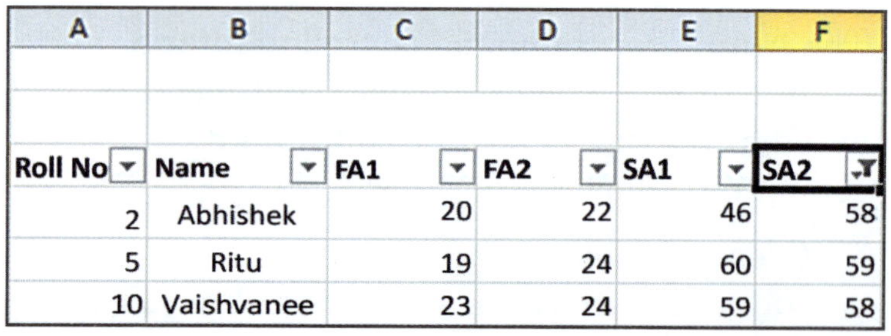

Fig. 2.15: Filtered data

When filtering is enabled but not applied, a drop-down menu arrow appears next to the column name. When a filter is applied to a particular column, the filter button appears next to the column name. When you bring the mouse pointer over this, the filter criteria is displayed as the **screen** tip (Fig. 2.16).

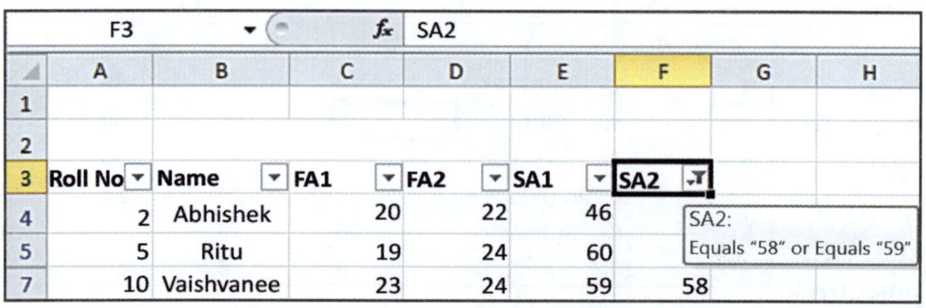

Fig. 2.16: Filter criteria

Quick Way

The shortcut key to filter data is **Ctrl+Shift+L.**

Quick Way

Click the **Clear** button in the **Sort & Filter** group of buttons under the **Data** tab to remove the filter.

If you edit the data within the selected range, click the **Reapply** button in the **Sort & Filter** group. The filter criteria is reapplied to the new data.

To remove the filter, click the arrow next to the column heading where filter was placed (SA2 here) and select **Clear Filter** from SA2 or check **Select All** option in the Filter drop-down menu.

Custom Filtering

The **Filter** command is used to filter data based on multiple conditions. For example, to display the rows where SA2 marks lie in the range of 20 to 50, follow these steps:

1. Select the range to be filtered. Click the **Filter** button in the **Sort & Filter** group.
2. In the **Filter** drop-down menu, click **Number Filters** option. A submenu containing various operations such as Equals, Does Not Equal, Greater Than, Less Than, Above Average, and Below Average appears (Fig. 2.17).
3. Choose the desired filter, say **Between**. The **Custom AutoFilter** dialog box is displayed. Fill in less than 50 and greater than 20 (Fig. 2.18).
4. Click **OK**. The rows that have SA2 marks between 20 and 50 is displayed (Fig. 2.19).

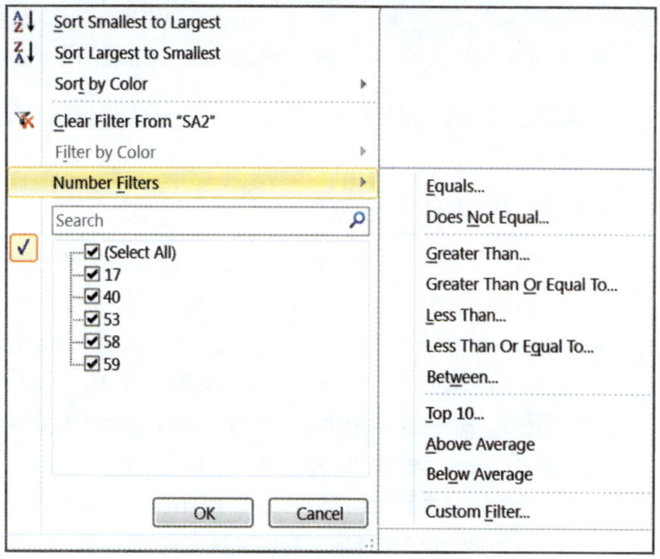

Fig. 2.17: Number Filters

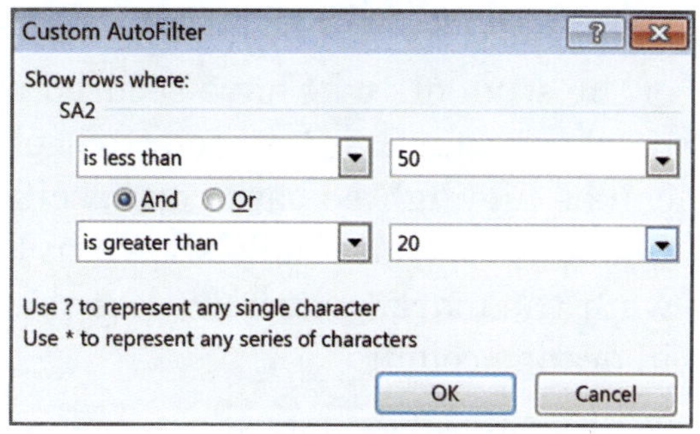

Fig. 2.18: Custom AutoFilter dialog box

The top scorers or low scorers in SA2 can also be filtered. Select the **Top 10** option from the **Number Filters** submenu. In the **Top 10 AutoFilter** dialog box (Fig. 2.20), customize the number of rows that you want to view by selecting Top/Bottom option.

Select **Above Average** or **Below Average** from the submenu to display rows with total marks above or below the average.

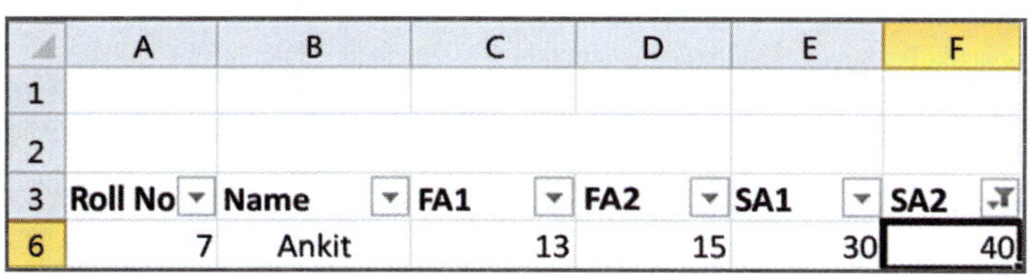

Fig. 2.19: Custom AutoFilter dialog box

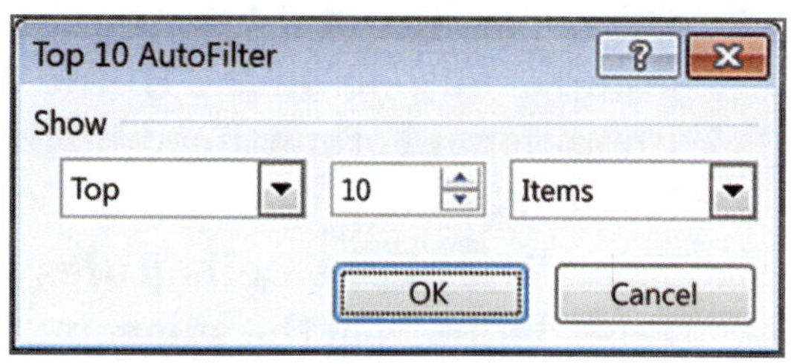

Fig. 2.20: Top 10 dialog box

Check your understanding!

State whether the following statements are true (T) or false (F).

1. Absolute referencing is based on the relative position of the cell in which the formula is being written. ☐
2. The Sort & Filter group of buttons appears on the Data tab. ☐
3. Filtering can be used to rearrange data in a particular sequence. ☐
4. Both cell formats and data values can be used to filter cells. ☐
5. The shortcut key to filter data is Ctrl+Shift+L. ☐

Conditional Formatting

Conditional formatting in MS Excel highlights important information in a spreadsheet. It allows users to set the cell's format according to the given conditions so that variations in data can be easily identified. Users can highlight selected cells or emphasize certain rows using this feature. The **Conditional formatting** command is in the **Styles** group of buttons under the **Home** tab.

Users can display data in a particular colour or style depending on a particular condition. For example, conditional formatting can be used to display the data of the students who have secured more than 50% marks in green colour. Selected cells, rows or columns can be highlighted based on specific condition(s). Consider the data table shown in Fig. 2.21 in which we want the marks which are less than 20, to be displayed in orange colour.

	A	B	C	D
1	Class Test - Social Science			
2				
3	Roll No	Name	History	Geography
4	1	Geeta	45	43
5	2	Ratan	34	39
6	3	Siddarth	49	26
7	4	Aparna	45	17
8	5	Vishnu	12	8
9	6	Amrit	38	45
10	7	Aditi	19	28
11	8	Karishma	40	45
12	9	Sudershan	42	41
13	10	Ritwik	33	36

Fig. 2.21: Selecting the range

To display select data in a specific colour (here, orange), follow these steps:

1. Select the range containing data. In the example given, the range is C4:D13.
2. Click **Conditional Formatting** in the **Styles** group of buttons on the **Home** tab. The Conditional Formatting drop-down menu appears (Fig. 2.22).
3. Select **Highlight Cells Rules** and choose **Less Than** from the submenu.

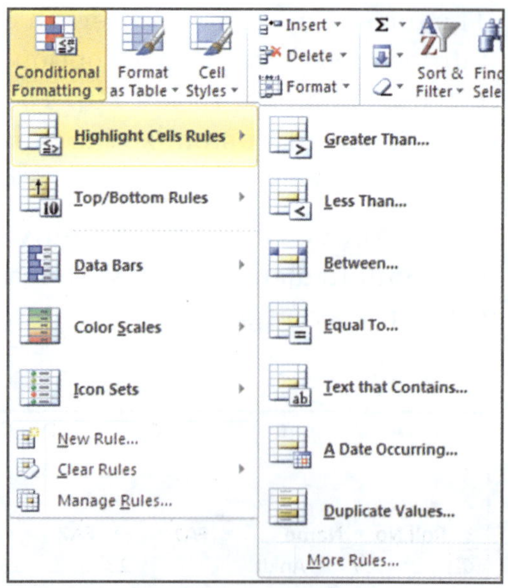

Fig. 2.22: Conditional Formatting

4. The **Less Than** dialog box appears. Type 20 in the text box labelled **Format cells that are LESS THAN** (Fig. 2.23).
5. Click the arrow in the **with** list box. Select the desired format option.

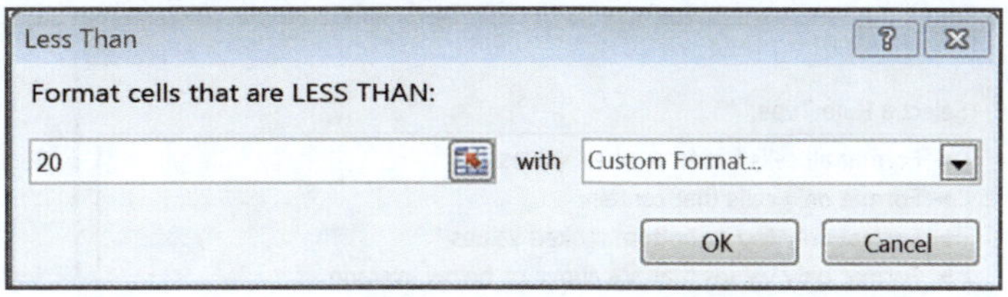

Fig. 2.23: Setting criteria in Conditional Formatting

6. If you want to have a format style of your own, click **Custom Format** option from the drop-down menu. The **Format Cells** dialog box is displayed (Fig. 2.24).
7. Select the desired font style and colour. Click **OK**. The **Less Than** dialog box appears again.
8. Click **OK**. You will see that all cell values with marks less than 20 are displayed in orange colour.

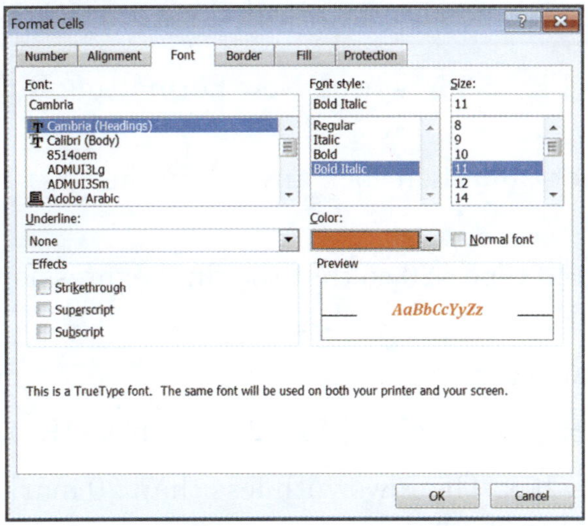

Fig. 2.24: Format Cells dialog box

	A	B	C	D
1	Class Test - Social Science			
2				
3	Roll No	Name	History	Geography
4	1	Geeta	45	43
5	2	Ratan	34	39
6	3	Siddarth	49	26
7	4	Aparna	45	*17*
8	5	Vishnu	*12*	*8*
9	6	Amrit	38	45
10	7	Aditi	*19*	28
11	8	Karishma	40	45
12	9	Sudershan	42	41
13	10	Ritwik	33	36

Fig. 2.25: Result of the criteria using Conditional Formatting

To clear Conditional Formatting, click the arrow next to the **Clear Rules** option in the **Conditional Formatting** drop-down menu. Choose any of the two options—**Clear Rules from Selected Cells** or **Clear Rules from Entire Sheet**.

To apply conditional formatting to selected rows, follow these steps:

1. Select the entire table shown in Fig. 2.26.
2. In the **Conditional Formatting** drop-down menu, click **New Rule**. The **New Formatting Rule** dialog box appears (Fig. 2.27).
3. In the **Select a Rule Type** section, click **Use a formula to determine which cells to format** (Fig. 2.28). You also have options to format rows having values above or below average or a particular value or having unique or duplicate values.

	A	B	C	D
1	Class Test - Social Science			
2				
3	Roll No	Name	History	Geography
4	4	Aparna	45	43
5	5	Vishnu	34	39
6	1	Geeta	49	26
7	2	Ratan	45	17
8	3	Siddarth	12	8
9	6	Amrit	38	45
10	7	Aditi	19	28
11	8	Karishma	40	45
12	9	Sudershan	42	41
13	10	Ritwik	33	36

Fig. 2.26: Conditional Formatting for selected rows

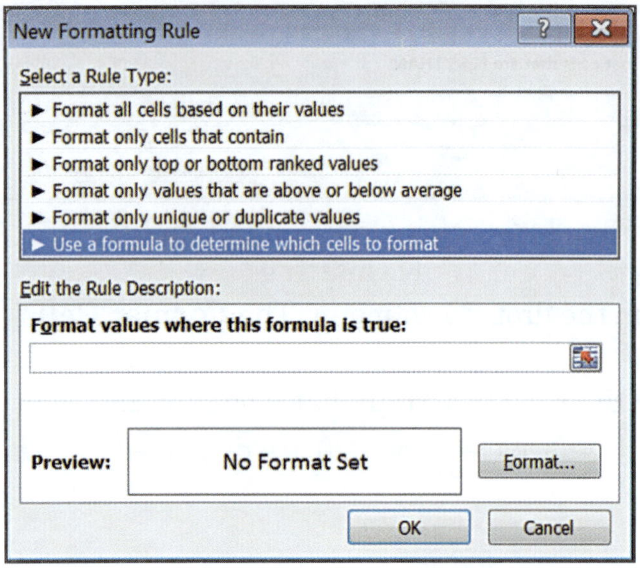

Fig. 2.27: Setting rules for selected rows

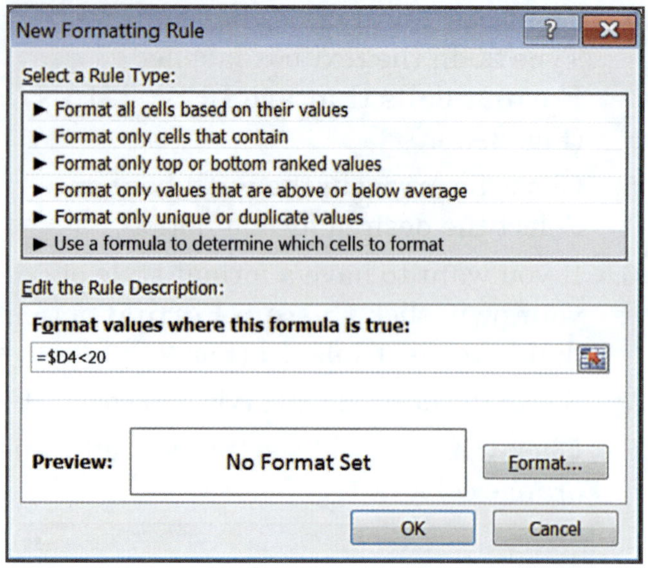

Fig. 2.28: Setting New Formatting Rule

4. In the **New Formatting Rule** dialog box, type = and then click any cell in the Geography column.
5. Delete the dollar sign before the row number and type <20 so that the final expression becomes =$D4<20.
6. Click **Format**. The **Format Cells** dialog box appears.
7. Click the **Fill** tab and choose orange as the background colour (Fig. 2.29). Click **OK**.
8. Click **OK** in the **New Formatting Rule** dialog box. The rows with less than 20 marks in Geography will be filled with orange colour (Fig. 2.30).

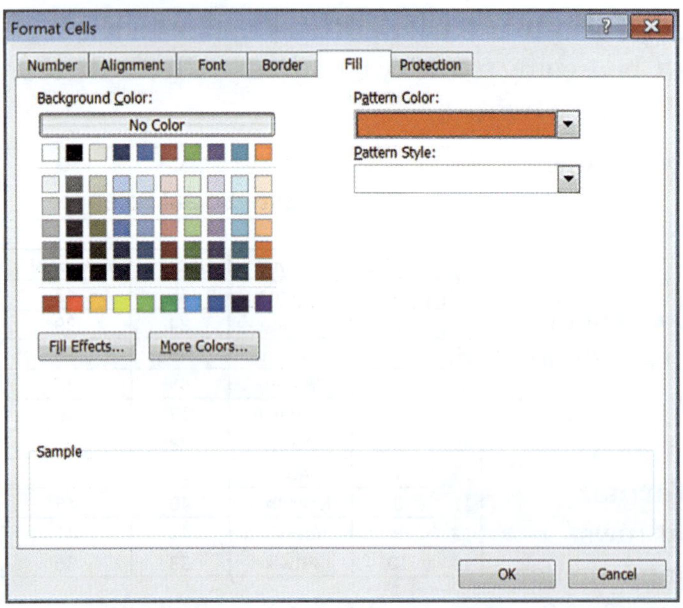

Fig. 2.29: Setting Fill criteria

	A	B	C	D
1	Class Test - Social Science			
2				
3	Roll No	Name	History	Geography
4	1	Geeta	45	43
5	2	Ratan	34	39
6	3	Siddarth	49	26
7	4	Aparna	45	17
8	5	Vishnu	12	8
9	6	Amrit	38	45
10	7	Aditi	19	28
11	8	Karishma	40	45
12	9	Sudershan	42	41
13	10	Ritwik	33	36

Fig. 2.30: Final Result of Conditional Formatting for selected rows

You should know!

MS Excel allows you to sort and filter data by cell colour also. To sort by cell colour, select **Cell Color** under **Sort On** in the **Sort** dialog box.

To filter data by cell colour, select **Filter By Color** in the **Filter** drop-down menu.

Thereafter, specify the colour and the data will be sorted/filtered.

Quick Way

You can copy the conditional formatting to other cells using the **Format Painter** tool under the **Home** tab.

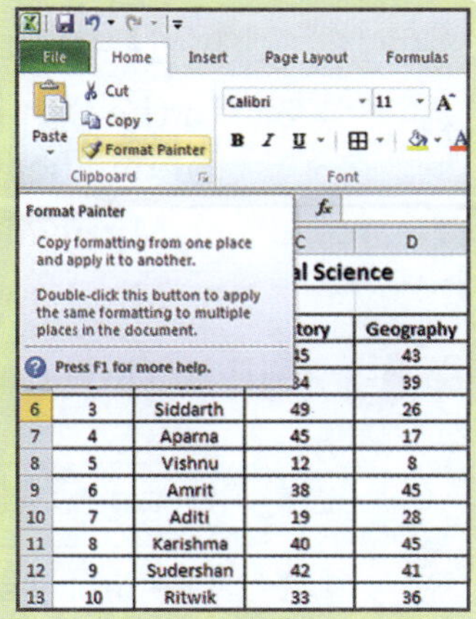

Quick Recap

1. The address of a cell used in calculating a formula is called a cell reference. There are three types of cell referencing techniques—relative, absolute and mixed.
2. Relative referencing is based on the relative position of the cell in which the formula is being written, with respect to the cell address appearing in the formula.
3. Absolute referencing is used when we do not want to change the address of the cell while copying the formula to another cell.
4. Mixed referencing is the combination of relative and absolute referencing. While implementing this, either the row or the column of the cell reference being used in the formula is fixed.
5. Sorting refers to arranging the data in ascending or descending order.
6. Data can be sorted on single or multiple column values.
7. Filtering displays selective data that meet the specified criteria for a column.
8. Conditional Formatting sets the cell's format according to the given conditions.

Exercises

A **Choose the correct option for each of the following.**

1. In ________________ referencing, the cell reference in a formula changes.

   a. Mixed b. Absolute c. Formula d. Relative

2. = $A$1 * B14 is an example of which type of referencing?

   a. Relative b. Absolute c. Mixed d. None of these

3. Sorting can be based on cell values of:

   a. Single column only c. Both single and multiple columns

   b. Multiple columns only d. None of these

4. Which of the following is the button to sort data in descending order?
   a. [Sort] – Sorting Data
   b. [Z↓A] – Sorting Data
   c. [A↓] – Sorting Data
   d. None of these
5. In the Sort dialog box, ______________ option is selected if the selected range consists of column headings in the top row of the selected range.
   a. My headers
   b. My Data
   c. My data has headers
   d. My headers have data

B Fill in the blanks using the words given below.

sorting   Mixed   conditional formatting   Sort & Filter   sorting   filtering

1. The process of arranging data in a particular order is called ______________ .
2. ______________ and ______________ of data helps to organize data.
3. When data is formatted according to the specific conditions, it is called ______________.
4. ______________ referencing is the combination of absolute and relative referencing.
5. The buttons to sort data are in ______________ group of buttons on Data tab.

C State whether the following statements are true (T) or false (F).

1. Data can only be sorted from the smallest to the largest values. ☐
2. A formula cannot be copied from one cell to another. ☐
3. H$3 is an example of mixed referencing. ☐
4. Data is not rearranged while filtering. ☐
5. You cannot copy filtered records. ☐

D Answer the following questions.

1. Name different types of cell referencing techniques.
2. How can data be sorted on multiple columns?
3. On what basis can filtering of data be done?
4. How do we get to know when filtering is turned on?
5. Define conditional formatting. How can it be copied from one cell to another?

Lab Activity

1. Your father has asked you to make a list of any eight families in the neighbourhood and create an Excel sheet containing their details:

   After creating the table, you have been asked to perform the following tasks:

   a. Display the details of families in alphabetical order of their names.
   b. Display the details of families in descending order of income.
   c. Display the data in descending order of male members.
   d. Display the income that is more than 50000 in yellow colour.

e. Highlight the rows of Business families with green colour.

f. Display the rows where the income is more than average income.

RSG Residential Society

S No.	Name	Female Members	Male Members	Income	Occupation
1	Gaba	3	4	95000	Business
2	Sachdeva	3	3	109000	Service
3	Pandit	2	5	98000	Mixed
4	Khan	4	2	145000	Farming
5	Batra	5	1	99000	Mixed
6	Zarin	3	2	134000	Service
7	Anand	1	1	155000	Farming
8	Sharma	2	3	140000	Service

Health Care Clinic

No.	Name	Age	Department	OPD_Date	Charges	Sex
1	Navin	44	Neuro	13-05-2014	500	M
2	Rakesh	55	Orthopaedic	20-10-2014	1000	M
3	Nimmi	4	Eye	10-07-2014	550	F
4	Jeet	19	Surgery	21-01-2014	200	M
5	June	61	ENT	17-02-2014	650	F
6	Penny	14	ENT	27-07-2014	550	F
7	Kunal	36	Cardiology	20-11-2014	500	M
8	Phoola	66	Gardiology	22-05-2014	300	F
9	Shipra	19	Cardiology	14-03-2014	900	F
10	Anuj	21	Paediatrics	19-10-2014	1400	M

2. Sushma is working in a healthcare clinic. She has been asked to create an Excel worksheet containing details of the patients visiting the hospital. Help her to perform the following tasks:
   a. Display the data in descending order of age.
   b. Highlight the data of the patients visiting the ENT department in green colour.
   c. Display the charges which are less than 300 in blue colour.
   d. Display the patients paying the maximum consultation charges in yellow colour.

Research Project

Explore the option of **Format only top or bottom ranked values** that appears in New Formatting Rule while setting the rules for selected rows in Conditional Formatting.

Teacher's Notes

1. Discuss why data should be organized.
2. Discuss why and in which situations should the data be sorted and/or filtered.
3. Discuss how conditional formatting helps to deliver a better worksheet.

LibreOffice Calc

Types of Cell Referencing

The **Types of Cell Referencing** in LibreOffice Calc is the same as that in MS Excel 2010.

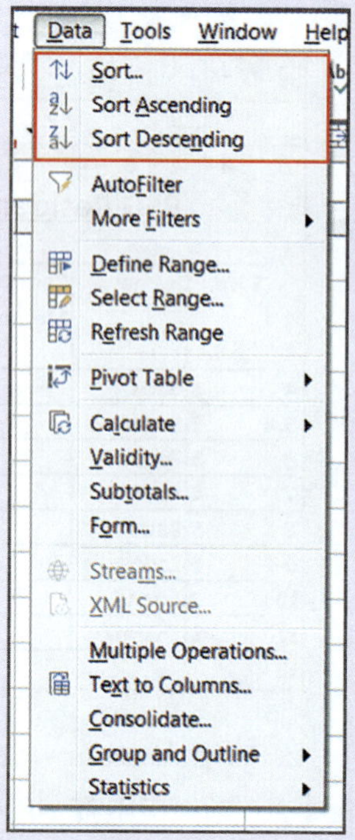

Sorting Data

To sort the data in LibreOffice Calc, follow these steps:

1. Select the cell or range of cells.
2. Click on the **Data** menu.
3. Choose the appropriate option.
   - **Sort** option helps to sort the data based on various criteria at the same time.
   - **Sort Ascending** option helps to sort the data in ascending order.
   - **Sort Descending** option helps to sort the data in descending order.

Alternatively, you can also use the commands from the **Standard** toolbar to sort the data.

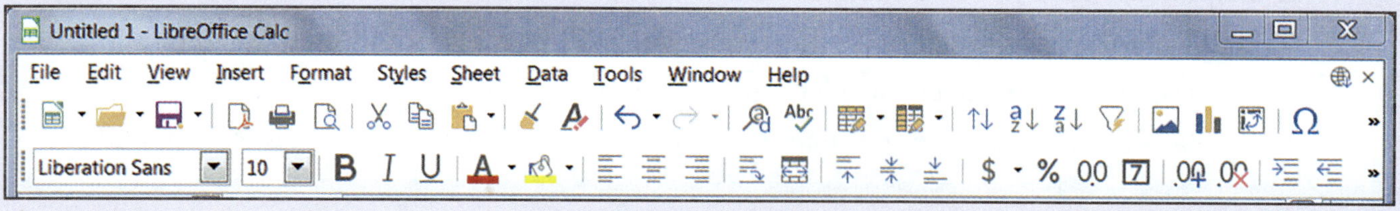

Standard toolbar

Filtering Data

This feature helps to retrieve and work with selected subset of data as the unwanted data is temporarily hidden from the view.

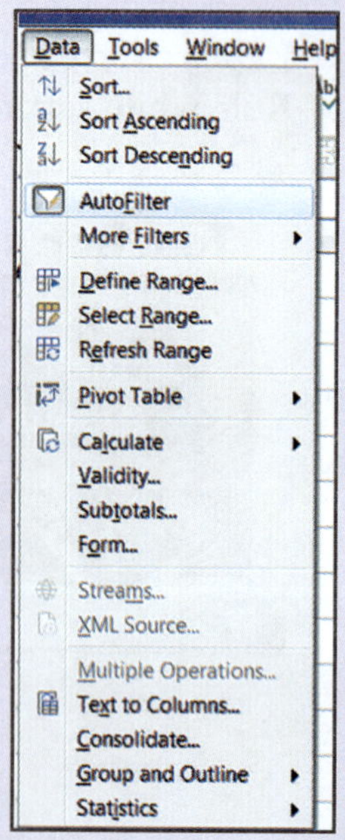

AutoFilter Command

To apply **AutoFilter** in LibreOffice Calc, follow these steps:

1. Select any cell from the range of cells.
2. Click on the **Data** menu.
3. Click on the **AutoFilter** option. The small arrows appear with every field name.
4. Click on the drop-down arrow next to the required field name and specify the condition.
5. Click on **OK**.

Alternatively, you can also click on the **AutoFilter** command from the **Standard** toolbar.

Custom Filtering

To apply **Custom Filter** in LibreOffice Calc, follow these steps:

1. Select any cell from the range of cells.
2. Click on the **Data** menu.
3. Click on the **More Filters** option. A pop-up menu appears.
4. Click on the **Standard Filter** option. The **Standard Filter** dialog box appears.
5. Choose the appropriate criteria to filter i.e. choose the field names, conditions, values and the operator (as shown).
6. Click on **OK** button.

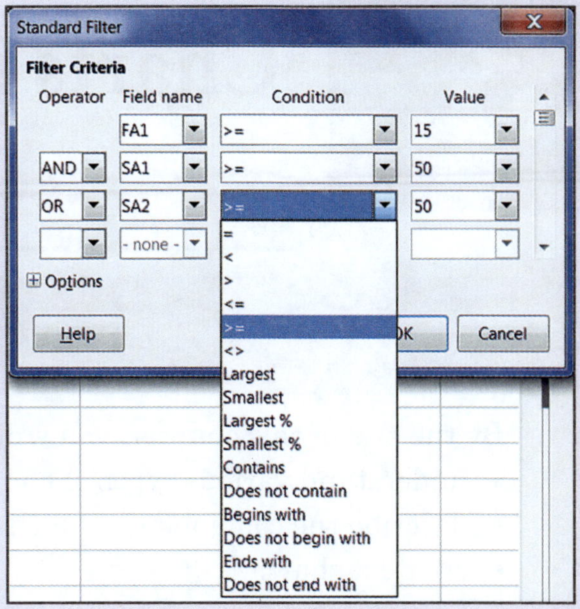

Conditional Formatting

To apply **Conditional Formatting** in LibreOffice Calc, follow these steps:

1. Select any cell from the range of cells.
2. Click on the **Format** menu.
3. Click on the **Conditional** option. A pop-up menu appears.
4. Choose the **Condition** option. The **Condition Formatting** dialog box appears.
5. Specify the condition and required style to apply. Click on the **Add** button to add more than one column for conditional formatting.
6. Click on **OK** button.

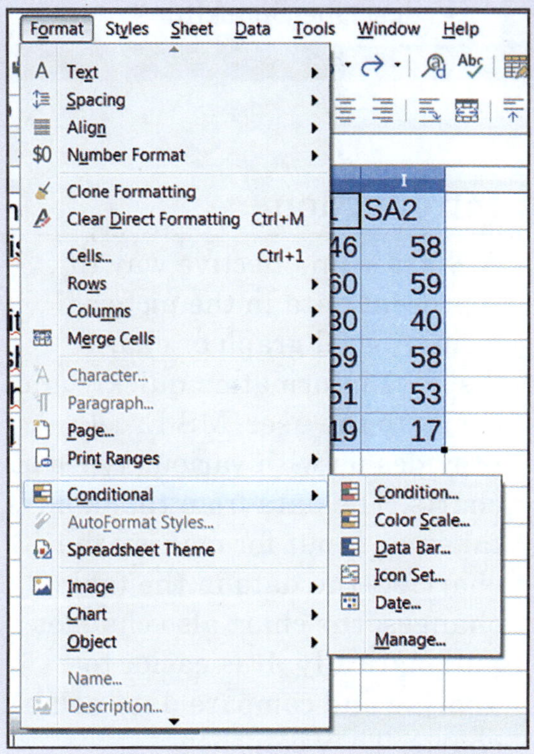

3 Charts in MS Excel 2010

Learning Objectives

By the end of this chapter, you will be able to:

- understand various types of charts.
- describe the components of a chart.
- create a chart.
- format a chart using chart tools.
- describe Sparklines.

Introduction

A chart is an effective way to represent data in the pictorial form. A good graph or chart displays information quickly and easily to the user. MS Excel provides us with various types of charts. The data from the table is taken as input for making the chart. As the data in the table changes, the chart also changes automatically. It is easier to analyse and compare data using charts. They can show relationships that are not easily understood by studying a list of numbers. Charts can also provide a convenient way to compare different sets of data.

Types of Charts

Excel provides us with different types of charts. To understand them, consider the table shown in Fig. 3.1 that shows the hobbies of people living in two residential societies.

	A	B	C	D	E	F	G
2							
3				Hobbies			
4							
5			Reading	Travelling	Sports	Painting	Dancing
6		Society A	25	32	23	11	9
7		Society B	30	27	19	11	13
8							

Fig. 3.1: Data table

Bar Chart

A bar chart displays data in the form of long, rectangular rods called bars of different heights, displayed either vertically or horizontally. So, comparisons between various data items can be made easily. In a bar chart, the categories are organized vertically and the values horizontally. The data displayed on the bar chart may include various types of information such as sales of a particular item over a period of time or the salaries of private and public school teachers, and so on. The information displayed through a bar chart helps users to analyse data and reach conclusions quickly and easily. The bar chart in Fig. 3.2 compares the hobbies of people in Society A (in blue) and Society B (in red).

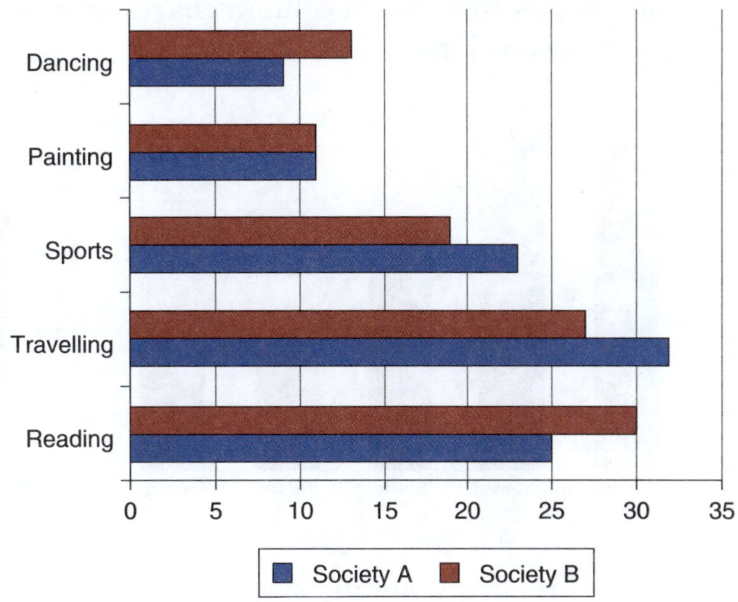

Fig. 3.2: Bar chart

Line Chart

It is the most basic type of chart and is used to depict related information. It is created by connecting a series of data points together with a line. This type of chart is often used to plot changes in data over a period of time such as change in fuel prices over a period of year, production or sales trends over a period of time, monthly temperature changes, effects of scientific experiments, etc. Usually, in a line chart, category is plotted along the horizontal or x-axis and data is plotted as individual points along the vertical or y-axis. A line chart is preferred when there are many data points or when data trends are important. Figure 3.3 shows a line chart for the data presented in Fig. 3.1.

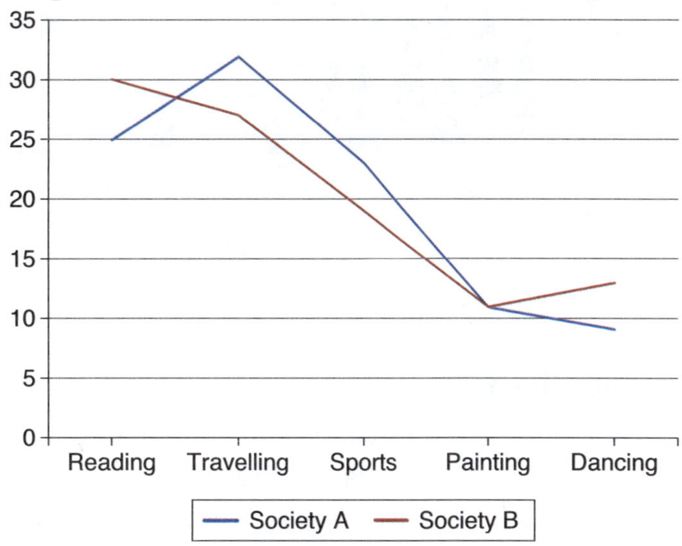

Fig. 3.3: Line chart

Column Chart

This is one of the most commonly used charts in which data is represented in the form of vertical bars. It is similar to a bar chart but the bars are placed vertically in this type of chart. The heights of the bars are proportionate to the value of data.

Generally, categories are organized along the horizontal axis and the values along the vertical axis (Fig. 3.4). Each data point in a series is represented by a column that rises from the x-axis. A column chart is used to show changes in data over a period of time or to illustrate comparisons between different data items. A column chart is preferred when height of individual points is more important than the trend in series.

The various subtypes of column charts available in Excel 2010 are—cylinder, cone and pyramid (Figs. 3.5–3.7).

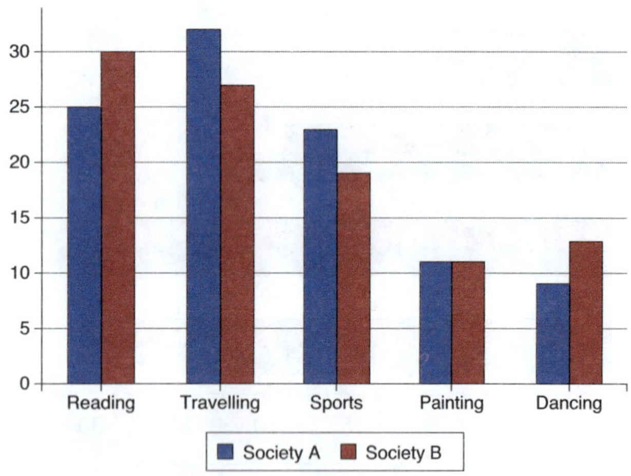

Fig. 3.4: Column chart

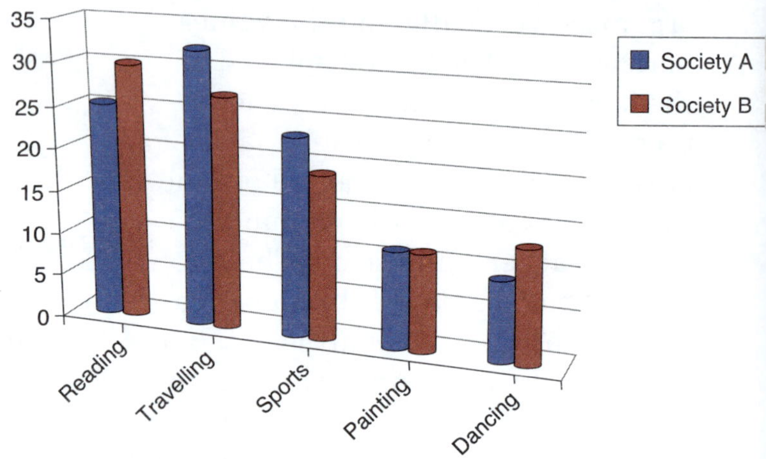

Fig. 3.5: Cylinder subtype of column chart

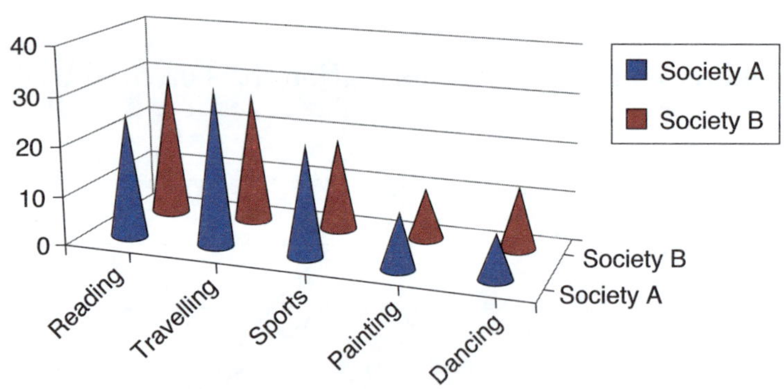

Fig. 3.6: Cone subtype of column chart

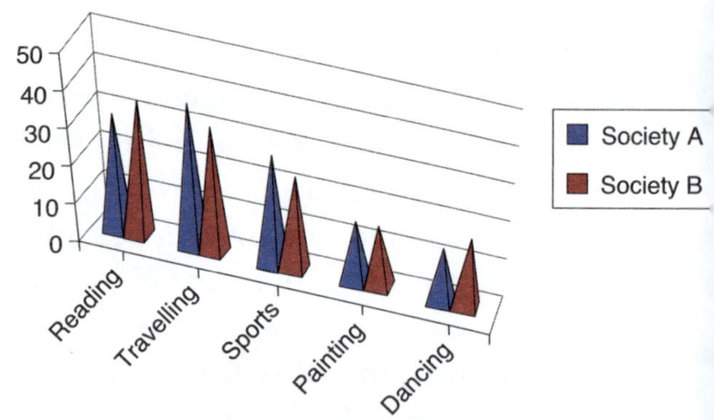

Fig. 3.7: Pyramid subtype of column chart

Pie Chart

A pie chart displays data in the form of a circle that is divided into sectors. Each sector represents a data value and the size of each sector is proportional to the value it represents. Hence, all the sectors are summed up together to make the full circle. In a pie chart, data is plotted for a single-data series. Pie charts are used in advertising and mass media.

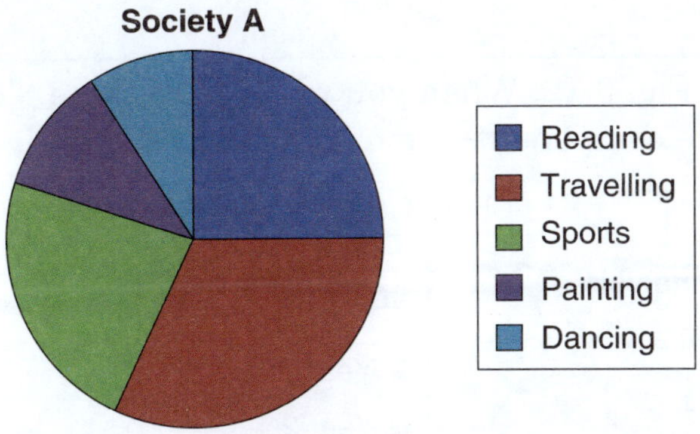

Fig. 3.8: Pie chart

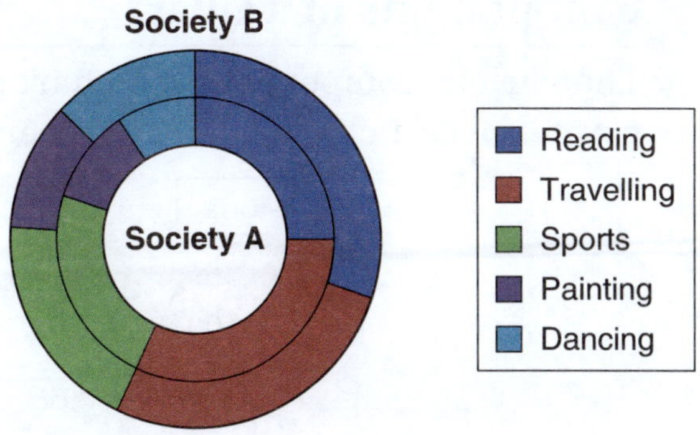

Fig. 3.9: Doughnut chart

Doughnut Chart

A doughnut chart is functionally identical to a pie chart. The difference is that unlike a pie chart, a doughnut chart may contain more than one data series. It displays data as a percentage of the whole. Each ring of a doughnut chart represents one data series (Fig. 3.9). The category groups or series groups are represented by individual doughnut slices as a percentage of the sum of all the values in the data series.

Area Chart

An area chart is used to display quantitative data graphically. It is based on a line chart but the area between the axes and the lines is filled with different colours. This colourful and visual display distinguishes data more clearly. Users can also plot one series on top of another. It is mainly used for representing sales and production figures.

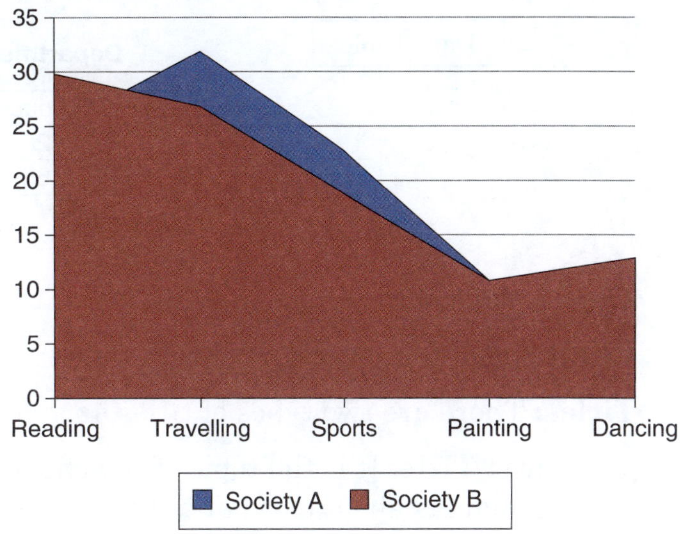

Fig. 3.10: Area chart

3D Surface Chart

It creates a three-dimensional view of data. It shows a three-dimensional surface that connects a set of data points. Unlike other charts, colours in surface chart are used to distinguish values and not each data series. A topographic map is an example of a 3D surface chart in which the same colour represents the same range of values.

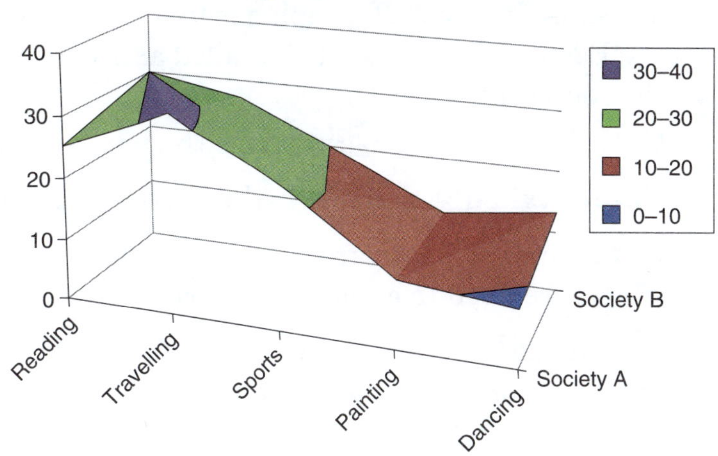

Fig. 3.11: 3D Surface Chart

Components of a Chart

The various components of a chart are shown in Fig. 3.12. When you move the mouse pointer over a chart object, a screen tip giving the component name is displayed.

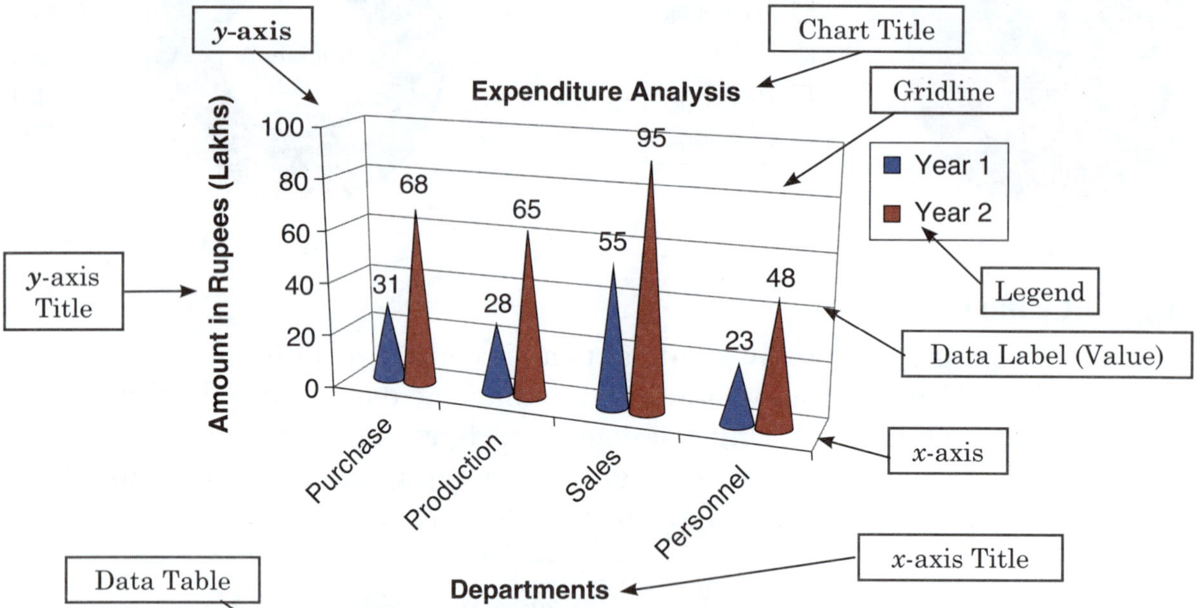

	Purchase	Production	Sales	Personnel
Year 1	31	28	55	23
Year 2	68	65	95	48

Fig. 3.12: Components of a chart

The key components of a chart are:

Chart Area: It refers to the area in which all the components or objects of the chart are placed.

Titles: There are two types of titles as given below:

a. **Chart Title:** It is the topic of the chart, usually given at the top. It lets us know what the chart is about or what data can be inferred from the chart. In Fig. 3.12, 'Expenditure Analysis' is the title of the chart.

b. **Axis Titles:** A 2D graph has two axes (*x* and *y*) while a 3D chart has three axes (*x*, *y* and *z*). Each axis is given a title, called axis title, which depicts the data series the respective axes represent.

Category Axis or *x*-axis: It is the horizontal axis of the chart.

Value Axis or *y*-axis: It is the vertical axis used to plot the value of each data point.

Data Series: These are the bars, sectors or other elements that represent data values which are used to create the chart.

Plot Area: It is the rectangular area or a window within the chart area bound by two axes for a 2D chart. 3D charts, on the other hand, have a base area constituted by the *x–y* plane. This is known as the **floor**. The vertical areas, that is, the *y–z* and *x–z* planes are known as the **walls**. The two walls and the floor constitute the plot area in a 3D chart. It contains the actual chart and includes the plotted data, data series and value axis.

Legend: It identifies the data series being represented by the chart. A unique colour, pattern or symbol is assigned to each data series so that it can be easily distinguished.

Gridlines: These are the lines that run across the plot area from each category on the *x*-axis and from each value on the *y*-axis. Although displaying of gridlines is optional, the exact value of each data point can be easily known if gridlines are displayed.

Data Label: It is the label that provides information about a data point on a chart.

Data Table: It is the table from where the input to create the chart is taken.

Check your understanding!

Fill in the blanks.

1. A ____________ chart uses vertical bars while a ____________ chart uses horizontal bars to represent data.
2. The ____________ is the horizontal axis and the ____________ is the vertical axis.
3. A chart is used to present data in a ____________ form.
4. In a ____________ chart, data is displayed as a circle that is divided into sectors.
5. A topographic map is an example of a ____________ chart.

Creating a Chart

The commands to create a chart are in the **Charts** group of buttons on the **Insert** tab (Fig. 3.13).

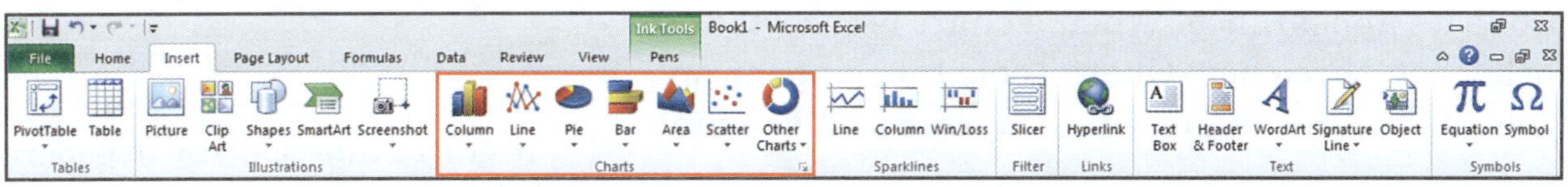

Fig. 3.13: Charts group of buttons

To create a chart in MS Excel 2010, follow these steps:

1. Enter the data in a worksheet. Refer to the table shown in Fig. 3.14 that shows the salary and donations of five employees of an organization. The range of the data is A1:C7.
2. Select the data range (A1:C7) and click on the **Insert** tab.
3. From the **Charts** group of buttons, choose any chart type, say **Bar Chart**.

	A	B	C	D
1	Name	Salary	Donation	
2				
3	Arvind	14000	200	
4	Sumita	25000	380	
5	Pushp	17000	400	
6	Vandana	29000	550	
7	Abhishek	33000	500	
8				

Fig. 3.14: Data in Excel

4. Click the arrow below the **Bar Chart** button and choose the desired subtype from the submenu. The chosen chart subtype will be displayed in the centre of the worksheet (Fig. 3.15). You can move it to any other location on the worksheet by clicking and dragging its white background. The size of the chart can be changed by dragging its corners.

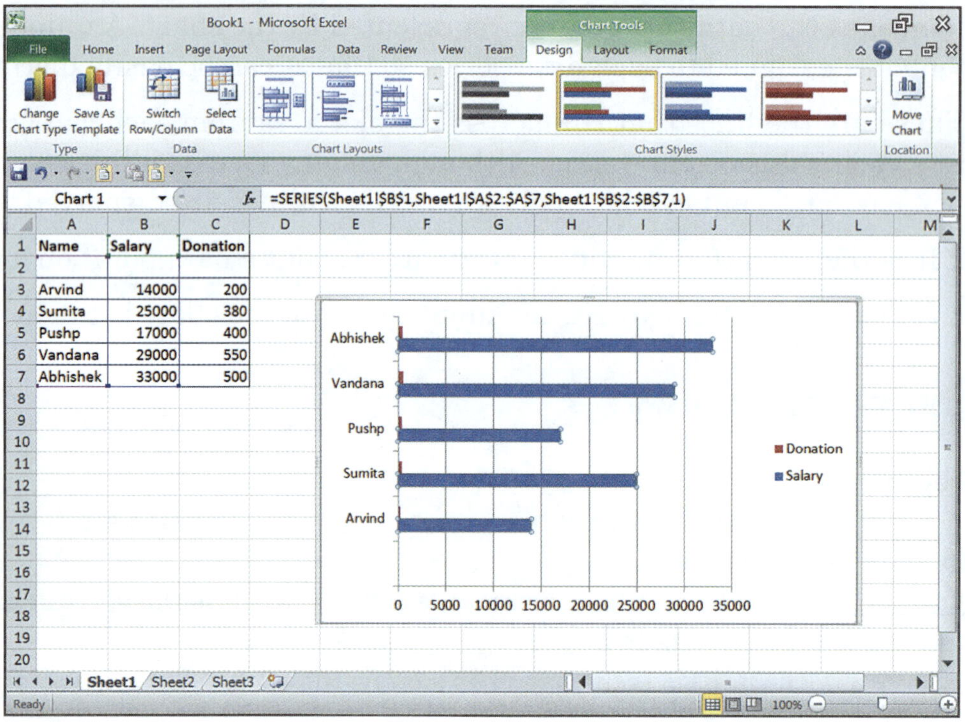

Fig. 3.15: Bar chart inserted on a worksheet

Formatting a Chart

MS Excel allows you to format a chart by changing its layout, design, style, location, etc. in order to improve its appearance. When a chart is inserted in a worksheet, three new Chart Tools tabs appear on the ribbon. These are **Design**, **Layout** and **Format**.

Quick Way

Select the data range that you want to represent on a chart and press F11 function key to generate the chart instantly.

Applying Chart Styles

The **Design** tab on the ribbon provides various chart style options in the **Styles** group of buttons. Click the arrow in the **Styles** group of buttons. All chart styles will be displayed as shown in Fig. 3.16. Click on any of the styles to give your chart the desired look.

PRACTICE TIME

Gather information about the number of girls and boys in each section of Class 7 in your school. Represent this data using a bar chart, column chart, line chart and pie chart. Which chart is easiest to read?

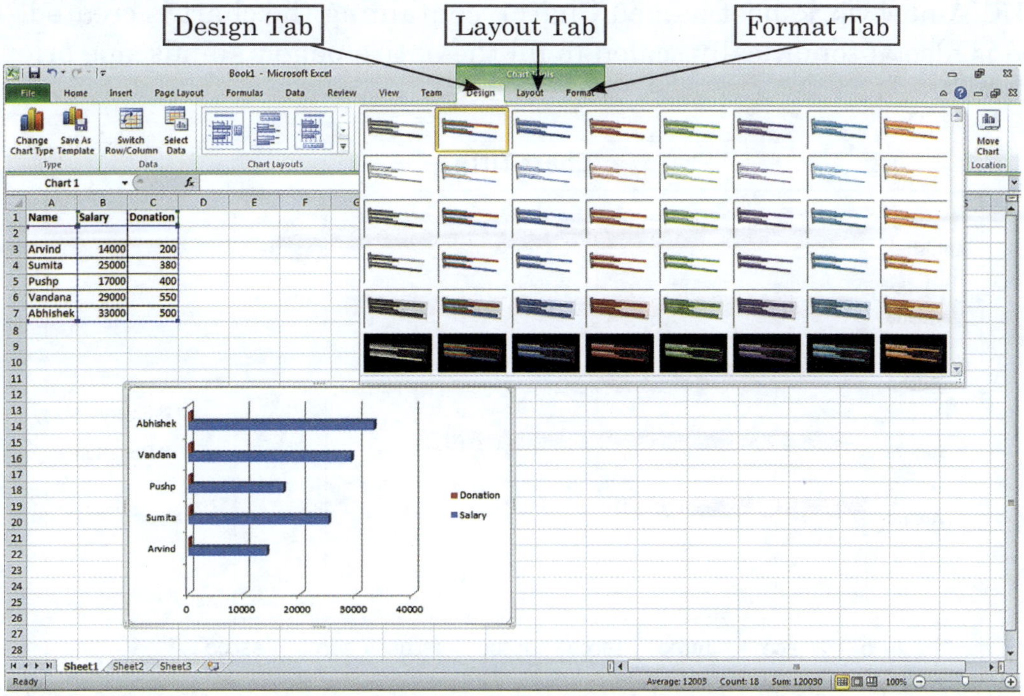

Fig. 3.16: Chart styles

Moving the Chart

You can move the chart from one location to another on the same worksheet or on a different worksheet.

1. Click the **Move Chart** button in the **Location** group of buttons on the **Design** tab (Fig. 3.17).

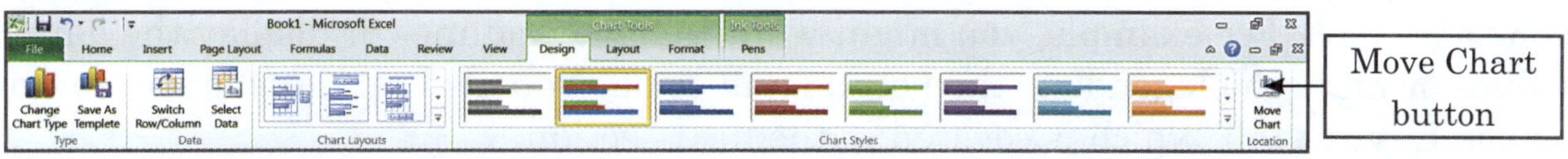

Fig. 3.17: Move Chart button on the Design tab

2. The **Move Chart** dialog box appears (Fig. 3.18).

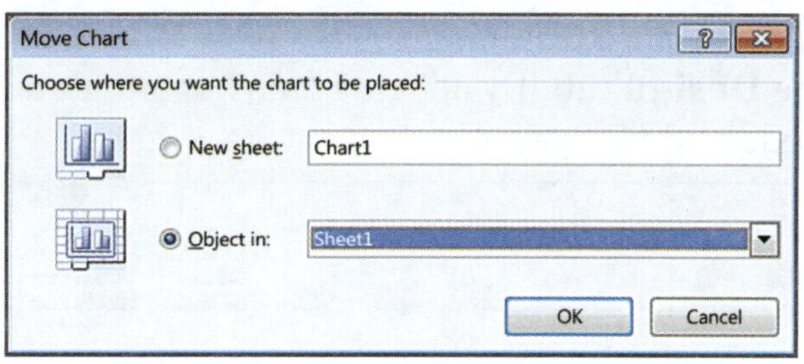

Fig. 3.18: Move Chart dialog box

3. The **Object in** radio button is already selected and you can choose any of the existing worksheets for the destination location of your chart. If you want to move the chart to a new worksheet, click **New sheet** radio button and type the name of the new worksheet, say Chart1.

4. Click **OK**. A new worksheet named Chart1, containing the chart is created. The chart inserted is also automatically scaled to fill the entire page in landscape orientation (Fig. 3.19).

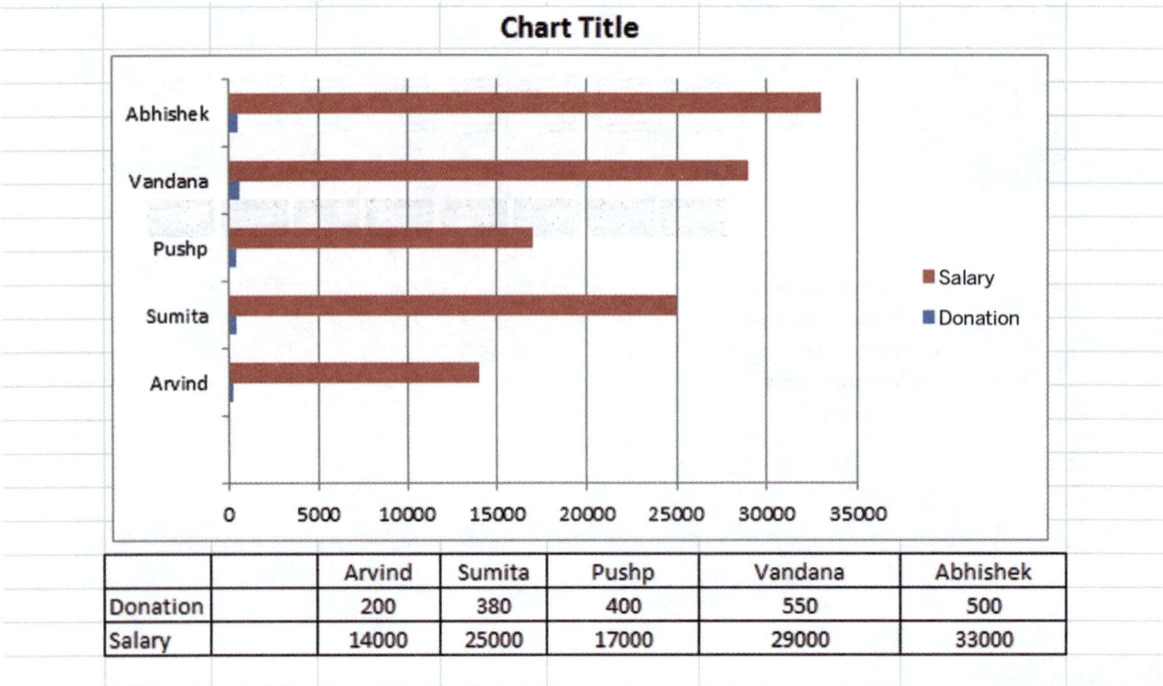

		Arvind	Sumita	Pushp	Vandana	Abhishek
Donation		200	380	400	550	500
Salary		14000	25000	17000	29000	33000

Fig. 3.19: Chart inserted in a new worksheet

5. You can double-click on the **Chart Title** in the new sheet to give a title to your bar chart.

6. In the **Layout** group of buttons on the **Design** tab, you can choose a desired layout of your bar chart. For example, you might want to have gridlines or display the data values or move the legends to the bottom and so on. You also get more layout options on the **Layout** tab, which is covered in the next section.

You should know!

You can swap the data over the axes using the **Switch Row/Column** button in the Data group of buttons on the **Design** tab. By clicking this button, data being charted on the *x*-axis will move to *y*-axis and vice versa.

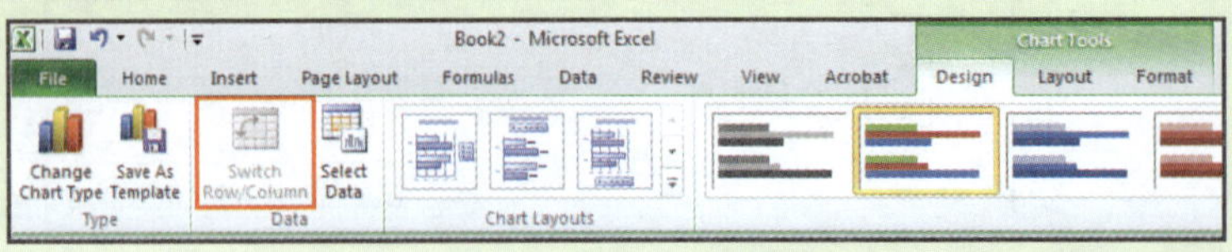

Changing the Layout

The **Layout** tab allows you to edit, that is, add or change the components of the chart (Fig. 3.20). You can change the titles, legends, data labels, background and other properties of the chart.

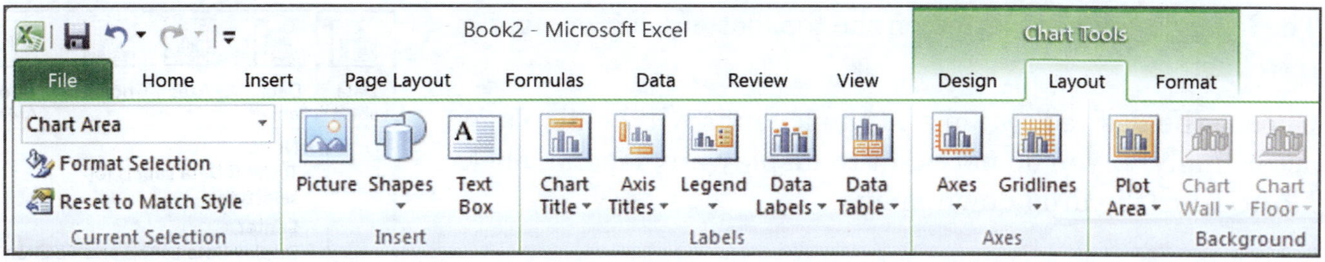

Fig. 3.20: Layout Tab

Chart Title

Click **Chart Title** in the **Labels** group of buttons on the **Layout** tab. The drop-down menu gives you the options as shown in Fig. 3.21.

If your chart does not contain any title, select the **None** option. Click the **Above Chart** option to add the title above the chart. The **Chart Title** text box is inserted above the chart. Double-click on it to add the title.

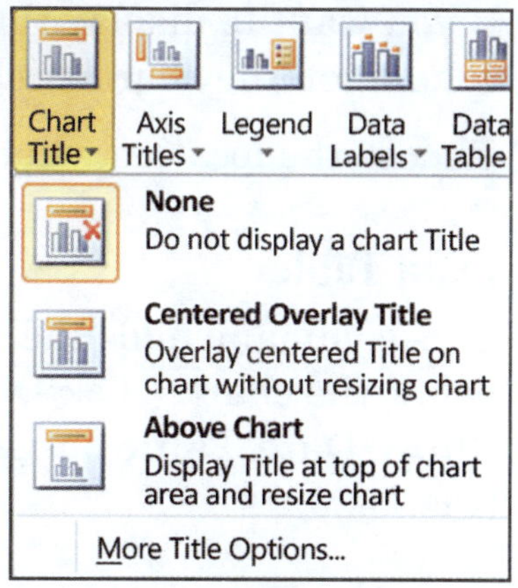

Fig. 3.21: Chart Title options

Axis Titles

This command allows you to add/edit titles along the *x*-axis and *y*-axis.

To add an *x*-axis title, click **Axis Titles**. Click **Primary Horizontal Axis Title** and from the submenu, choose the option **Title Below Axis**. The *x*-axis title text box appears below the axis. Double-click on it and type the new title.

To add a *y*-axis title, click **Primary Vertical Axis Title** from the **Axis Title** submenu (Fig. 3.22). Choose the desired layout of title from the submenu. The *y*-axis title text box is inserted. Double-click to type the new title.

Legend

Click on **Legend** button and a drop-down menu containing various options for inserting the legends with respect to the chart is displayed (Fig. 3.23).

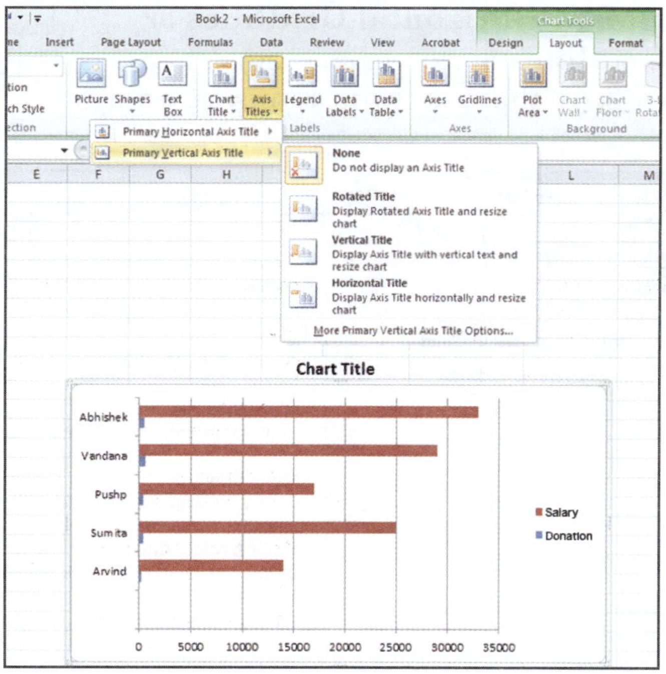

Fig. 3.22: Axis submenu

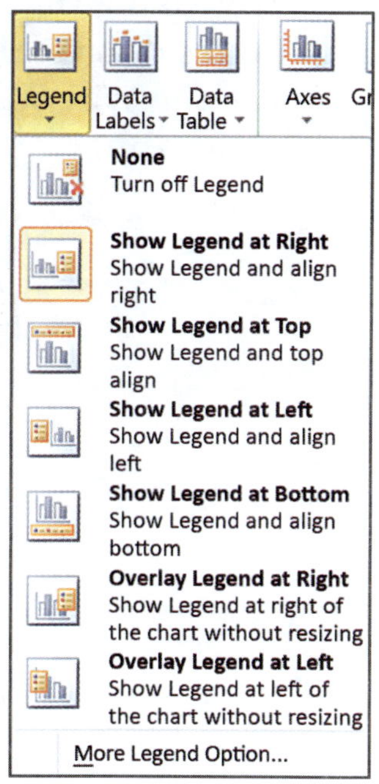

Fig. 3.23: Legend options

The legends can be inserted on the top, bottom, left or right of the chart.

Choose the desired option and the legends will be displayed accordingly. If you do not want to display any legend, click **None** from the drop-down menu.

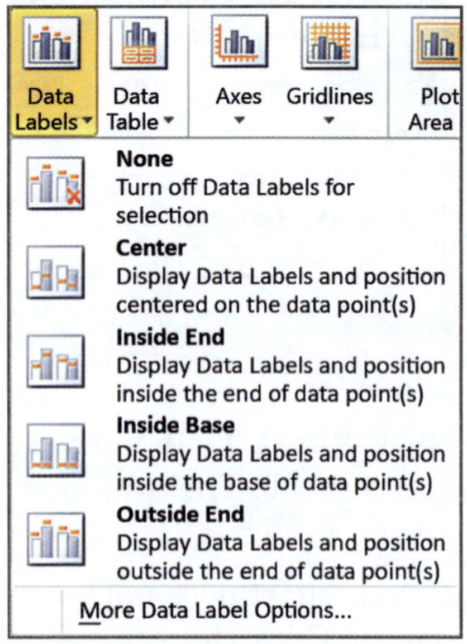

Fig. 3.24: Data Labels menu

Data Labels

If you want to display the value of each data point or column on the chart, click **Data Labels** button (Fig. 3.24).

Choose the location where you want to place the labels.

Data Table

This command adds the table on which the chart is based below the chart. Click **Data Table** button and then select **Show Data Table** option from the drop-down menu (Fig. 3.25).

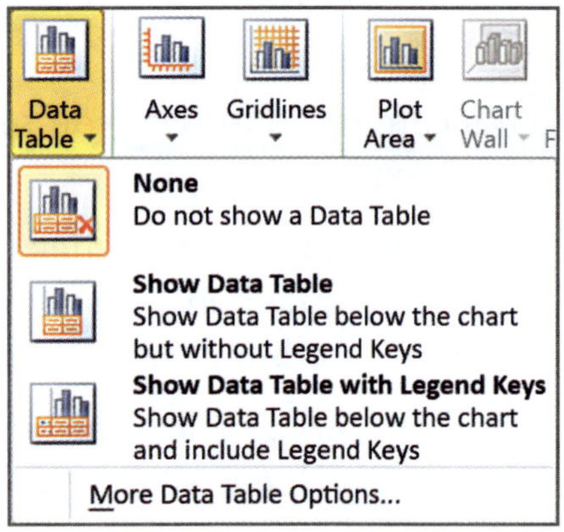

Fig. 3.25: Data Table menu

Gridlines

This command in the **Axes** group of buttons turns gridlines on or off. Gridlines are of two types—major gridlines and minor gridlines. Major gridlines are darker gridlines and placed at a distance while minor gridlines are lighter and are closer. You can choose the gridlines that you would like to display for different axes by using the **Primary Horizontal Gridlines** or **Primary Vertical Gridlines** option (Fig. 3.26). Then, choose the type of gridlines that you want to insert from the submenu.

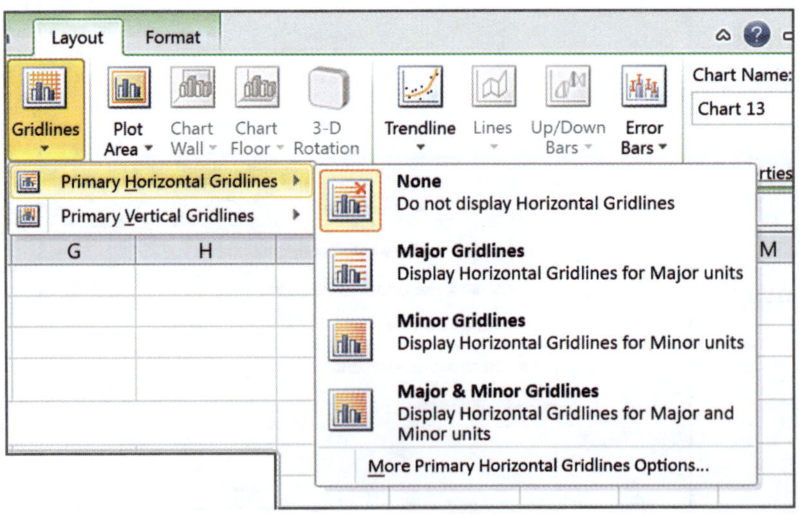

Fig. 3.26: Gridlines menu

You should know!

You can even insert pictures and text to a chart. The buttons to insert pictures, shapes and text are in the **Insert** group of buttons on the **Layout** tab.

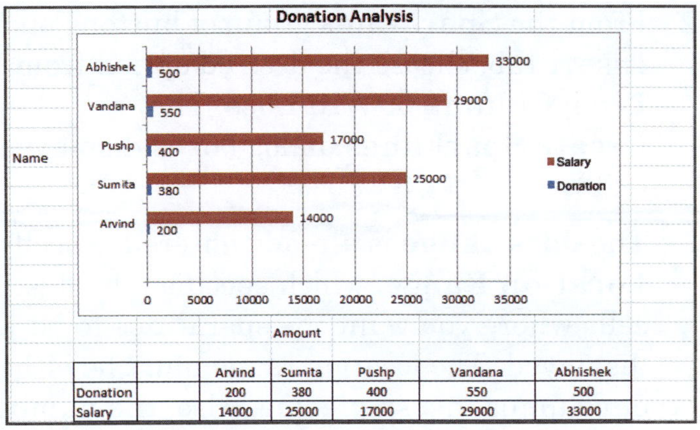

Fig. 3.27: Chart with all the components

Figure 3.27 shows the chart inserted on the new sheet with all the components discussed above.

Chart Formatting

Various options for formatting text and numbers in a chart are available on the **Format** tab. This helps to improve the appearance of the chart. You can change the background colour, style and pattern, format the titles and legends, edit the border style and colour, etc. using the commands on the **Format** tab (Fig. 3.28).

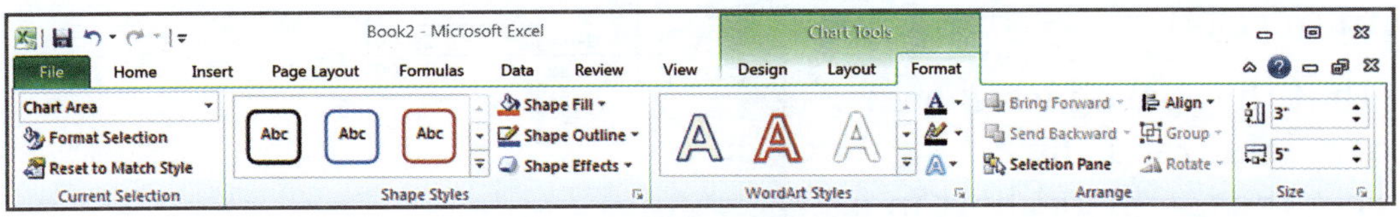

Fig. 3.28: Format tab

From the **Shape Styles** group of buttons on the **Format** tab, choose the style that you want to apply to your chart. You can select the desired background colour by clicking the **Shape Fill** command and then selecting the desired colour from the colour palette. Similarly, desired **Shape Outline** and **Shape Effects** can be applied to the chart.

Quick Way

You can access formatting options instantly by double-clicking any particular chart component.

Every chart has text in the forms of titles, data or legends. The **WordArt Styles** group of buttons has commands to change the font style, colour and other effects.

Sparklines

Sparkline, a new feature in MS Excel 2010, helps show and analyse data trends. A sparkline is a miniature chart embedded in a single spreadsheet cell that provides visual representation of the data. Consider the table shown in Fig. 3.30.

1. Select the data range. In the example given, it will be B2:C8.

2. From the **Sparklines** group of buttons on the **Insert** tab, choose the desired option from **Line**, **Column** or **Win/Loss**. The **Create Sparklines** dialog box is displayed (Fig. 3.29).

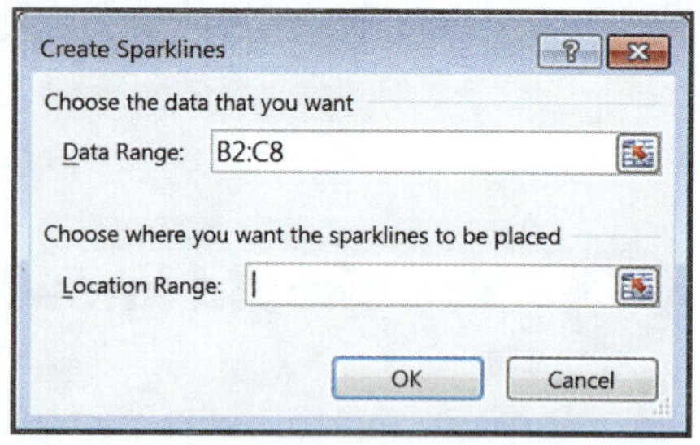

Fig. 3.29: Create Sparklines dialog box

3. The **data range** is already entered. Specify the **Location Range**, which specifies the destination cells where you want the sparklines to be displayed. The location range must be either rows or columns in a single line. Also, the number of rows/columns should be two more than the number of rows/columns in the data range. For example, the data in the selected range is in five rows, so seven cells in a single column or single row should be selected for the data range.

4. Click **OK**. The sparklines will be displayed. Increase the row width to have a clear look at them. Figure 3.30 contains two options of sparklines—**Line** (row 11) and **Column** (row 14).

   Notice that the sparklines show change in data trends by displaying the complete chart in a single cell for entire data range. So, you can have comparative analysis of the data by using this feature.

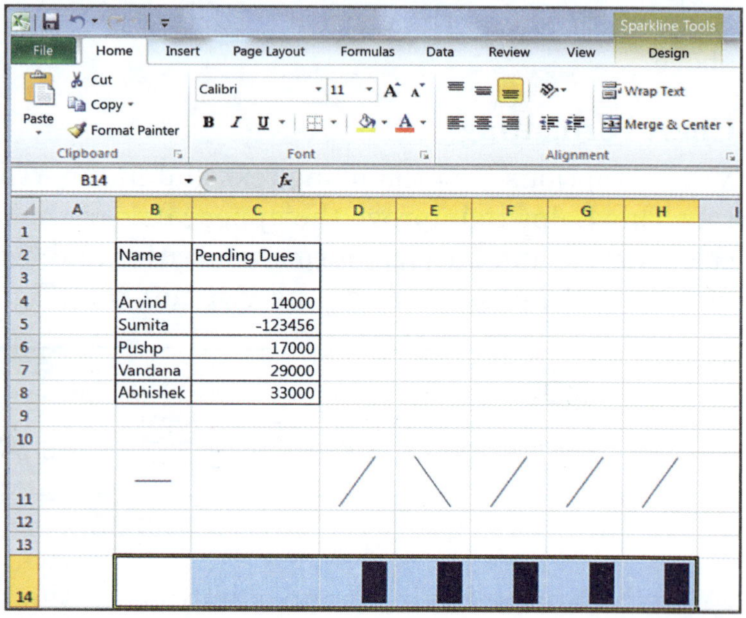

Fig. 3.30: Sparklines inserted on the worksheet

Quick Recap

1. A chart is a pictorial representation of data.
2. Some of the charts provided by MS Excel are bar, line, column, pie, doughnut, area and 3D surface.
3. Column and bar charts compare values across categories.
4. Pie charts and doughnut charts show the relationship of the parts to the whole.
5. Line charts show changes in data over a period of time.
6. The various components of the chart are—chart area, chart title, axis titles, *x*-axis, *y*-axis, data series, plot area, legends, gridlines, data labels and data table.
7. Chart area includes the area in which all the components or objects of the chart are placed.
8. Chart title refers to the topic of the chart, usually given at the top.
9. Axis title is the data series that the axis represents.

10. Data series refers to the bars, slices or other data points that represent data values on a chart.
11. Plot area is the area or a window within the chart area, bounded by the axes.
12. Legend identifies the data series being represented in the chart, by assigning a unique colour, pattern or symbol to each data series.
13. Gridlines are the lines that run across the plot area from each category on the x-axis and from each value on the y-axis.
14. Data label is the label that provides information about a data point on a chart.
15. A sparkline is a miniature chart embedded in a single spreadsheet cell and is helpful to analyse data trends.

Exercises

A **Choose the correct option for each of the following.**

1. Which chart will be the most effective in comparing the tuition fee of private and public schools?

   a. Bar chart b. Pie chart c. Area chart d. Doughnut chart

2. Which of the following is not a subtype of column chart?

   a. Cylinder b. Circle c. Cone d. Pyramid

3. Which chart contains the data for a single-data series?

   a. Column b. Bar c. Line d. Pie

4. Which of the following is used to identify the data series being represented in the chart?

   a. Data Label b. Plot area c. Chart d. Legends

5. When the chart is inserted in the worksheet, which of the following tabs do not appear on the ribbon?

   a. Design b. View c. Layout d. Format

B **Fill in the blanks using the words given below.**

bar	line	F11	area	sparklines

1. In a ____________________ chart, the categories are organized vertically and the values horizontally.
2. The ____________________ chart is created by connecting a series of data points.
3. A(n) ____________________ chart is used to display quantitative data graphically.
4. The ______________ feature introduced in MS Excel 2010 is used to analyse data trends.
5. The shortcut key to generate a chart is ____________________.

C **State whether the following statements are true (T) or false (F).**

1. All the sectors summed up together in a pie chart make up the full circle. ☐
2. A chart can never be inserted in a separate sheet. ☐
3. A data table can be inserted with the chart. ☐
4. You cannot change the title of the chart once it is inserted. ☐
5. In a bar chart, x-axis is the category axis. ☐

D **Match the following.**

Column A	Column B
1. Sparkline	a. Contains all the chart components
2. Layout tab	b. Information on a data point
3. Chart area	c. Chart in a single cell
4. Legend	d. Edit chart components
5. Data label	e. Identification of a data series

E **Answer the following questions.**

1. Define a chart. Name any five components of a chart.
2. Distinguish between a bar chart and a column chart.
3. What is the sparkline feature of MS Excel 2010? Write the steps to create a sparkline with the line option.
5. Write the steps to move a chart to a different worksheet.
6. Give one point of difference between chart area and plot area.

Fun Time!

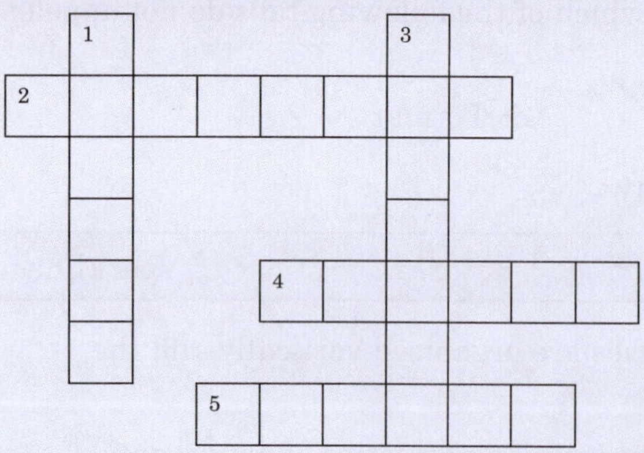

Solve the crossword using the clues given below.

ACROSS

2. Like a pie chart, but may contain more than one data series
4. The horizontal axis of a chart
5. Identifies the data series being represented by the chart

DOWN

1. Like a bar chart, with the bars placed vertically instead
3. Uses colours to distinguish values instead of data series

Lab Activity

1. Your class teacher has to show the class performance through a pie chart. The adjacent table shows the names of the students and marks scored by them. Help her to complete the chart.

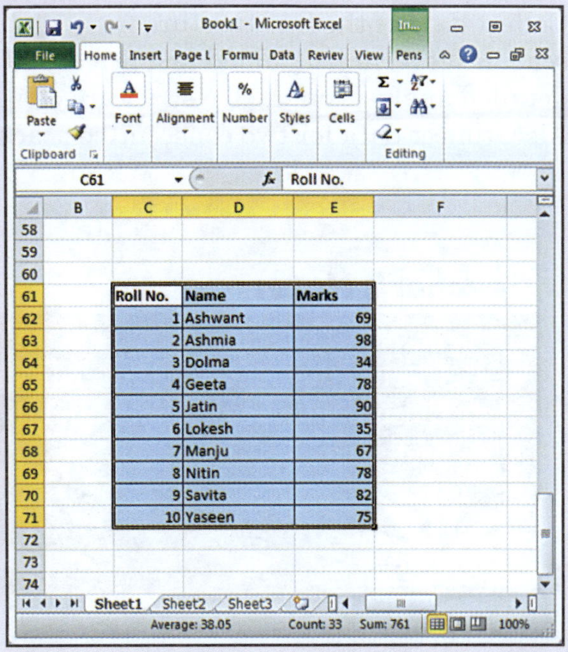

Roll No.	Name	Marks
1	Ashwant	69
2	Ashmia	98
3	Dolma	34
4	Geeta	78
5	Jatin	90
6	Lokesh	35
7	Manju	67
8	Nitin	78
9	Savita	82
10	Yaseen	75

2. Amit and Manjeet are working in the Sales department of a garment company. The adjacent table gives the sales figures of both for the past six months. Compare their performances through an appropriate chart.

	Amit	Manjeet
Jan	12000	10000
Feb	9870	9980
Mar	12000	16000
Apr	6790	5647
May	2094	3481
Jun	10710	11999

3. The adjacent table shows the average rainfall in a city during the monsoons over last 10 years. Show the variations by inserting a line chart on a separate worksheet.

Year	Rainfall (in mm)
2004	564
2005	590
2006	678
2007	450
2008	589
2009	710
2010	679
2011	599
2012	648
2013	744
2014	654

4. The following table gives the percentage of number of students, male and female, dropping out of school. Insert an appropriate chart to illustrate the given data.

	2000	2001	2002	2003	2004	2005	2006	2007	2008	2009	2010	2011	2012
Total	10.9	10.7	10.5	9.9	10.3	9.4	9.3	8.7	8.0	8.1	7.4	7.1	6.6
Male	12.0	12.9	11.8	11.3	11.6	10.8	10.3	9.8	8.5	9.1	8.5	7.7	7.3
Female	9.9	9.5	9.2	8.4	9.0	8.0	8.3	7.6	7.5	7.0	6.3	6.5	5.9

Research Project

Collect data of the fee structure from 10 different students of your locality studying in different schools (government, aided and private schools). Form a table in MS Excel and then have a detailed analysis on the fee structure of all these schools using appropriate charts for illustration. Also, collect data for two consecutive academic sessions and show the data trends.

Teacher's Notes

1. Discuss the importance of charts in data analysis.
2. Discuss all types of charts and the situations in which a particular chart should be preferred.

LibreOffice Calc

Types of Charts

The **Types of Charts** in LibreOffice Calc is the same as that in MS Excel 2010.

Components of a Chart

The **Components of a Chart** in LibreOffice Calc are the same as that in MS Excel 2010.

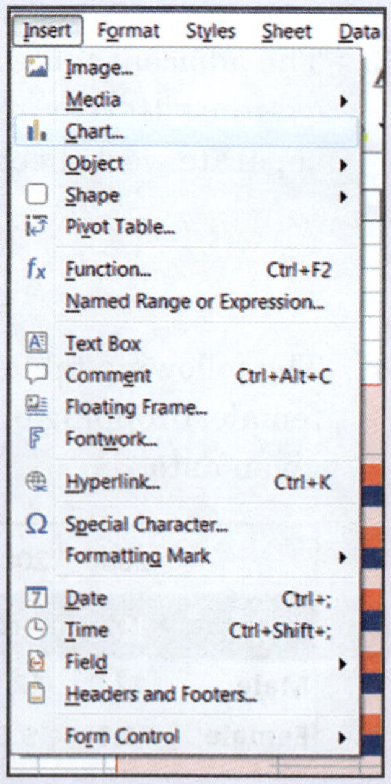

Creating a Chart

To create a chart in LibreOffice Calc, follow these steps:

1. Select the data range.
2. Click on the **Insert** menu.
3. Click on the **Chart** option. The **Chart Wizard** dialog box appears.
4. Choose the chart type, data range, data series and chart elements in each step of the wizard. Click Next button to move to Next step.
5. Finally, click on **Finish** button.

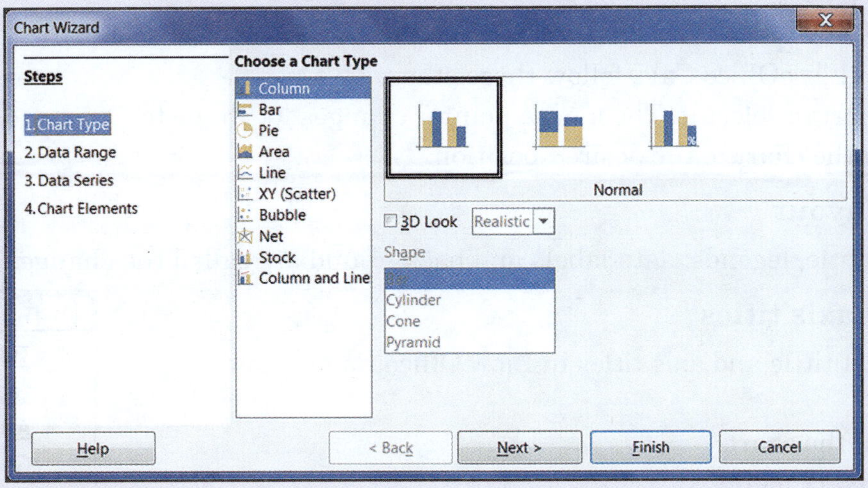

Chart Tools

LibreOffice Calc helps us to change the layout, design, style and location of the drawn chart.

Applying chart styles

To change the chart type or chart style, follow these steps:

1. Double-click on the chart.
2. Click on the **Format** menu.
3. Click on the **Chart Type** option. The **Chart Type** dialog box appears.
4. Choose the appropriate chart type and chart style.
5. Click on **OK** button.

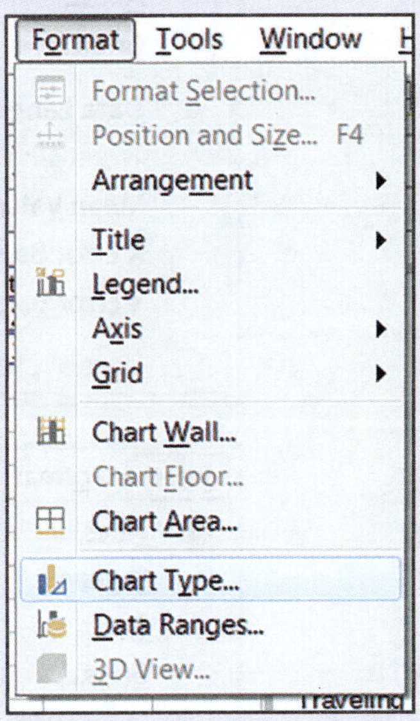

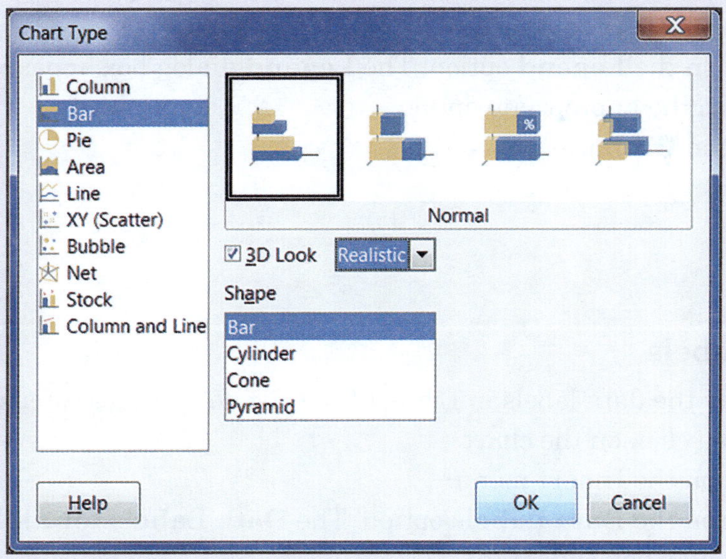

Alternatively, you can also use the **Formatting** toolbar to change the chart styles.

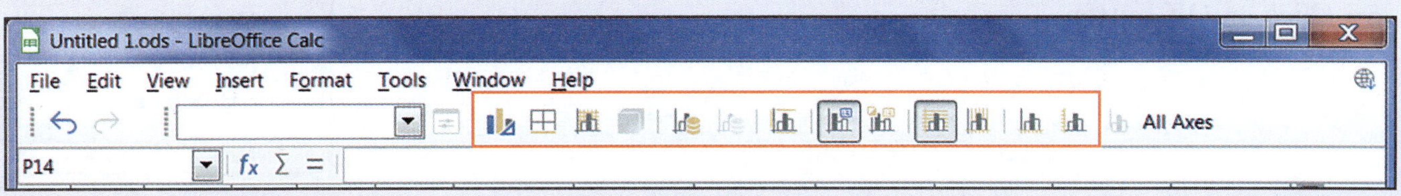

Moving the chart

To move a chart in LibreOffice Calc, follow these steps:

1. Click on the chart to select it. The mouse pointer changes its shape to four-headed arrow.
2. Click and drag the chart to the desired position.

Changing the layout

The change in the title, legends, data labels and background are called the changes in the layout.

Chart title and axis titles

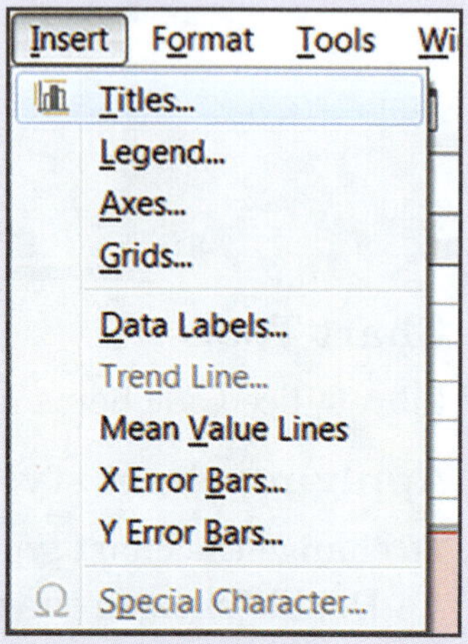

To change the chart tittle and axis titles in LibreOffice Calc, follow these steps:

1. Double-click on the chart.
2. Click on the **Insert** menu.
3. Click on the **Titles** option. The **Titles** dialog box appears.
4. Specify the appropriate titles for chart, x-axis and y-axis.

Legend

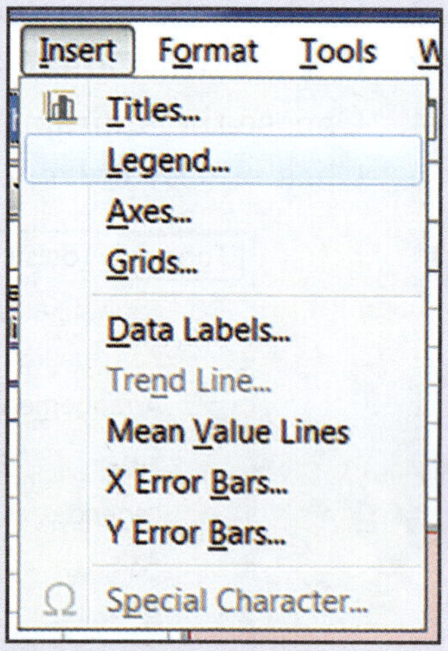

To change the position of the legend in LibreOffice Calc, follow these steps:

1. Double-click on the chart.
2. Click on the **Insert** menu.
3. Click on the **Legend** option. The **Legend** dialog box appears.
4. Choose the appropriate option.
5. Click on **OK** button.

Data Labels

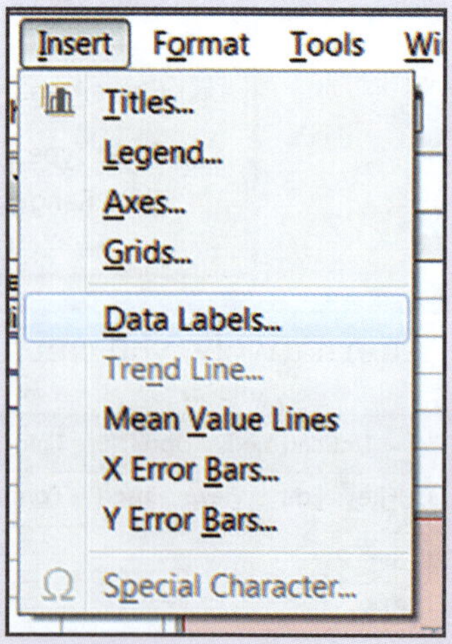

To display the data labels in LibreOffice Calc, follow these steps:

1. Double-click on the chart.
2. Click on the **Insert** menu.
3. Click on the **Data Labels** option. The **Data Labels for all Data Series** dialog box appears.
4. Choose the appropriate option.
5. Click on **OK** button.

Gridlines

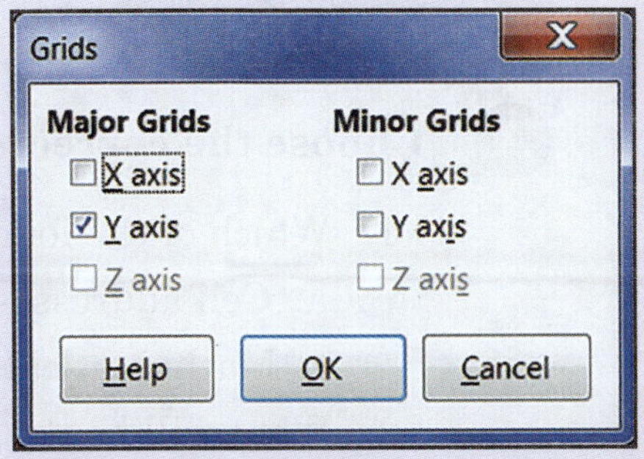

To display the gridlines in LibreOffice Calc, follow these steps:

1. Double-click on the chart.
2. Click on the **Insert** menu.
3. Click on the **Grids** option. The **Grids** dialog box appears.
4. Choose the appropriate option.
5. Click on **OK** button.

Chart Formatting

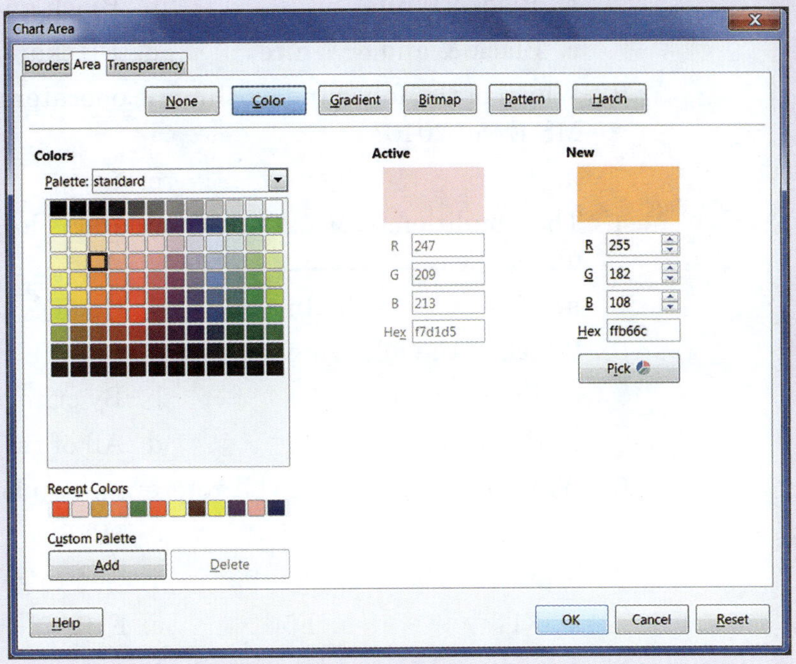

To change the background colour, style and pattern in LibreOffice Calc, follow these steps:

1. Double-click on the chart.
2. Click on the **Format** menu.
3. Click on the **Format Selection** option. The **Chart Area** dialog box appears.
4. Choose the appropriate colour and line style.
5. Click on **OK**.

Sparklines

Unlike MS Excel 2010, LibreOffice Calc does not support Sparklines feature.

Worksheet

A Choose the correct option for each of the following.

1. Which of the following can be the constituents of a formula in MS Excel?
   a. Cell addresses b. Constant values
   c. Mathematical operators d. All of the above
2. What will be the output if you type = "Black"&"and"&"White" in the formula bar?
   a. Black&White b. Black and White
   c. Black & and & White d. BlackandWhite
3. Which of the following arithmetic operators has the highest precedence in MS Excel 2010?
   a. + b. ^ c. * d. /
4. The Conditional formatting command is located in the Styles group of buttons under the __________ tab.
   a. File b. Insert c. Home d. Data
5. Which of the following is a type of filter?
   a. By list values b. By criteria
   c. By format d. All of the above
6. Which of the following cell references can be included in relative reference?
   a. $F6 b. A5 c. $B$6 d. None of the above
7. Name the shortcut key that is pressed to generate a chart.
   a. F11 b. F5 c. F10 d. F15
8. A topographic map is an example of a __________ chart.
   a. Line chart b. Pie chart c. Area chart d. Surface chart
9. Which of the following is an optional feature of a chart?
   a. Gridlines b. Category axis c. Data Table d. Both a. and c.
10. Which chart is preferred to view monthly temperature variations?
    a. Pie chart b. Line chart c. Bar chart d. Surface chart

B Unscramble the words to fill in the blanks.

1. The __________ cell shows the result of the formula that you have entered but the actual formula is seen in __________. (EITVAC/RAB UMALRFO)
2. This process of placing one string after another is called __________ . (NIOANTTAECCON)
3. In __________ referencing, the relative position of rows and columns changes when you copy a formula. (ELTIRAEV)
4. Using __________ feature, you can display data in a particular colour or style depending on a particular condition. (TIONCONIDLA GFNORTMTAI)
5. __________ is an effective way to represent data in pictorial form. (STCHRA)
6. Category axis is the __________ axis of the chart. (X)

7. An ________________ chart is used to display quantitative data graphically. (AAER)
8. Two walls and the floor constitute the ________________ of a 3D chart. (TPLO AAER)
9. The Sparklines group of buttons is under the ________________ tab. (TINSRE)
10. The value of each data point on the chart is represented by ________________. (AADT RIESSE)

C **State whether the following statements are true (T) or false (F).**

1. A formula in MS Excel always starts with the $ sign. ☐
2. Auto-editing of result is possible in MS Excel 2010. ☐
3. In MS Excel 2010, the evaluation of a formula is always carried out from left to right. ☐
4. Only numeric data can be sorted. ☐
5. You can access formatting options instantly by double-clicking the particular chart component. ☐

D **Label all the sorting and filtering commands in the toolbar given below.**

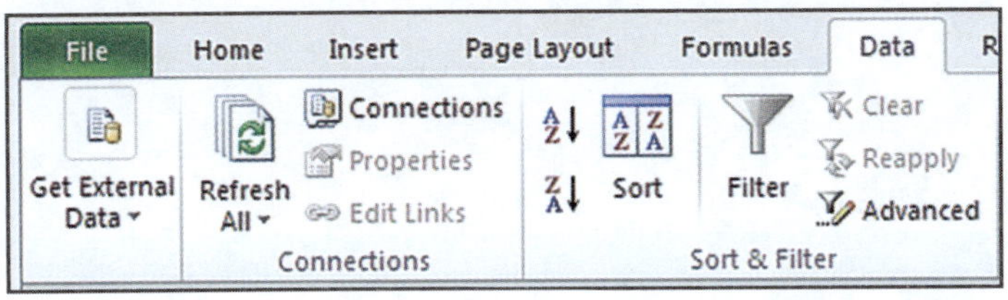

E **Label the category axis, value axis, data labels and legends in the following chart.**

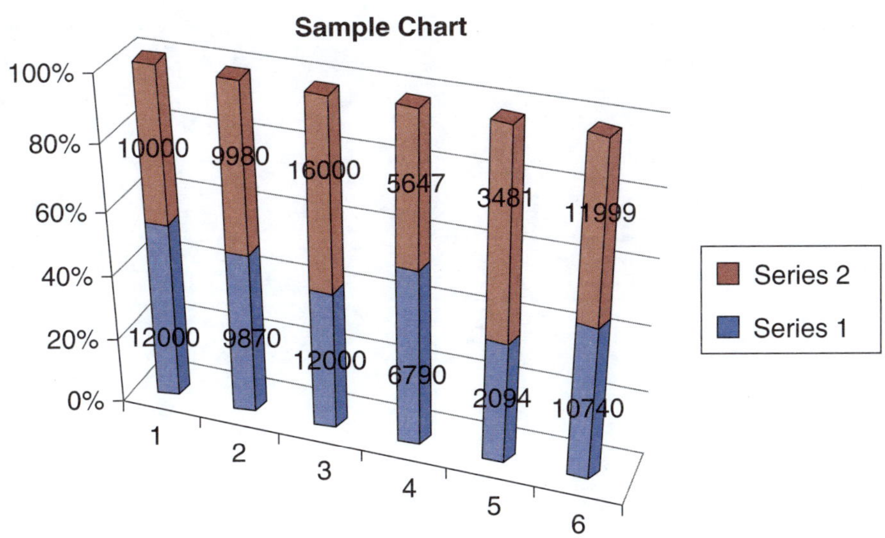

F **Answer the following questions.**

1. Name any three constituents of formula available in MS Excel.
2. Explain any two ways by which you can remove the filter.
3. What will be the output if you apply filter criteria "beginning with M" to a field containing data values: Sunita, Babita and Mamata?

4. Explain absolute referencing with an example. Which character is used to convert absolute referencing into relative referencing?
5. Differentiate between a pie chart and a doughnut chart.
6. What is the use of the sparkline feature of MS Excel 2010?

Projects

Go to your school library and collect information on the number of books in each category—Thrillers, Poetry, Love stories, Historic novels, Science fiction and Autobiographies. The information should contain the number of books, average cost, popularity status (on a grade point of 1–10) and average number of books issued in each category. Thereafter, sort the data in descending order of their popularity status. Also, filter data for each category. Insert an appropriate chart to depict the collected information.

4 Looping with QBASIC

Learning Objectives

By the end of this chapter, you will be able to:

- Use the While...Wend statement.
- Use the Do....While and Do...Until loops.
- Use the For....Next statement.
- Use the Exit command.

Warm Up

Label all the parts of the QBASIC window.

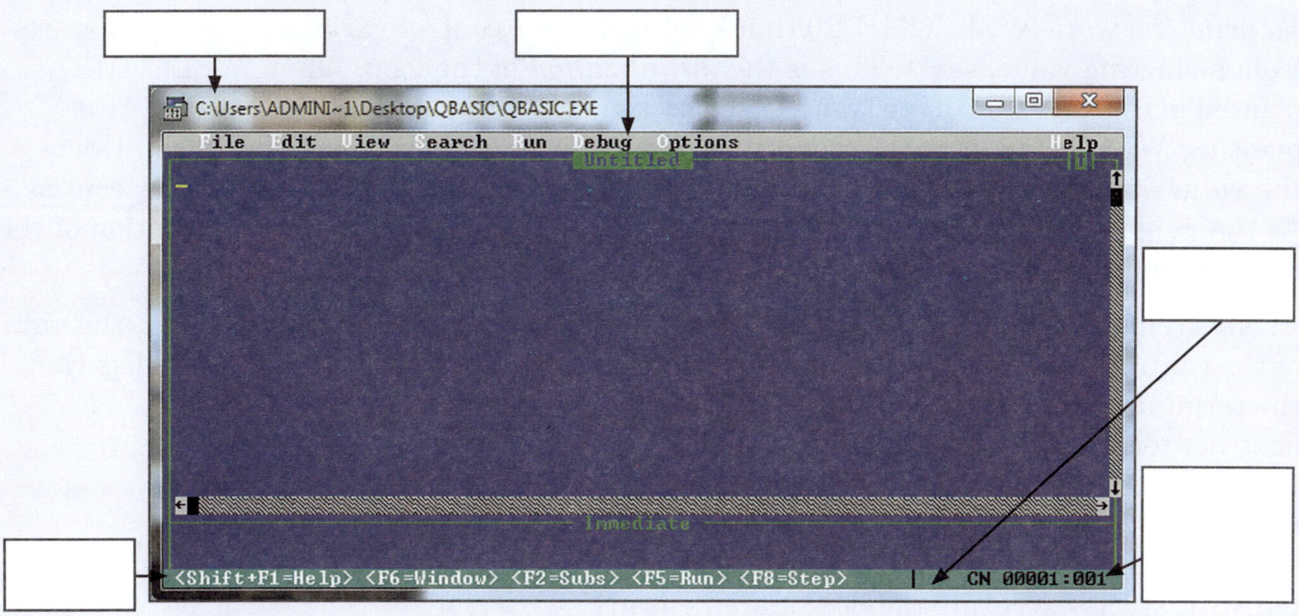

Introduction

What will you do to print the word 'WELCOME' 20 times? One option is to give the command `PRINT "WELCOME"` 20 times. This is obviously not a practical solution. Instead, you can use looping statements. 'Looping' means repeated execution of a statement or a set of statements. These statements are much better to use as they make the program flexible, reduce the number of instructions and save memory space.

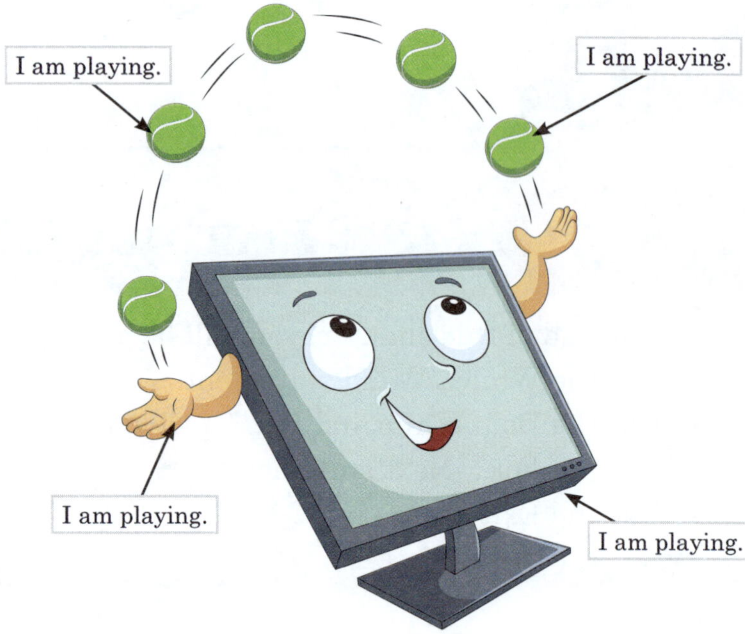

The statements used for looping in QBASIC are WHILE...WEND, DO WHILE...LOOP, DO UNTIL...LOOP and FOR...NEXT LOOP.

All looping statements must have the following four components:

a. **Initialization**—the value from where the loop starts
b. **Termination**—the value at which the loop ends
c. **Step up/down**—specifies how the loop moves forward or backward
d. **Body of the loop**—the statements inside the loop that are to be executed repeatedly.

To print the word 'WELCOME' 20 times, let us have a control variable, ctr, which starts from a starting value, say 1. This is the *initialization* of the loop. When 'WELCOME' is printed once, the value of ctr is increased by the step value (default value is 1). After printing 'WELCOME' for the second time, the value of ctr becomes 2, and so on. Hence, the value of ctr is increased every time the statement PRINT "WELCOME" is executed. As the value of ctr reaches 20, the termination point reaches and further execution of the body of the loop stops.

Always remember that the loop must move either forward or backward. That is, the value of the control variable should change every time the body of the loop is executed so that the termination condition is reached. If the loop does not terminate, it is called an **endless loop**. If such a condition arises, you can end this type of loop by pressing **Ctrl+Break**. This stops the current execution of the loop and QBASIC starts executing the next statement in the program.

You should know!

A control variable is used to keep track of the number of times the loop is executed.

While...Wend

Syntax:

```
WHILE condition
     Statement(s)
WEND
```

The block of statements between WHILE and WEND constitutes the body of the loop. This body of the loop is executed only if the condition given after the WHILE keyword evaluates to True. When the condition becomes False, the execution of the loop stops.

Consider the following example to print all even numbers from 10 to 20.

```
CLS
NUM = 10
WHILE NUM <= 20
     PRINT NUM
     NUM = NUM + 2
WEND
```

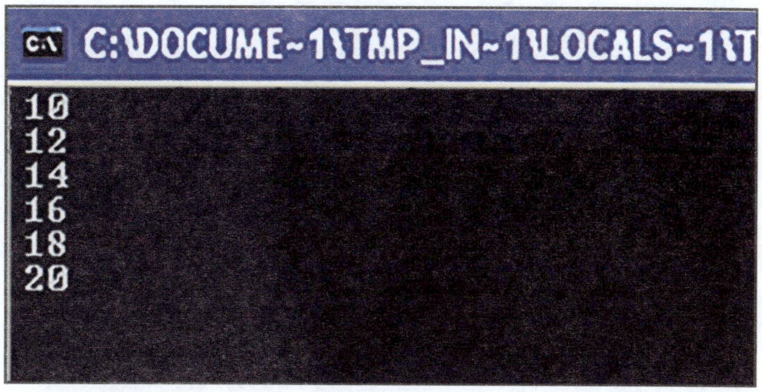

Output

Here, the statements

`PRINT NUM and NUM = NUM + 2`

constitute the body of the loop. The value of the control variable, NUM is initialized to 10. Since the value of NUM is less than 20, the condition becomes True and hence the body of the loop is executed, thereby printing 10. Thereafter, NUM is incremented by 2 and so the value of NUM is now 12. This new value of NUM is again compared with 20. The process continues till the value of NUM becomes more than 20 and the condition evaluates to False. This stops further execution of the loop.

Hence, the output of the above program will be as shown in the output.

PRACTICE TIME

Harsh wants to print all odd numbers between 50 and 100 using the WHILE...WEND statement. Help him to complete the task.

SOLUTION

```
CLS
VAR = 51
WHILE VAR < 100
    PRINT VAR
    VAR = VAR + 2
WEND
```

DO WHILE...LOOP

Syntax:

```
DO WHILE condition
     Statement(s)
LOOP
```

Here, the condition evaluates either to True or False. The statement(s) between the keywords DO WHILE and LOOP form the body of the loop which is executed repeatedly as long as the condition evaluates to True.

Consider the example which prints multiples of 5 between 50 and 20 in the reverse order.

```
MULTIPLE = 50
DO WHILE MULTIPLE >= 20
     PRINT MULTIPLE
     MULTIPLE = MULTIPLE - 5
LOOP
```

In the given program, the variable MULTIPLE is initialized with the value 50. For the loop to be executed, the condition MULTIPLE >= 20 has to be True. To begin with, the value of MULTIPLE is 50, the condition evaluates to True and so the statement PRINT MULTIPLE is executed. After printing the value of MULTIPLE, its value is decreased by 5 and it becomes 45. The condition is again tested and the entire execution process is repeated again and again till the condition becomes False. The output of the above program is as shown in the output screen.

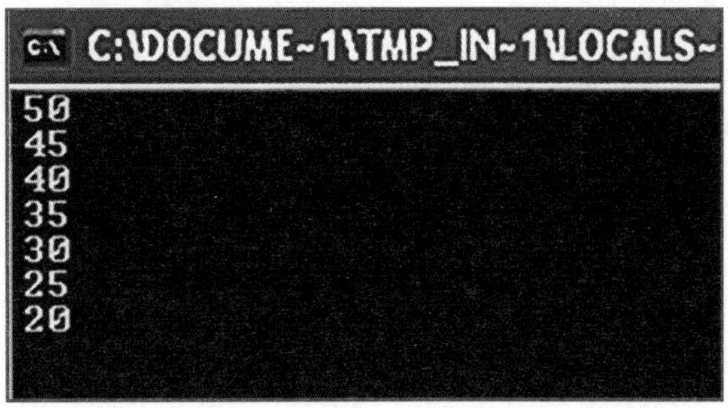

Output

DO UNTIL...LOOP

Syntax:

```
DO UNTIL condition
     Statement(s)
LOOP
```

This looping statement is similar to the DO WHILE...LOOP. The only difference is that unlike DO WHILE... LOOP, this loop executes till the time the condition is False.

Let us display numbers from 20 to 10 using the DO UNTIL...LOOP.

```
Number = 20
DO UNTIL Number < 10
     PRINT Number
     Number = Number - 1
LOOP
```

Here, the body of the loop will be executed till the time the condition, Number < 10, is False. The variable Number is initialized with 20 and so the program will print numbers from 20 to 10. As the value of Number becomes less than 10, the condition becomes False and the loop terminates.

You should know!

You can write the WHILE and UNTIL statements at the end of the loop also. The syntax then becomes

```
DO
    Statement(s)
LOOP WHILE condition
```

```
DO
    Statement(s)
LOOP UNTIL condition
```

Since the condition is given at the end of the loop, the loop will be executed at least once in all circumstances, whether the condition is True or False. This is because the condition is evaluated after the body of the loop is executed at least once.

FOR...NEXT LOOP

In all the loops discussed till now, the initialization, termination and step up/down statements are given separately. The FOR...NEXT looping statement provides a simpler way to create a loop. In this statement, the initialization, termination and step up/down statements are given together.

Syntax:

```
FOR control variable=initial value to termination value STEP index value
    Statement(s)
NEXT control variable
```

The FOR...NEXT statement works in the following manner:

a. The control variable is first assigned an initial value and a final termination value. The set of statements between the FOR and NEXT statements constitute the body of the loop and are executed if the value of the control variable lies between the initial value and the termination value. The NEXT statement increases the value of the control variable by the index value specified after the keyword STEP. The index value or the step value is optional and can be positive or negative. The default index value is 1. Thereafter, the control shifts back to the FOR statement.
b. The new value of control variable is compared against the final value specified in the FOR statement. If the value lies between the initial value and the final value, the whole process is repeated otherwise the statement after the NEXT statement is executed.

Consider the following example to display the word 'WELCOME' 5 times.

```
FOR A = 1 to 5
PRINT "WELCOME"
NEXT A
```

Here, A is the counter-looping variable that has been initialized to 1. The last value of the counter variable is set to 5. Since the index value is not specified, the default index value 1 will be taken as step value. With each execution of the loop, the counter variable will be increased by 1. Hence, the loop will run 5 times printing the word 'WELCOME' each time as shown in the adjacent output screen.

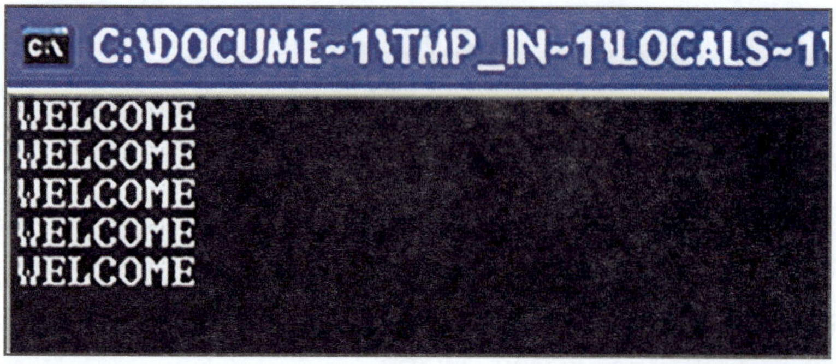

Output

Now, alter the previous program in the following manner:

```
FOR A = 1 to 5 STEP 2
     PRINT "WELCOME"
NEXT A
```

Here, the index value is set to 2. So, the counter variable A will be increased by 2 with each execution of the loop. Hence, the loop will now execute 3 times.

EXIT Command

The EXIT command or the EXIT statement in QBASIC is used to stop the execution of the loop before the termination condition is reached.

PRACTICE TIME

Anju is making her son learn the table of 7. Help her print the table of 7 using FOR...NEXT loop.

SOLUTION

```
REM To print table of 7
CLS
NUM = 7
FOR VAR = 1 TO 10
     PRINT NUM; "*"; VAR; "="; NUM*VAR
NEXT VAR
END
```

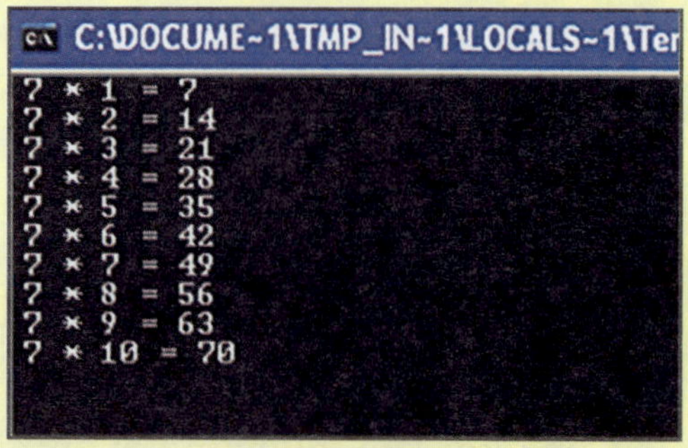

Syntax:

```
EXIT FOR        — In case of FOR...NEXT loop
```

or

```
EXIT DO         — In case of DO WHILE...LOOP and DO UNTIL...LOOP
```

For example,

```
    FOR P = 150 to 100 STEP - 5
        PRINT P
        IF (P + 10 = 130) THEN EXIT FOR
    NEXT P
```

Here, the execution of the loop will stop as soon as the IF condition evaluates to True. Hence, the output of the this program will be as shown here.

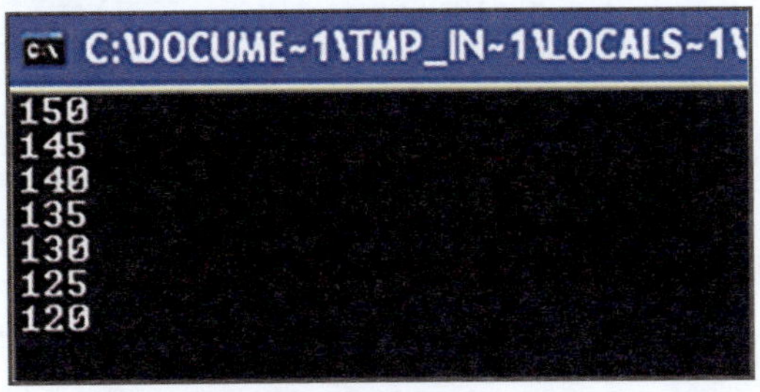

Output

You should know!

The EXIT command does not work with WHILE...WEND loop.

Quick Recap

1. Looping means repeated execution of a statement or a set of statements.
2. The four components of a loop are initialization, termination, step up/down and body of the loop.
3. Initialization is the value from where the loop starts.
4. Termination is the value at which the loop ends.
5. Step up/down specifies how the loop execution moves forward or backward.
6. Body of the loop refers to the statements that are to be executed repeatedly.
7. The looping statements in QBASIC are WHILE...WEND, DO WHILE...LOOP, DO UNTIL...LOOP and FOR...NEXT.
8. The WHILE...WEND and DO WHILE...LOOP looping statements are executed till the condition is True.
9. The DO UNTIL...LOOP is executed till the condition is False.
10. While using the FOR...NEXT loop, the initialization, termination and step up/down are given in one single statement.
11. The FOR...NEXT statement is executed till the time the value of the control variable lies between the initial value and the final value.
12. The EXIT command is used to stop the execution of FOR...NEXT, DO WHILE...LOOP or DO UNTIL...LOOP statements.

Exercises

A Choose the correct option for each of the following.

1. The statements that are executed repeatedly till the condition is True, form the ____________ of the loop.

   a. Initialization b. Termination c. Body d. None of these

2. The DO UNTIL...LOOP is executed till the condition is ____________.

   a. True c. Either True or False b. False d. Neither True nor False

3. The FOR...NEXT loop will be executed till the control variable is ____________ the initial value and the final value.

   a. Less than b. Greater than c. In between d. None of these

4. The execution of which of the following looping statements can be stopped by using the EXIT command?

   a. DO WHILE...LOOP c. DO UNTIL...LOOP
   b. FOR....NEXT d. All of these

5. You can stop the execution of an endless loop by pressing ____________.

   a. Ctrl+Alt b. Ctrl+Break c. Alt+Break d. Shift+Break

B Fill in the blanks using the words given below.

initialization control step endless Ctrl+Break termination

1. ____________ is the point from where the loop starts and ____________ is the point where the loop ends.
2. In a FOR...NEXT loop, you may not specify the ____________ value.
3. ____________ is the shortcut used to stop further execution of the loop.
4. If the loop does not terminate, it is called an ____________ loop.
5. The ____________ variable keeps track of the number of times the loop is executed.

C State whether the following statements are true (T) or false (F).

1. The step value can only have a positive number. ☐
2. The FOR...NEXT statement cannot be stopped with the EXIT command. ☐
3. Every loop must have a terminating condition. ☐
4. In a FOR...NEXT loop, the default step value is 0. ☐
5. The statements between WHILE and WEND constitute the body of the loop. ☐

D Identify the errors in the following programs.

1.
```
DO WHILE
    PRINT A
    A = A*4
LOOP
```

2.
```
FOR MEMBER = 75 TO 20 STEP 15
PRINT MEMBER
NEXT MEMBER
```

3.
```
X = 5
DO UNTIL X < 9
X = X + 1
WEND
PRINT X
```

E Answer the following questions.

1. Name the looping statements used in QBASIC.
2. What are the components of a looping statement?
3. Differentiate between a DO WHILE...LOOP and DO UNTIL...LOOP.
4. What is the use of STEP in a FOR...NEXT statement? Is it necessary to give STEP in every FOR...NEXT statement?
5. What is the default STEP value in a FOR...NEXT loop? Is it possible to have a negative value in STEP?

Lab Activity

1. Lata's mathematics teacher asks her to write a program in QBASIC that displays the factorial of a number. Help her to complete the task.
2. Sameer works as a manager in a sales firm. He wants to display the weekly sales of his salesmen. Develop a program in QBASIC that accepts sales figures for all six working days of the week and finally displays the total weekly sales made by each salesman.
3. The teacher asked Ashu to make a program in QBASIC that accepts a number and prints the following series till that particular number.

   1, 4, 9, 16, 25...n

   Help Ashu to complete the task.
4. Dhruv wants a program that accepts a number and prints its square and cube. He wants the program to continue till the time the user enters 0. Create a program for him.
5. Sushant wants a program that accepts a number and checks whether the number entered is a prime number or not. Create a program for him.

Research Project

Write a program to print the Fibonacci series.

1, 1, 2, 3, 5, 8, 13,...

[***Hint***: *You can research on the internet to learn about the 'Fibonacci Series'.*]

Teacher's Notes

1. Discuss the importance of using looping statements.
2. Demonstrate the use of all the looping statements covered in the chapter giving different examples.

5 Information and Communication Technology

Learning Objectives

By the end of this chapter, you will be able to:

- understand Information and Communication Technology.
- know about e-commerce.
- know about e-governance.
- know about e-learning.

Warm Up

State whether the following sentences are true (T) or false (F).

1. VoIP is the service that allows users to speak to other people using an internet-enabled computer. ☐
2. A smart phone can be used to connect to social media apps. ☐
3. It is not possible to buy clothes and shoes in online shopping stores. ☐
4. Google Drive, a service used to store files securely on the cloud, is a paid service. ☐
5. Real-time collaboration allows multiple users to work on a single file at the same time. ☐

Introduction

Information and Communication Technology (ICT) refers to technologies that provide access to information through telecommunications. Modern information and communication technologies have connected people all over the world at all times through various means. In this chapter, you will study various applications of ICT and how they have affected the society.

You should know!

The term, Information and Communication Technology, was first coined by Dennis Stevenson in 1997.

Information and Communication Technology (ICT)

ICT is an **umbrella term** that includes any communication device or application, such as, radio, television, mobile phones, smart phones, satellite systems, networks and network devices. The term even includes various services and applications such as broadband services, videoconferencing, e-commerce, e-learning, etc. Also, any form of information from all over the world is gathered, stored, shared and distributed with the help of ICT.

> **Word Web**
> **umbrella term:** term that covers wide range of things

In the past few decades, ICT has made communication a very fast and simple process. People can communicate with anyone across the world and at any time using technologies such as instant messaging, chat rooms, videoconferencing, etc. Social networking sites such as Facebook and Twitter allow users from all over the world to be in touch with each other all the time. You will find applications of ICT in almost all spheres of life such as education, business, healthcare, agriculture, governance, art, employment, transport, space and environment study, etc.

Advantages of ICT

1. People from all over the world stay connected to each other through emails, SMSs, mobile applications such as WhatsApp and social networking sites such as Facebook and Twitter. Like-minded people form groups and can collectively work for a cause.
2. ICT has made distance learning possible. Various e-learning sites provide study materials and tutorials. Also, many universities are now conducting online courses and examinations. This is very helpful for students who cannot attend a regular course in schools and colleges.
3. Through ICT, payment of bills, making reservations, paying taxes, applying for driving license or passport can be done conveniently from home. Even online complaint cells and helpline services have been set up by the government to redress public grievances providing transparency in the system.
4. ICT has lowered expenses and improved cash flow in the market. Online money transactions are very convenient and a fast method for payments or transfer of money. Online trading enables smaller investors to coordinate their own trading plans. E-banking services allow access to one's bank accounts at a mouse's click. Online shopping enables consumers to search for low-priced goods and get them delivered at their homes.

Disadvantages of ICT

1. More and more people are becoming victims of online frauds. Criminals steal the identity and bank account details of people and then execute unauthorized money transfers and purchases.
2. Personal profiles of people posted on various social networking sites are being misused.
3. A lot of time gets wasted on messaging, mobile applications and social networking sites. In many cases, these are being overused to the level of addiction causing reduced concentration levels.

Electronic Commerce (E-commerce)

Electronic commerce or e-commerce is the buying, selling and exchange of goods and services over computer networks, predominantly on the internet. The transactions, exchange of data for such business transactions and terms of sale are all performed electronically.

Fig. 5.1: Shopping on the internet

This is one of the most effective and efficient ways of conducting business nowadays. The web is rapidly becoming a multibillion-dollar source of revenue for the world's businesses.

Companies set up websites that provide details of their products and services. Consumers then buy the desired products using credit cards, debit cards, net banking, cash-on-delivery, etc. But e-commerce sites need to implement extra security features to prevent online frauds.

Word Web

encrypting: putting the information for communication in a code that is not understood by all

Some of the security measures adopted by e-commerce sites are as follows:

1. Authenticating people to carry on the transactions
2. Controlling access to resources for registered or selected users
3. Encrypting communication
4. Ensuring the privacy and effectiveness of transactions

You should know!

Secure Sockets Layer (SSL) is the most widely used security technology used by web browsers.

Categories of e-commerce

E-commerce can be divided into four main categories. These are as follows:

- **Business-to-Business (B2B)**: In this category of e-commerce, companies do business with each other. For example, manufacturers selling to distributors or wholesalers selling to retailers fall into this category. Thousands of companies who sell their products to other companies in this manner have discovered that web is a quick way to reach the consumers at any point of time.
- **Business-to-Consumer (B2C)**: In this category of e-commerce, businesses sell their products to the general public, typically of through catalogues and utilizing the shopping-cart software. There are several websites such as *flipkart.com* and *amazon.com,* where companies provide information directly to actual consumers who can order products and services directly from the site. Be it buying clothes, footwear, accessories, household items or even booking a holiday, with e-commerce all these purchases can be done round the clock and just at a click of the mouse.

- **Consumer-to-Business (C2B)**: In this category of e-commerce, a consumer posts his project online with a detailed business proposal containing a set budget. The interested companies review the consumer's proposal and bid on the project. The consumer then reviews the bids and selects the best option. This category is often referred to as *Digital Middlemen*.
- **Consumer-to-Consumer (C2C)**: In this category of e-commerce, individual consumers put up items for sale through auctions, free classifieds and forums on certain websites. The interested consumers can bid on such sites to purchase any item. eBay's auction service is a very good example of this category, where person-to-person transactions take place every day since 1995.

Other than the categories of e-commerce discussed here, G2G (Government-to-Government), G2E (Government-to-Employee), G2B (Government-to-Business), B2G (Business-to-Government), G2C (Government-to-Citizen), C2G (Citizen-to-Government) are other forms of e-commerce that involve transactions with the government. These deliver services that include procurement of items, filing of taxes, business registrations, renewal of licenses, etc.

Advantages of e-commerce

1. It is available round the clock and 365 days a year.
2. The buying and selling can be done from any place where Internet connection is available.
3. Customers can select the desired product from the choices given by different providers. Also, the products and services can be delivered at home.
4. The process of buying and selling is fast and convenient.
5. E-commerce is cost-efficient for businesses as it helps in reducing costs.

Disadvantage of e-commerce

1. Extra security measures have to be taken to avoid online fraud and misallocation of funds.

Check your understanding!

State whether the following statements are true (T) or false (F).

1. ICT is a specific term that applies to the technology used by mobile phones and smart phones. ☐
2. Online frauds have become more common with increased use of ICT. ☐
3. E-commerce companies encrypt their data for security purposes. ☐
4. ICT is not preferred by most people as it is very expensive and difficult to use. ☐
5. A B2C e-commerce company sells products directly to consumers through the Internet. ☐

E-Governance

E-governance or electronic-governance is an emerging trend to re-invent the manner in which the government functions. In the term electronic-governance, the word 'electronic' implies 'technology-driven'. It is the use of modern information and communication technologies such as Internet, smart phones, mobiles, local networks, etc. by the government to improve its effectiveness, transparency, efficiency and service delivery. Through e-governance, government services are made available to the citizens in a convenient, efficient and transparent manner, thereby promoting democracy. It also enables participation of citizens in government affairs and matters, and enhances their economic and social opportunities, so that they can make better lives for themselves and for the coming generations. With the ongoing era of digital economy, governments all over the world have recognized information technology as an effective tool in promoting the economic activities and developing human resources of their countries.

Advantages of e-governance

1. It improves transparency.
2. It provides information speedily to all citizens and allows direct interaction with them.
3. It improves efficiency.
4. It improves delivery of public services such as transportation, power, health, water, security and municipal services.

Disadvantages of e-governance

1. Despite the government's efforts to ensure safety of data, e-governance websites may get attacked by hackers. This leads to online frauds.
2. Internet-enabled hardware devices, such as routers, advanced servers and security systems, constitute costly infrastructure. Many developing countries may not be able to afford this technology.

E-governance in India

In India, the aim is to redefine governance in the ICT age so as to provide smart governance to the citizens. Several significant initiatives have been taken at the Centre and the State level in this direction. The website shown in Fig. 5.2 is the home page of National Portal of India.

Some of the initiatives taken by the Central and State governments are listed below:

1. Both the Central and State governments have taken steps to extensively promote the use of Information Technology (IT) in managing its internal processes. Various online services are being provided to the citizens of India. The applications that have been implemented are targeted towards providing G2B, G2C and B2G services with emphasis on the use of local language.

2. The ministries/ departments have kept a provision of about 3 to 5 per cent of their annual budgets to be spent on IT-related services.

3. The government has enacted the IT Act 2000, which provides legal status to the information and transactions carried on the Internet.

4. The Ministry of Information and Communications Technology has set up a Centre for E-Governance (CEG) at Electronics Niketan, New Delhi. It showcases several e-governance applications deployed in various states and also provides technical consultation to people.

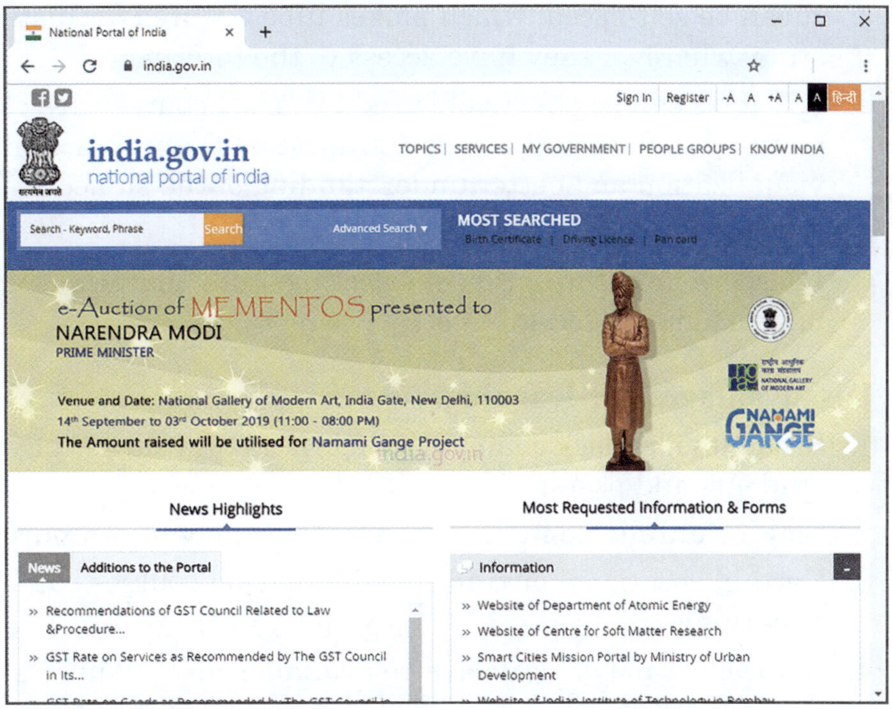

Fig. 5.2: E-governance page of the National Portal of India *(http://india.gov.in/)*

5. Some of the e-governance projects operational across India are: Bhoomi, Stamps Registration and Archiving (SARITA), Versatile Online Information for Citizen Empowerment (VOICE), e-Seva and VidyaVahini

E-Learning

E-learning is the use of electronic media and ICT to enable people to learn anytime and anywhere. It includes providing course material, trainings, guidance from experts and conducting examinations. It is being accepted as the next evolution of the training and education industry.

E-learning includes numerous types of media to deliver text, audio, video, images, animations, etc. It facilitates the learning and delivery process for both teachers and students.

Advantages of e-Learning

1. E-learning can occur in and out of classrooms, with or without instructors.

2. E-learning can be done as per the student's convenience, at any time, making it a flexible learning process.

Fig. 5.3: Learning using the internet

3. It can be self-paced, which makes it best suited for distance learning. Students can study wherever they have access to the internet.
4. ICT tools can be effectively used to enrich courseware content with multimedia features such as audio, video, graphics, 3D animation, etc. This results in better visualization and better understanding of the subject.
5. It reduces travel cost and time.
6. Learners have the option of selecting study material that meets their level of understanding and interest.

Disadvantages of e-learning

1. Students may lack competitive spirit as they do not have social interaction with fellow students and peers.
2. Slow or unreliable internet connections may be a hindrance.
3. Certain vocational or traditional hands-on courses can be difficult to simulate with e-learning.
4. Instructors may not always be available on demand.

Quick Recap

1. Information and Communication Technology (ICT) is the technology that provides access to information through telecommunications.
2. ICT provides access to information through any communication device or application such as, radio, television, mobile phones, smart phones, satellite systems, networks and network devices.
3. Electronic commerce or e-commerce is buying, selling and exchange of goods and services over computer networks, predominantly on the internet.
4. The four categories of e-commerce are Business-to-Business (B2B), Business-to-Consumer (B2C), Consumer-to-Business (C2B) and Consumer-to-Consumer (C2C).
5. E-governance refers to the use of ICT by government to improve its effectiveness, efficiency and service delivery.
6. E-learning is the use of electronic media and ICT to enable people to learn anytime and anywhere by providing course material, trainings, guidance from experts and conducting examinations.

Exercises

A **Choose the correct option for each of the following.**

1. Which of the following communication devices can be included under ICT?

   a. Mobile phones b. Radio c. Networks d. All of these

2. Which of the following is not a category of e-commerce?
   a. B2B   b. C2B   c. C2C   d. None of these
3. In which of the following categories of e-commerce companies do business with each other?
   a. B2B   b. C2B   c. B2C   d. C2C
4. Which of the following categories of e-commerce utilizes shopping-cart software?
   a. B2B   b. C2B   c. B2C   d. C2C
5. In which city is the Centre for E-Governance (CEG) set up by the Government of India?
   a. Mumbai   b. New Delhi   c. Kolkata   d. Chennai

B **Fill in the blanks using the words given below.**

ICT   e-governance   C2B   fraud   E-Learning

1. E-commerce is also referred to as a subset of ______________ .
2. In the ______________ category of e-commerce, a consumer posts his project online with a detailed business proposal.
3. E-commerce sites need to implement extra security features to prevent ______________ .
4. Through ______________ , government services are made available to citizens electronically.
5. ______________ allows you to study at any time and at any place.

C **State whether the following statements are true (T) or false (F).**

1. Today, distance learning is possible because of ICT. ☐
2. For e-commerce, you have to go to an electronics store to buy and sell goods. ☐
3. You can do online shopping only during daytime. ☐
4. The IT Act 2000 provides legal status to the information and transactions carried on the Internet. ☐
5. E-learning can be done outside the classrooms. ☐

D **Expand the following.**

1. ICT ______________________________
2. VOICE ______________________________
3. SARITA ______________________________
4. CEG ______________________________
5. C2B ______________________________

E **Answer the following questions.**

1. What do you mean by ICT?
2. Give two advantages and two disadvantages of ICT.
3. Write any two initiatives that the government has taken to promote e-governance in India.
4. Write any two advantages of e-learning.
5. Name the various categories of e-commerce.

Fun Time!

Solve the crossword using the clues given below.

ACROSS

3. The use of ICT by the government (12)
4. The most widely used security technology by web browsers (20)
5. An example of a B2C company (8)

DOWN

1. The buying and selling of goods and services over the internet (10)
2. The umbrella term that includes any communication device or application (3)
3. The practice of using codes to save information for security purposes (11)

Research Project

List out four e-learning and e-commerce websites. Explore and describe the convenience that they provide.

Teacher's Notes

1. Discuss about ICT and its various applications in different spheres of our lives.
2. Discuss how e-commerce has made shopping easy.
3. Discuss what all things should be kept in mind to avoid online fraud.

Worksheet

A Choose the correct option for each of the following.

1. Initialization is the value from where the loop ____________.
   a. Starts b. Ends c. Continues d. None of these
2. Termination is the value at which the loop ____________________.
   a. Starts b. Ends c. Continues d. None of these
3. The default index value or the step value for a FOR...NEXT loop is __________.
   a. 0 b. 1 c. –1 d. Any of these
4. Which of the following is an umbrella term that includes any communication device or application?
   a. E-commerce b. E-governance c. ICT d. None of these
5. ________________ is the process by which information is stored in the form of a code that is not understood by all people.
   a. Authenticating b. Encrypting c. Decoding d. Authorizing
6. Which of the following types of media are included in e-learning modules?
   a. Audio b. Video c. Images d. All of these
7. What are the components of a looping statement?
   a. Initialization b. Termination c. Body of the loop d. All of these
8. If the loop does not terminate, it is called an ____________ loop.
   a. Endless b. Never ending c. Constant d. None of these
9. Which of the following services and applications can be included in ICT?
   a. Broadband services c. e-commerce
   b. Videoconferencing d. All of the above
10. In which of the following categories of e-commerce do individual consumers put up items for sale through auctions?
   a. B2B b. B2C c. C2C d. C2B

B Unscramble the words to fill in the blanks.

1. ______________________ means repeated execution of a statement or a set of statements. (OPLNGOI)
2. A ______________________ is used to keep track of the number of times the loop is executed. (ONOCLTR ARVILEAB)
3. The ______________________ command does not work with WHILE...WEND loop. (TEXI)
4. ______________________ is the use of electronic media and ICT to enable people to learn anytime and anywhere. (ENEARLGNI)
5. ______________________ is the buying, selling and exchange of goods and services over computer networks. (EMRCMECOE)
6. ______________________ is the most widely used security technology used by the web browsers. (REECUS OTSCSKE AYLRE)

7. ________________________ of the loop refers to the statements that are to be executed repeatedly. (YBDO)
8. Step up/down specifies how the ________________________ moves forward or backward. (OOLP)
9. In e-commerce, all transactions are performed ________________________ (EYLLLEACCATINOR)
10. ________________________ refers to technologies that provide access to any type of information through telecommunications. (CTI)

C **State whether the following statements are true (T) or false (F).**

1. A step variable is used to keep a track of number of times the loop is executed. ☐
2. E-commerce sites need to implement extra security features to prevent online frauds. ☐
3. The block of statements between WHILE and WEND constitutes the termination statements. ☐
4. The new value of the control variable is compared against the final value specified in the FOR statement. ☐
5. To shop online, payment can be done through credit cards only. ☐

D **Answer the following questions.**

1. Write a program to print the product of any 10 natural numbers which are accepted from the user. The program should terminate if the sum becomes a multiple of 5.
2. Write a program to print table of 19 using the FOR...NEXT loop.
3. Write a program to print all the even numbers from 100 to 10 using the WHILE...WEND loop.
4. Why is e-commerce becoming a multibillion dollar source of revenue?
5. Give two advantages and two disadvantages of e-governance.

Projects

Research the e-governance projects taken up by the central government of India and make a detailed PowerPoint presentation on any two projects.

6 Introduction to HTML

Learning Objectives

By the end of this chapter, you will be able to:

- understand HTML—a markup language.
- understand HTML tags, elements and attributes.
- know the structure of an HTML document.
- create and view an HTML document.
- define BODY Element <BR> tag.

Warm Up

Log on to the internet. Access three of your favourite websites. Compare the three websites on the basis of colour and size of the text, the background used, the kind of content available, the number of buttons, etc. Note the differences between them. Discuss the differences in the classroom.

Introduction

In this chapter you will learn how to create a website using HyperText Markup Language (HTML). It is easy to learn and use. Also, no prior knowledge of programming is required for it.

HTML was invented by Tim Berners Lee in 1990 and its first version called HTML 1.0 was released in 1991. Some other versions are HTML 3.2, HTML 4.01, XHTML and the latest HTML 5 was released in 2011.

HTML—A Markup Language

Hyper**T**ext **M**arkup **L**anguage or HTML is the computer language used to create documents, called web pages, on the World Wide Web. These web pages, which can be viewed in a web browser, include both text and graphics. HTML is basically used to define the structure and layout of a web page. It defines how the content of the page is to be presented or displayed in the browser.

Let us understand the terms **HyperText** and **Markup**.

HyperText means highlighted text. This highlighted text or image is linked to any other web page, thus creating a hyperlink. Each web page of a website has hyperlinks so that you can browse from one page to another.

HTML is also a markup language, a language consisting of markup tags. These tags describe how the content will be displayed on the web page. For example, the <b> tag displays the text in bold. You will learn about HTML tags in the next section. Two tools are required to create HTML documents: (a) an HTML **Editor** to create and save a web page, and (b) a **web browser** to view it. The purpose of a web browser is to read HTML documents and display them as web pages. To display the web pages in the browser, you write the HTML code in an HTML Editor. **Notepad** is a very basic text editor which is excellent for HTML coding. Apart from this, WordPad and Text Edit are also used as HTML editors. As the viewer of a web page, you cannot see the HTML code in the browser. Instead, you only see the result of the markup tags used in the code.

Before we start coding in HTML, let us discuss the various components that make up the HTML code: tags, elements and attributes.

HTML Tags

HTML tags are used to identify HTML elements. A **tag** is a piece of code that instructs the browser how to display a particular text or image. A tag name is a keyword surrounded by angular brackets (< and >). For example, <b> is the tag to display the text in bold.

Generally, HTML tags come in pairs. The first tag in the pair is called the **ON** tag or the **Opening** tag. The second tag is preceded by a forward slash (/) before its name. This tag is called **OFF** tag or the **Closing** tag. The content is enclosed between the opening tag and the closing tag. Hence, the general format of the tag is:

```
<tag name>content</tag name>
```

For example,

```
<b>MOTHERLAND</b>
```

The above code will display the word, MOTHERLAND, in bold. That is, it will appear as

MOTHERLAND

on the web page in the browser.

HTML Elements

A web page is made up of HTML elements. The opening tag, closing tag and the content in between together form an HTML **element**. In other words, an HTML element is everything between the opening and the closing tag, including the tags. In the previous example, <b>, MOTHERLAND and </b> form an HTML element.

There are two types of elements in HTML: container elements and empty elements.

a. **Container elements:** These elements have both opening (or ON) and closing (or OFF) tags. For example, <b>, </b>, <u>, </u>, <font> and </font> are container elements.

b. **Empty elements:** These have an opening tag, but do not have a closing tag. Empty elements usually perform a particular function. For example, <br>, also known as the line break tag, is an empty element that displays the text in a new line. <hr> is another empty element that draws a horizontal line in the browser. It is also known as horizontal rule.

HTML Attributes

Attributes provide additional information about the elements. An HTML tag may have several attributes that specify the additional effects to be applied to the content enclosed between the tags. For example, you may like to specify the font style, colour and alignment or apply borders to your table or image, and so on. These attributes are always specified in the opening tag. For example, to display the text (say MOTHERLAND) in red colour, you will use the following code:

```
<font color = "red">MOTHERLAND</font>
```

Here, color is the attribute of the font tag.

Structure of an HTML Document

The various components that make up an HTML document are elements, tags and attributes. Each HTML document starts with an <html> tag and ends with an </html> tag. A browser will interpret the entire code written between these tags as an HTML document.

It is the HTML element that defines the document as an HTML file. It is a container element. This element contains only the <head> and <body> elements. They, in turn, can contain other elements. A standard HTML document is divided into two distinct sections: head and body.

Head

The <head> provides information about the document page and is the first element contained inside the <html> element. The <head> element is a container element that includes identification and supplementary information about the document. Most of this information is not displayed as no text is put inside the head element. It contains the <title> element which specifies the title of the web page that you are creating.

Title

The <title> element is a container element because it has an opening (<title>) and closing (</title>) tag. In between these tags, the title is written. This title is displayed in the title bar of the browser window.

Body

This section contains the main content of the web page which includes text and graphics. The text enclosed in the <body> element is displayed on the web page according to the tags and attributes in which the respective content is enclosed.

To sum up, the basic structure of an HTML document will be as follows:

```
<html>
<head>
     <title>.................</title>
</head>
```

```
<body>
..................
..................
</body>
</html>
```

Points to Remember While Writing HTML Code

HTML is a very simple language, but the following points should be kept in mind while writing the code of an HTML document:

1. The tag names and attribute names are not case-sensitive. For example, <TITLE> and <title> are the same. However, as a convention, lower case is generally used to write the tags in an HTML document. Also, remember that the values of the attributes may be case-sensitive.

2. There is no relevance of spaces between the tags. For example, the following three statements will give the same result:

   a. `<b> MOTHERLAND</b>`

   b. `<b>     MOTHERLAND     </b>`

   c.
   ```
   <b>
   MOTHERLAND
   </b>
   ```

However, there should be no space before, after or in between the tag names, that is, between the opening and closing angular brackets, < and >, in a tag. That means the following statements are incorrect:

```
<t i t l e>
<   title>
<title  >
<  title  >
```

3. HTML elements can be nested. This is done in order to apply more than one effect to a particular text or graphic. Care has to be taken that the element that is opened first will be closed later. Consider following example to underline the text and also display it in bold.

   ```
   <b> <u>MOTHERLAND </u> </b>
   ```

   Here, note that the, <b> tag was typed first, followed by the <u> tag. The closing of these tags is always done in the opposite order. Hence the </u> tag was typed first, followed by the </b> tag.

4. It is strongly recommended that you create the HTML document in a proper order with line breaks (using the **Enter** Key) and indents (using the **Tab** key). Even though no change in the browser window is seen, as it does not matter how you structure the HTML document, it definitely helps in understanding, modifying and debugging the code.

Check your understanding!

Fill in the blanks.

1. HTML stands for ______________________________.
2. An HTML document is divided into two sections: _______________ and ____________.
3. A _________ is a piece of code that instructs the browser how to display an image or text.
4. HTML tags and attribute names are not ________________.
5. __________________ is an example of an empty element.

Creating an HTML Document

As discussed before, you need an HTML editor to create an HTML document. In fact, you can type the code in any word processor like WordPad, MS Word and Notepad, In this chapter, we will use Notepad to write all HTML codes. Follow these steps to create an HTML document:

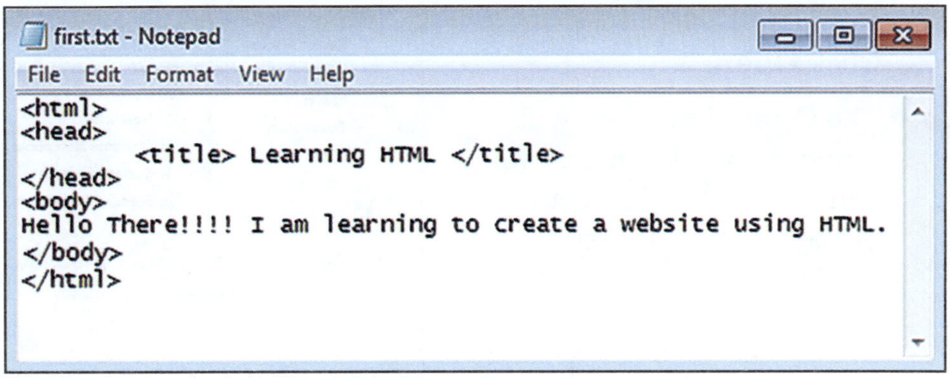

Fig. 6.1: Notepad window

1. Click **All Programs** from the **Start** menu.
2. From the **Accessories** submenu, select **Notepad**. The Notepad window will appear.
3. Type the HTML document as shown in Fig. 6.1.
4. To save the file, select **Save As** option from the **File** menu. The **Save As** dialog box appears (Fig. 6.2).
5. Choose the location where you want to save your file. Type the name with an extension *.htm* or *.html* in the **File name** text box. Click the **Save** button.

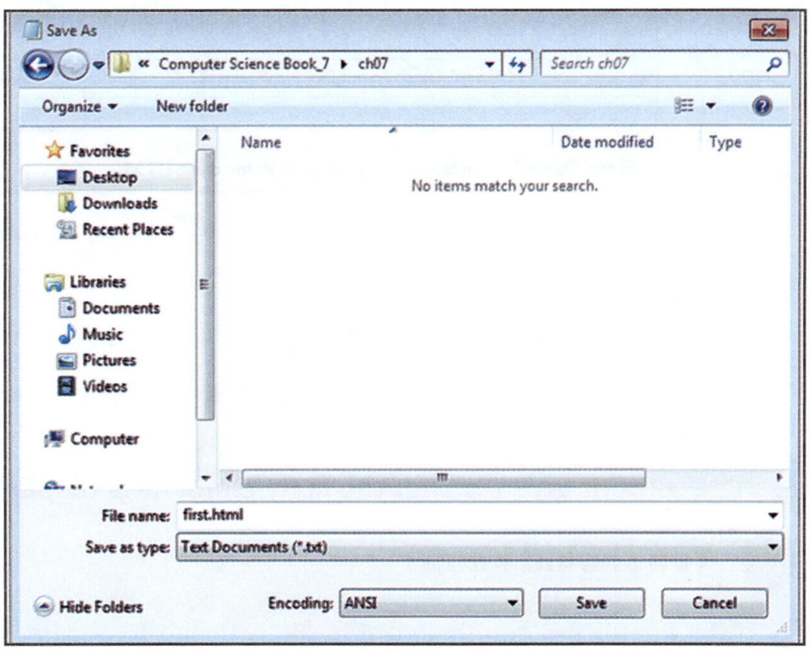

Fig. 6.2: Save As dialog box

Viewing HTML Documents in a Web Browser

To view an HTML document, open any web browser (Internet Explorer).

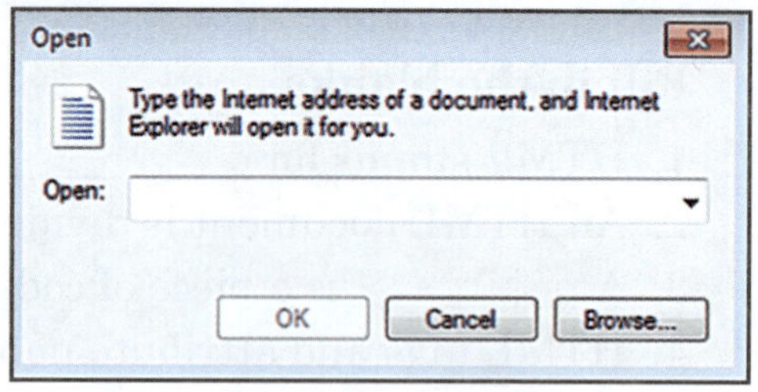

Fig. 6.3: Open dialog box

Follow these steps to view an HTML document in a web browser:

1. Select **Open** option from the **File** menu.
2. The **Open** dialog box is displayed (Fig. 6.3). Click the **Browse** button.
3. The Windows Internet Explorer window appears (Fig. 6.4). Choose the path where your file has been stored and select your file. Click **Open**.
4. The **Open** dialog box will reappear. Click **OK** and you will see the HTML document in the browser (Internet Explorer).

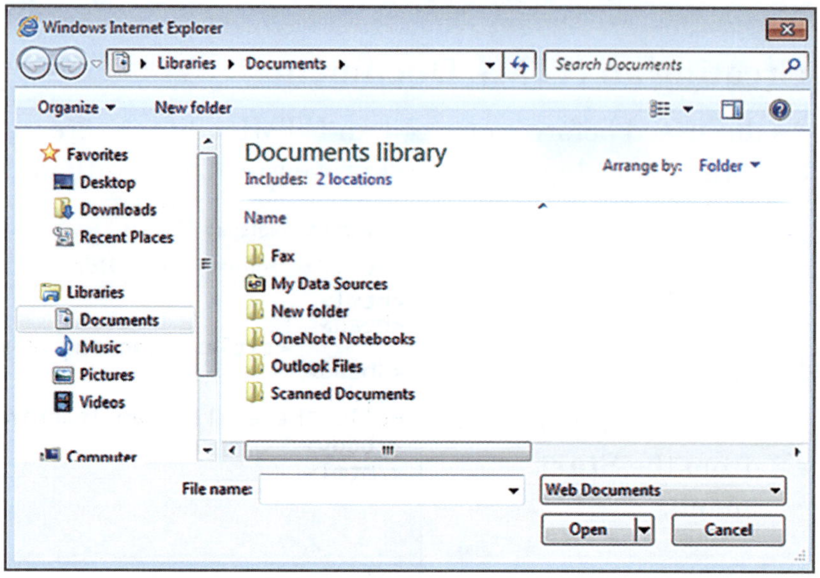

Fig. 6.4: Windows Internet Explorer window

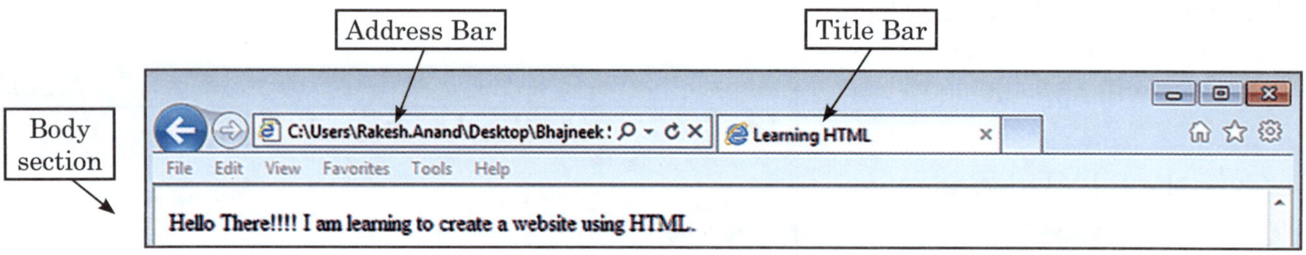

Fig. 6.5: Web page in browser window

As can be seen from Fig. 6.5:

a. The complete path with the file name is displayed in the address bar.

b. The text between the <title> and </title> tags is displayed on the title bar of the browser window.

c. The content given within the body element is displayed in the body part of the browser.

You should know!

If the menus are not displayed in the Internet Explorer, press the **Alt** key to view the menu bar.

PRACTICE TIME

Kunjal wants to create a simple web page on Fast Foods. Give her the step-by-step instructions to complete the task.

SOLUTION

1. Open **Notepad**.
2. Type the following HTML code:

```
<html>
<head>
<title> Fast Foods</title>
</head>
<body>
Fast foods are becoming increasingly popular due to various reasons.
It is fast to cook and easy-to-eat food, and our taste buds love
them. Fast food is actually very harmful. It causes obesity and other
lifestyle-related diseases. Fast food is harmful because it is fried
in oil, which increases cholesterol levels in our body. Also, raw
materials in fast foods don't have any nutritional value.
</body>
</html>
```

3. Select **Save As** option from the file menu. Type the name of the file in the File name text box, say 'fast food.html'.
4. Open **Internet Explorer** or any other browser.
5. Select **Open** option from the **File** menu.
6. The **Open** dialog box is displayed. Click **Browse**.
7. Select the file 'fast food.html' and click **Open**.
8. In the **Open** dialog box, click **OK** to view the web page.

Body Element

The <body> element is one of the basic HTML elements. As it has both ON and OFF tags, it is a container element. The entire content (text and graphics) that has to be displayed on the web page is enclosed between the opening and closing tag of the <body> element. You might like the web page that you are creating to have specific properties. For example, you may want to specify the background colour, margins, text colour, etc. All these properties of a web page can be set through the attributes of the body element. The <body> element has a number of attributes to control and format the page display. Some of these attributes are discussed below.

bgcolor

This attribute is used to set the background colour of the web page. The value of this attribute can be a colour name or a RGB hexadecimal code. For example,

```
<body bgcolor = "red">    or    <body bgcolor = "#223344">
```

You should know!

All colours are made up of three primary colours—red, green and blue. These colours are represented as hexadecimal values. In a hexadecimal value, the first two digits represent the amount of red, the second two digits represent the amount of green and the last two digits represent the amount of blue contained in the colour.

background

This attribute is used to display an image in the background of an HTML document. The value of this attribute is the complete path and file name of the image file that you want to insert as the background. For example,

```
<body background = "C:\desktop\a.jpeg">
```

text

This attribute is used to set the text colour of the document and its value can be the name of the colour or a hexadecimal RGB code. For example,

`<body text = "yellow">` or `<body text= "#006600">`

leftmargin, topmargin, rightmargin and bottommargin

These attributes are used to set all the four margins—top, bottom, left and right margins of a web page. The values of these attributes are numeric and the unit is pixels. For example,

`<body leftmargin = "80">` or `<body topmargin = "95">`

You should know!

You can use more than one attribute for an element by separating each attribute with a space. For example,

```
<body text="green" bgcolor="yellow" topmargin="80">
```

Consider the following example that uses the body element with its attributes. Type the following HTML code in Notepad, save the document as *politics.html* and then open it in a browser.

HTML code

```
<html>
<head>
     <title> Politics in India</title>
</head>
<body bgcolor="Blue" text = "yellow" leftmargin="60" topmargin= "75"
rightmargin="60">
India is the largest democracy in the world with the largest number of
political parties taking part in the election campaign. In the 1996
```

```
national elections, almost 600 million people voted and an average of
26 candidates competed for each of the 543 territorial constituency
seats. Elections are held at national level and state level. Elections
are also held for city, town and village councils. There are different
political issues in Indian politics, at national level and at regional
or state level. Some communities just demand more economical and
social rights for their communities, while others demand more autonomy
for their cultures within the Indian states. With all its problems
India survives as a single state with democratic character.
</body>
</html>
```

Politics.html will appear in the web browser as shown in Fig. 6.6.

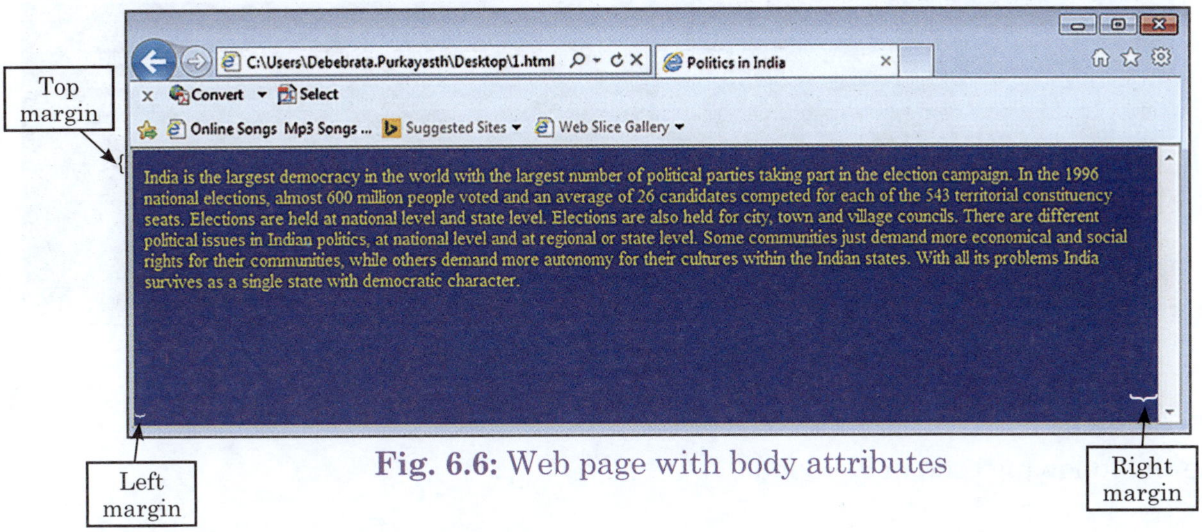

Fig. 6.6: Web page with body attributes

If you use the background attribute instead of bgcolor and give the complete path with file name as its value, the browser will place the image specified in the value as the background.

HTML code (with background attribute)

```
<html>
<head>
     <title> Politics in India</title>
</head>
<body background="file:///C:/Users/Mohini/Desktop/images.jpg" text =
"yellow" leftmargin="60" topmargin= "75" rightmargin="60">
India is the largest democracy in the world with the largest number
of political parties taking part in the election campaign. In the
1996 national elections, almost 600 million people voted and an
average of 26 candidates competed for each of the 543 territorial
constituency seats. Elections are held at national level and state
level. Elections are also held for city, town and village councils.
There are different political issues in Indian politics, at national
```

```
level and at regional or state level. Some communities just demand
more economical and social rights for their communities, while others
demand more autonomy for their cultures within the Indian states.
With all its problems India survives as a single state with
democratic character.
</body>
</html>
```

Figure 6.7 shows the output with the attributes applied.

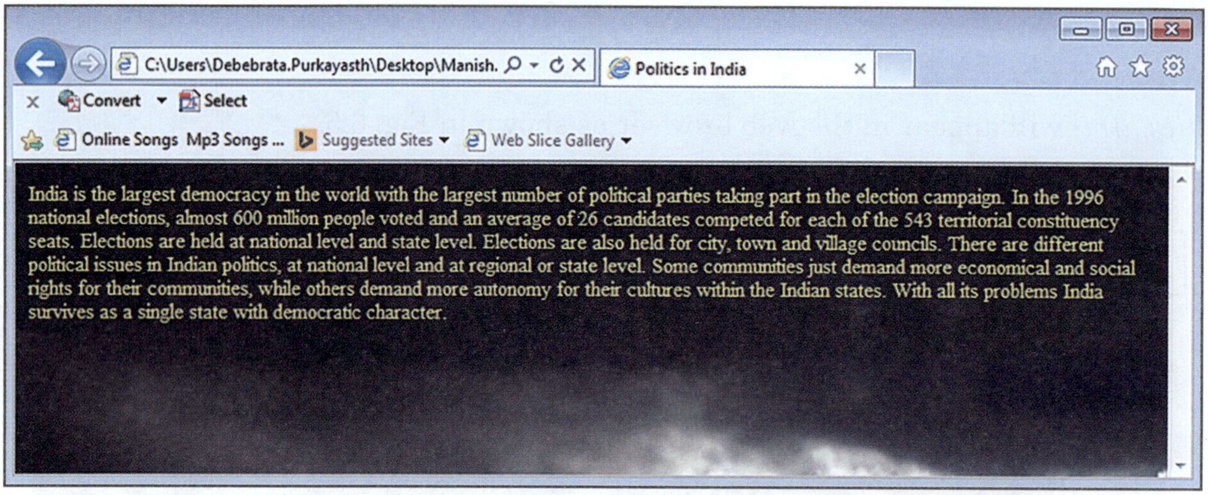

Fig. 6.7: Web page with background image

 element

Type the following code in Notepad.

```
<html>
<head>
     <title> Understanding line breaks </title>
</head>
<body>
     O wild West Wind,
     thou breath of Autumn's being,
     Thou, from whose unseen presence the leaves dead are driven,
     like ghosts from an enchanter fleeing,
</body>
</html>
```

Save the file and view it in the browser (Fig. 6.8). You will see that the entire text is displayed in a single line.

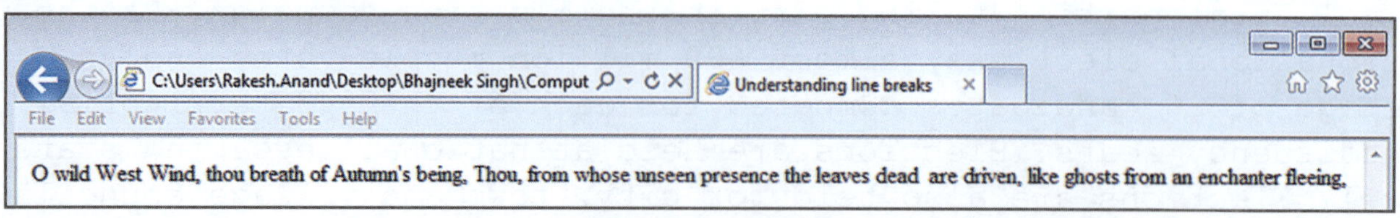

Fig. 6.8: Display of content in web browser

This is because the browser does not recognize the formatting features of a text editor. So, pressing an **Enter key** for a new line in the code has no effect in the browser. The <br> element is used in such cases to insert line breaks. That is, if you want your text to appear in a new line or want some blank lines between the text, the <br> element is used. This is an empty element as it does not have an OFF tag.

Now type the above code containing the <br> element after every line of text content. When you save the file and view it in the browser (Fig. 6.9), you will see the text with line breaks.

```
<html>
<head>
     <title> Understanding line breaks </title>
</head>
<body>
     O wild West Wind, <br>
     thou breath of Autumn's being, <br>
     Thou, from whose unseen presence the leaves dead are driven, <br>
     like ghosts from an enchanter fleeing, <br>
</body>
</html>
```

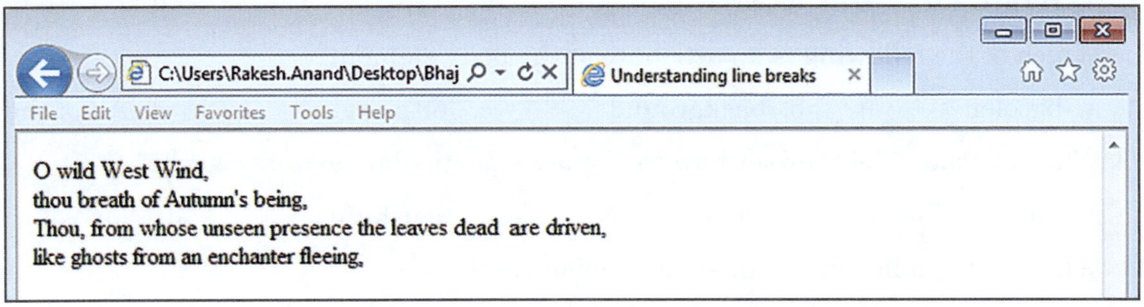

Fig. 6.9: Text with <br> element

You can also use the <br> tag to have multiple line breaks. Insert 4–5 <br> tags after the first line of the text and view the page in the browser. Do you see more number of line breaks?

Quick Recap

1. HyperText Markup Language or HTML is the language used to create web pages.
2. A browser is used to view web pages. Some examples of browsers are Internet Explorer, Google Chrome, and Mozilla Firefox.
3. HTML defines how the content of the page is to be presented or displayed in the browser. HTML code is written in HTML editor.
4. A tag is a piece of code that instructs the browser how to display a particular text or image. A tag name is a keyword surrounded by angular brackets (< and >).
5. HTML tags generally come in pairs. The opening tag, closing tag and the content in between together form an element.
6. Elements are of two types—container elements and empty elements.
7. Container elements are the elements that have both opening and closing tags.

8. Empty elements are the elements that have an opening tag but do not have a closing tag.
9. Tag names and attribute names are not case-sensitive.
10. HTML files are saved with the extension *.htm* or *.html*.
11. A standard HTML document is divided into two distinct sections: HEAD and BODY.
12. The <head> element includes identification and supplementary information about the HTML document.
13. The <body> element contains the main content of the web page which includes text and graphics. Some attributes of <body> element are bgcolcor, background, leftmargin, topmargin, rightmargin and leftmargin.

Exercises

A **Choose the correct option for each of the following.**

1. Which of the following is not an HTML version?

   a. HTML 1.0 b. XHTML c. HTML 5 d. HTML 6

2. Which of the following is an attribute of the body element?

   a. bgcolor b. background c. leftmargin d. All of the above

3. What instructs the browser how to display a particular text or image?

   a. Tag b. Element c. Attribute d. None of the above

4. Which of the following is an empty element?

   a. <html> b. <body> c.
 d. <head>

5. Which attribute of the body tag is used to set the top margin of the web page?

   a. Top b. margintop c. topmargin d. topandmargin

B **Fill in the blanks using the words given below.**

tag	attributes	website	Tim Berners Lee	*.htm* or *.html*

1. ________________ invented HTML.
2. A ________________ consists of multiple web pages linked to each other through hypertext.
3. HTML files are saved with the extension ________________ .
4. A ________________ is a piece of code that instructs the browser how to display a particular text or image.
5. ________________ are the properties associated with each tag.

C State whether the following statements are true (T) or false (F).

1. HTML can include both text and graphics. [ ]
2. HTML tags are always in pairs. [ ]
3. The tag names and attribute names in HTML are case-sensitive. [ ]
4. An ON tag has a forward slash before its name. [ ]
5. Empty elements do not require an OFF tag. [ ]

D Answer the following questions.

1. Differentiate between a container element and an empty element.
2. Name any two web browsers.
3. How is bgcolor different from background attribute of the body tag?
4. Name two distinct parts of an HTML document.
5. Write the attributes of the body tag with their functions.

Lab Activity

1. Sahil wants to create a web page on the rulers of India. Help him do so. Set all the page margins as 60 pixels. Also, insert a suitable background image of the web page. The title of the page should be 'Rulers of India'.
2. Help Shreya create a colourful web page on the artists of India.
3. Sukanya wants to create a website on types of plants. Help her do so. The background colour should be green and the text should be in red colour.

Research Project

Create a web page on the previous year's achievements of your school for your school website using HTML. Explore different web page layouts on the Internet and try using them in your creation.

Teacher's Notes

1. Discuss all the HTML tags with their attributes.
2. Discuss the need of a text editor.

7 Displaying Text in HTML

Learning Objectives

By the end of this chapter, you will be able to:

- describe the use of the <hr> and the <comment> tags in HTML
- use various formatting elements in HTML such as paragraph, heading, font and other markup elements

Warm Up

Give one-word answers to the following:

1. This person invented HTML ____________________
2. This is the latest version of HTML ____________________
3. This is used to create an HTML document ____________________
4. This is used to view an HTML document ____________________
5. Each HTML document starts with this tag ____________________

Introduction

In the previous chapter, you studied the basic structure of an HTML document. You also created a web page using the basic elements of HTML, that is, head, title and body.

In this chapter you will learn the basic elements to display the HTML text in various formats in a web browser. Let us discuss elements that help in better presentation of information on the web page such as <hr>, <comment>, <font>, <p> and <center> elements.

Horizontal Rule

The <hr> element is used to create a horizontal line on the web page. This is also called **Horizontal Rule** in HTML. It is an empty element as it has no OFF (or closing) tag. The <hr> element has the following attributes:

You should know!

The default value of the size attribute of <hr> element is 2 pixels.

Size: Size specifies the thickness of the horizontal line in pixels. For example, the following statement will draw a line that has a width of 8 pixels in the browser window.

```
<hr size="8">
```

You should know!

If an inch is divided into 72 equal parts, each part is called a pixel.

Width: This attribute takes the horizontal width of the line as its value. This value can be provided in two ways:

- *In pixels:* For example, the statement <hr width="100"> will draw a line which is 100 pixels wide.
- *In percentage of page width:* For example, <hr width="60%"> will draw a line that will cover 60% of the width of the web page horizontally.

Align: It specifies the side of the web page according to which the line will be aligned. So, the value of this attribute can either be left, centre or right.

For example,

```
<hr align="right">
```

will right align the line.

Color: It specifies the colour of the line. The value of this attribute can be either the name of a colour or a hexadecimal RGB code.

For example,

```
<hr color="green">
```

will draw the line in green colour.

You should know!

In HTML 5, the <hr> element represents a thematic break between paragraph-level elements. No visible line is drawn in the browser.

Noshade: This attribute does not have any value. Specifying it along with the <hr> element displays a solid line without any shading in the browser.

For example,

```
<hr noshade>
```

To sum up all the attributes that we have learnt, let us draw a horizontal line in the browser, which is red, centre-aligned and covers 50% of the page width. The command required will be as follows:

```
<hr size="50%" align="center" color="red">
```

Figure 7.1 shows the output of this command.

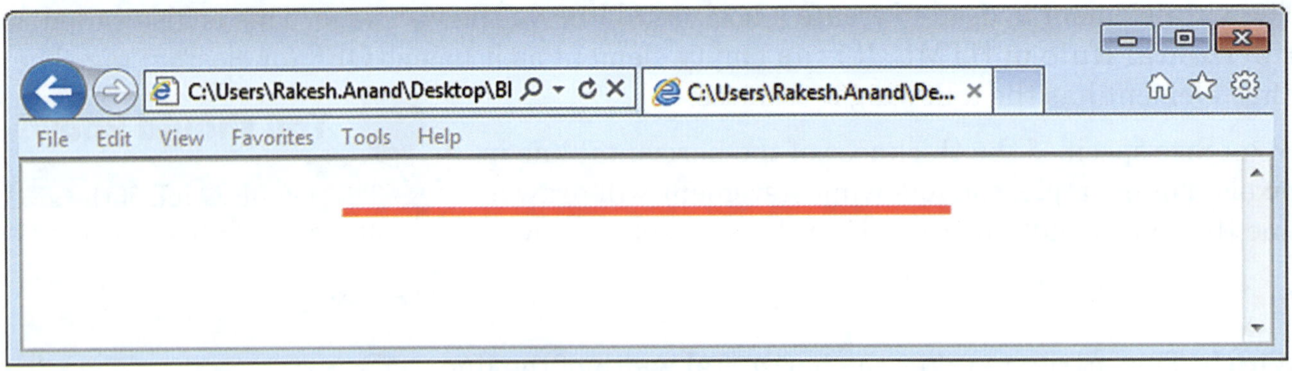

Fig. 7.1: Red horizontal bar

Comment Element (<!-->)

A comment is a statement given in HTML code that is meant to have only a reference to a particular code. It is ignored by the browser and hence is not displayed. Comments are used just to write small explanations of the HTML code, which helps in better understanding and easy modification of the document by anyone in the future.

The syntax of the comment tag is

```
<!--and-->
```

For example,

```
<!--This is a comment entry-->
```

Here, the statement 'This is a comment entry' will not be displayed in the browser.

Center Element (<Center>)

The centre element is used to place the text in the centre of the web page, between the left and the right margins. In other words, the text or image enclosed between <center> and </center> is aligned in the centre of the web page. It is a container element. For example,

```
<center>I AM IN THE CENTRE.</center>
```

You should know!

The <center> element has become obsolete and is not available in HTML 5. Instead, we use CSS (Cascading Style Sheets) in the code.

Check your understanding!

Fill in the blanks.

1. The ____________ element is used to create a horizontal line on the web page
2. <hr align="left"> will ____________ align the rule.
3. The hr element is an ____________ element.
4. 1 pixel is equal to ____________ part of an inch.
5. ____________ are not displayed in the browser.

Text Elements in HTML

There are some basic elements used to display text in the browser like paragraph, font, heading, etc. These elements make the web page appear structured and different sections of the page are easily distinguishable.

Paragraph <p>

The paragraph element is used to display multiple lines of text, that is, a paragraph in HTML. It is defined by <p> and </p> tags. When the text enclosed between these two tags is displayed in the browser, a blank line is inserted before and after the enclosed text.

Align is the attribute of the paragraph element that is used to align it in the centre, left or right of the web page. Hence, the value of the align attribute can be either of the following:

- center: Aligns the text in the centre
- left: Aligns the text to the left side of the web page
- right: Aligns the text to the right side of the page
- justify: Aligns the text from both left and right side of the page

The syntax of the <p> element is

```
<p align="value">
```

where value can be left, right, centre or justify.

As an example, type the following HTML code in Notepad, save the document as an HTML file and open it in the browser.

```
<html>
<head>
  <title>Learning alignments</title>
</head>
<body>
  <p align="left">
  Positive thinking requires a lot of mental workout. The more you work
  for it, the better you will be at it. Although it is not possible to
  think positive all the time, you should try that majority of your
  thoughts reflect good and happy things. It will certainly make you
  more positive and a more happy person in life.
  </p>
  <br>
  <p align="right">
  Generally, people don't think positive because they might not be
  aware of the right tools for becoming a positive person. You must
  learn skills like building up your self confidence, encouraging
  yourself and others for adopting a positive attitude, good habits,
  doing meditation, exercising regularly and above all, being in the
```

```
        company of positive people. You should also try to bend more
        towards spiritualism.
        </p>
        <br>
        <p align="center">
        You will definitely start loving life by thinking of life as an
        adventure. Every time you step out of your house, just think that
        you are going out for an adventure. Think about how the
        possibilities are endless. There are possibilities to meet new
        people, to help the needy, to reach your workplace at time and even
        to impress your boss by your work.
        </p>
        <br>
        <p align="justify">
        It is very important that you change your thoughts by developing
        good habits and adopting a positive attitude. Do not let anything
        overpower you such that it becomes an obsession. It is easier to
        break a habit when you first notice it. So, instead of waiting for
        years and years to leave that habit, you should take immediate
        measures to stop it. Otherwise, it will become more and more
        difficult for you to come out of your obsession. Surveys have shown
        that obsession is one of the most dangerous thing to happen for
        oneself and for others.
        </p>
    </body>
    </html>
```

In the browser, the HTML document will be as shown in Fig. 7.2.

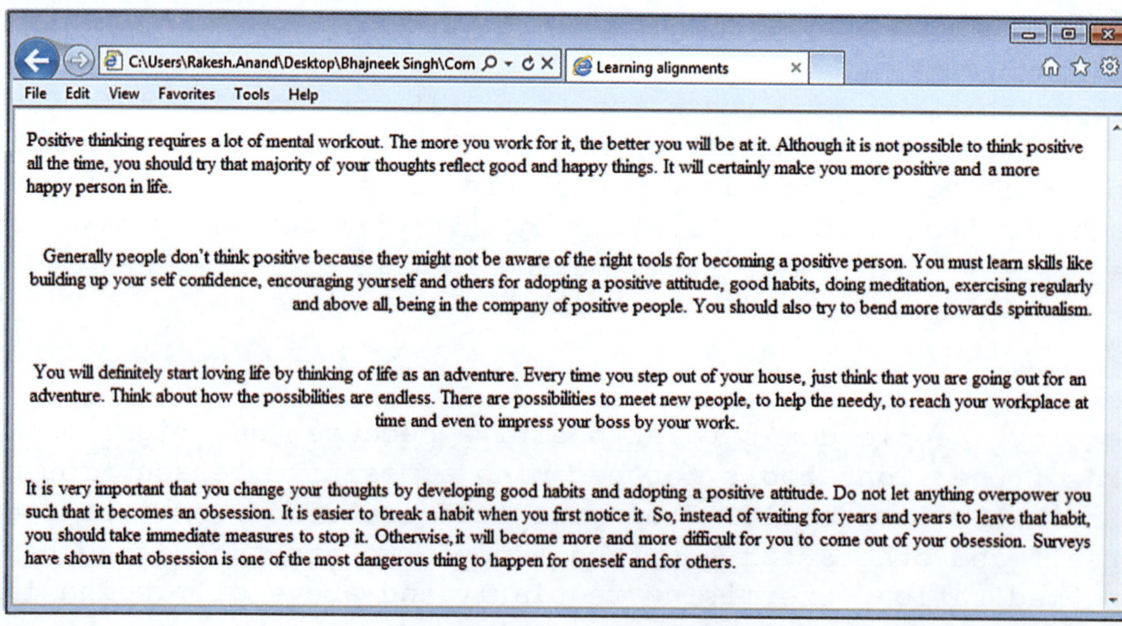

Fig. 7.2: Values of align attribute

Heading <hn>

The heading element of HTML displays different levels of headings in an HTML document. It is a container element and the text enclosed between the ON and OFF tags is displayed differently from the main text.

HTML provides six heading levels, H1 to H6. H1 displays the heading in the largest size of 24 points whereas H6 displays the smallest size of 8 points. The syntax for using heading element is as follows:

```
<hn>heading text</hn>
```

where *n* is the heading level and it can take values from 1 to 6.

As an example, type the following HTML code and view it in the browser.

```
<html>
<head>
<title>Use of heading styles</title>
</head>
<body>
<h1>There is no substitute for hard work</h1>
<h2>There is no substitute for hard work</h2>
<h3>There is no substitute for hard work</h3>
<h4>There is no substitute for hard work</h4>
<h5>There is no substitute for hard work</h5>
<h6>There is no substitute for hard work</h6>
</body>
</html>
```

When viewed in a browser, the web page looks as shown in Fig. 7.3.

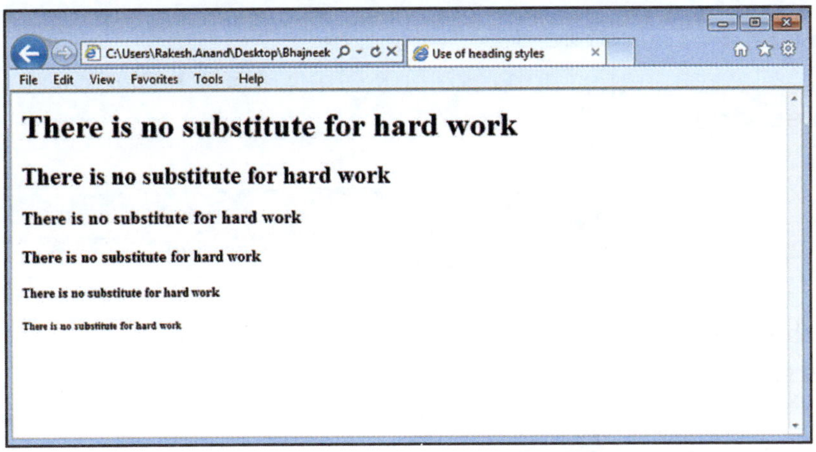

Fig. 7.3: Displaying different heading styles

Font Element (<font>)

The <font> element is used to display the text in a particular font style, size and colour. It is a container element containing <font> and </font> tags. The three attributes of <font> element are as follows:

Size: It is used to specify the size of the text. The smallest font size is 1 and the largest font size is 11.

For example,

```
<font size="5">FANTASTIC HOLIDAY</font>
```

Color: This attribute is used to set the colour of the text. The value of this attribute can either be the name of the colour or the RGB colour code in hexadecimal. For example,

```
<font color="red">FANTASTIC HOLIDAY</font>
```

Or

```
<font color="FF0000">FANTASTIC HOLIDAY</font>
```

Face: It is used to specify the typeface or the name of the font. For example,

```
<font face="arial">FANTASTIC HOLIDAY</font>
```

To understand the various attributes of the font element, write the following HTML code in Notepad and see the corresponding web page in the web browser.

```
<html>
<head>
<title>Changes in font (size, text and colour)</title>
</head>
<body>
<center>
  <font face="Monotype Corsiva" size="11" color="pink">
  <B>Be Strong</B>
  <br> <br> <br>
  </font>
  <font face="MV Boli" size="10" color="#C054BB">
  People will always hate you, break you; but how you handle them, is
  what <B>Makes You</B>
  </font>
</center>
</body>
</html>
```

The web page in the browser window will be as shown in Fig. 7.4.

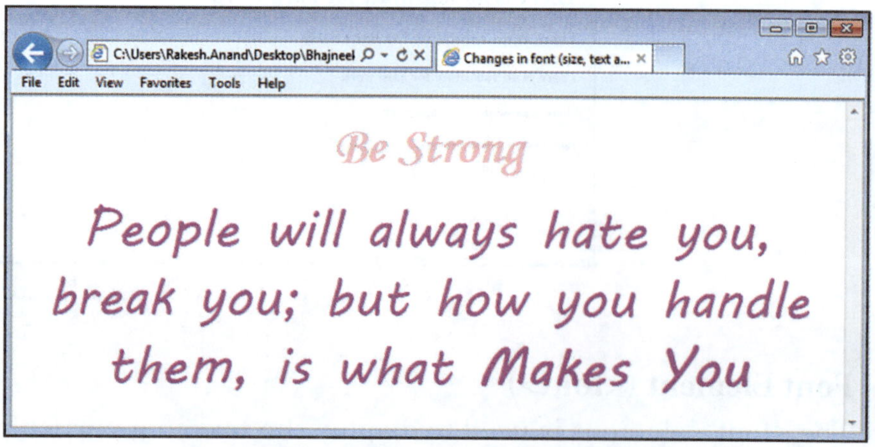

Fig. 7.4: Font face, colour and size

Physical Markup Elements

The physical markup elements (bold, italic and underline) change the appearance of the text. All of these are container elements.

Bold: The bold element is used to emphasize text. Enclose the text that is to be displayed in bold between the <b> and </b> tags. For example,

```
<b>SILENCE PLEASE</b>
```

Underline: This element underlines the text enclosed between the <u> and </u> tags. For example,

```
<u>SILENCE PLEASE</u>
```

Italics: The text enclosed between the <i> and </i> tags is displayed in italics. For example,

```
<i>SILENCE PLEASE</i>
```

Type the code given below in Notepad and see the effect of physical markup elements in the browser.

```
<html>
<head>
<title>Font Style</title>
</head>
<body>
   <b>SUCCESS</b>
   <br> <br>
   <u>There is no shortcut to success.</u>
   <br> <br>
   <i>Always remember</i>
</body>
</html>
```

The output of this code is shown in Fig. 7.5.

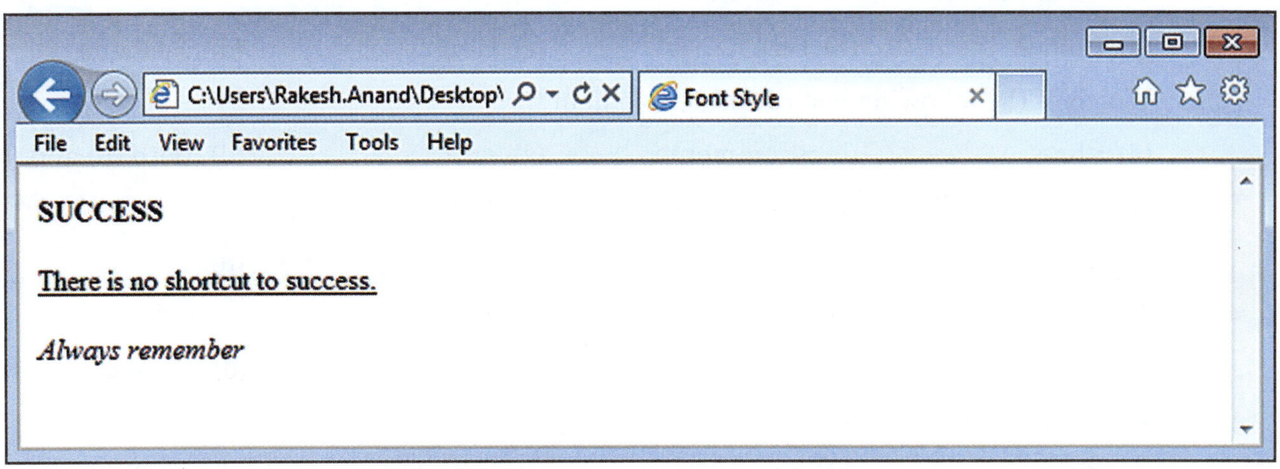

Fig. 7.5: Bold, Underline and Italic

These tags can be nested or combined to apply multiple effects to a particular text. For example, if to underline text and also make it bold, the following statement can be used:

```
<b><u>SILENCE PLEASE</u></b>
```

Quick Recap

1. The <hr> element is used for creating a horizontal line on the web page.
2. The attributes of the <hr> element are size, width, colour, align and noshade.
3. A comment given in HTML code is ignored by the browser and is not displayed. You use comments just to write small explanations of the HTML code, which helps in better understanding and easy modification of the document by anyone in future.
4. The comment tags are <!--and-->.
5. The paragraph element is used to display multiple lines of text.
6. Paragraph element is defined by <p> and </p> tags.
7. Align is the attribute of the paragraph element that is used to align it in centre, left or right of the web page.
8. The heading element of HTML displays different levels of headings in an HTML document.
9. The font element is used to display the text in a particular font style, size and colour.
10. The attributes of font element are face, size and colour.
11. The physical markup elements (bold, italic and underline) change the appearance of the text.

Exercises

A **Choose the correct option for each of the following.**

1. Which of the following is NOT an attribute of <hr>?

   (a) Colour (b) Size (c) Height (d) Noshade

2. Which of the following is a container element?

   (a) <hr> (b) <comment> (c) <u> (d) Both (b) and (c)

3. How many levels of headings are possible in HTML?

   (a) 4 (b) 5 (c) 6 (d) 7

4. Text written after which of the following tags is not shown in the browser?

   (a) <!— (b) <!- (c) <-! (d) None of the above

5. Which tag is used to display text in italics?

   (a) <itl> (b) <i> (c) <u> (d) <italics>

B **State whether the following statements are true (T) or false (F).**

1. The <hr> element can draw a line only in black colour. ☐
2. There are 7 attributes of the font element. ☐
3. Color is the attribute of font element. ☐
4. You can left align a paragraph. ☐
5. <b> is an empty element. ☐

C **Identify the tag/element.**

<u> <hr> <font> <center> comment element

1. To display the text in the centre of the web page. ____________________
2. To draw a horizontal line in the browser ____________________
3. The element that is ignored by the browser ____________________
4. To underline the text ____________________
5. To display the text in a particular size ____________________

D **Answer the following questions briefly.**

1. Write the advantages of using comments in the HTML code.
2. Write the HTML code to display your school's name and address in italics, underline the text and give it yellow colour on the web page.
3. Write the statement to draw a solid line on the web page. The line should be of size 10 pixels, in red colour and centre aligned.
4. Identify the errors in the following statements:
   - <font color="orange" align="center">
   - <p align=right>
5. Write an HTML code to prepare a web page on World Environment Day. Try to use all the tags learnt in this chapter.
6. What is the use of the noshade attribute in the <hr> element?
7. List all the attributes of the font element.
8. What values can the align attribute of <p> element have?
9. Explain the two ways, giving examples, in which the color attribute of the <hr> element can be given values.
10. Give the two ways in which the horizontal length of the line can be specified.

Fun Time!

Identify all HTML elements and tags in the word grid.

H	A	S	H	U	O	I
F	C	O	L	O	U	R
T	O	Y	D	R	H	T
C	E	N	T	E	R	R
R	B	H	T	L	M	B
H	N	N	P	F	A	C

Lab Activity

1. Create the web page that gives the benefits of examination. Create a suitable layout of the web page with appropriate font colour, size and face. Make the page look presentable.
2. Meeta wants her students to create a web page containing one paragraph each on any two of their hobbies. Each paragraph should be of a different colour and centre aligned from the left and right side of the page. There should be a heading—'Hobbies' at the top. The name of each hobby should be the sub-headings.
3. Sushant has a keen interest in creating web pages. It is his friend Raunak's birthday and he wants to create a web page containing a few lines on their friendship. Since his friend's favourite colour is yellow, so he wants the background of the page to be yellow. The heading 'Happy Birthday Raunak' should be in bold face and underlined. He also wants the line to appear in the centre of the page and a horizontal line after each line of text. The text should be in red colour and the horizontal line in blue colour. At the bottom right of the page, he wants to write his name. Help him create the web page.
4. Create a web page 'My Family'. Choose a suitable font style, size and colour of the text for each member of the family.

Research Project

Find out the HTML version on your system. Does your browser support all HTML 5 elements? Also, find out the additional key features that HTML 5 provides as compared to the previous one.

Teacher's Notes

1. Discuss various elements covered in this chapter and their attributes.
2. Demonstrate the effect of all the values of the align attribute of the <p> element.
3. Encourage students to create web pages using different font styles, colours and sizes.
4. Demonstrate all the levels of the heading element with an example.

Worksheet

A **Choose the correct option for each of the following.**

1. Which of the following is an incorrect code statement?
   a. < body> b. <body> c. <b> Hello </b> d. <b><u> Hello </u></b>
2. Which of the following are components of an element in HTML?
   a. ON tag b. OFF tag c. Content between ON and OFF tag d. All of the above
3. Which of the following attributes is used to insert an image in the background?
   a. Bgcolor b. backgroundcolor c. background d. None of the above
4. In which year was the first version of HTML released?
   a. 1990 b. 1991 c. 1992 d. 1993
5. What are the properties associated with each tag called?
   a. Element b. ON c. Attribute d. None of the above
6. Which of the following cannot be the value of the align attribute of <p> element?
   a. Right b. Bottom c. Left d. Center
7. In which of the following ways can the horizontal width of the line in a web page be specified?
   a. In pixels b. In percentage c. Both a and b d. Neither a nor b
8. Which of the following is not an attribute of <font> element?
   a. Color b. Style c. Size d. Face
9. Which of the following is a container element?
   a. <h4> b.
  c. <hr> d. None of the above
10. In <hn> tag, what is the range of values of n?
    a. 2–8 b. 1–8 c. 2–6 d. 1–6

B **Unscramble the words to fill in the blanks.**

1. A ______________________ is used to view a web page. (BWE SWRBERO)
2. ______________________ is the latest version of HTML. (TLMH 5)
3. ______________________ element is used to insert line breaks. (b>r<)
4. The HTML code is written in an ______________________ . (MHTL RDEIOT)
5. ______________________ element is also called horizontal rule. (RH)

C **State whether the following statements are true (T) or false (F).**

1. HTML tags are enclosed in angular brackets. ☐
2. You can view an HTML document by typing the complete path and file name in the address bar. ☐
3. Empty elements have both ON and OFF tags. ☐
4. <hr> is a container element. ☐
5. The text enclosed between <!--and--> is not displayed in the browser. ☐

D **Identify the address bar and title bar in the following figure.**

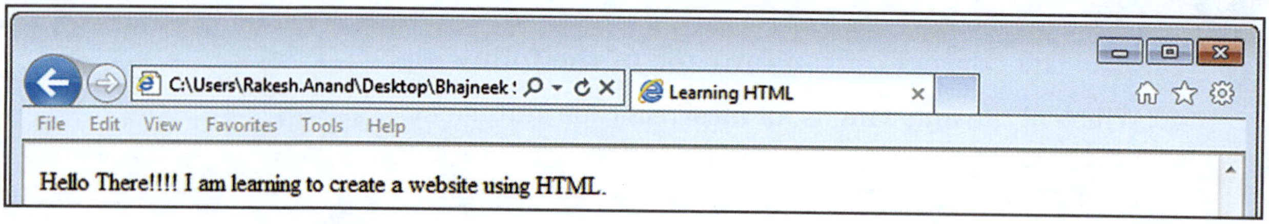

E **Application-based questions.**

1. Aarav wants to have blue colour as the background of his page. Give the command to do so without using the colour name.
2. Nikita wants to have 50 pixels as left and right margins of her page and a picture in the background. Write the HTML statement to do so.
3. What is the error(s) in the following statement:

   <body background="file:///C:/Users/Mohini/Desktop/images.jpg" text = "red" left margin="60" top margin= "75" right margin="60">

F **Answer the following questions.**

1. Explain the structure of an HTML document.
2. What is the use of body tag? How can you insert an image in the background of an HTML document?
3. What is the difference between the <p> and the <br> elements?
4. Name the three physical markup elements.
5. What is the use of the comment element in HTML?

Projects

Create a web page on the rivers of India. Find out information about all the major rivers of India and display information about each river in a different style and colour. Mention your name at the bottom of the web page.

8 More on Flash 8

Learning Objectives

By the end of this chapter, you will be able to:

- import image files.
- create and modify an instance of a symbol.
- group the outline and fill of an object.
- use the Eyedropper tool.
- transform objects.
- use gradients.
- work with text in Flash.

Warm Up

Fill in the blanks.

1. The opening screen of Flash 8 is divided into ________________ columns.
2. The ________________ tool is used to paint objects on the stage.
3. The three modes of the Pencil Tool are ________________, ________________ and ________________.
4. The two options of Zoom Tool are ________________ and ________________.
5. The shortcut key to insert a frame is ________.

Introduction

You have learnt quite a bit of Macromedia Flash 8 in Class 6. You had explored the **Tools Panel**, **Timeline** and also applied animations to objects using frame-by-frame animation.

In this chapter, you will study some more tools and advanced features of Flash 8. You will also learn to create gradients, enhance symbols and animate text.

Importing Image Files

Flash 8 allows you to import and use images created in other applications. JPEG, GIF, PNG images and various other file formats can be imported into Flash for use. Follow these steps to do so:

1. Select **Import** option from the **File** menu.
2. Click **Import to Stage** from the submenu (Fig. 8.1). The **Import** dialog box appears (Fig. 8.2).
3. Select the drive and folder where your image file is saved. Select the file to be inserted and click **Open**.
4. The image is added to the Stage.

You should know!

The graphic files that you want to import must be at least 2 pixels × 2 pixels in size.

Quick Way

The shortcut key to import a picture in Flash is **Ctrl+R**.
To import an image directly into the library, choose **Import to Library** from the **Import** submenu.

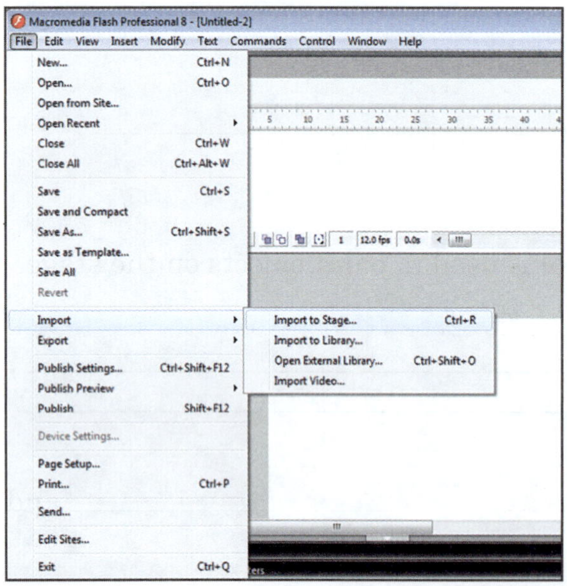

Fig. 8.1: Import to Stage option

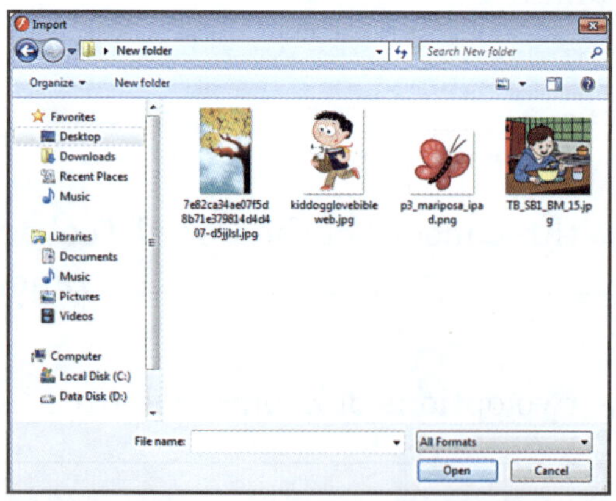

Fig. 8.2: Import dialog box

This image can be used in the same way as with other objects. These imported images are added to the Flash library as **assets**. An **asset** is a non-Flash item that has been imported and stored for future use. Assets can be converted to symbols and stored in the **Flash library**.

Creating Symbols

A **symbol** is any object that is stored within the movie. It is reusable and is stored in the **Flash Library**. This means it can be inserted in the movie multiple number of times. This is done by the use of an **instance**. Each time you insert a symbol in the movie, it is the instance of the symbol that gets inserted.

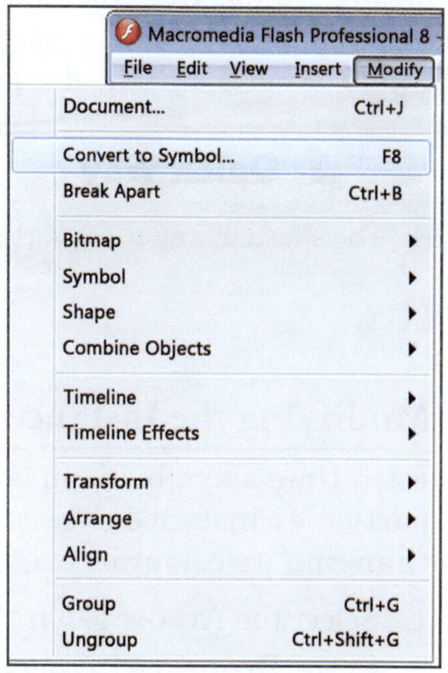

Fig. 8.3: Modify menu

Hence, we can say that an instance is the occurrence of the symbol. Even if we change the instance, the original symbol is not affected. There are the three types of symbols available in Flash 8:

- Movie clip
- Button
- Graphic

Any drawing that you create on the Stage can be changed into a symbol. The steps to change a drawing into a symbol are:

1. Draw an object (say, a hut) on the Stage.
2. Click the **Arrow Tool** and select the object (the hut).
3. From the **Modify** menu (Fig. 8.3), select **Convert to Symbol** option. The **Convert to Symbol** dialog box appears (Fig. 8.4).
4. Type a name that you want to give to your symbol.
5. A symbol can be a movie clip, a button or any graphic. Since your object is a drawing, so choose **Graphic** option.
6. Click **OK**. On the right side of the Stage, you will see the Flash library with the name and picture of the recently inserted symbol, that is the hut here.

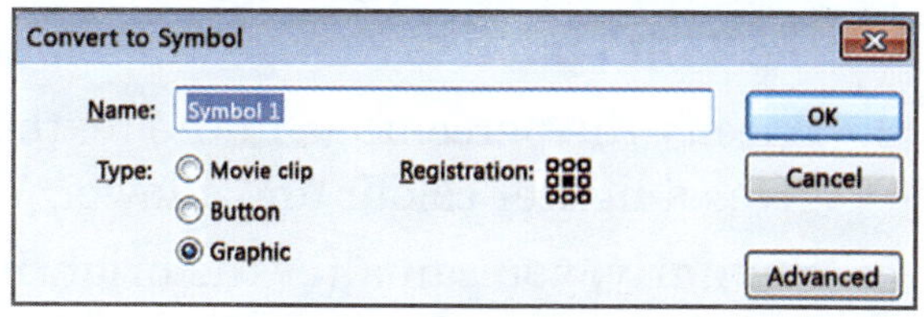

Fig. 8.4: Convert to Symbol dialog box

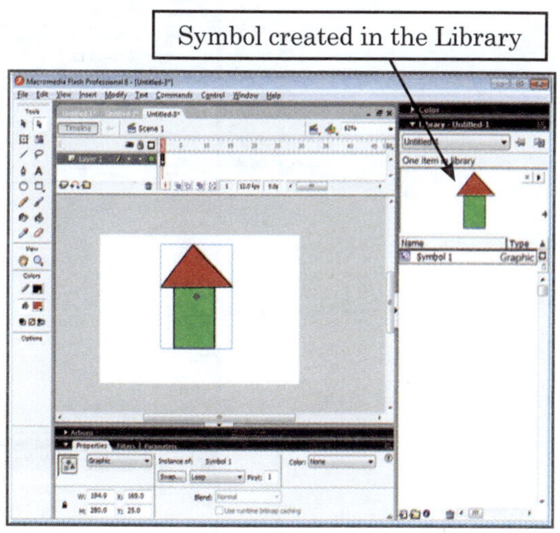

Fig. 8.5: Library panel

You should know!

If the Flash Library panel is not visible, click the **Library** option in the **Window** menu.

After the symbol is created, its instance has to be added in the movie. Click and drag the desired symbol from the Library panel onto the Stage. The instance of the symbol is inserted. Flash 8 allows you to insert multiple instances of a symbol. You can even resize, rotate or move a particular instance without affecting other instances.

Quick Way

The shortcut key to convert an object to symbol is **F8**. Press **Ctrl+L** to open the Library panel.

Modifying the Instance of a Symbol

Each time a symbol is inserted, an instance of the symbol is created. Once a particular instance is inserted, Flash allows users to modify its properties by changing its colour or brightness. Follow the steps given below to modify an instance:

1. Select the **Arrow** tool from the **Tools Panel** and select the instance to be modified.
2. In the **Property Inspector** window, click the drop-down menu arrow for the **Color** in the Color list box.
3. You will find the following options: None, Brightness, Tint, Alpha and Advanced. Select the **Tint** option to change the colour shade (Fig. 8.6).
4. Specify the percentage in the textbox. You will notice that a higher percentage of Tint gives a lighter colour and a lower percentage gives a darker colour.
5. Similarly, you can alter the brightness/transparency of the instance by selecting the **Brightness** or **Alpha** option.

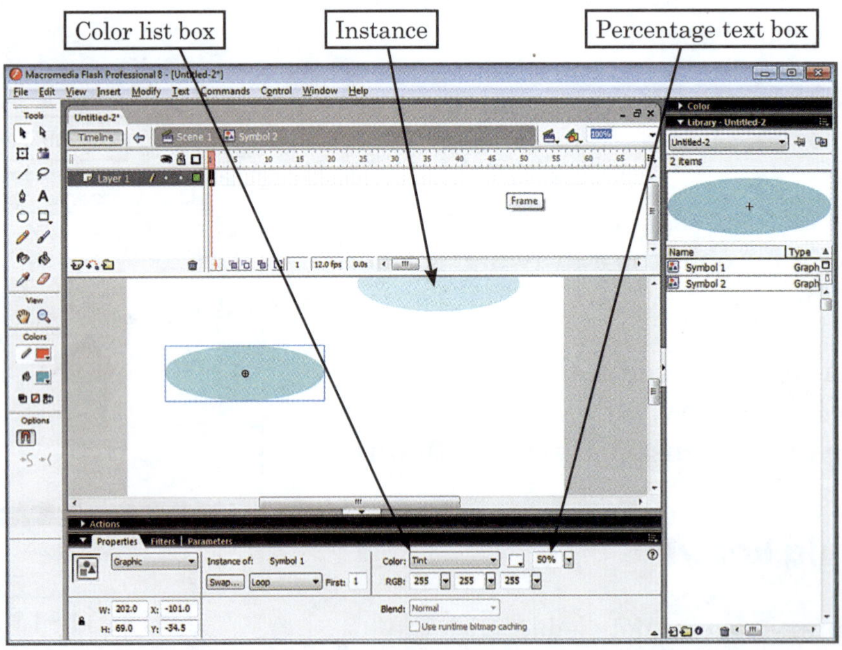

Fig. 8.6: Changing the colour shade of an instance

Grouping Outlines and Fill

When an object is drawn in Flash, two distinct objects are created—one is the outline and the other is the fill. In order to move both the objects together, they need to be grouped into a single object. Follow these steps to group the outline and the fill (Fig. 8.7):

1. Click the **Arrow** tool from the **Tools Panel**.
2. Click and drag to select both the outline and the fill.
3. Select **Group** option from the **Modify** menu.
4. To ungroup the outline and the fill, select **Break Apart** option from the **Modify** menu.

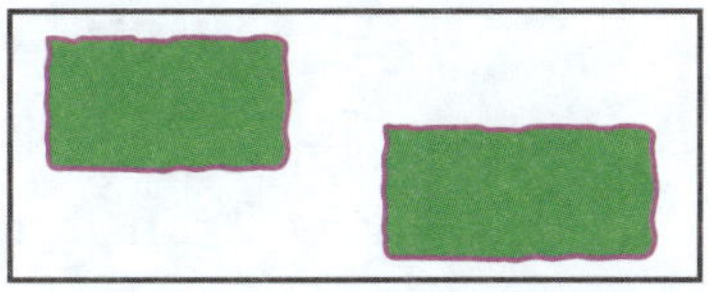

Fig. 8.7: (a) Outline and Fill grouped together

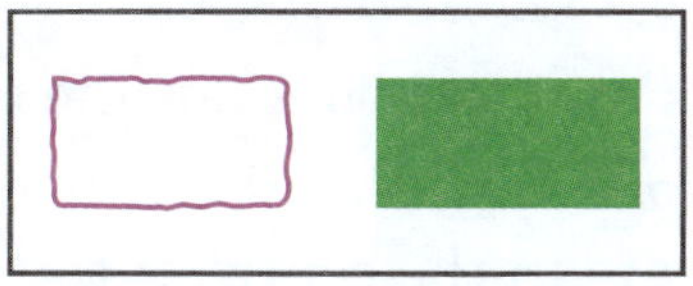

Fig. 8.7: (b) Outline and Fill ungrouped

Quick Way

The shortcut key to group the objects is **Ctrl+G**. To break apart the grouped objects, the shortcut key is **Ctrl+B**.

Eyedropper Tool

The **Eyedropper** tool is used to copy the outline and fill properties from one object and immediately paste them to another object. It is a useful tool to copy custom colours and gradients for outline or fill colour. Instead of recreating them again, they can be copied and reused in multiple objects. Both colours and style from existing lines, strokes and files can be picked and fills applied to other objects. Users can pick up a colour from one object using the **Eyedropper** tool and fill this colour in another object using the **Paint Bucket** tool.

Follow these steps to use the **Eyedropper** tool:

1. Select **Eyedropper** tool from the **Tools Panel**. The pointer changes to an eyedropper.
2. Click the outline or filled area whose properties you want to copy.
3. a. Clicking the stroke or outline, changes the tool automatically to an **Ink Bottle** tool.
   b. Clicking the filled area changes the tool automatically to a **Paint Bucket** tool with its **Lock Fill Modifier** turned on.
4. Click the line or fill where the copied properties are to be applied.

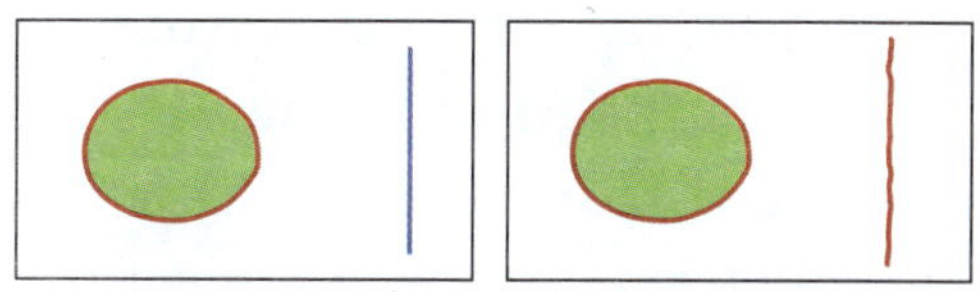

Fig. 8.8: Eyedropper tool

You should know!

The **Eyedropper** tool also allows users to apply an image as a fill in combination with **Paint Bucket** tool.

In Fig. 8.8, the outline properties of the oval are copied using the **Eyedropper** tool and applied to the line in the adjacent figure.

Transforming Objects

Transforming an object means to modify the object by changing its shape, size, colour, position and orientation on the Stage. If a gradient was applied to the object, it can be changed in different ways. In this section, you will learn various methods of transforming an object.

Free Transform Tool

Free Transform tool helps to move, scale, rotate, compress, stretch or skew an object on the Stage. Follow these steps to compress the drawing using the **Free Transform** tool:

1. Draw an object on the Stage. You can even import a picture if you wish to.
2. Select the object and click **Free Transform** tool.
3. Double-click on the object so as to select both outline and fill.
4. As the object is clicked, a **Central handle**, also called the **Transformation Point**, appears in the centre of the selected object.
5. As the pointer is moved over different parts of the selection, it changes to indicate which transformation function is available. For example, to move the object, the pointer changes to a cross whereas to rotate an object, the pointer changes to a curved arrow.

Quick Way

The shortcut key to use Free Transform tool is Q.

Moving an Object: Follow these steps to move an object from one place to another on the Stage (Fig. 8.9):

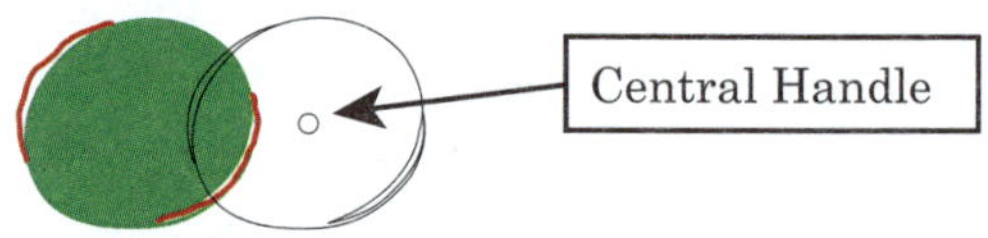

Fig. 8.9: Rotating an object

1. Select the object to be moved.
2. When the pointer is positioned over the selected object, the pointer changes to a cross (×).
3. Click and drag the object to a new position and release the left mouse button.

Rotating an Object: Follow these steps to rotate an object (Fig. 8.10):

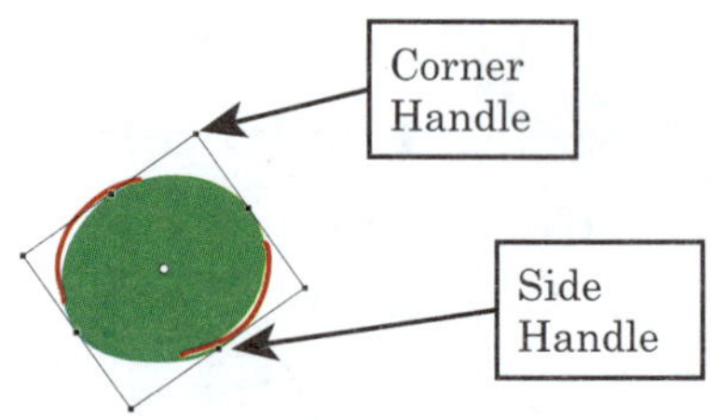

Fig. 8.10: Rotating an object

1. Select the object to be rotated.
2. From the **Modify** menu, select **Transform** option.
3. Select **Rotate and Skew** from the submenu.
4. Click the corner handle of the object. A curved arrow called the **Rotation Handle** ( ) appears.
5. Drag this **Rotation Handle** by the desired angle to rotate the object. The outline of the object becomes visible as it is rotated.
6. To end the rotation, release the mouse button and click anywhere outside the selected object.

Quick Way

To rotate a selected object, select the **Free Transform** tool and position the mouse pointer on any of the four corner handles. When the pointer changes to a curved arrow, click and drag to rotate the object.

Flipping an Object: Flipping an object means to invert it either horizontally or vertically. Follow these steps to flip an object (Fig. 8.11):

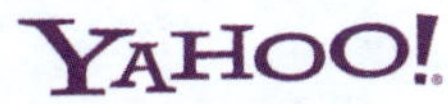

Fig. 8.11 (a): Original image

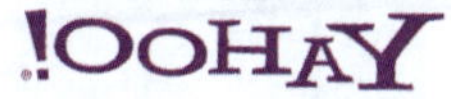

Fig. 8.11 (b): Flipped image

1. Select the object that you want to flip.
2. Select **Transform** from **Modify** menu.
3. Select **Flip Vertical** or **Flip Horizontal**. Accordingly, the selected object will be flipped.

In Fig. 8.11, the image on the left is flipped horizontally. Notice the flipped image in Fig. 8.11 (b).

Scaling an Object: Scaling an object means to change the size of the object. To scale the selected object, click on its corner handles and drag it diagonally or horizontally in the desired direction. Release the mouse button when the desired size is obtained.

You should know!

The Free Transform tool cannot transform symbols.

Gradients

A gradient is a multicoloured fill in which one colour slowly changes to another. These gradients can be used to fill closed objects on the Stage.

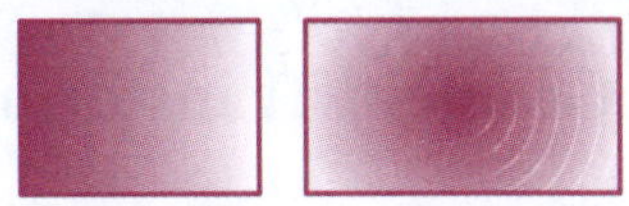

Fig. 8.12: Linear and Radial Gradients

Creating a New Gradient

Flash allows users to create two types of gradients—**Linear** and **Radial**. A linear gradient changes colour from the starting point to the end point in a straight line whereas in a radial gradient the change of colour is in the outward direction, in concentric circles, starting from the central point. Figure 8.9 shows linear and radial gradients.

Quick Way

The shortcut key to open the Color Mixer is **Shift+F9**.

Follow these steps to create a new gradient:

1. Select an object on the Stage.
2. Select **Color Mixer** option from the **Window** menu (Fig. 8.13). The **Color Mixer Panel** is displayed on the top right corner of the Flash window (Fig. 8.14).
3. Click the drop-down arrow of the **Type** list box and choose either of the gradients — Linear or Radial.
4. Click and drag the **Left Color Marker** and **Right Color Marker** to choose the desired colours (Fig. 8.15). You will see that the change of colour is reflected in the selected object also. A new gradient has been created.

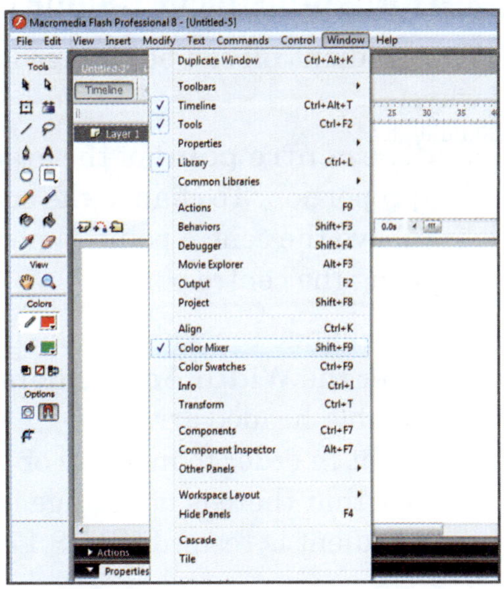

Fig. 8.13: Window menu

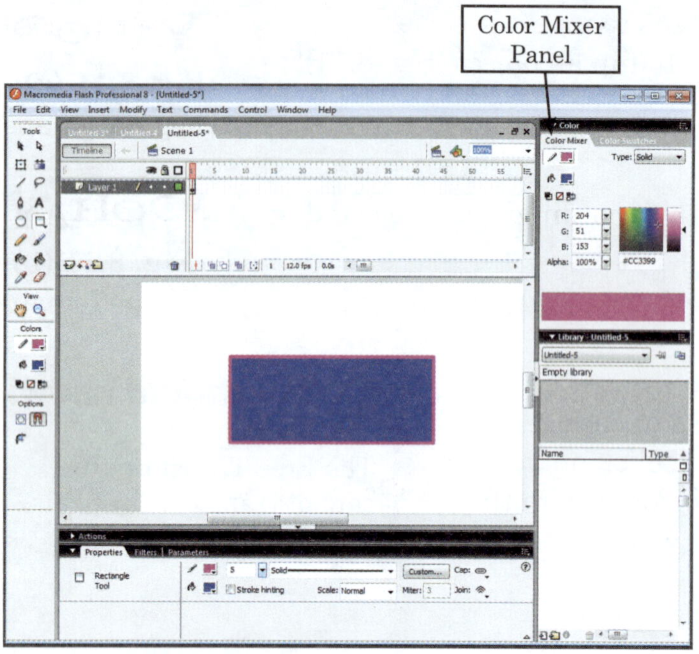

Fig. 8.14: Color Mixer option

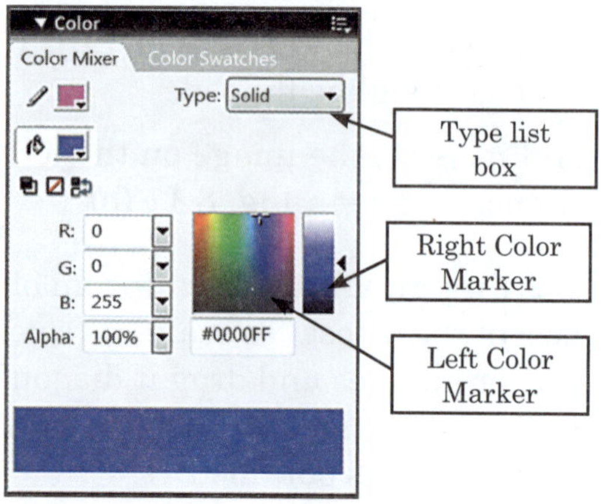

Fig. 8.15: Color Mixer Panel

Gradient Transform Tool

After creating a gradient, Flash 8 gives the option to transform the applied gradient by adjusting its size, direction, rotation or center. To modify the gradient fill of an object, first select the **Gradient Transform** tool. Then, click inside the object that has gradient as fill. The transformation of linear and radial gradient is discussed below.

Linear Gradient: See the figure showing linear gradient. The two vertical lines on either side of the object indicate the direction of the fill. The line on the right has a **Gradient Rotate Handle** (◌) and a **Width Adjustment Handle** (⟷) (Fig. 8.16).

The gradient fill can be changed in the following ways:

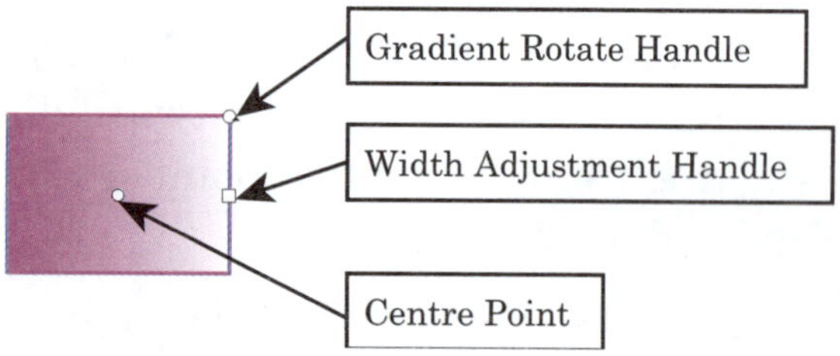

Fig. 8.16: Linear fill with handles

a. The **centre point** of the gradient is the point where the colour mixing is in equal proportion. To change the centre point of the gradient fill, bring the mouse pointer above the centre point. When the cursor changes to a four arrow cursor (✛), click and drag the centre point.

b. To change the width of the gradient fill, position the mouse pointer over the **Width Adjustment Handle**. The pointer will change to a double-headed arrow (⟷). Drag the adjustment handle to left or right in order to increase or decrease the gradient width. You will see that there is no change in the size of the object. Only the gradient is resized (Fig. 8.17).

Fig. 8.17: Changing the width of the gradient

c. To rotate the gradient fill, position the pointer over the **Rotation Handle** (◌). The pointer changes to (⟲). Now drag the **Rotation Handle** clockwise or anticlockwise by the desired angle (Fig. 8.18).

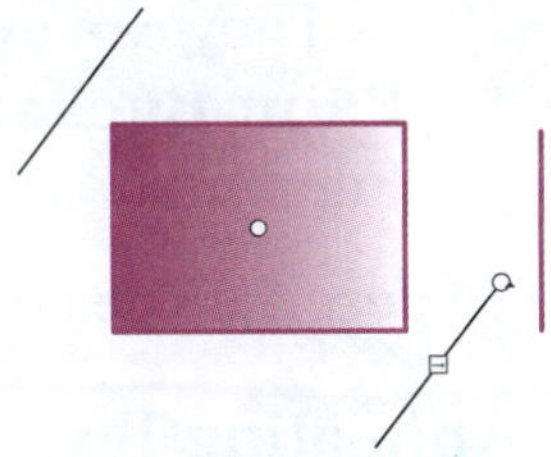

Fig. 8.18: Rotating the gradient fill

Radial Gradient: Select the **Gradient Transform** tool and click on an object filled with a radial gradient. An ellipse appears around the selected object as shown in Fig. 8.19:

Any one or all of the following actions can be performed:

a. Drag the **Centre Point** to adjust the centre of the gradient.

b. Drag the radius **Adjustment Handle** to increase or decrease the radius of the gradient.

c. Drag the **Diagonal Resize Handle** to change the gradient size proportionately.

d. Drag the **Gradient Rotate Handle** clockwise or anticlockwise to rotate the gradient at the desired angle.

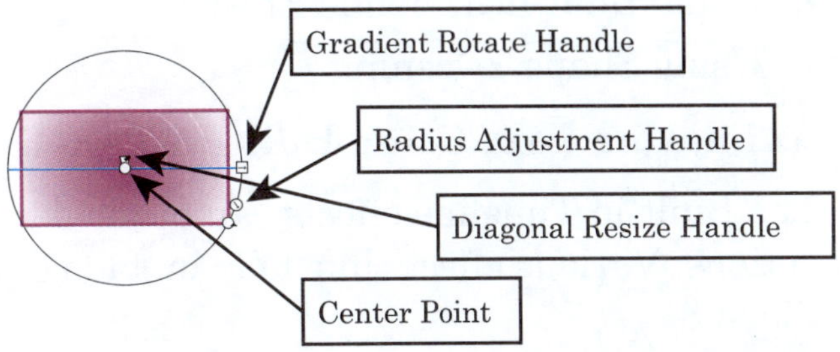

Fig. 8.19: Radial Gradient

Working With Text in Flash

You have already learnt about the text tool in Class 6 which is used for inserting text on the Stage. You applied formatting effects like font colour, size and style to the entered text. After the text has been added to the Stage, various text effects can be applied. However, before the text can be animated or letters reshaped, it needs to be converted into a basic shape. After this, the Selection tool can be used to reshape it. Characters can even be filled with gradients.

You should know!

Once a text character is converted into a shape, it cannot be edited as text.

Converting Text Into Basic Shapes

Follow these steps to convert the text into a basic shape:

1. Select the text.
2. Select **Break Apart** option from the **Modify** menu. A single text block is broken into multiple text blocks and each character has its own separate text block.
3. Again select **Break Apart** from the **Modify** menu. Now, the characters can no longer be considered as text. So, no text formatting effects, that is, font colour, size, style, etc. can be applied. Each individual character is independent. These shapes can now be resized or reshaped, like other shapes, by moving the pointer to the edge of any character and dragging

Fig. 8.20: Broken text

Fig. 8.21: Text converted to basic shapes

it. They can even be filled with colour or gradient with another colour/gradient using the **Paint Bucket** tool. For example, the alphabet I and Y have been formatted as shown in Fig. 8.21.

To deselect the shapes, click outside the converted text block.

Animating Text

In Class 6, you had animated text using frame-by-frame animation. In that process, each character was added in a different frame. In this chapter, you will animate text using two new methods:

- Using Built-in Timeline Effects
- Using Shape Tweening

Animating Text Using Built-in Timeline Effects

The Built-in Timeline effects can be used to create animations by selecting just a few options. Various effects like fade in, fade out and explode can be applied using this feature of Flash 8.

Follow these steps to to create animations using Built-in Timeline effects in Flash:

1. On a new Flash document, click **Text** tool.
2. Type any word, say ANIMATIONS@@@ on the Stage.
3. Right click the text and select **Timeline Effects** from the **drop-down** menu (Fig. 8.22).
4. From the **Effects** submenu, choose the desired effect, say **Blur**.

Quick Way

Press **Ctrl+Enter** to preview the animation in a separate window.

5. The **Blur** dialog box appears (Fig. 8.23). The dialog box shows the preview of the selected animation with default settings like Effect Duration, Resolution, Scale, etc. You can change the settings if you want and then click **OK**. The Timeline window will now show frames and animations.
6. Save the file and press the **Enter** key to play the movie.

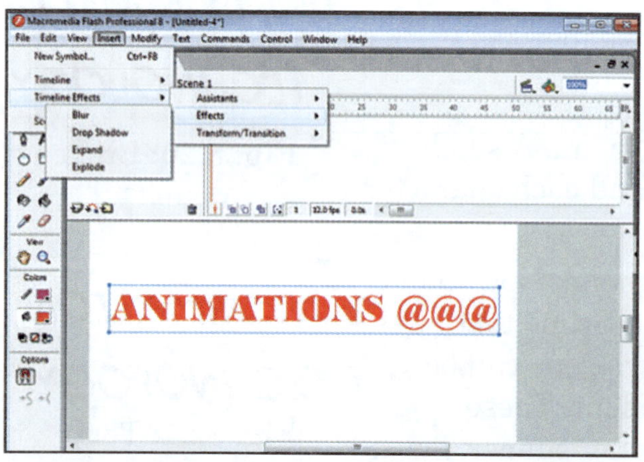

Fig. 8.22: Timeline Effects Option

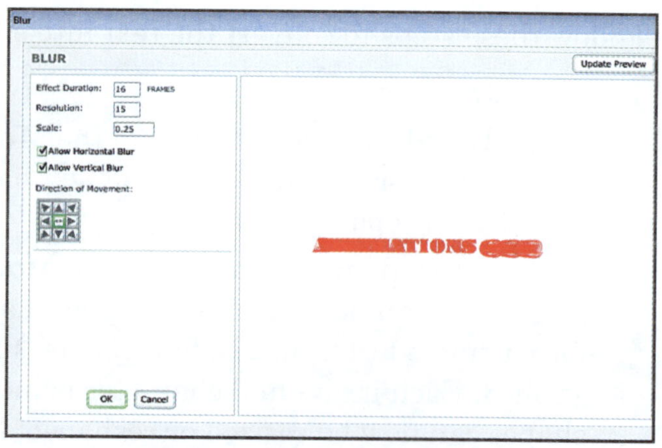

Fig. 8.23: Blur dialog box

Animating Text Using Shape Tweening

This is another method to animate text. Follow these steps to apply shape tweening to the selected text:

1. Open a new Flash document.
2. Select Frame 1. Use the **Text** tool to write FRIENDSHIP (Fig. 8.24). You may apply desired font colour, style and size.
3. Click the **Arrow** tool in the **Tools Panel**.
4. Select the text and choose **Break Apart** option from the **Modify** menu.
5. Again select **Break Apart** from the **Modify** menu.
6. Select frame 55 (Fig. 8.25) and insert a keyframe by pressing **F6**.
7. Delete the old text.
8. Select **Text** tool and type IS LIFE. You can apply the desired font colour, size and style to the text.
9. With frame 55 still selected, click the **Arrow** tool and select the latest typed text.
10. Select **Break Apart** from the **Modify** menu twice (Fig. 8.26).

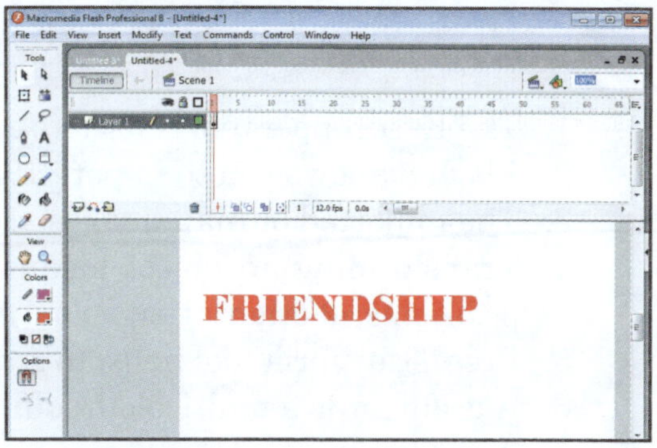

Fig. 8.24: Text in frame 1

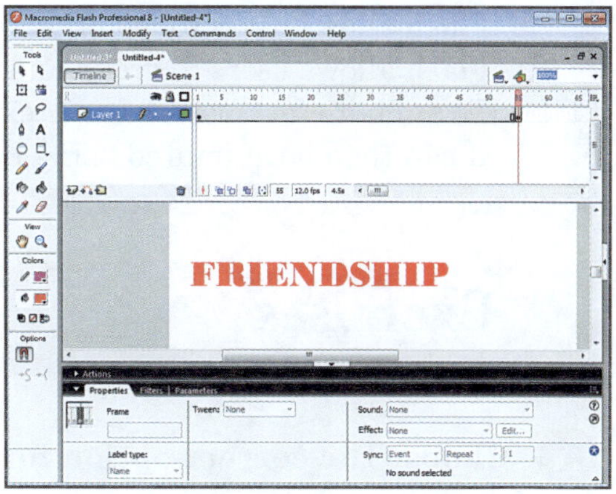

Fig. 8.25: Keyframe at frame 55

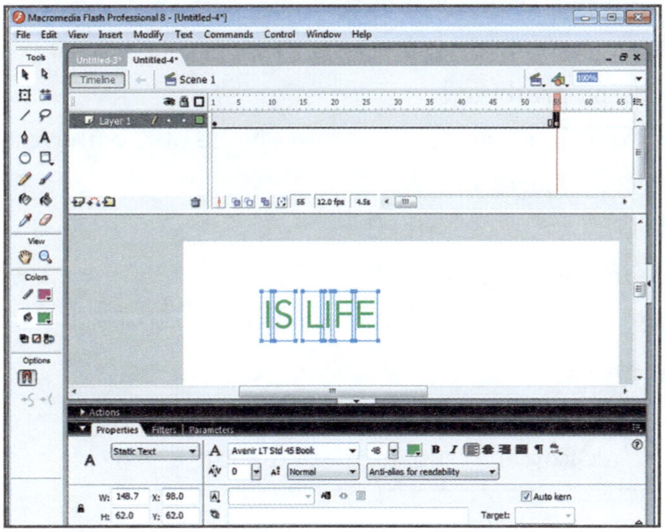

Fig. 8.26: Broken or ungrouped text

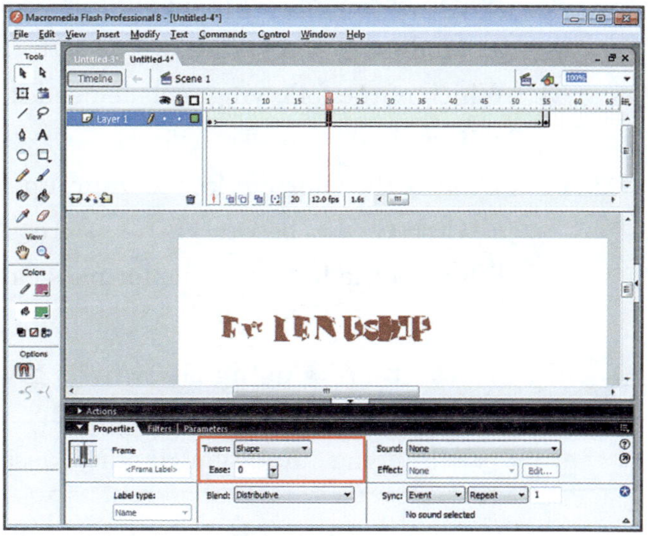

Fig. 8.27: Animated text with Shape Tweening

11. Select any frame between frame 1 and frame 55.
12. From the **Property Inspector** window, click the arrow next to **Tween** option. From the drop-down menu select **Shape** (Fig. 8.27).
13. Save the file and press **Enter** to play the movie.

You should know!

Before playing the movie, make sure that Frame 1 is selected.

Quick Recap

1. The Eyedropper tool is used to copy the fill and outline properties from one object to another.
2. Flash 8 allows you to import JPEG, GIF, PNG and various other file formats into Flash.
3. The imported bitmap images are added to the Flash library as assets.
4. Transforming an object means to modify the object by changing its shape, size, colour, position and orientation on the Stage.
5. Free Transform tool helps to scale, rotate, compress, stretch or skew an object on the Stage.
6. A gradient is a multicoloured fill in which one colour slowly changes to another.
7. A gradient in Flash is of two types—linear and radial.
8. The Gradient Transform tool is used to transform the gradient applied to an object.
9. Flash allows users to modify the properties of an instance.
10. Flash allows users to group and ungroup the outline and the fill of an object.
11. To animate text or reshape a text character, the text needs to be converted into basic shape. It can then be animated using Built-in Timeline options or Shape Tweening.

Exercises

A Choose the correct option for each of the following.

1. Which of the following is considered as transforming an object?
   a. Rotation b. Flipping c. Moving d. All the above
2. Which of the following menu items contains the Transform option?
   a. Modify b. Window c. File d. Image
3. Which of the following tools is used to edit the gradient?
   a. Gradient b. Transform c. Gradient Transform d. None of the above
4. What is the shortcut key to ungroup selected objects?
   a. Ctrl+G b. Ctrl+B c. Alt+G d. Alt+B
5. Which of the following file formats can be imported into Flash?
   a. *.jpeg* b. *.gif* c. *.png* d. All of the above

B Fill in the blanks using the words given below.

Flipping Rotation Handle assets Ink Bottle transformation point

1. If you copy the outline using an Eyedropper tool, the tool automatically changes to an ____________ tool.
2. The imported images are added to the Flash library as ____________ .
3. ____________ an object means to invert it either horizontally or vertically.
4. The central handle of the selected object is also called ____________ .
5. You will drag the ____________ in clockwise or anticlockwise direction to rotate a gradient fill.

C **State whether the following statements are true (T) or false (F).**

1. The Eyedropper tool is used to copy properties of one object to another. ☐
2. An asset cannot be converted into a symbol. ☐
3. The instance of a symbol in Flash cannot be modified. ☐
4. To animate text or reshape a text character, it needs to be converted into a basic shape. ☐

D **Give one word for each of the following.**

1. It helps to scale, rotate or skew an object on the Stage. ____________
2. A multicolour fill. ____________
3. This tool helps to copy a fill and is used along with the Eyedropper tool. ____________
4. It is a type of gradient in concentric circles. ____________
5. Shortcut to group selected objects. ____________

E **Answer the following questions.**

1. In which situations is the Eyedropper tool used?
2. Write the steps to import an image into Flash. Assume that the name of the file is *image.jpeg* and is stored in C:\Desktop.
3. What is a gradient? How is a linear gradient different from a radial gradient?
4. Write the steps to group the outline and fill of an object. Why is it required?
5. Write the steps to convert text into basic shapes.

Lab Activity

1. Somil wants to import a picture *flower.jpeg* into Flash but does not know how to do the task. Give him the steps to complete his task.
2. Gaurangi is fond of jewellery designing. She has saved a symbol of a ring in the Flash library. She wants to change the colour and brightness of the symbol. Help her to complete the task.
3. Prabhnoor wants to write the names of his five friends, convert the text into symbols and then animate them using Timeline effects. Help him to complete the task.
4. Saumya, a teacher in a playschool, wants that when she narrates a nursery rhyme in the class the lyrics should be projected on the screen of the interactive board. Take any nursery rhyme and animate the text using Shape Tweening.

Research Project

Write a short poem on yourself and then apply various animation effects to it.

Teacher's Notes

1. Discuss all the tools of the Tools Panel and their uses.
2. Demonstrate to the students how to apply animations to text using Timeline Effects and Shape Tweening. The teacher may first demonstrate frame-by-frame animations that the students had studied in Class 6.

9 Introduction to OpenShot Video Editor

Learning Objectives

By the end of this chapter, you will be able to:

- use OpenShot Video Editor.
- understand the components of OpenShot user interface.
- create a movie.
- save and export a movie.
- add transitions and effects.

Introduction

You have already learned to create animated movies using Flash. While creating such movies, the still images or pictures were placed one after another in such a manner that while playing the animation, the characters or objects appeared to be moving. What if you want to show the actual movement of characters by capturing their video and also add some still images, text, or audio files?

When multiple audio and video clips are joined together and played in sequence, you get a movie. Movie making is becoming increasingly popular these days. It involves combining videos and images in a desired sequence, and then adding audio, titles, or any other text. Let us learn movie making by using a simple yet powerful tool called OpenShot Video Editor (Version 2.4.4).

About OpenShot Video Editor

OpenShot Video Editor is one of the most widely used video editors. It is used to create, edit, and view movies. It is a free and open-source software with a user-friendly interface. Images, videos, audio, and text captions can be used while creating movies using this application. As the user can create videos, film, and animations, OpenShot Video Editor can be described as a combination of a video editing and animation creation application.

Some of the distinct features of OpenShot Video Editor are:

- It can be used on multiple operating systems like Windows, Linux, and Mac OS.
- It provides a free, stable, and user-friendly interface.

- It is a cross-platform application that allows projects to be saved in one operating system and opened in another.
- It supports almost all video (.mov, .mpeg4, .wmv, etc.), audio (.wav, .au, .mp3, etc.), and image (.jpeg, .png, etc.) formats.
- It integrates the desktop with its user interface. This integration is a key feature of OpenShot. To add an audio, video, or image file to the project in OpenShot, simply drag it from the desktop and drop it in the OpenShot user interface.
- It provides unlimited tracks and layers for videos.
- It supports both 2D and 3D animated titles and effects.

Cool Tip

OpenShot Editor can be downloaded from https://www.openshot.org/download/. Specify the operating system on which you want to install and click the **Download** button.

You should know!

OpenShot was created in August 2008 by Jonathan Thomas, a software developer from North Texas (United States of America).

- It has options for clip resizing, scaling, trimming, snapping, rotation, and cutting.
- Audio can be added, mixed or edited to an animation or video.
- Most advanced features of digital video effects including brightness, gamma, hue, greyscale, etc. are all included in the application.
- Previews of imported videos can be seen in a separate **Preview** window.

Starting OpenShot Video Editor

To start OpenShot Video Editor, click **Start ▸ Programs ▸ OpenShot Video Editor**. Alternatively, double-click the OpenShot shortcut icon () on the desktop. The user interface of OpenShot Video Editor appears as shown in Fig. 9.1.

The OpenShot user interface contains the following components:

- **Menu bar:** It contains the various menu options—File, Edit, Title, View, and Help.
- **Main toolbar:** It is present just below the Menu bar. It contains the commands to perform common operations like Open, Save, Undo, Redo, and export a video project.
- **Project Files panel:** This panel displays all the audio, video, and image files that have been added to project. By default, all the files are displayed under the **Show All** tab. To see video, audio, and image files separately, click on the respective tabs in the **Project Files** panel.
- **Filter textbox:** This component allows users to filter the list of items in the project just by typing a few characters. As the characters are typed in the **Filter** textbox, the files which have those sequence of characters in their names are displayed in the **Project Files** panel.
- **Video Preview window:** This window allows users to view the video being created. It has buttons to play, pause, rewind, fast forward, and move to end or beginning of the video.
- **Function tabs:** These tabs allow users to switch between **Project files**, **Transitions**, and **Effects**. Transitions and effects are discussed later in the chapter.

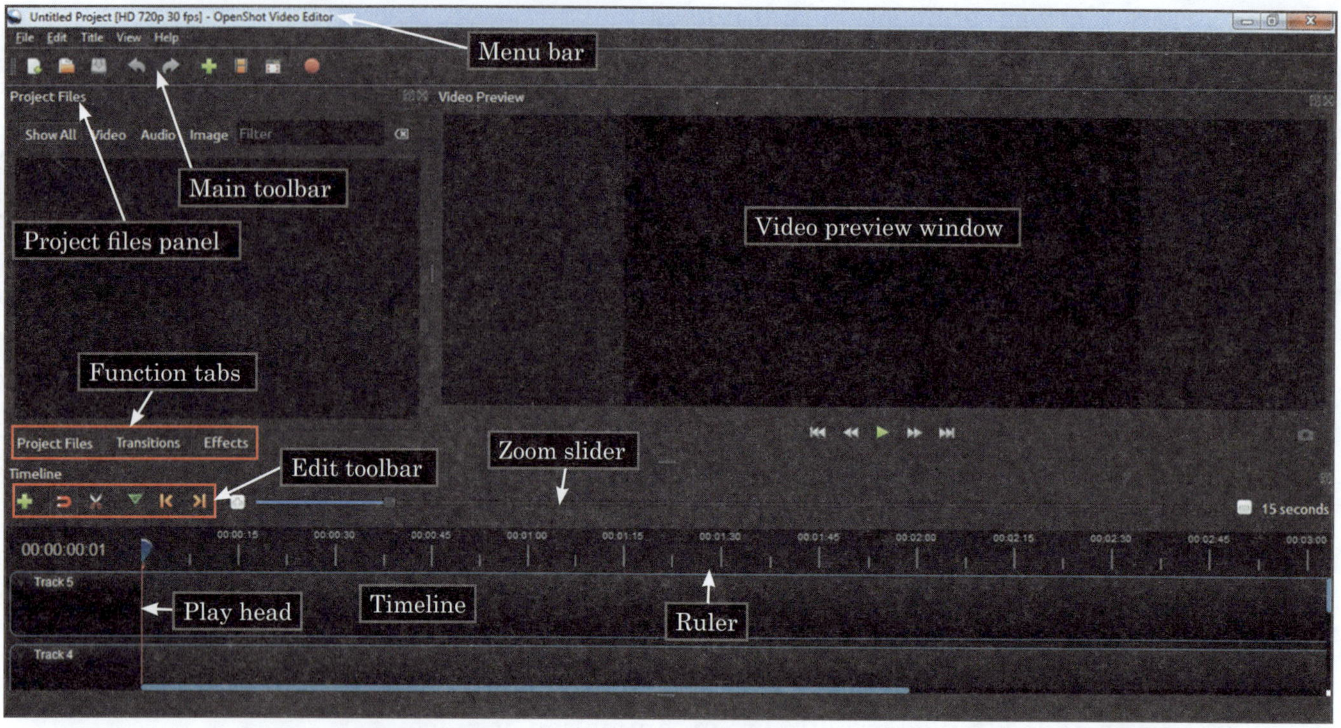

Fig. 9.1: User interface of OpenShot Video Editor

- **Edit toolbar:** It is present below the **Function** tabs. The commands on this toolbar help us to work on the audio-video clips and images that have been added on to the **Timeline**. It contains buttons to add audio, snap the video clips, insert markers, jump between markers, and many more.
- **Timeline:** It contains various tracks on which video clips, images, audio files with added transitions, and effects can be placed. The clips or files added to the timeline can be arranged and rearranged in the desired sequence. They can also be overlapped to create automatic transitions. There is a horizontal **ruler** on the timeline that shows the timescale. The red vertical line with a blue balloon on the top is called the **play head**.
- **Zoom slider:** It allows the user to adjust the timescale of the video timeline.

Check your understanding!

1. Name any two video and any two audio formats supported by OpenShot Video Editor.

   audio ____________________ ____________________

   video ____________________ ____________________

2. Which of the following statements are true about OpenShot Video Editor?

   a. It provides unlimited tracks and layers for videos. ☐

   b. It can be used only on Windows operating system. ☐

   c. To insert a video file, drag a video file from the desktop to the OpenShot interface. ☐

   d. It is a cross-platform application. ☐

Creating a Movie

To create a movie, a new project has to be started. A movie project is a file that contains information about the arrangement of various pictures, audio/video clips, transitions, text, and other effects. When the OpenShot Video Editor is started, it opens with a blank project by the name '*Untitled Project*'. To open a new project, users may select **New Project** option from the **File** menu.

Once the blank project is started, creating a movie consists of five steps:

1. Importing video, image, and audio files
2. Arranging videos and photos on the timeline
3. Adding music to the timeline
4. Previewing the project
5. Saving and exporting the video Each of these steps is discussed in detail in the coming section of the chapter.

Importing video, image, and audio files

To import or add various files to your project, open the project and follow the steps given below:

1. Click the **Import Files** button (➕) on the **Main Toolbar**. The **Import File...** dialog box opens (Fig. 9.2).
2. Browse and select the desired video, audio or image file.
3. Click the **Open** button. The selected file will be added to the **Project Files** panel. Likewise, any number of audio, video, and image files can be added as shown in Fig. 9.3. The files will be dragged from here and placed on the timeline as per the desired sequence.

Once the file is inserted in the project, it can be viewed by right-clicking on the file and then selecting the **Preview File** option (Fig. 9.4).

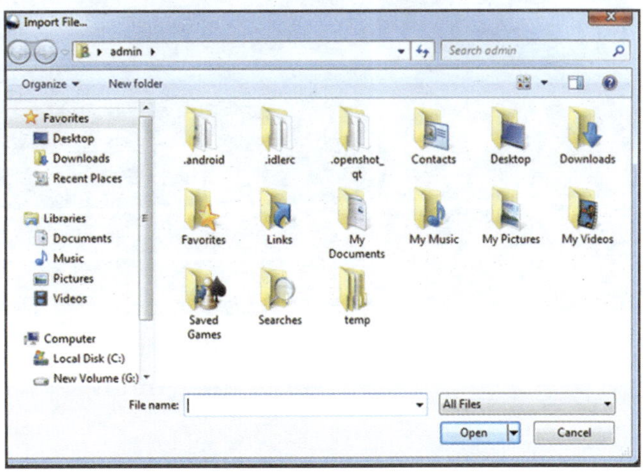

Fig. 9.2: Import File... dialog box

Quick Way

The shortcut key to open the **Import Files** dialog box is Ctrl+F.

You should know!

To add a file to the current project, drag the files from their location and drop them in the OpenShot user interface. It gets added to the **Project Files** panel.

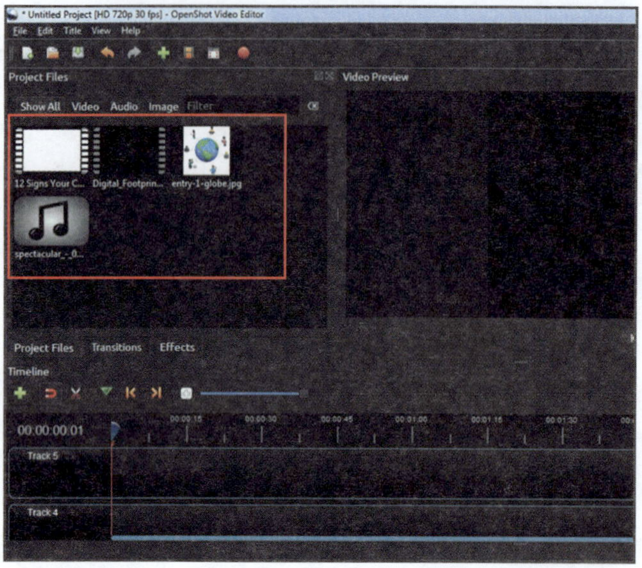

Fig. 9.3: Files added to the project

Fig. 9.4: Files added to the project

The **Preview window** appears. Click the **Play** button ( ) on the bottom left of the **Preview** window. The video will start playing (Fig. 9.5).

To remove any of the inserted files from the project, right-click that file in the **Project Files** panel and select the **Remove from Project** option (Fig. 9.6).

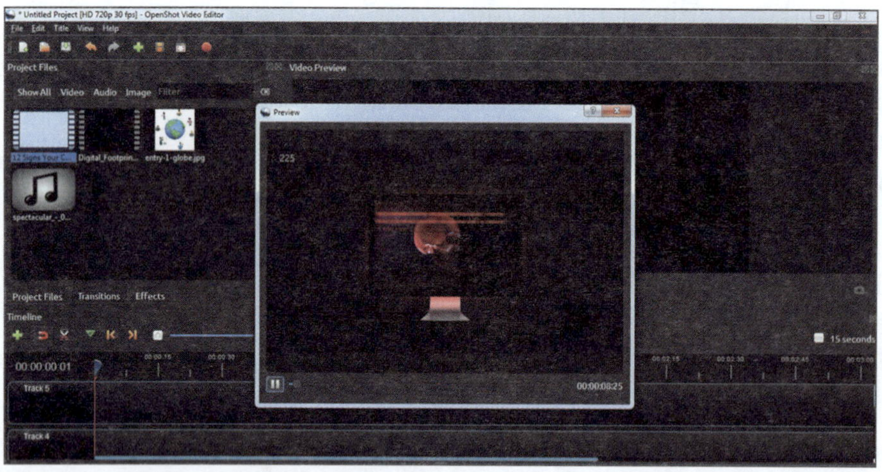

Fig. 9.5: Inserted video being played in the Preview window

Fig. 9.6: Remove from Project option

Arranging videos/photos/images on the timeline

Once the required files are inserted in the project, the next step is to arrange the videos and images in the desired sequence on the timeline. For this, drag each photo/video onto any track in the timeline. It represents the final video and, hence, the sequence of the files being placed needs to be in desired order. OpenShot Video Editor will automatically create a smooth fade between two clips. The clips can be dragged and dropped from one position to another to rearrange them on the timeline. The size of the added clips can also be altered by placing the mouse pointer on its edges and then dragging it to the required timeframe. Figure 9.7 shows the timeline with two video clips added on **Track 5**.

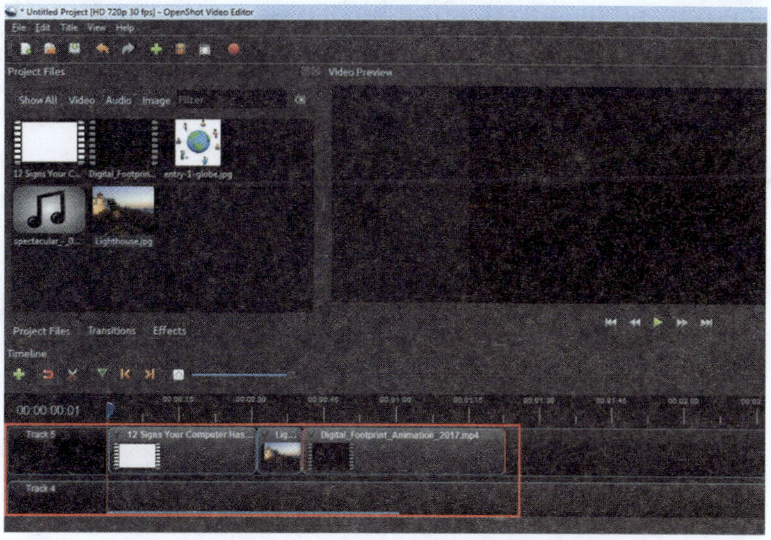

Fig. 9.7: Files added to the **Timeline**

Adding music to the timeline

Every video has a music or some sound along with it. To add another audio to the video, drag the audio file from the **Project Files Panel** to the **Timeline**. If the audio file is to be played in between the video clips that have been added to the timeline, then it has to be placed it on the same track where the videos have been placed. However, if the audio is to be played in the background, add it to a different track. In Fig. 9.8, the audio file is added on to **Track 4**. If the music is too long, it can be shortened by clicking the right edge of your music clip and resizing it.

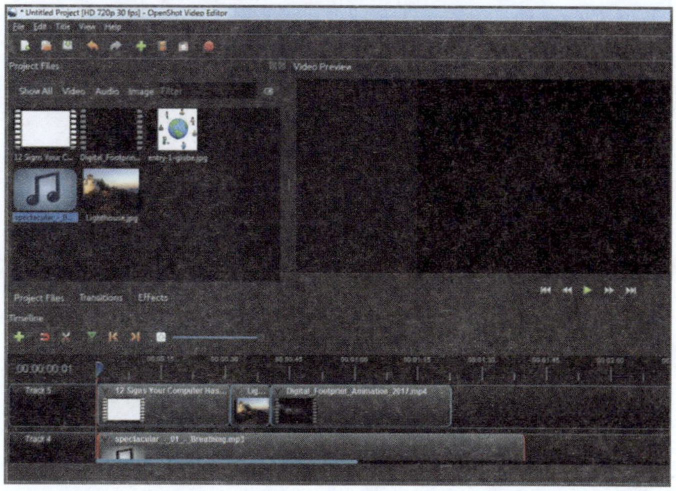

Fig. 9.8: Adding the audio clip to the timeline

Previewing the project

To preview the project, click the **Play** button ( ) under the **Video Preview** window. The movie project will be played in the same sequence as the audio–video clips or images have been placed on different tracks in the **Timeline**. Make sure that the **Play head** is positioned in the

Fig. 9.9: Previewing the movie

beginning of the timeline before you click the **Play** button. The **Playback Control** buttons at the bottom of the **Video Preview** window allow us to pause, rewind, fast forward, and move to the beginning or end of the movie.

Saving and Exporting the video

To save the project file, follow the steps given below:

1. Click **Save Project As** option from the **File** menu. The **Save Project As...** dialog box is displayed (Fig. 9.10).
2. Browse for the drive and folder in which the file is to be saved.
3. Type the name of the project (*firstproject*) in the **File name** text box.
4. Click the **Save** button. The project will be saved with the extension *.osp*.

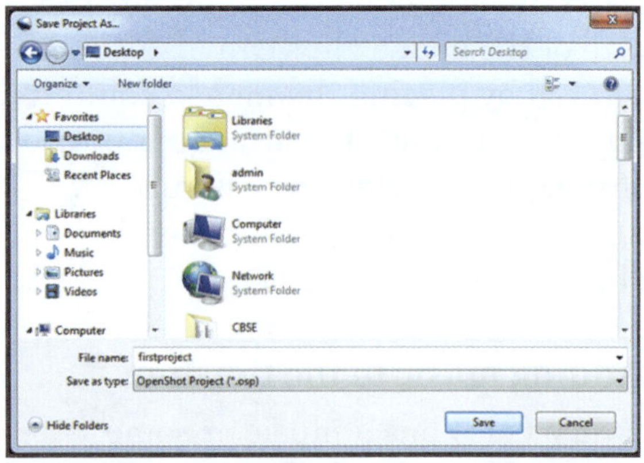

Fig. 9.10: Save Project As... dialog box

The saved movie project can be edited or viewed using the OpenShot Video Editor application. However, the movies should be able to play on any media player. So, the project has to be saved in a format that can play on any media player like Windows Media Player or VLC media player. This process of converting the project to a video format is known as **exporting a project**.

Follow these steps to export a project:

1. Click the **Export Video** option from the **File** menu. The **Export Video** dialog box appears (Fig. 9.11).
2. Specify the name of the file in the **File Name** text box. By default, the name of the file being exported will be same as the project file. In our example, the default file name will be *firstproject*.
3. Browse for the folder where you want to save the movie. By default, the exported movie will be saved in the same folder where the project file is saved.
4. By default, the **Profile** selected is *All Formats*, so the video can be played using all media formats like DVD, Blue ray disc, web, etc.
5. The **Target** is the format in which the movie will be saved. The default video format is *MP4*. Any other format can be selected from the list box.
6. Similarly select the desired **Video profile** (resolution) and **Quality** of the video from the respective list boxes.

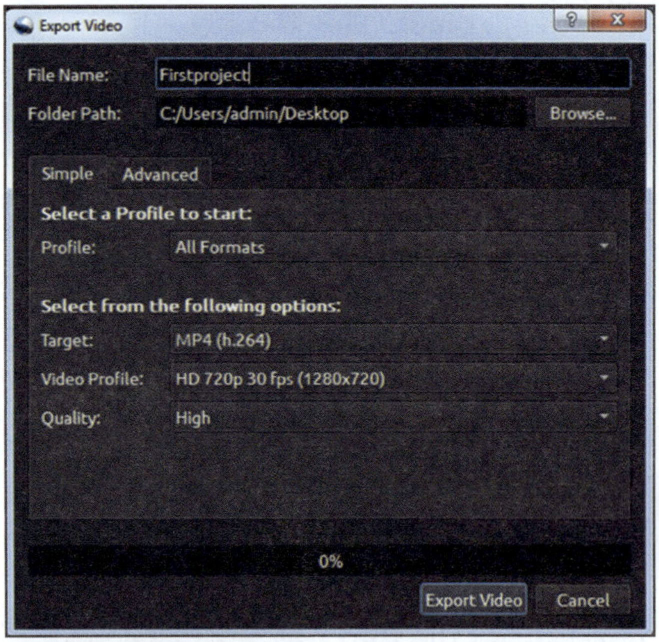

Fig. 9.11: Export Video dialog box

7. Finally, click the **Export Video** button. The OpenShot progress bar appears that shows the status of the movie being saved and exported (Fig. 9.12).

The process of exporting converts the OpenShot project into a single video file that can be played in almost all the video players and can be uploaded on a website as well. Once the file is exported and converted to video format (.mp4, .mpeg, .mov, etc.), the movie becomes uneditable. That means the file saved in this format cannot be edited. It can only be viewed using a media player. To edit the movie, open the *.osp* file, make changes, save it, and then export it again.

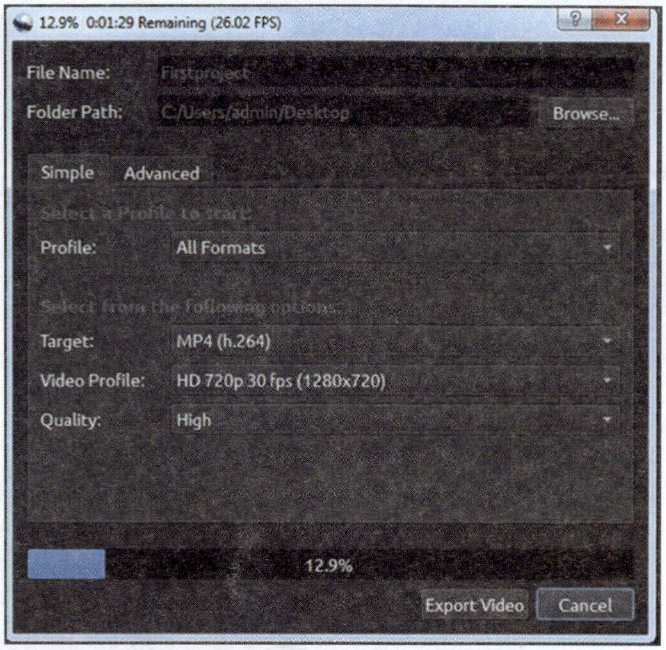

Fig. 9.12: Progress bar

Applying Transitions

A video transition determines how the movie will navigate from one video clip or image to another when it is being played. OpenShot Editor allows the application of transition effects within a single video clip as well. To add transition to the videos and images added in the timeline, follow these steps:

1. Click the **Transitions** tab below the **Project Files** panel.
2. The **Project Files** panel shows icons of various transitions given by OpenShot video editor like *Fade, Circle in to out, Circle out to in, Wipe left to right* and many more (Fig. 9.13).
3. Click and drag the desired transition from the **Project Files** panel to the **Timeline**. Place it on the video clip or image where the transition is to be applied.
4. Place the **Play head** in the beginning and then click on the **Play** button below the **Video Preview** window to play the movie. You will see that the selected transition is applied on the clip/image (Fig. 9.13).

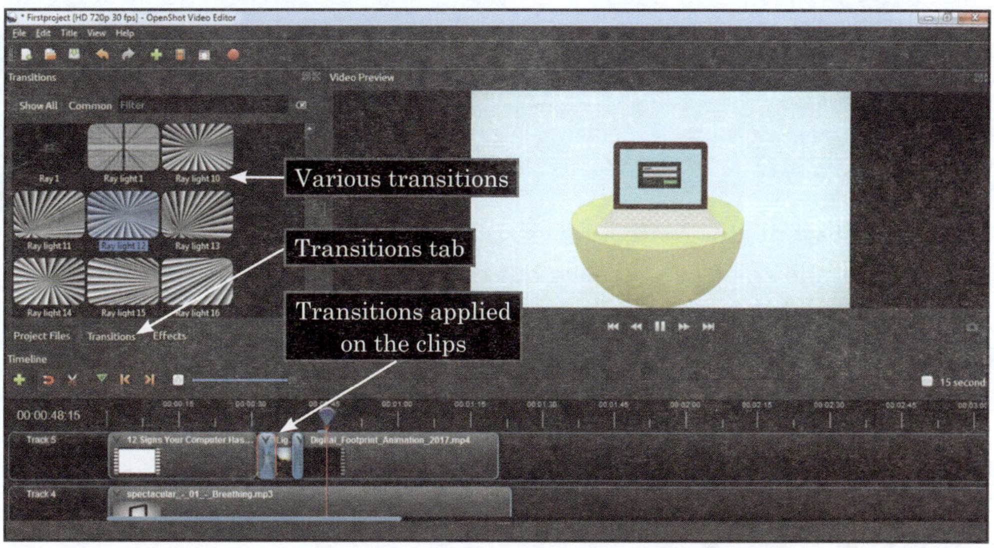

Fig. 9.13: Applying transitions

To remove the transition, right-click on the applied transition on the **Timeline** and select the **Remove Transition** option.

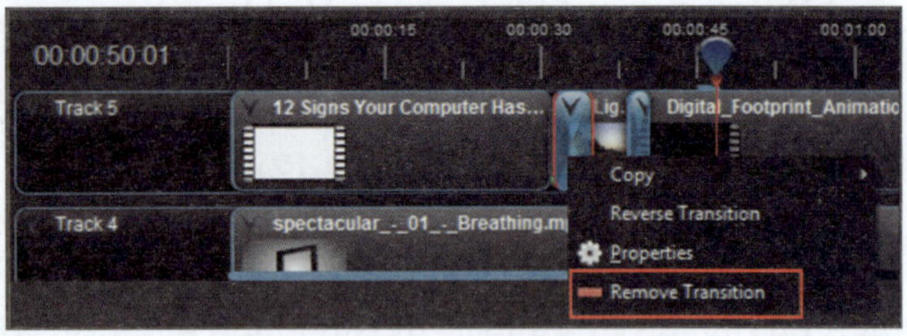

Fig. 9.14: Removing transitions

Applying Effects

OpenShot Video Editor allows users to add various effects to the video clips and images. To add an effect to a video clip or image that has been added on the **Timeline**, follow these steps:

1. Click the **Effects** tab. Various effects like *Bars Blur* and *Color Shift* are displayed in the **Project Files** panel.

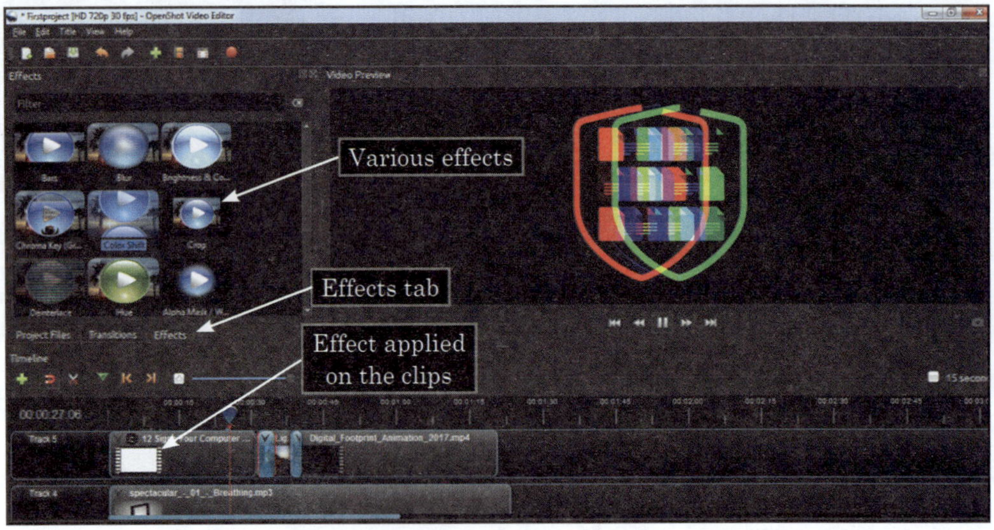

Fig. 9.15: Adding effects

5. Click and drag the desired effect and place it on the video clip or image on the timeline on which the effect has to be applied. The selected effect (*Color Shift*) is applied on the video clip or image on the **Timeline**.
6. To view the effect, position the **Play head** in the beginning of the clip and click the **Play** button. The figure shows the video clip with the added effect (*Color Shift*).

To remove the applied effect, right-click it and select the **Remove Effect** option from the pop-up menu.

Check your understanding!

1. Sumit wants to create a movie using OpenShot Video Editor. His friend told him to follow the steps given below but they are not in the correct order. Help Sumit to rearrange them in a proper sequence so that he can start creating the movie.
   - Add music to the Timeline.
   - Importing video, image, and audio files.
   - Save and export the video.
   - Arrange videos and photos on the timeline.
   - Preview the project.
2. Manju has applied the transition (Fade) to a video clip on the Timeline. Now, she wants to remove the applied transition. How can she complete the task?

Quick Recap

1. OpenShot Video Editor is a combination of a video editing and animation creation application. It is a free and open-source software that allows us to create, edit, and view movies.
2. Some of the components of OpenShot Video Editor User Interface are Menu bar, Main toolbar, Project files panel, Timeline, Video Preview window, and Function tabs.
3. Creating a movie using OpenShot Video Editor consists of: importing video, image, and audio files; arranging videos and photos on the timeline; adding music to the timeline; previewing the project; and saving and exporting the video.
4. Timeline is one of the most important components of the user interface. It contains various tracks on which the video clips, images, audio files with added transitions and effects can be placed in the desired sequence.
5. The movie project is saved with an extension *.osp*.
6. The process of saving the project in a format that can play on any media player like Windows Media Player or VLC media player is known as exporting a project.
7. Various transitions and effects to the video clips and images can be added.

Exercises

A **Fill in the blanks using the correct words.**

.osp | exporting | Play head | Movie making | Timeline

1. ______________ involves combining videos and images in a desired sequence.
2. ______________ contains various tracks on which the video clips, images, and audio files can be placed in a desired sequence.
3. The red vertical line with a blue balloon on the top is called the ______________ .
4. A movie project in OpenShot Video Editor is saved with the extension ______________ .
5. The process of saving a project in a video format like .mp4 is known as ______________ a project.

B **State whether the following statements are true (T) or false (F).**

1. OpenShot Video Editor is a combination of a video editing and animation creation application. ☐
2. There is no separate window in OpenShot video editor to view the inserted videos. ☐
3. There is only one track in the Timeline of OpenShot video editor. ☐
4. Once the video clip is inserted in a movie project, it cannot be removed. ☐
5. The size of the clips added to the Timeline can be altered. ☐

C Match the following.

Column A	Column B
1. Timeline	a. Fade
2. Video Preview window	b Tracks
3. Exported file	c. Playback control buttons
4. Transition	d. Blur
5. Effects	e. Uneditable

D Answer the following in one word.

1. Name the component that allows the user to filter the list of items in the project just by typing a few characters.
2. Name the feature that determines how the movie will navigate from one video clip or image to another when it is being played.
3. Name the button that should be clicked to preview the movie project.
4. Name any two effects that can be added to a video clip inserted on the Timeline.
5. The shortcut key to open the Import File dialog box.

E Answer the following questions.

1. OpenShot Video Editor is a cross-platform application. What do you mean by the given statement?
2. Name any five components of OpenShot Video Editor user interface.
3. Can an image be removed from the Project File panel? If yes, how?
4. What is the difference between exporting and saving a movie?
5. Write the steps to export a video.

Lab Activity

1. Riaz is going for his friend's birthday party. He wants to gift him a movie that showcases their friendship over the years. He has collected some pictures and videos for the movie. Help him create the movie.
2. On Father's day, Kuhu wants to gift her father a movie showcasing their relationship. She has collected lot of pictures and videos for the same. Help her to create a video using OpenShot Video Editor.

Research Project

Other than OpenShot Video Editor, which other software can be used to make movies? Make a list of at least five such software packages and also mention their key features.

Teacher's Notes

The teacher should demonstrate the entire process of making the movie in OpenShot Video Editor. (S)he may announce the topic in the class and ask the students to search and collect some related audio, video, and image files that can be used to create a movie in the class.

Worksheet

A Choose the correct option for each of the following.

1. Which of the following is the shortcut key to use Free Transform tool?
   a. P b. Q c. F d. T
2. To which tool does the Eyedropper tool change to when you copy the Stroke of an object?
   a. Brush Tool b. Paint Bucket tool
   c. Ink Bottle Tool d. None of the above
3. Which of the following image formats can be imported into Flash?
   a. JPEG b. GIF c. PNG d. All of the above
4. In Flash, which of the following is true about transforming objects ?
   a. We can modify the object by changing its shape but not its size
   b. We can modify the object by changing its shape but not its colour
   c. We can change the gradient
   d. We can modify the object by changing its colour but not its size
5. What do we mean by scaling an object in Flash?
   a. Changing the size of an object
   b. Changing the orientation of the object
   c. Changing the colour of the object
   d. None of the above
6. Which of the following is NOT true about OpenShot Video Editor?
   a. Free and open source software
   b. Allows to use Images, videos, audio and text
   c. Both a. and b. d. Neither a. nor b.
7. Which of the following component of OpenShot Video editor interface displays all the audio, video and image files that have been added to the project.
   a. Filter text box b. Projects File Panel
   c. Video Preview window d. Edit toolbar
8. Who created OpenShot Video Editor?
   a. Mark Zuckerberg b. Tim Berners Lee
   c. Jonathan Thomas d. Bill Gates
9. Which of the following video formats are supported by OpenShot Video Editor?
   a. .mov b. .mpeg4 c. .wmv d. All of the above
10. Which of the following is the shortcut key to open the Import Files dialog box in OpenShot Video Editor?
    a. Ctrl + F b. Ctrl + I c. Ctrl + M d. Ctrl + T

B Unscramble the words to fill in the blanks.

1. An ________________ is a non-Flash item that you import and store for future usage. (SETAS)
2. A ________________ is a multicoloured fill in which one colour slowly changes to another. (DTGAIREN)

3. The central handle of the selected object in Flash is also called ____________________ of the object. (RMNRSATFAONOIT TPONI)
4. The Eyedropper tool allows to apply an image as a fill in combination with __________________ tool. (ATIPN BEKCUT)
5. To create a new gradient in Flash, select the _________ option from the Window menu. (ROOCL IEMRX)
6. _____________button is clicked to preview the project in Project Preview Window in OpenShot Video Editor. (LPYA)
7. The movie project in OpenShot Video Editor is saved with an extension ___________ . (OPS)
8. In OpenShot Video Editor interface, various effects to the video clips can be applied by clicking on the __________ tab. (TFFSECE)
9. A video ___________determines how the movie will navigate from one video clip or image to another when it is being played. (ORNNAITTSI)
10. In the Timeline, the red vertical line with a blue balloon on the top is called the __________. (LPYA DEHA)

C **State whether the following statements are True (T) or False (F).**

1. If you click the filled area, the Eyedropper tool automatically changes to the Paint Bucket tool with its Lock Fill modifier turned on. ☐
2. The shortcut key to import a picture in Flash is Ctrl + R. ☐
3. The Free Transform tool cannot rotate an object. ☐
4. A linear gradient does not change colour. ☐
5. Once a text character is converted into shape, it cannot be edited. ☐
6. OpenShot Video editor cannot be downloaded from Internet by paying a nominal price. ☐
7. The visual effects cannot be applied to images in OpenShot video editor. ☐
8. Once a file has been inserted in a movie project, it cannot be removed. ☐
9. Zoom slider is used to adjust the timescale of video timeline in OpenShot Video Editor. ☐
10. OpenShot Video editor supports 3D animation effects. ☐

D **Give one word for the following.**

1. This tool helps to copy fill and stroke from one object to another.
2. This tool helps to modify the gradient fill of an object.
3. Which frame should be selected before previewing the movie?
4. The place where the imported bitmap images are added in Flash.
5. Two types of gradients in Flash
6. Which software is a combination of a video editing and animation creation application?
7. Any one effect that can be applied to a video clip in OpenShot Video Editor.
8. Any one audio format supported by OpenShot Video Editor.

E Label the following components in the figure given below:

Function tabs   Timeline   Filter textbox

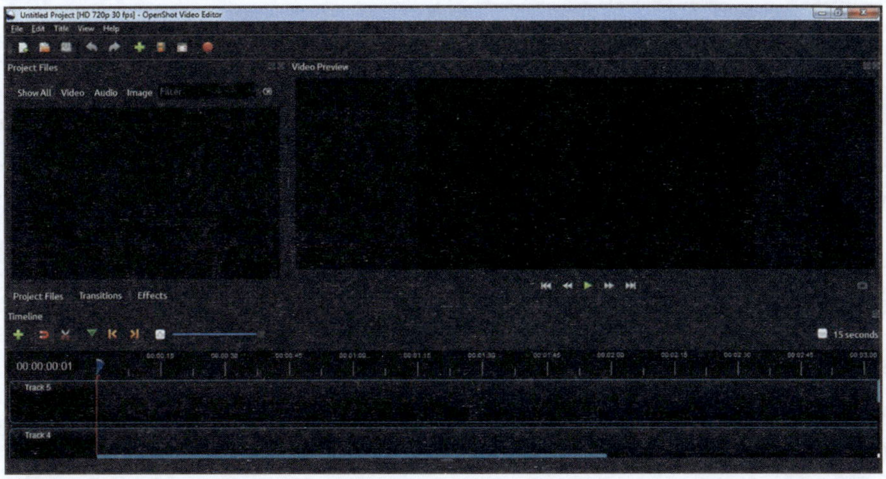

F Application Based Questions

1. Create an animated movie in Flash that shows a butterfly coming from one end of the screen and sitting on a flower.
2. Create a movie in OpenShot Video Editor that shows the achievements of your school in various inter school competitions. Also, put the photographs of the teachers involved in the competitions. Give appropriate title, credits and captions in your movie.

G Answer the following questions

1. Write the steps to change the centre point and width of the gradient.
2. How can we convert the text in Flash into basic shape?
3. Write steps to create a new gradient.
4. What all can be done to an object using the Free Transform tool?
5. Why OpenShot Video editor is considered as a cross platform application?
6. Give any four features of OpenShot Video Editor.
7. What is the use of Filter textbox in OpenShot Video Editor user interface?
8. What do you mean by exporting a movie project?

Projects

1. In the course of your study, you have learnt to create both animated movies using Flash and motion pictures using OpenShot Video Editor. Form a comparative report on both the software. You may include the following information in your report:
   - Key features
   - Advantages / Disadvantages
   - Versions Available
   - Situations in which you will prefer one to the other

Assessment 1

Chapters 1–5

(Maximum Marks: 40)

A **Choose the correct option for each of the following.** **(6 × 1 = 6)**

1. Initialization is the value from where the loop ______________.

   a. Starts b. Ends c. Continues d. None of these

2. Which of the following formula shows absolute referencing of cells?

   a. G1 b. $G$1 c. $G1 d. 1$G

3. In which of the following forms will you find text on a chart in MS Excel?

   a. Legends b. Titles c. Data d. All of the above

4. Which of the following is an invalid step value in the context of looping constructs in QBASIC?

   a. 0 b. 1 c. -1 d. 100

5. If the loop doesn't terminate, it is called an ______________ loop.

   a. Endless b. Never ending c. Constant d. None of these

6. Which of the following falls into the category of E-Commerce?

   a. B2B b. C2B c. C2C d. All of the above

B **Fill in the blanks.** **(6 × 1 = 6)**

1. Using ____________________ feature in MS Excel, you can display data in a particular colour or style depending on a particular condition.
2. In a 3D chart, the base area constituted by the xy plane is known as ____________________ and the vertical areas, that is, the yz and xz planes are known as ____________________.
3. ____________________ is the vertical axis used to plot the value of each data point on a chart.
4. The ____________________ loop in QBASIC is executed till the condition is False.
5. ____________________ is the use of electronic media and ICT to provide education anytime and anywhere.
6. ____________________ of the loop refers to the statements that are to be executed repeatedly.

C **State whether the following statements are true (T) or false (F).** **(5 × 1 = 5)**

1. A formula results in a new value from an existing range of values. ☐
2. In MS Excel, when you bring the mouse pointer over a filter, the filtering criteria is displayed. ☐

3. Plot area of a chart does not include data series. ☐
4. Initialization is the value from where the loop starts. ☐
5. E-governance is of no help to people of the country. ☐

D **Give one word for each of the following.** **(5 × 1 = 5)**

1. Button to remove filter in MS Excel
2. A type of chart which is used to display graphically quantitative data and is based on a line chart.
3. This is the point where the loop ends.
4. Most widely used security technology by web browsers.
5. Buying and selling on the Internet.

E **Give one point of difference between each of the following.** **(4 × 1 = 4)**

1. AutoFilter and Sorting
2. Bar chart and column chart
3. WHILE...WEND and DO...WHILE
4. B2B and B2C in the context of E-Commerce

F **Give the shortcut keys for the following.** **(2 × ½ = 1)**

1. To filter data in MS Excel 2. To create a chart instantly

G **Identify the error in the following QBASIC code:** **(1)**

```
X = 10
DO WHILE X < 45
X = X + 1
PRINT X
WEND
PRINT X
```

H **Answer the following questions.**

1. What can be the reason if you see a couple of #s in a cell? How will you resolve the problem? (2)
2. Define sorting in MS Excel. (2)
3. What is an endless loop in QBasic? How can you stop the execution of an endless loop? (2)
4. Write a program in QBASIC to accept ten numbers and display the message 'WELL DONE' every time a multiple of 8 is entered. (3)
5. 'ICT is considered as an indispensable part of our lives today'. Give any two points to justify the given statement. (3)

ASSESSMENTS

Assessment 2

Chapters 6–9

(Maximum Marks: 40)

A Choose the correct option for each of the following. **(6 × 1 = 6)**

1. In which year was HTML 5 released?

   a. 2009 b. 2010 c. 2011 d. 2012

2. Which of the following is a container element?

   a. <title> b. <hr> c.
 d. None of these

3. Which of the following always has to be a part of an HTML document?

   a. <font> b.
 c. <hr> d. <title>

4. What do we mean by flipping an object?

   a. Inverting the object horizontally only

   b. Inverting the object vertically only

   c. Inverting the object either horizontally or vertically

   d. None of the above

5. What should be the minimum size of the graphic files to be imported in Flash?

   a. 2*2 pixels b. 4*4 pixels c. 2*2 inches d. 4*4 inches

6. On which of the following operating systems, OpenShot Video Editor cannot be installed?

   a. Windows b. Linux c. Mac OS d. None of the above

B Fill in the blanks. **(6 × 1 = 6)**

1. The first version of HTML was ____________________ .
2. A ____________________ is a piece of code that instructs the browser how to display a particular text or image.
3. The ____________________ element is used to place the text in the horizontal centre of the web page.
4. The ____________________ tool in Flash is used to copy the properties of one object to another.
5. OpenShot Video editor can be downloaded from ______________.
6. The _____________ in OpenShot Video Editor contains various tracks on which the video clips, images, audio files with added transitions and effects can be placed.

C **Match the following.** **(6 × ½ = 3)**

Column A	Column B
1. Import a file in OpenShot	a. Ctrl + R
2. <b>	b. Draws a horizontal line
3. <hr>	c. Q
4. Import a picture in Flash	d. Ctrl + F
5. Free Transform tool	e. Adjusts the timescale
6. Zoom Slider	f. Physical markup tag

D **Give one word for each of the following.** **(5 × 1 = 5)**

1. Name of the person who invented HTML
2. This bar gives the title of the web page
3. An attribute of <hr> tag that gives solid line
4. A tool used to change the multicolour fill of objects
5. A combination of a video editing and animation creation application

E **Give one point of difference between each of the following.** **(5 × 1 = 5)**

1.
 and <p>
2. HEAD and BODY section of an HTML document
3. Saving and Exporting a movie in OpenShot Video Editor
4. Flipping and Scaling an object in Flash
5. Linear and Radial Gradient

F **Give one characteristic each of the following.** **(4 × 1 = 4)**

1. <html> element
2. Web browser
3. Timeline in OpenShot video editor
4. Gradients in Flash

G **Application-based questions**

1. Create a web page that contains your resume, that is, your name, address, date of birth, contact number, hobbies and interests, class in which you are presently studying and the name of your school. Do the following on the web page that you create: (4)
   a. Background colour: Yellow b. Title of the page: Myself
   c. Details (name, address, DOB, etc.): Green colour, size 4, bold
2. Write the steps to animate the text ASSESSMENT in Flash. (3)
3. Write steps to import a video file in OpenShot Video Editor movie project. (2)

H **Answer the following questions.**

1. Name any two versions of HTML. (1)
2. Explain the integration feature of OpenShot Video Editor. (1)

Model Test Paper-1

Chapters 1 to 5

(Maximum Marks: 60)

A Choose the correct option for each of the following. **(1 × 10 = 10)**

1. Which sign always precedes the formula?

   a. * b. % c. # d. =

2. Which of the following menu items are not added in the Menu Bar when the chart is inserted in an Excel sheet?

   a. Layout b. Insert c. Design d. Format

3. What is the shortcut key for AutoSum in MS Excel?

   a. Alt + = b. Ctrl + = c. Shift + = d. None of these

4. Which of the following is not an option in the AutoSum drop down menu?

   a. Count Numbers b. Count
   c. Average d. Max

5. Which of the following is Date and Time function?

   a. TODAY b. LEN c. MAX d. LCM

6. Which of the following is an umbrella term?

   a. E-commerce b. E-governance c. ICT d. None of these

7. Which of the following commands in QBASIC is used to stop further execution of the program?

   a. QUIT b. EXIT c. BYE d. None of these

8. What are the components of a loop?

   a. Initialization b. Termination c. Body of the loop d. All of these

9. eBay's auction service is an example of which category of e-commerce?

   a. C2C b. B2B c. B2C d. C2B

10. Which of the following loop executes till the time the given condition is false?

    a. WHILE...WEND b. DO WHILE...LOOP
    c. DO UNTIL...LOOP d. None of the above

B Fill in the blanks **(1 × 5 = 5)**

1. Filter on the selected range of cells in MS Excel is reapplied by clicking on the ________ button.

2. The conditional formatting command in MS Excel is in the ________ tab.
3. ________________ displays information about data points on an Excel chart.
4. ___________ command is used to stop the execution of the loop.
5. ICT provides access to information through ____________ .

C **State whether the following statements are true or false.** **(1 × 5 = 5)**

1. Formula in MS Excel can only be given in the Formula Bar. ☐
2. Auto-editing feature of Excel automatically changes the formula in MS Excel. ☐
3. A step value of a loop in QBASIC can never be negative. ☐
4. You can do arithmetic operations on a text value in MS Excel. ☐
5. E-Learning facilitates the learning and delivery process only for students and not for teachers. ☐

D **Give one word for each of the following.** **(1 × 5 = 5)**

1. Predefined formulas to perform certain operations
2. Output of the following statement in MS Excel ="Break"+"Free"
3. The chart that is used to plot data for a single data series.
4. The command in QBASIC that can be used to exit the loop prematurely.
5. Buying and Selling over a computer network.

E **Give one point of difference between each of the following pairs.** **(5 × 2 = 10)**

1. C2B and C2C with respect to E-Commerce
2. Sorting and Filtering
3. E-Commerce and E-Governance
4. DO WHILE...LOOP and FOR...NEXT LOOP
5. Line chart and Area chart

F **Write any two features of each of the following.** **(5 × 2 = 10)**

1. ICT
2. Loops in QBASIC
3. Charts in MS Excel
4. Absolute Referencing
5. Function Library in MS Excel

G **Answer the following questions briefly.**

1. What is the benefit of AutoSum feature of MS Excel? (1)
2. How can sorting be done on multiple columns in an Excel worksheets? (2)
3. What is a Secure Sockets layer? (1)
4. What are the two ways to remove filtering of cells in a worksheet? (2)
5. List any two advantages of E-governance. (2)
6. Which loop(s) will be executed at least once irrespective of whether the condition is true or false? (2)

H **Application Based Questions**

1. Write a program in QBASIC that accepts a number and checks whether it is a prime number or not? (5)

Model Test Paper-2

Chapters 6 to 9

(Maximum Marks: 60)

A **Choose the correct option for each of the following.** **(1 × 10 = 10)**

1. What is the full form of HTML?
   a. Hypertext Madeup Language
   b. Hypertext Markup Language
   c. Highlighted Text Markup Language
   d. Highlighted Text Makeup Language
2. Which of the following is not an attribute of <font>element?
   a. face b. align c. color d. size
3. Which of the following is true about HTML elements?
   a. There are three types of elements in HTML
   b. The container elements have an opening and a closing tag
   c. The empty elements have an opening and a closing tag
   d. The tag names of elements are case sensitive.
4. Which of the following is the correct comment tag?
   a. <! and !> b. <- - and - -> c. <! - - and - -> d. None of the above
5. Which of the following is a physical markup element?
   a. <b> b. <font> c. <hr> d. <center>

6. The images imported and added to the Flash library are called ___________.
   a. Sets b. Assets c. Liabilities d. Assessments
7. Which of the flowing statements are true for animating text in Flash?
   a. The text to be animated has to be converted to basic shape
   b. It can be animated using Shape tweening
   c. Both a and b
   d. Neither a nor b
8. In OpenShot Video Editor, which component allows the user to adjust the timescale of the video timeline?
   a. Filter textbox b. Zoom Slider c. Projects Panel d. Timeline
9. The effects that are seen when the movie navigates from one video clip or image to another is called ______________.
   a. Transition b. Animation c. Gaming d. Jumping
10. Which of the following can be created using OpenShot Video Editor?
   a. Videos b. Films c. Animations d. All of the above

B **Fill in the blanks** **(1 × 5 = 5)**

1. The HTML files are saved with an extension ______________.
2. The default value of size attribute of <hr> element is ______________.
3. There are ____________ types of gradients in Flash.
4. The shortcut key to break apart grouped objects is ______________.
5. OpenShot Video Editor provides ___________ tracks and layers for videos.

C **State whether the following statements are true or false** **(1 × 5 = 5)**

1. The physical markup elements change the appearance of the text. ☐
2. backgroundcolor is the attribute of <body> element. ☐
3. In Flash, we have the option to preview the animation in a separate window. ☐
4. Once a video is exported into a video format, it cannot be edited. ☐
5. Only one audio file can be added in a movie being created in OpenShot Video Editor ☐

D **Give one word for each of the following.** **(1 × 5 = 5)**

1. Who invented HTML?
2. A type of element having only the ON tag.
3. A tool used to compress an object in Flash

4. The type of gradient in which the colour changes in concentric circles.
5. The extension in which a movie project in OpenShot Video Editor is saved.

E **Give one point of difference between each of the following pairs.** **(5 × 2 = 10)**

1. BGCOLOR and background attribute of <body> element
2. Eyedropper tool and Paint Bucket tool
3. Empty element and container element
4. Timeline in Flash window and Timeline in OpenShot Video Editor
5. Applying effects and applying transitions to a video clip in OpenShot Video editor

F **Write any two features of each of the following.** **(3 × 2 = 6)**

1. Headings in HTML
2. Text animation in Flash
3. Transitions in OpenShot Video Editor

G **Label the following components in the user interface window given below. Also write one function of each.** **(2 × 2 = 4)**

1. Video Preview Window
2. Playback Control buttons

H **Answer the following questions briefly.**

1. What is the use of Eyedropper tool in Flash? (1)
2. What do you mean by 'hypertext' and 'markup' in HTML? (2)
3. Who created OpenShot video editor? (1)
4. What do you mean by comments? How can you give comments in HTML? (2)
5. In how many ways can we align a paragraph in HTML? Name them (2)
6. Write the steps to add Blur effect to the image in a movie being created in OpenShot Video Editor? (2)

I **Application Based Questions**

1. Write the steps to change the center point and width of a gradient. (2)
2. Create a movie named Tribals of India using OpenShot Movie Editor. You may use the internet to search and download the images and videos of various Indian tribes. (3)

TCS iON PRESENTS

NCO

SOF NATIONAL CYBER OLYMPIAD 2018-19

CLASS 7

QUESTION PAPER SET A

DO NOT OPEN THIS BOOKLET UNTIL ASKED TO DO SO

Total Questions: 50 | Time: 1

Guidelines for the Candidate

1. You will get additional ten minutes to fill up information about yourself on the OMR Sheet, before the start of the exam.
2. Write your **Name, School Code, Class, Section, Roll No.** and **Mobile Number** clearly on the **OMR Sheet** and do not forget to s
   We will share with you your marks/result and updates on your mobile number.
3. The Question Paper comprises three sections:

   Logical Reasoning (10 Questions), **Computers and Information Technology** (35 Questions) and **Achievers Section** (5 Questi

   Each question in Achievers Section carries 3 marks, whereas all other questions carry one mark each.
4. All questions are compulsory. There is no negative marking. Use of calculator is not permitted.
5. There is only ONE correct answer. Choose only ONE option for an answer.
6. To mark your choice of answers by darkening the circles on the OMR Sheet, use **HB Pencil** or **Blue / Black ball point pen** only. E

   Q.16: Which of the following is a type of printer?

A.	Cathode Ray Tube	B.	Light Emitting Diode
C.	Thermal Flatbed	D.	Liquid Crystal Display

   As the correct answer is option C, you must darken the circle corresponding to option C on the OMR Sheet. 16. Ⓐ Ⓑ ●
7. Rough work should be done in the blank space provided in this booklet.
8. Return the OMR Sheet to the invigilator at the end of the exam.
9. Please fill in your personal details in the space provided on this page before attempting the paper.

SOF

SCIENCE OLYMPIAD FOUNDATION

Inspiring Young Minds Through Knowledge Olympiads

Name:..

Section:.............. SOF Olympiad Roll No.:........................ Contact No.:...

1. Select a figure from the options which will continue the same series as established by the Problem Figures.

Problem Figures

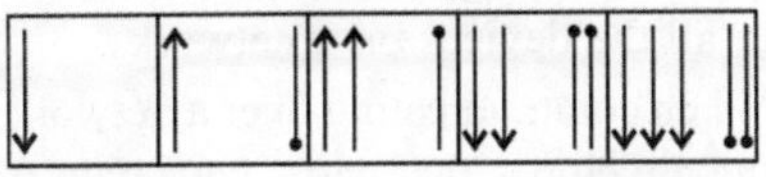

A. 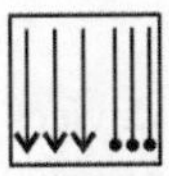

B. 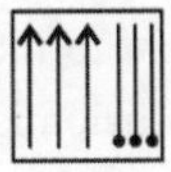

C. 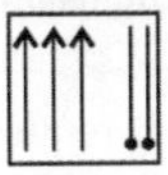

D. 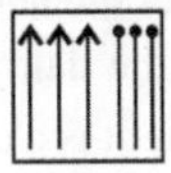

2. Select the odd one out.

A. 

B. 

C. 

D. 

3. In a certain code language, 'REPAIR' is written as 'FSBQSJ'. How is 'EXAMINATIONS' written in the same language?

A. YFNBOUJBPJOT

B. YFNBOJUBPJTO

C. YFNBOJUBJPTO

D. YFNBOJBUJPOT

4. Select the correct water image of the given figure.

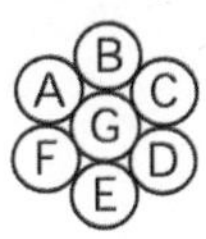

A. 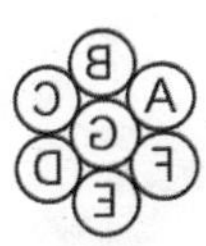

B. 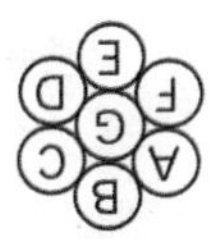

C. 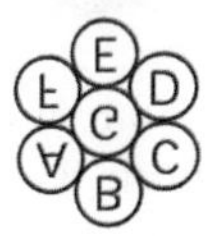

D. 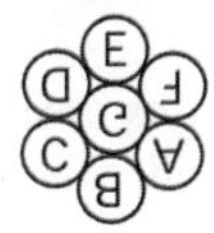

5. Five boys took part in a race. Raj finished before Mohit but behind Garv. Avinash finished before Sumit but behind Mohit. Who finished the race at second position?

A. Raj

B. Garv

C. Mohit

D. Sumit

6. *P* is 600 km eastward of *O* and *Q* is 800 km north of *O*. *R* is exactly in the middle of *Q* and *P*. The distance between *Q* and *R* is

A. 1000 km

B. 500 km

C. 400 km

D. 300 km

7. If L stands for '+', M stands for '–', N stands for '×' and P stands for '÷', then value of 14 N 10 L 42 P 2 M 8 is

A. 90

B. 103

C. 153

D. 212

8. Select a figure from the options in which the given figure is exactly embedded as one of its parts.

A. 

B. 

C. 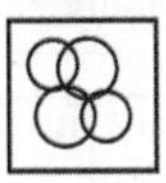

D. 

9. Select a figure from the options which satisfies the same condition of placement of the dots as in the given figure.

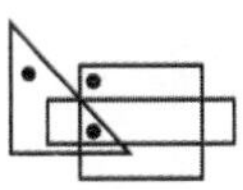

A. 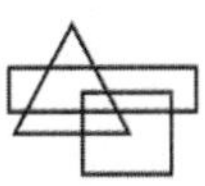

B. 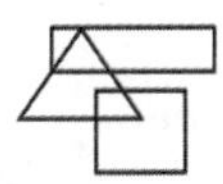

C. 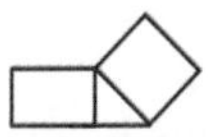

D. 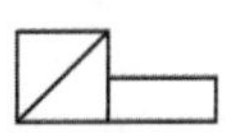

10. How many triangles are there in the given figure?

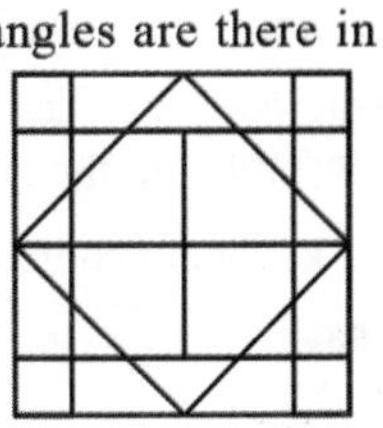

A. 16

B. 18

C. 20

D. None of these

11. Which of the following steps is the correct way to display the given dialog box, if you want to create the separate document for each copy of the letter and send them directly to the printer after completing the mail merge in MS-Word 2010?

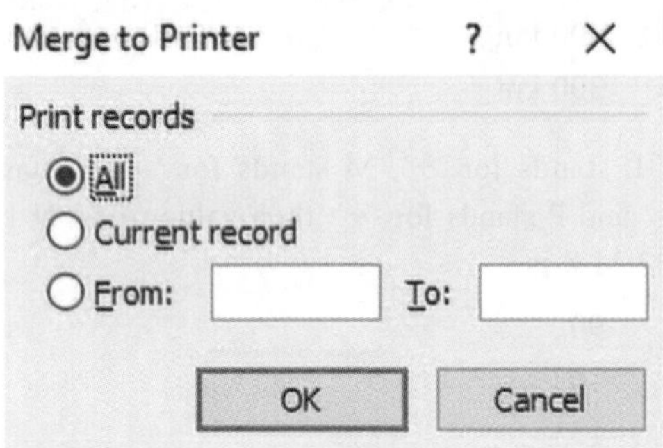

A. Mailings tab → Finish group → Finish and Merge drop down → Print documents
B. Mailings tab → Finish Group → Insert merge field document → Print documents
C. Mailings tab → Create tab → Finish and Merge drop down → Print documents
D. Mailings tab → Preview Results → Insert merge field document → Print documents

12. What is the keyboard shortcut to print the current date in a particular cell in MS-Excel 2010?

A. Ctrl + D
B. Ctrl + N
C. Ctrl + ;
D. Ctrl + %/5

13. Which of the following statements hold(s) true with respect to Macros in MS-Word 2010?

Statement 1: Macros can be assigned to a command button and can be added to the Quick Access Toolbar.

Statement 2: The keyboard shortcut to view the macros is Ctrl + F8.

A. Only Statement 1
B. Only Statement 2
C. Both Statement 1 and Statement 2
D. Neither Statement 1 nor Statement 2

14. Which of the following statements is INCORRECT regarding the networking terms?

A. A hub is a hardware that broadcasts the messages to all the devices on a network.
B. When communicating over a network, packets are the envelopes that carry your data from one end point to the other.
C. Collision is an attempt by two devices to transmit over the network at the same time usually resulting in the data being lost.
D. Client is a computer that handles requests for data, email, files, and other network services from other computers.

15. Which of the following features of MS-PowerPoint 2010, will insert text as a link to any MS-Word document file?

A. 
B. 
C. 
D. Both A and B

16. Many engineering design applications like architectural plan of a building or designs of aircraft or a car, often require high quality, perfect graphical output on large sheets. Which of the following devices plots such designs or graphs on a sheet of paper that can be spread and fixed over a table, where paper does not move and the pen holding mechanism provides all motions?

A. 
B. 
C. 
D. 

17. Sabita has created a school presentation comprising of 30 slides. Now, she wants to divide these 30 slides into 2 groups of presentation in such a way that:

- 20 slides to be presented to her teachers
- 10 slides to be presented to her class mates

Which of the following features of MS-PowerPoint 2010 will she use for this purpose?

A. 
B. 
C. 
D. 

18. Which of the following options when clicked, will convert the data shown in Figure 1 into the data shown in Figure 2 in MS-Excel 2010?

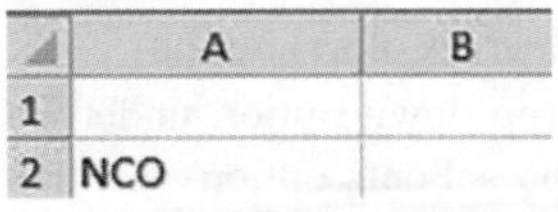

Figure 1

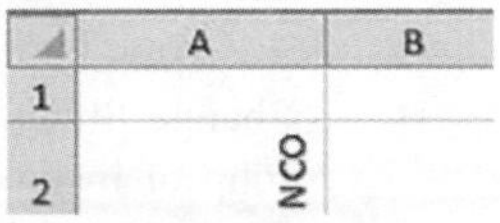

Figure 2

A. 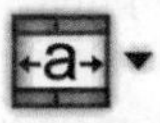
B. 
C. 
D. 

19. When you click on ___________, the symbol marked as (1) appears on the status bar in MS-Excel 2010.

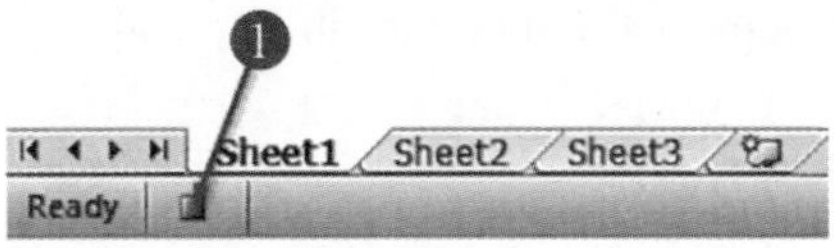

A. Sort and Filter
B. Record Macro
C. View Macros
D. Insert Cells

20. Select the INCORRECT match of QBASIC functions with their outputs.

A. N = 100 MOD 30 – 10
PRINT N
B. N = SQR(729) – 27
PRINT N
C. N = LEN("") – 1
PRINT N
D. PRINT LEFT$ ("NCO", 1) – N

21. The given icon is used to ___________in a mail merged document of MS-Word 2010.

A. Make changes to the list of recipients
B. Add a greeting line to your document
C. Add any field from the recipient list
D. Start a mail merge

22. What will be the output of the following QBasic code?

```
NUM = 10
DO WHILE (NUM <19)
PRINT NUM
NUM = NUM + 3
LOOP
```

A. 13
16
19
B. 13
16
19
21
C. 10
13
16
19
D. 10
13
16

23. Which of the following is NOT an E-commerce website?

A. Alibaba.com
B. RELIANCE Communications
C. ebY
D. JABONG COM

24. Which of the following options would replace the question mark (?) to enable the filtering feature in MS-Excel 2010?

Home tab → ? → Click on 'Sort & Filter' → Filter

A. Filtering group
B. Editing group
C. Cells group
D. Styles group

25. Which of the following features of Windows 7 is used to add the special characters, such as ©, ĉ etc?

A. Math input Panel
B. Sticky Notes
C. Private Character Editor
D. Character Map

26. Which of the following statements is CORRECT for Program File virus?

A. It infects executable/program files like .exe and .com files.
B. It is loaded in memory as soon as a program executes.
C. Sunday virus is an example of program file virus.
D. All of these

27. What would be the output of the following QBASIC code?

```
F$ = MID$("Predefined colour name", 16, 4)
PRINT F$
```

A. lour

B. ur n

C. name

D. r nam

---

28. The keyboard shortcut to bookmark a page of Google Chrome window is ____________, and to show/hide bookmark bar, press ___________.

A. Ctrl + D, Ctrl + ⇧ Shift + B

B. Ctrl + B, Ctrl + Tab + B

C. Ctrl + B, Ctrl + ⇧ Shift + D

D. Ctrl + D, Ctrl + ⇧ Shift + D

---

29. Observe the following diagrams [(a) and (b)] given below and replace the labels marked as X and Y with their respective Language Processor software.

(a)

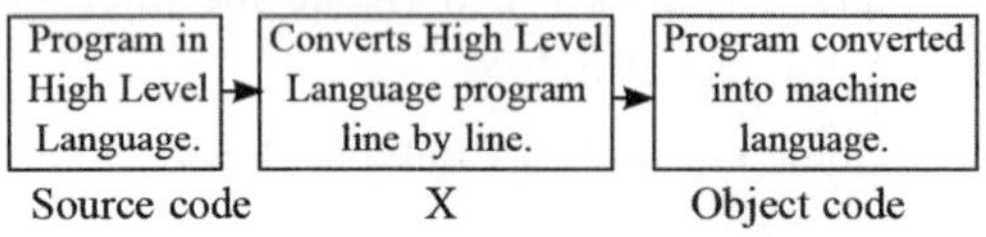

(b)

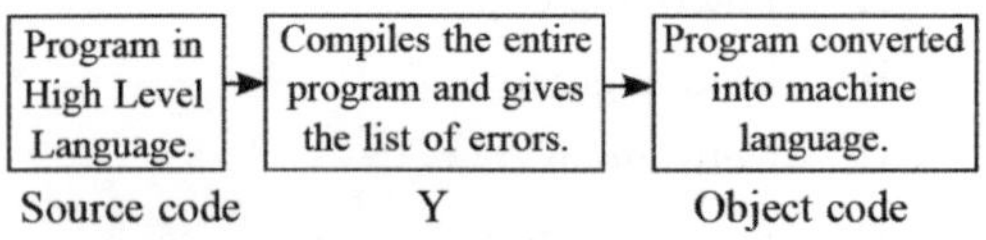

A. X- Assembler, Y- Utilities

B. X- Interpreter, Y- Compiler

C. X- Interpreter, Y- Assembler

D. X- Compiler, Y- Utilities

---

30. Which of the following statements hold(s) true about second generation of computers?

Statement-1: In this generation, magnetic cores were used as the primary memory, and magnetic tape and magnetic disks as secondary storage devices.

Statement-2: All the high-level languages like C, C++, DBASE etc., were used in this generation.

A. Only Statement 1

B. Only Statement 2

C. Both Statement 1 and Statement 2

D. Neither Statement 1 nor Statement 2

31. Which of the following steps is used to create New theme colors of your choice in MS-Word 2010?

A. Styles group of View tab → Click on Style option → 'Create New Theme Colors' option

B. 'Change Styles' drop down option under Styles group of Insert tab → Fonts option → Click on 'Create New Theme Colors' option

C. Insert tab → 'Paragraph Spacing' option → 'Create New Theme Colors' option at the lower end

D. 'Change Styles' drop down option under Styles group of Home tab → Colors option → 'Create New Theme Colors' option

---

32. Which of the following computers was developed by Maurice Wilkes at the University of Cambridge Mathematical Laboratory in England?

A. EDSAC

B. EDVAC

C. UNIVAC I

D. IBM-650

---

33. Which of the following is NOT an online storage service?

A. 

B. 

C. 

D. 

---

34. Intel 4004 was the _________ .

A. First single chip microprocessor

B. First multi-tasking operating system

C. Portable micro-computer for general purpose

D. One of the first generation device

---

35. Which of the following Control Panel items is used to change the Power button from Shut down to Log off in start menu of Windows 7?

Note : (A snapshot is shown here (as a hint), to show you one of the intermediate steps to change the power button action in start menu).

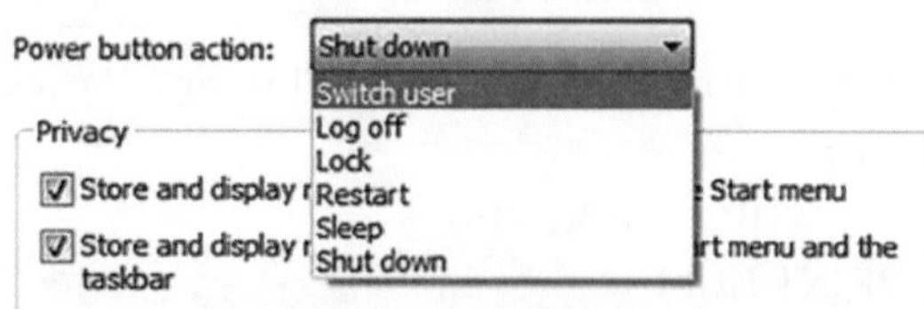

A. Indexing Options

B. Taskbar and Start Menu

C. Display

D. Personalization

36. Identify the following icon.

- It is a/an computer program/app that renders a 3D representation of Earth, based on satellite imagery.
- Users can explore the globe by entering addresses and coordinates in this app, by downloading it in their smartphones.

A. Earth Sky
B. Google Earth
C. Earth Map
D. Google Globe

37. A____________ is a device that measures information arising from physical interaction with its environment. These are used in robotics, computer hardware and security systems. A common application of this device is in touchscreen devices on mobile phones and computing. It appears in everyday life such as elevator buttons and lamps which dim or brighten by touching the base.

A. Myo Armband
B. Smart Watch
C. Tactile Sensor
D. Civic Vision

38. Which of the following is a virtual assistant developed by Google that is available on mobile and smart home devices, it was initially debuted as a part of Google's messaging app Allo, and its voice-activated speaker Google Home?

A. 

B. 

C. 
D. 

39. Which of the following features of Page Layout tab of MS-Excel 2010 has the option to align the edges of the triangles from diagonal to the left (as the transformation shown from Figure 1 to Figure 2)?

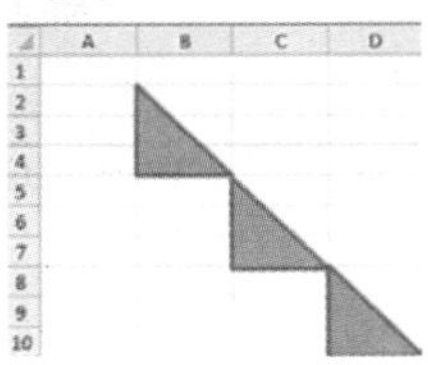

Figure 1

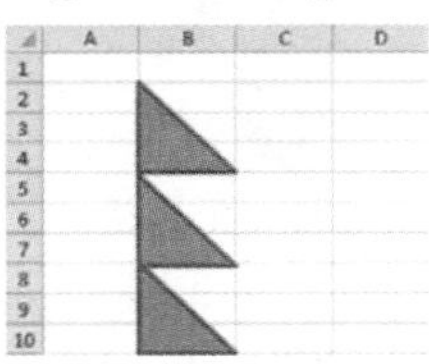

Figure 2

A. 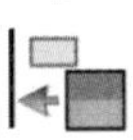
B. 
C. 
D. 

40. In which of the following storage devices, the access time varies according to the storage location?

A. Random access storage device
B. Sequential access storage device
C. Primary access storage device
D. Secondary access storage device

41. Match the following technologies in Column- I with their descriptions in Column-II.

	Column-I		Column-II
(a)	Holographic Computing	(i)	It is a high-resolution screen technology developed by Apple.
(b)	Retina Display	(ii)	It is a wireless technology which is also known as P-ISM.
(c)	5 Pen PC Technology	(iii)	It is used for presenting laser generated 3D images of objects in a real environment.

A. (a)-(iii), (b)-(i), (c)-(ii)
B. (a)-(ii), (b)-(i), (c)-(iii)
C. (a)-(i), (b)-(ii), (c)-(iii)
D. (a)-(iii), (b)-(ii), (c)-(i)

42. Now-a-days, a new interface is adopted by computing devices that allows its users to control games and apps when the controlling device is moved in the air. Which technology is followed by such interfaces?

A. Gesture sensing
B. Air sensing
C. Air manevvering
D. Steering

43. Identify the following.

- It is used for reading out text information to blind persons.
- It is also used in translation systems to convert entered text into spoken words, in a language selected by user.

A. Speech synthesizer
B. Digitiser
C. Equalizer
D. Voice Reproduction System

44. Which of the following connects the CPU to various internal components and to expansion cards for graphics, networking and sound?

A. Ports
B. Chipset
C. Buses
D. Registers

45. Identify the following technology.

- It includes method for acquiring, processing, analyzing and understanding digital images, and extraction of data from the real world in order to produce numerical or symbolic information, *e.g.*, in the form of decisions.
- It deals with how computers can be made for gaining high-level understanding from digital images or videos.

A. Language processing
B. Computer Vision
C. Optical Mounted vision
D. Multi-Line vision

ACHIEVERS SECTION

46. Observe the given QBASIC code and identify the line number (marked as 1 to 10) with an error.

Line **QBASIC code**

```
1.  X = 55
2.  IF X >= 1 AND X <= 9 THEN
3.     PRINT "SINGLE DIGIT NUMBER"
4.  ELSEIF X >= 10 AND X <= 99 THEN
5.     PRINT "2-DIGIT NUMBER"
6.  ELSE   X >= 100 AND X <= 9999 THEN
7.     PRINT "3-DIGIT NUMBER"
8.  ELSE
9.     PRINT "4-DIGIT NUMBER AND ABOVE"
10. END IF
```

A. Line 2
B. Line 4
C. Line 6
D. Line 9

47. Functions of X , Y and Z are given below. They are the icons present under Slide Master view in MS-Powerpoint 2010. Identify X, Y and Z.

X : It is used to rename the Custom Layout.
Y : It is used to preserve the selected master.
Z : It is used to switch the slide orientation between portrait and landscape.

A. X :  Y:  Z : 

B. X :  Y:  Z: 

C. X:  Y:  Z: 

D. X:  Y:  Z: 

48. Which of the following is the correct order of steps to change the Cursor blink rate from fast to slow using a slide bar as shown in the given image in Windows 7?

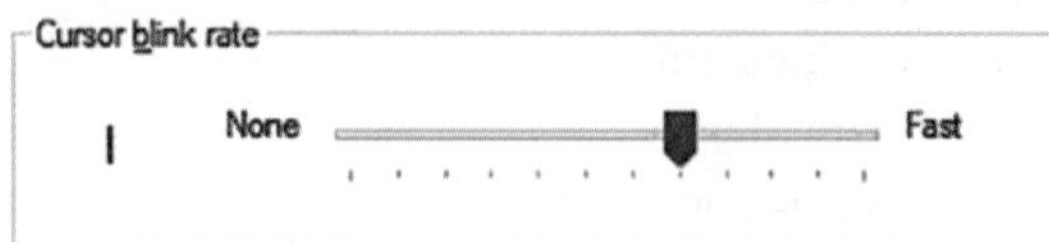

A. Control Panel → Keyboard → Keyboard Properties dialog box → Speed tab → Cursor blink rate
B. Control Panel → Mouse → Mouse Properties dialog box → Buttons tab → Cursor blink rate
C. Control Panel → Display → Preview Properties dialog box → Speed tab → Cursor blink rate
D. Control Panel → Fonts → Fonts Properties dialog box → Organise tab → Cursor blink rate

49. Identify the following computer virus.

- It is a type of malware that is based on the ability to translate, edit and rewrite its own code.
- It can change its internal structure, rewrite and reprogram itself each time it infects a computing system, thus making antivirus scanner quite difficult to detect it.

A. Boot Sector Virus
B. Resident Virus
C. Stealth Virus
D. Metamorphic Virus

50. A link is a communication pathway that transfers data from one device to another. For a communication to occur, two devices must be connected in some way to same link at same time. In the given diagram, a mainframe is connected to a workstation with a link, which type of connection is established here?

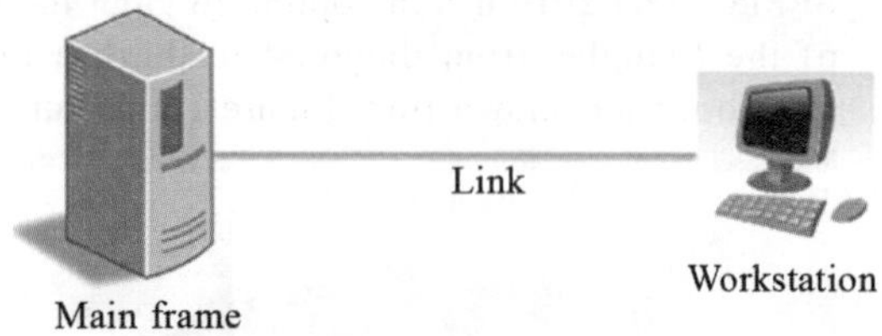

A. Timeshared connection
B. Spatially shared connection
C. Point-to-point connection
D. Multipoint connection

SPACE FOR ROUGH WORK

NCO | SET-A | CLASS-7

1.	(B)	2.	(D)	3.	(B)	4.	(C)	5.	(A)	6.	(B)	7.	(C)
8.	(A)	9.	(A)	10.	(D)	11.	(A)	12.	(C)	13.	(A)	14.	(D)
15.	(D)	16.	(C)	17.	(B)	18.	(C)	19.	(B)	20.	(C)	21.	(C)
22.	(D)	23.	(B)	24.	(B)	25.	(D)	26.	(D)	27.	(B)	28.	(A)
29.	(B)	30.	(A)	31.	(D)	32.	(A)	33.	(D)	34.	(A)	35.	(B)
36.	(B)	37.	(C)	38.	(C)	39.	(A)	40.	(B)	41.	(A)	42.	(A)
43.	(A)	44.	(C)	45.	(B)	46.	(C)	47.	(C)	48.	(A)	49.	(D)
50.	(C)												

SOF SCIENCE OLYMPIAD FOUNDATION

National Office: Plot 99, First Floor, Sector 44 Institutional area, Gurgaon -122 003 (HR) India

Email: info@sofworld.org | Website: www.sofworld.org

Regd. Office: 406, Taj Apt., Ring Road, New Delhi-110 029

Note: Please address all communication to the National Office only.

Windows 10

Windows 10 is the most recent version of the operating system from Microsoft Corporation. It is an improved version of Windows 7 and Windows 8.1. It provides both the traditional desktop interface (Start button, Start menu) as in Windows 7 and the colourful tile-based interface as in Windows 8.1 (Fig. 1).

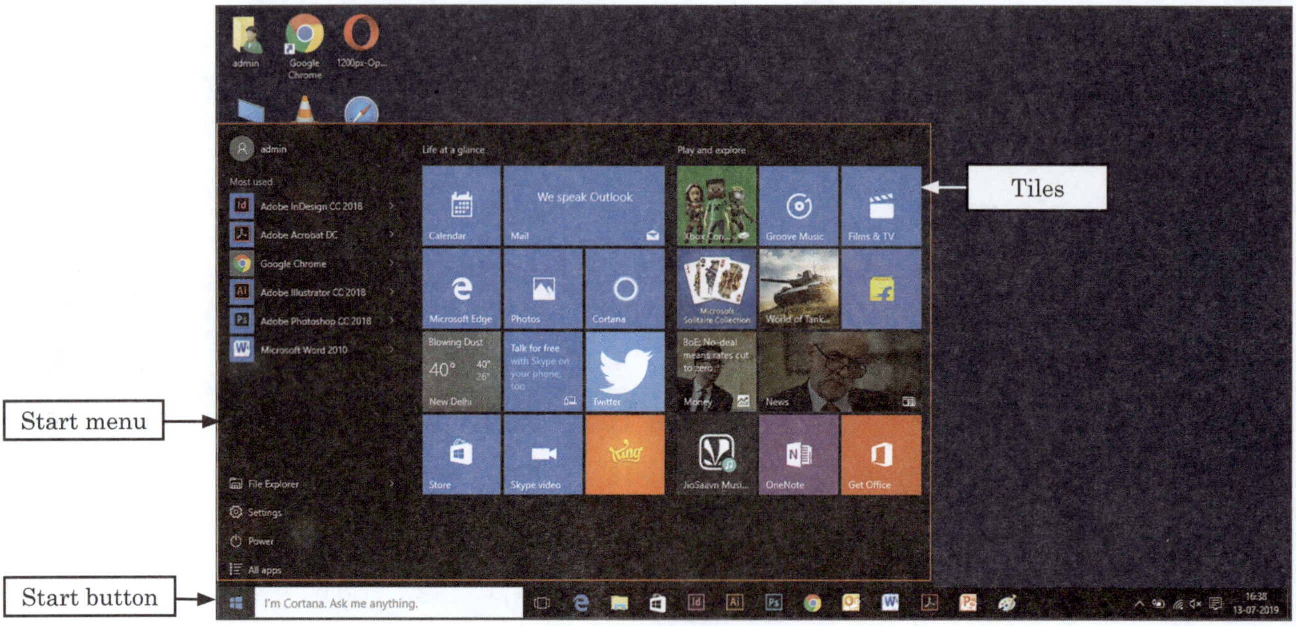

Fig. 1: Windows 10 Start screen

The most common editions of the Windows 10 operating system are Windows 10 Home, Windows 10 Pro and Windows 10 Education edition. The Windows 10 operating system supports touchscreen devices like smartphones and tablets.

Features of Windows 10

The new features specific to Windows 10 are as follows:

- It provides Start menu. Unlike Windows 7, the Start menu shows live tiles that provide updated information.
- It gives access to the Windows Store app that helps to search and download the required software or games.
- It provides Microsoft Edge as its default web browser.
- The virtual assistant Cortana helps us to search for information on the system or from the internet.
- It allows users to create virtual desktops with different screens.

The combination of Start menu with live tiles has made it very user-friendly and popular. Users can also customize the appearance of the Windows 10 desktop as in the previous version of Windows operating systems.

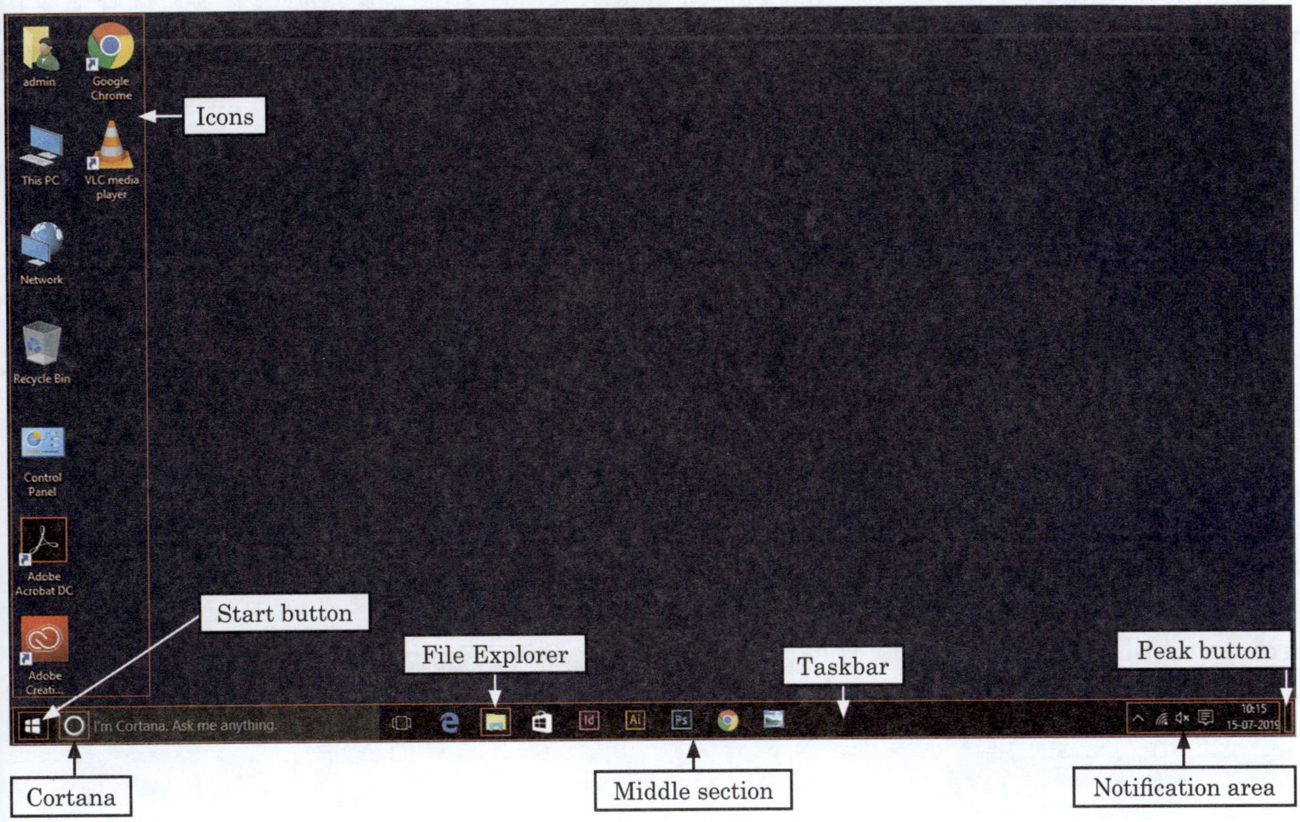

Fig. 2: Windows 10 desktop

MS Excel 2013

Let us learn how to format, sort and filter data, and create charts in MS Excel 2013.

Cell and Range References

Cell and Range references in MS Excel 2013 can be described in the same way as in MS Excel 2010. Here are examples of cell addresses and range references:

- The cell in column D and row 6 D6
- The range of cells in column F and rows 7 through 17 F7:F17
- The range of cells in row 8 and columns A through F A8:F8
- All cells in row 8 8:8
- All cells in columns A through D A:D

Using Formulas

To enter a formula for a specified set of values, type the equal to (=) sign in the formula bar followed by the formula. To calculate the sum, follow these steps:

1. Click the cell in which you want the sum to be displayed.
2. Type the formula beginning with an equal to (=) sign (Fig. 3).
3. Click the or press the Enter key to view the result.

MS Excel 2013 allows users to work with both text and numeric formulas. The use of the mathematical operators is also the same. Once a formula is applied, Excel allows the results to be auto-edited. To extend the formula to fill the range of cells, the **AutoFill** feature of MS Excel can be used.

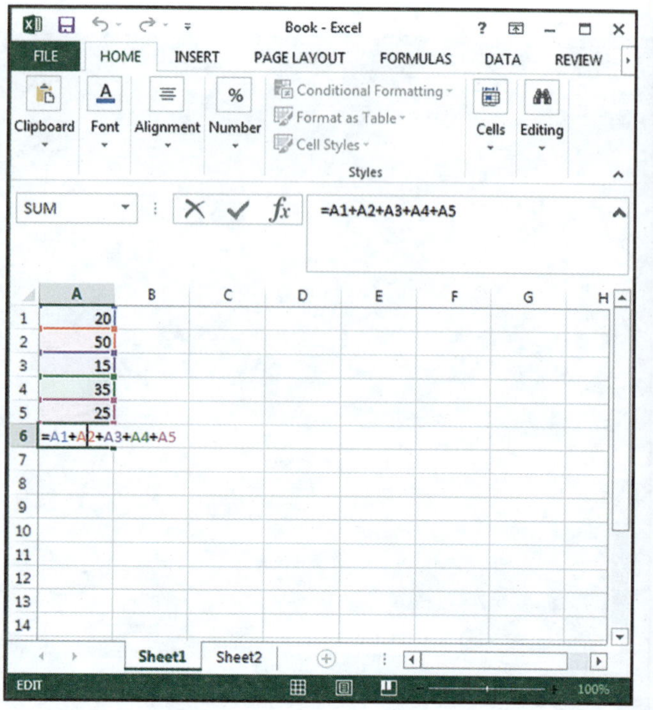

Fig. 3: Using formulas

Autosum Feature

To use the AutoSum feature, follow these steps

1. Select the cell and click **AutoSum** in the **Editing** group of buttons on the **Home** tab (Fig. 4).
2. Press the Enter key or click **AutoSum** button again to view the result.

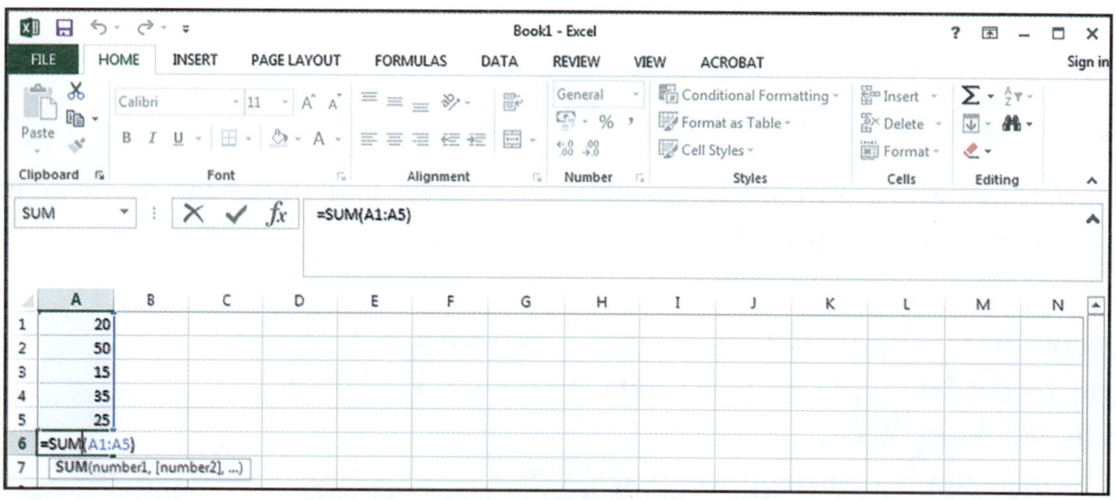

Fig. 4: Using the Autosum feature

Function Library

The functions are present in the Function Library group of buttons on the Formula tab, as in Excel 2010 (Fig. 5). The functions included are also the same.

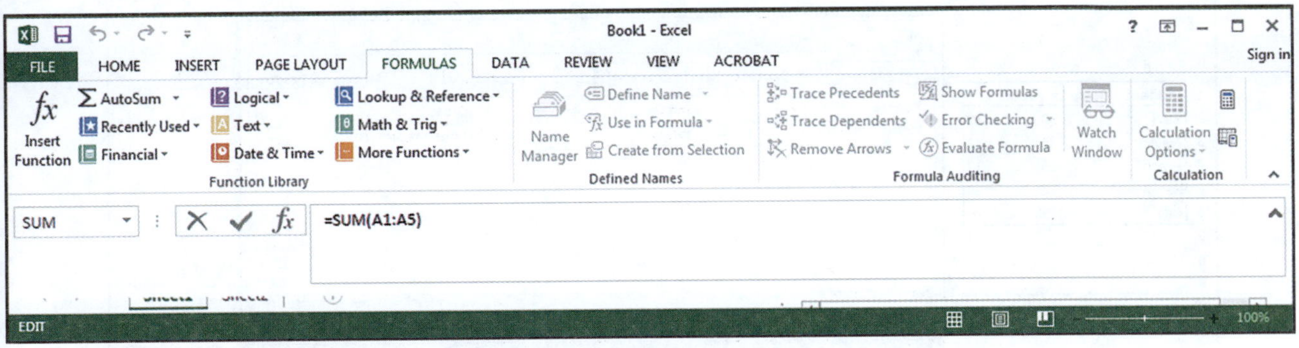

Fig. 5: The Function Library

Sorting Data

To sort data according to the values in a single column only, follow these steps:

1. Select the cell in the column according to which you want to sort the data.
2. Depending on how you want to sort the data, click the button to sort data in ascending/descending order (Fig. 6 and 7).

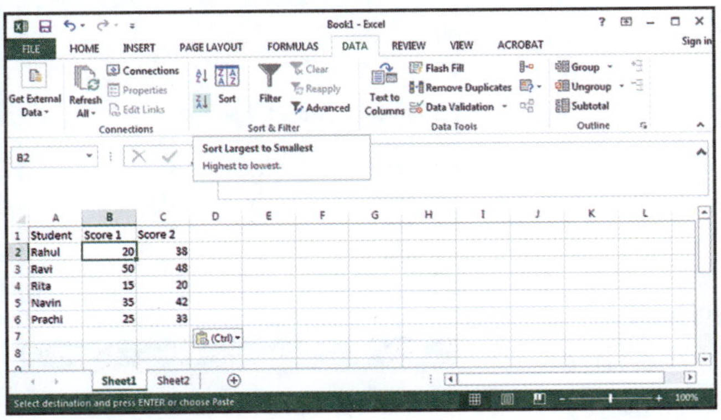

Fig. 6: Sorting data in descending order

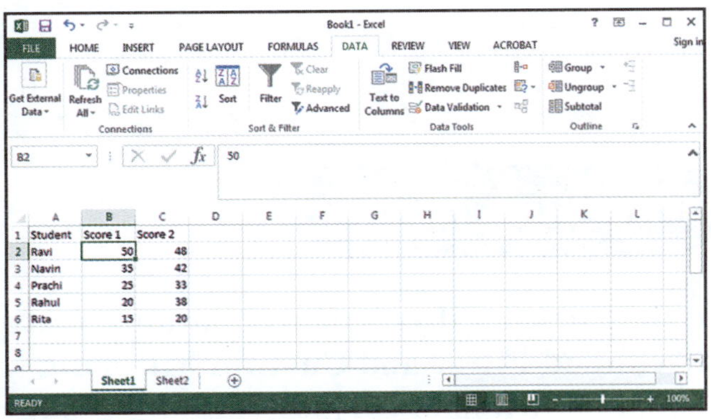

Fig. 7: Sorted data

Sorting data on multiple columns

1. Select the range of cells that need to be sorted.
2. Click **Sort** button in the **Sort & Filter** group of buttons on the **Data** tab. The **Sort** dialog box appears (Fig. 8).
3. Under **Column** section, choose the column to be used to sort the data. Under **Order**, then choose A to Z to sort the data in ascending order.

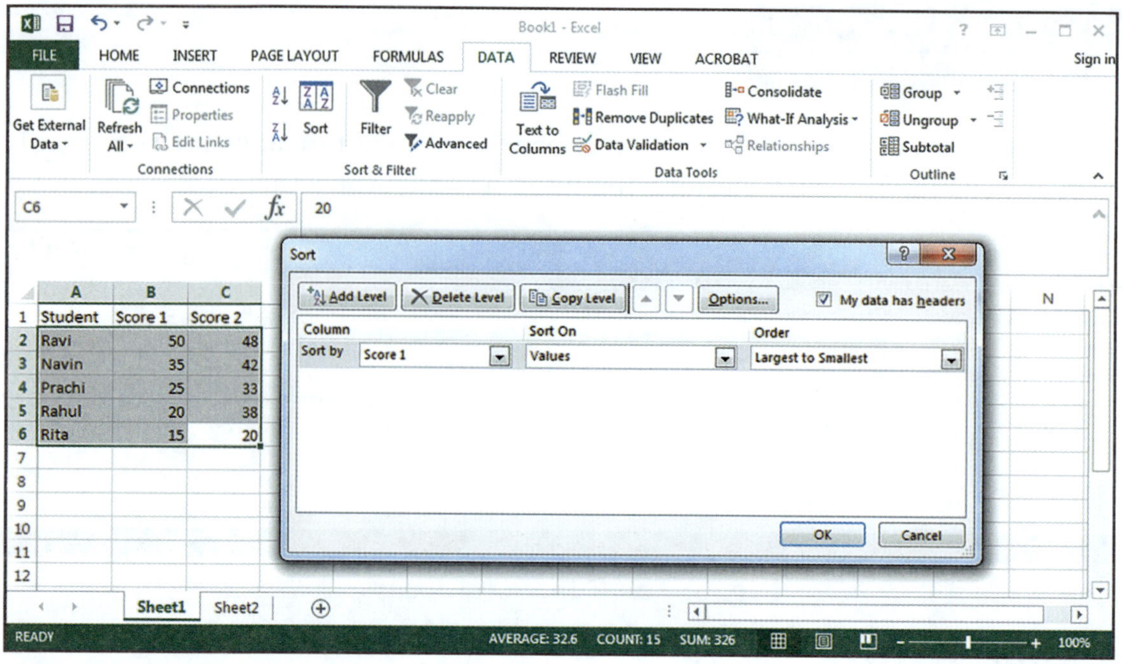

Fig. 8: Using the Sort dialog box to sort data on multiple columns

4. Click **Add Level** button on the top left corner of the dialog box. A new row appears Select the column for **Then by** list box in **Column** section. Under **Order**, select **Largest to Smallest**.
5. Click **OK** to see the sorted data (Fig. 8).

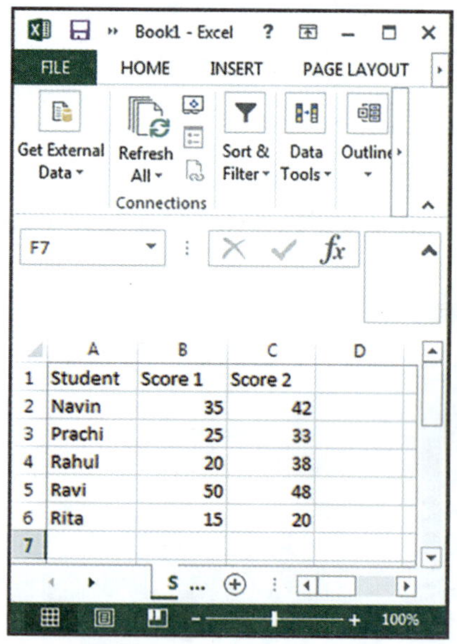

Fig. 9: Sorted data

Filtering Data

In the **Sort & Filter** group of buttons, **AutoFilter, Advanced Filter** and **Custom Filtering** are the three commands available to filter data ranges (Fig. 10).

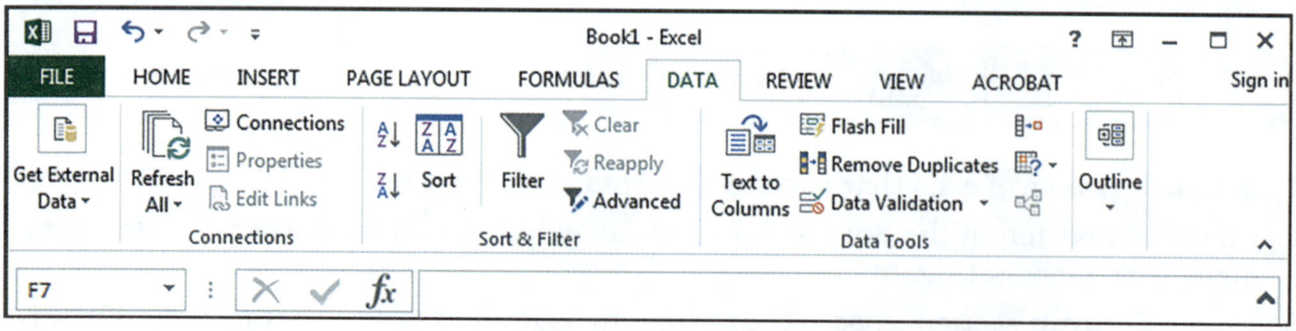

Fig. 10: Data filtering commands

AutoFilter Command

To use the AutoFilter command, follow these steps:

1. Select any cell in the range.
2. Under the **Data** tab, click the **Filter** button in the **Sort & Filter** group of buttons. Small arrows are seen next to each column heading with the filter icon (Fig. 11).
3. Click the arrow in the column header to choose the filter for the column. A drop-down menu is displayed (Fig. 12).
4. You will see that **Select All** option is checked. Deselect **Select All** and select only the numbers that are to be displayed.
5. Click **OK** to see the filtered data (Fig. 13).

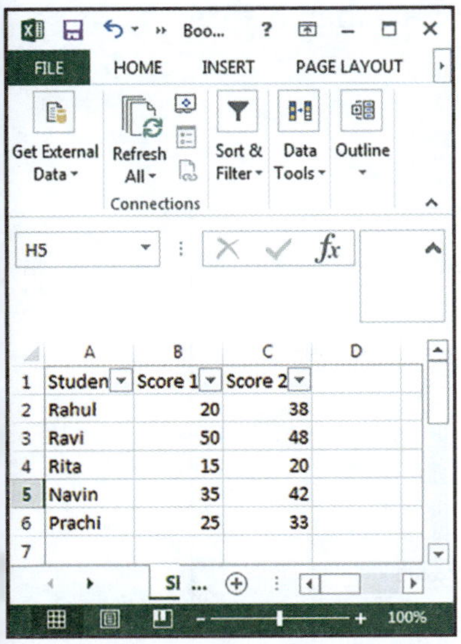

Fig. 11: Cell range for autofiltering data

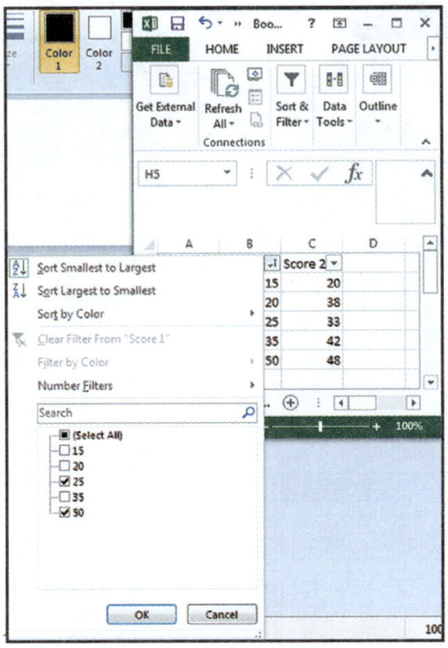

Fig. 12: Drop-down menu for data filtering

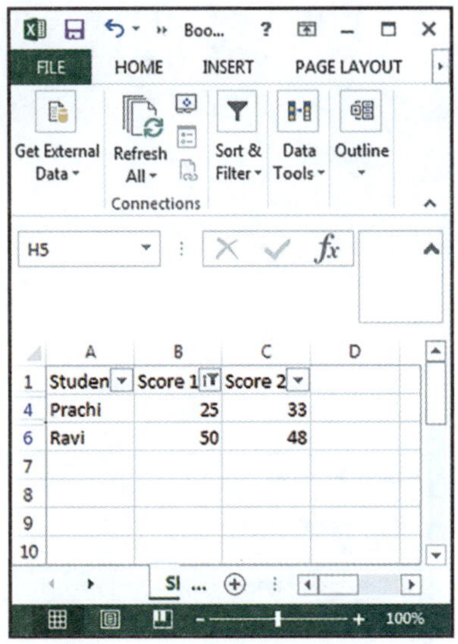

Fig. 13: Filtered data

Custom Filtering

To filter data based on multiple conditions, follow these steps:

1. Select the range to be filtered. Click the **Filter** button in the **Sort & Filter** group (Fig. 14).
2. In the **Filter** drop-down menu, click **Number Filters** option (Fig. 15).
3. Choose the desired filter, say **Between**. The **Custom AutoFilter** dialog box is displayed. Fill in the necessary values (Fig. 16).
4. Click **OK** to see the filtered data (Fig. 17).

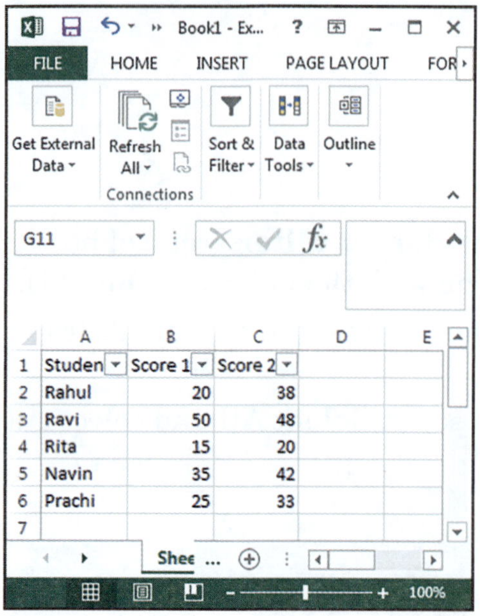

Fig. 14: Cell range for custom filtering data

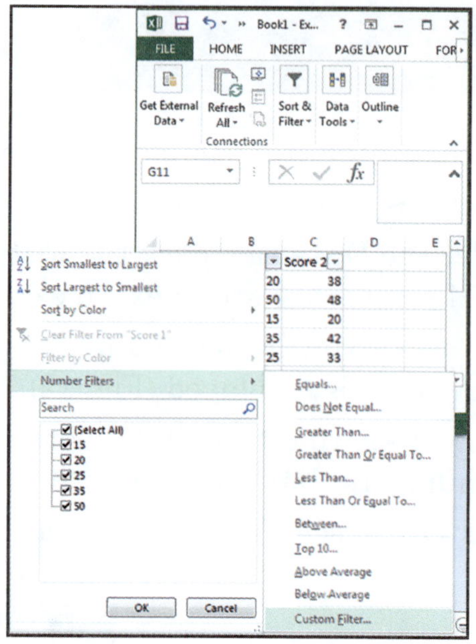

Fig. 15: Number filters

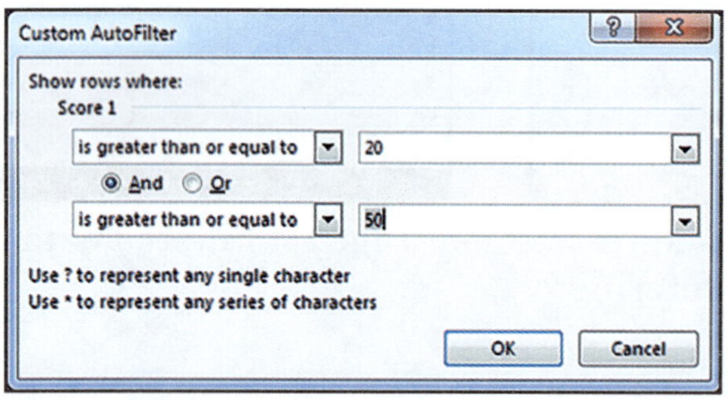

Fig. 16: Custom AutoFilter dialog box

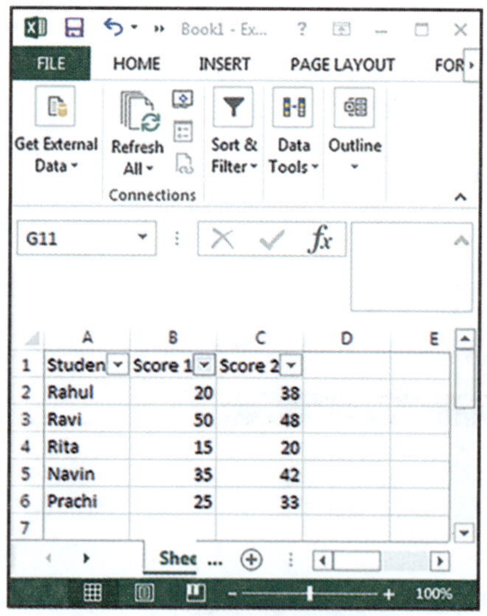

Fig. 17: Filtered data

Conditional Formatting

The **Conditional formatting** command is in the **Styles** group of buttons under the **Home** tab (Fig. 18). Users can display data in a particular colour or style depending on a particular condition.

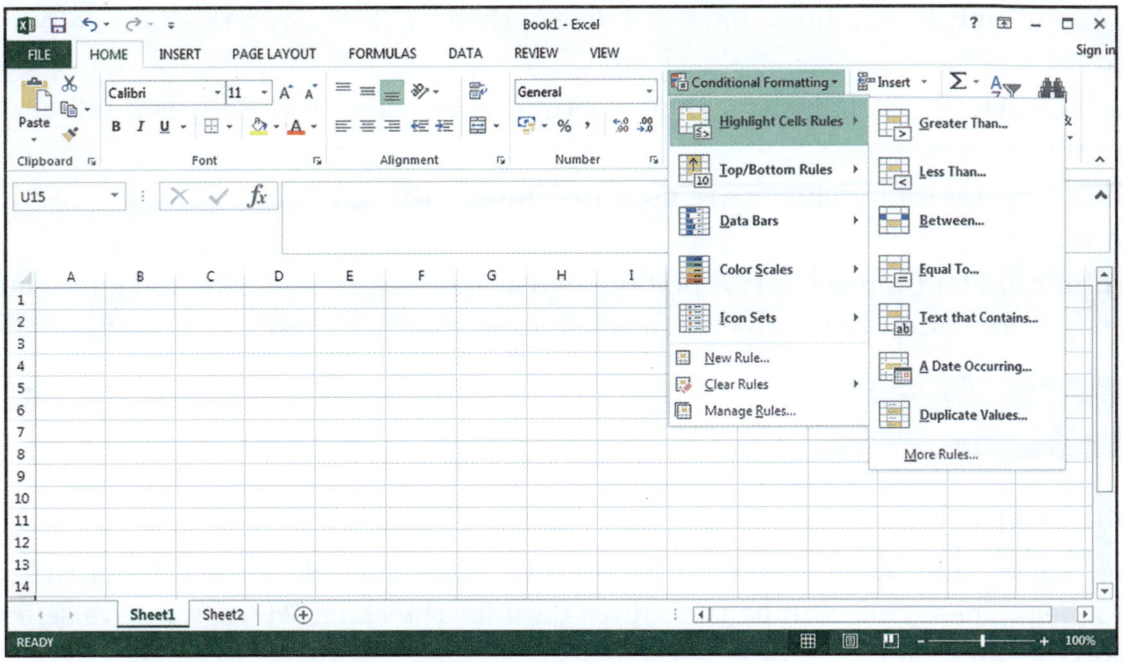

Fig. 18: Conditional Formatting

Charts in MS Excel 2013

It can often be difficult to interpret Excel Workbooks that contain a lot of data. Charts help in creating quick graphical representation of data to visualize comparisons and trends.

Types of Charts

The commands to create a chart are in the **Charts** group of buttons on the **Insert** tab (Fig. 19).

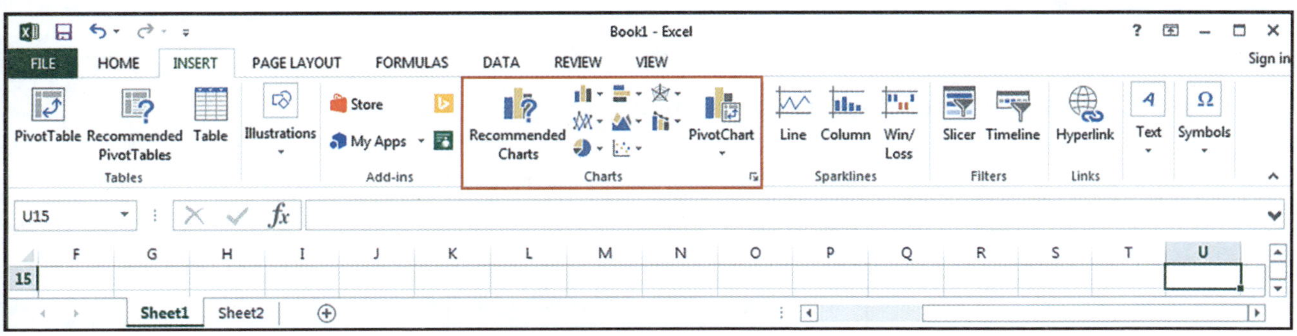

Fig. 19: Creating Charts

MS Excel 2013 offers quite a few additional types of charts. These are:

- **XY (scatter) and bubble chart:** Scatter charts are typically used for showing and comparing numeric values, like scientific, statistical, and engineering data.

- **Bubble chart:** In a bubble chart, the size of the bubbles shows the data points in the data series.
- **Stock chart:** Stock charts can show fluctuations in data, like daily rainfall or annual temperatures.
- **Radar charts:** Radar charts are used to compare the aggregate values of several data series.
- **Combo charts:** Combo charts combine two or more chart types to make the data easy to understand, especially when the data is widely varied.

To Insert a Chart

Follow the steps given below to insert a chart in an Excel worksheet:

1. Select the cells for which you want to create a chart, including the column titles and row labels. These cells will be the source data for the chart. Here, we have selected cells A1:F6 (Fig. 20).

	A	B	C	D	E	F	G
1	Genre	2008	2009	2010	2011	2012	
2	Classics	₹ 18,580	₹ 49,225	₹ 16,326	₹ 10,017	₹ 26,134	
3	Mystery	₹ 78,970	₹ 82,262	₹ 48,640	₹ 49,985	₹ 73,428	
4	Romance	₹ 24,236	₹ 131,390	₹ 79,022	₹ 71,009	₹ 81,474	
5	Sci-Fi & Fantasy	₹ 16,730	₹ 19,730	₹ 12,109	₹ 11,355	₹ 17,686	
6	Young Adult	₹ 35,358	₹ 42,685	₹ 20,893	₹ 16,065	₹ 21,388	
7							
8							

Fig. 20: Selecting cells A1:F6

2. From the Insert tab, click the desired Chart command. Here, we have selected Column chart command (Fig. 21).

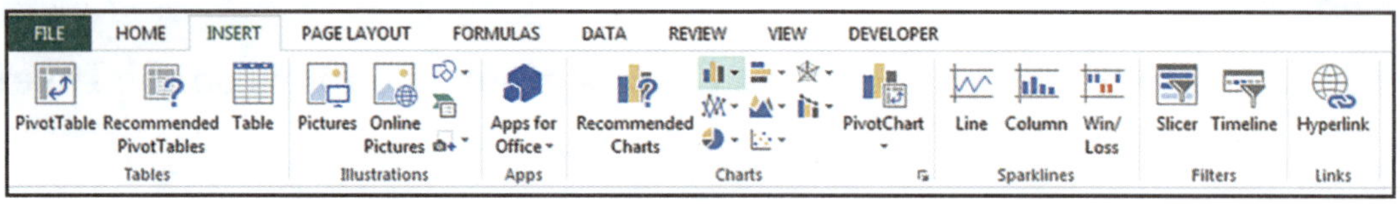

Fig. 21: Click the Column chart command

3. Choose the desired chart type from the drop-down menu (Fig. 22).

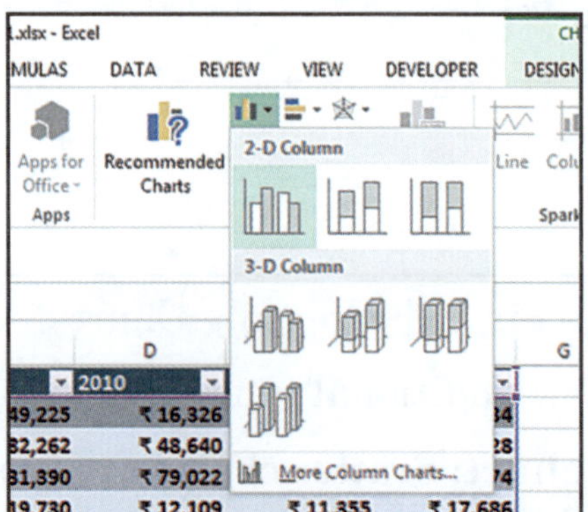

Fig. 22: Choosing a chart type

4. The selected chart will be inserted in the worksheet (Fig. 23).

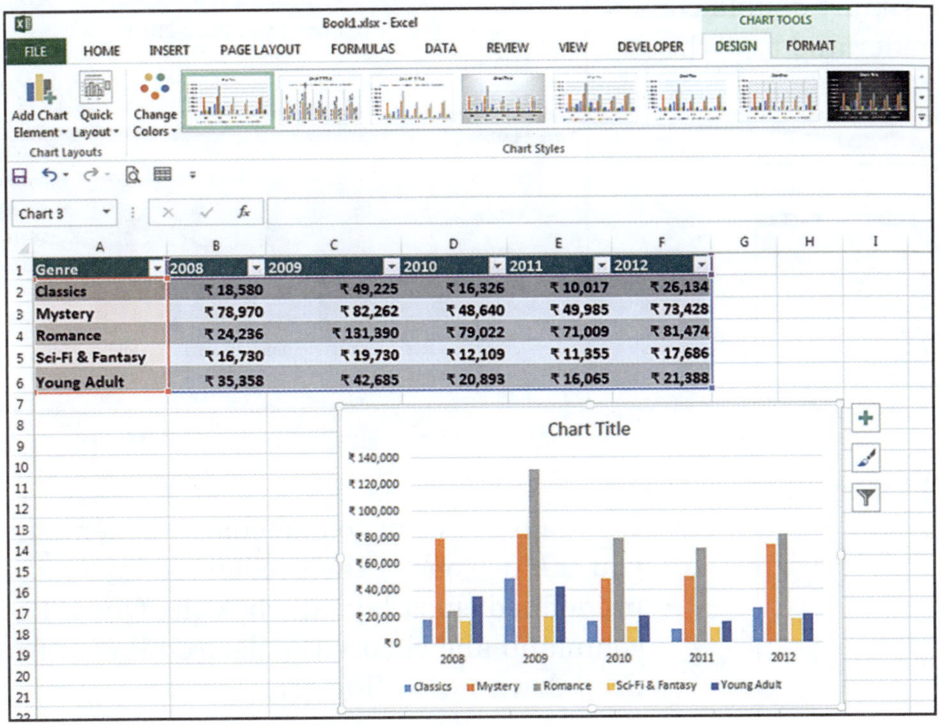

Fig. 23: The inserted chart

If you are not sure which type of chart to use, the Recommended Charts command (Fig. 24) will suggest several different charts based on the source data.

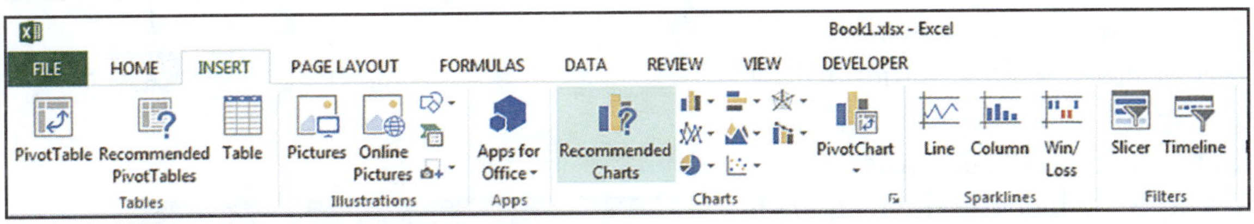

Fig. 24: Recommended Charts

Chart Layout and Style

After inserting a chart, there are several things you may want to change about the way your data is displayed.

It is easy to edit a chart's layout and style from the Design tab.

- Excel allows you to add chart elements such as chart titles, legends and data labels. Adding these elements make your chart easier to read. To add a chart element, click the Add Chart Element command (Fig. 25) on the Design tab and choose the desired element from the drop-down menu.

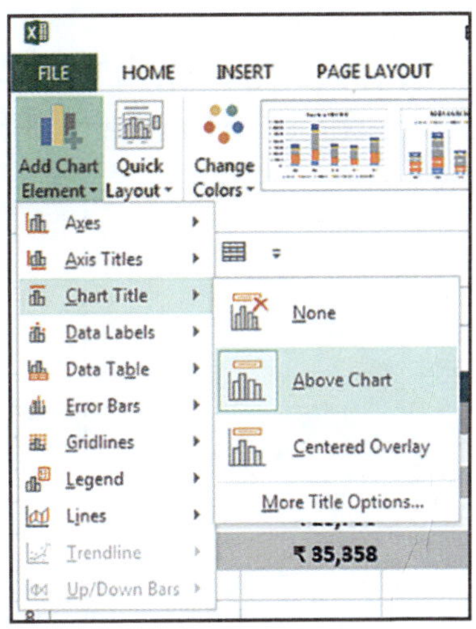

Fig. 25: Adding a chart title

- To edit a chart element like a chart title, simply double-click the placeholder and type the new name (Fig. 26).

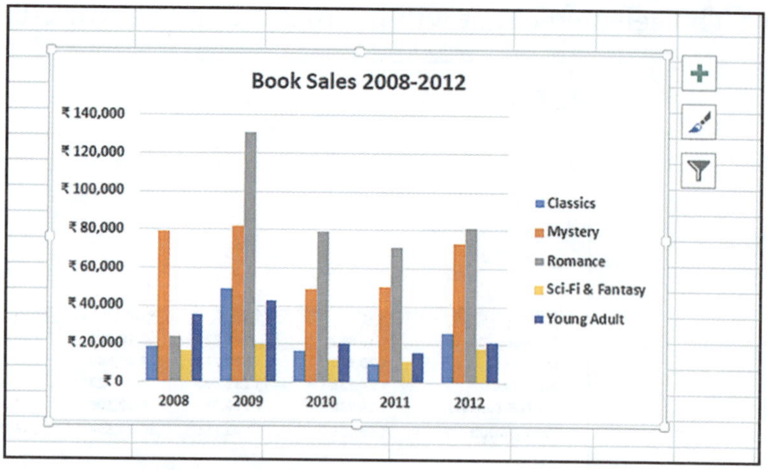

Fig. 26: Editing the chart title placeholder text

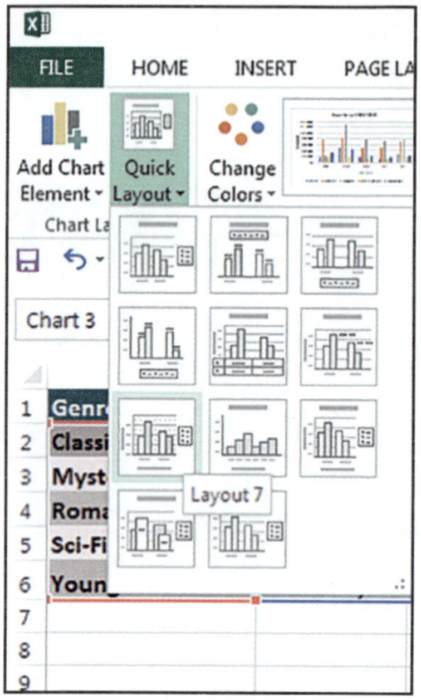

Fig. 27: Choosing a chart layout

- If you do not want to add chart elements individually, you can use one of the predefined layouts. To add a predefined chart layout, click the Quick Layout command and choose the desired layout from the drop-down menu (Fig. 27).

- Excel also includes several different chart styles, which allow you to quickly modify the look and feel of your chart. To change the chart style, select the desired style from the Chart Tools group (Fig. 28).

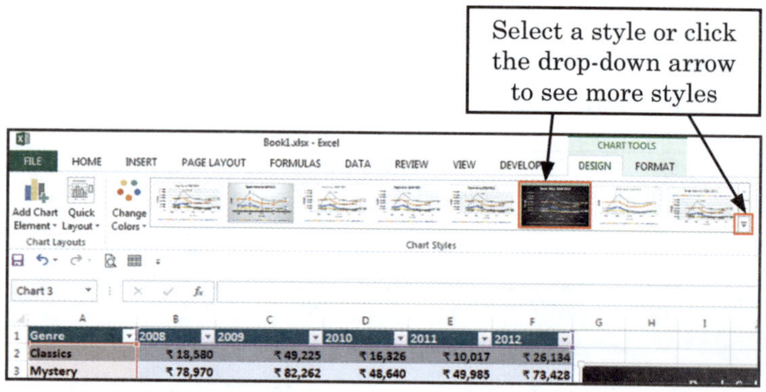

Fig. 28: Choosing a chart style

You can also use the chart formatting shortcut buttons to quickly add chart elements, change the chart style and filter the chart data.

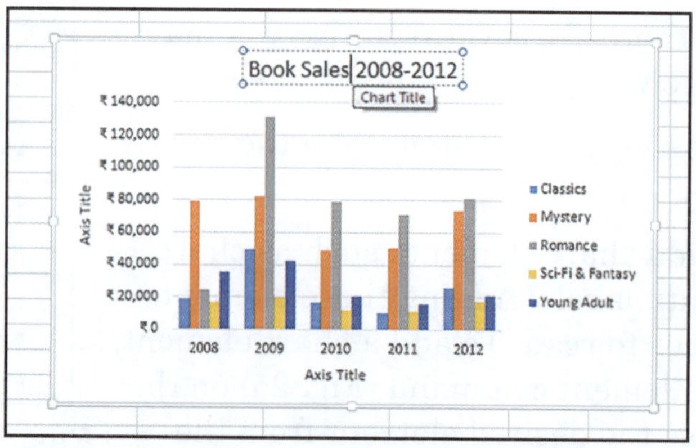

Fig. 29: Chart formatting shortcuts

Update on Animate CC

You have learnt about Macromedia Flash in this book. You know that it is a software used to create animations. However Macromedia Flash was taken over by Adobe, Inc. and was subsequently renamed as Adobe Flash Professional. Today, it is known by the name of **Adobe Animate**. Various versions of this animation software have been released by Adobe but in this section we shall be discussing about Adobe Animate CC.

The salient features of Animate CC are as follows:

1. It is a computer animation program that is also used for multimedia authoring. So it can be used for creating animated videos, games, websites and its related applications like online videos and apps.
2. It also allows to create vector graphics, that is scaled drawings and diagrams
3. Animations created in Adobe Animate CC can be published for HTML 5, Flash Player (.swf), Scalable Vector graphics(.svg) and many more.
4. It can be published for multiple platforms like desktop, mobile and television.
5. The Virtual Camera feature helps us to add more dramatic effects in our animation.
6. We can sync audio in our animations.
7. It has got a large variety of fonts that can be applied to the text inserted in the animation.

Components of Animate CC User Interface

The main components of Animate CC user interface are:

- **Menu Bar:** It is present on the top of the interface window and contains options to perform various tasks.
- **Tools Panel:** It contains various tools to create and edit the drawings
- **Properties Panel:** The various options in this panel allow us to set the properties of the currently selected tool or object.
- **Stage:** This is the workspace where we actually work, that is we create and edit drawings.
- **Layers Panel:** It is used to create and manage layers.
- **Timeline:** It is used to set the sequence of frames.
- **Library Panel:** It is used to manage symbols

Figure 30 shows the Animate CC user interface.

UPDATES

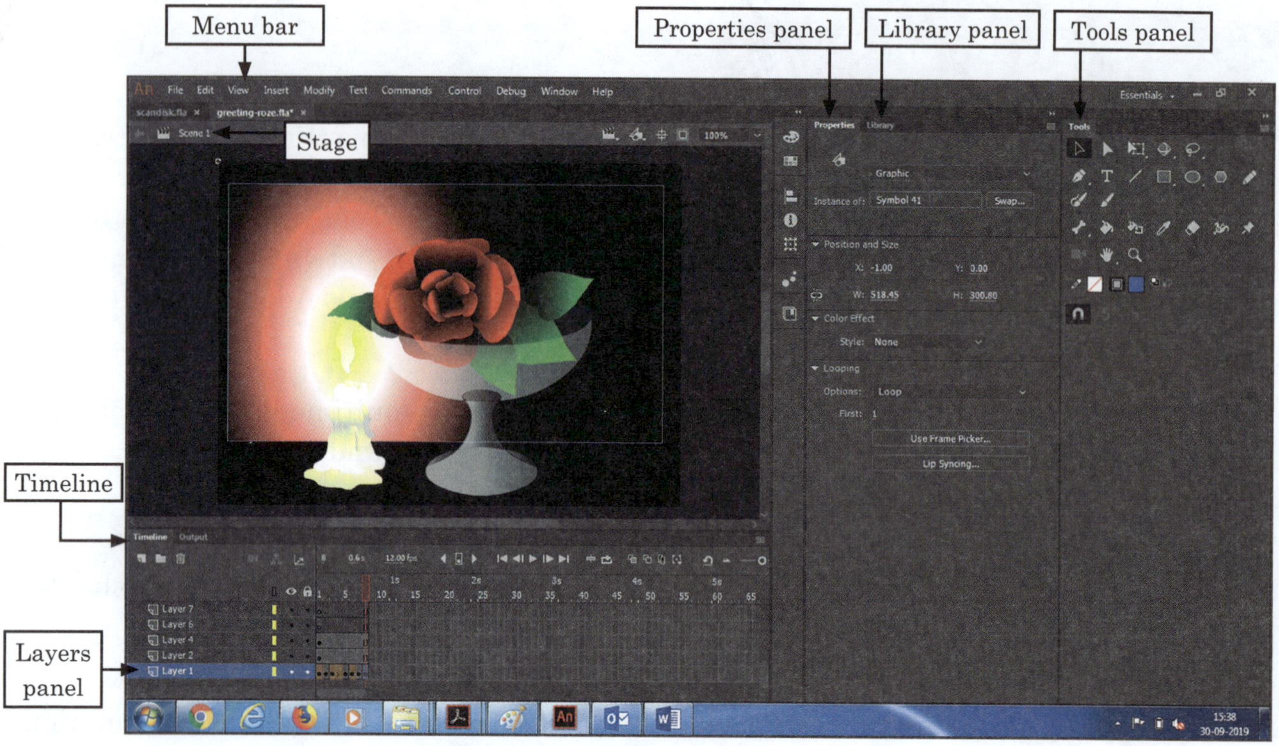

Fig. 30: Adobe Animate CC interface